COLLECTIVE VENGEANCE

JOSEPH STANLEY

A 27-Year-Old Coerced Abortion Jeopardizes a
Supreme Court Nomination

COLLECTIVE VENGEANCE

PALMETTO
PUBLISHING
Charleston, SC
www.PalmettoPublishing.com

Copyright © 2024 by Joseph Stanley

All rights reserved
No portion of this book may be reproduced, stored in a retrieval system, or transmitted in any form by any means–electronic, mechanical, photocopy, recording, or other–except for brief quotations in printed reviews, without prior permission of the author.

This is a fictional story. The characters, organizations, and events in this book are fictitious. Any similarity to persons, living or dead, or to actual organizations or events is coincidental and not intended by the author.

Printed in the United States of America

Paperback ISBN: 979-8-8229-4160-1
eBook ISBN: 979-8-8229-4161-8
Audiobook ISBN: 979-8-8229-4501-2

Acknowledgements

Collective Vengeance would not be available without the help and patience of my partner and spouse of forty years, Patty. She has always been there with and for me. To this day, she is my inspiration, my advocate, my collaborator, and the love of my life.

I owe thanks to my alpha and beta readers (Patty, Kathy, Mary, Mary Jo, Roz, Bill, Mike, Mark, Jane, Jennifer, Patrick, David, Heather, Matt, Cindy, Ellie, Bonnie B., Bonnie G, and Greg.) for offering their time and recommendations as *Collective Vengeance* made its way through multiple drafts. I must also express special appreciation to Ellie Brown (Ellie Brown Branding) for her work in creating and establishing my author identity and assistance with the book's cover design.

Thanks to Liz (project manager) and the rest of the team at Palmetto Publishing for their editing, design, and support work. It takes a number of skilled professionals to bring a book to market and I couldn't have accomplished this endeavor without them.

Table of Contents

Preface — 1
Introduction — 3

2019
Chapter 1 - The Nomination — 5

1992
Chapter 2 - A Girl Scorned — 8
Chapter 3 - David — 12
Chapter 4 - Ryleigh's Petition — 16
Chapter 5 - Confidant — 19

1993
Chapter 6 - Delivery — 22
Chapter 7 - Impasse — 26
Chapter 8 - Groundwork — 30
Chapter 9 - Collective Vengeance — 35

2005
Chapter 10 - Attica — 40

2019
Chapter 11 - Brooklyn Heights — 45
Chapter 12 - Ryleigh's Selections — 50
Chapter 13 - Chandler's Candidate — 55
Chapter 14 - Strong-Armed Enforcer — 61
Chapter 15 - At Odds — 65
Chapter 16 - Plantation Secrets — 68

Chapter 17 – Soho Office	74
Chapter 18 – Interview	76
Chapter 19 – The Collective Project	83
Chapter 20 – First Assignment	87
Chapter 21 – Backgrounding	92
Chapter 22 – Chance Encounter	95
Chapter 23 – Bryant Park	97
Chapter 24 – Ethan Brode, Reporter	102
Chapter 25 – Adira Tomasz—Executive Assistant	105
Chapter 26 – The Algonquin	107
Chapter 27 – Advisors	112
Chapter 28 – Debriefing	116
Chapter 29 – Assignment Lydia	121
Chapter 30 – Lucas Mathers, Senator	124
Chapter 31 – Ethan and Lydia	128
Chapter 32 – Illicit Enticements	134
Chapter 33 – Roy Covington	139
Chapter 34 – Lydia Outcome	142
Chapter 35 – First Strike	146
Chapter 36 – Reaction	149
Chapter 37 – Call to Action	151
Chapter 38 – A Shot across the Bow	157
Chapter 39 – Mayday	160
Chapter 40 – Modifications	164
Chapter 41 – Morning Encounter	172
Chapter 42 – Orientation	175
Chapter 43 – Defensive Preparation	182
Chapter 44 – Ominous Encounter	188
Chapter 45 – Lines in the Sand	193
Chapter 46 – Scheming	197
Chapter 47 – Connecting	202
Chapter 48 – Sunday Respite	209

Chapter 49 - Regrouping	212
Chapter 50 - Gathering Intelligence	218
Chapter 51 - Storm's Edge	223
Chapter 52 - Second Strike	233
Chapter 53 - Return Volley	235
Chapter 54 - Turning Tables	241
Chapter 55 - Imagine	244
Chapter 56 - Cutting Ties	251
Chapter 57 - Press Conference	254
Chapter 58 - Concerning Decisions	262
Chapter 59 - Coming Clean	271
Chapter 60 - A Provocative Morning	278
Chapter 61 - Resolution	281
Chapter 62 - Reunion	287
Chapter 63 - Disturbance	291
Chapter 64 - Taking Charge	294
Chapter 65 - Reports	300
Chapter 66 - Scheduling	306
Chapter 67 - Conflicted	310
Chapter 68 - Eleventh-Hour Distraction	314
Chapter 69 - En Route	320
Chapter 70 - Waiting	327
Chapter 71 - Waylaid	329
Chapter 72 - Reassignments	336
Chapter 73 - Recovering	338

2020

Chapter 74 - A Toast	341
Counter Vengeance	344
Serial Vengeance	345
About Joseph Stanley	347

Preface

I discovered a joy in being a writer, a teller of stories, emotions, and dreams, later in life. It began with journaling assignments as part of counseling for depression as I faced retirement and multiple life-changing decisions. Little did I know journaling would evolve into writing free verse, short stories, and novels.

One of the first free-verse poems I wrote was titled "Storms." It reflected my feeling of facing a never-ending onslaught of storms as I worked to cope with depression. Eventually, I learned that storms are a part of life, at least for me. When they come, it feels like they will never end. My counseling and journaling taught me that I could face the storms. That I could win the battles if I believed in myself.

"Storms" was the genesis for *Collective Vengeance*, in which Samantha, Jack, and their team face a never-ending series of storms or obstacles, just as I have with my depression.

And so I wanted to share what I call the genesis or origin of *Collective Vengeance*. If you enjoy the verse, you can find my published collection, *My Verse*, and obtain an e-book copy with personal reflections on my website at www.stanleywrites.com.

COLLECTIVE VENGEANCE

Storms

Storms of emotion consume and scar
Leaving us damaged, perhaps forever
Unable to condone, dismiss, or forgive
Craving vengeance evermore

They seize my mind and soul
I fear the maelstrom and turbulence
Feeling helpless and torn
Desperate, seeking definition and reference

As they whisper deception
I struggle to resist their attraction
They promise peace, if only I surrender
Masking their wrath, pretending to be the exception

Self-belief is the shield I carry
Believing the best of myself is my sword
The storm must be battled and conquered
Then my soul might be calmed and restored

The thought of battle is frightening
The thought of loss depressing
The storm looms and taunts
It is never ending

—Joseph Stanley, 2018

Introduction

Alexander Hamilton once defined the judicial branch of government as the least dangerous branch of government. The passage of time has rendered this opinion obsolete.

Judges take an oath stating they will be impartial, but they are human, with biases shaped by their life experiences and outside influences.

The importance of Supreme Court appointments is that they weigh heavily in determining our personal rights. Recent divisive revisions have caused serious aftereffects felt by political ideologies of the right and the left.

Samantha Mieras has reason to fear a particular Supreme Court appointment, knowing how dangerous it could become because of political influence and interference.

CHAPTER 1

The Nomination

November 2019

Samantha Mieras's life was about to be torn apart by sudden uncertainties and turmoil. She would be standing at the edge of a precipice, facing conflict and fears she had worked to restrain over the past twenty-seven years.

Exhausted from a long day of tedious investment meetings, she found her patience stretched like a taut rubber band as she struggled to navigate one of New York City's maddening traffic jams. *What the hell's going on? Get off the damn road if you can't drive.* She took a deep breath, trying to regain a level of composure. *Calm down, Sam; it's just another day of insanity. Ranting won't help.* CNN interrupted her inner monologue with a breaking-news alert.

We've just received notice from the Supreme Court's public information office. Chief Justice Robert Wheeler was admitted to Sibley Memorial Hospital in Washington, DC, this afternoon. The press release states Justice Wheeler is battling Stage 4 pancreatic cancer and has been receiving treatment for the past four months. Medical experts say chances of surviving a Stage 4 diagnosis are low, with life expectancy ranging from three to six months.

Confidential sources at the White House believe President Lawrence will fill Wheeler's eventual vacancy with an ultraconservative candidate to fulfill a campaign pledge. Chief Judge David Jaymes on the Second Circuit Court of Appeals in New York tops the president's list of prospective nominees. Appointing Jaymes would create an unstoppable conservative majority, placing existing precedents on individual rights and other hot-button issues in the lethal crosshairs of revisionists. We will update this story as more details become available and now return to our regular programming.

Sam's heart raced as her eyes grew wide. She slammed her hands against the steering wheel, screaming, "What the fuck. This can't be happening. Not now. Never! Damn it!"

In an instant, terrifying memories flooded her mind at the possibility of her rapist ascending to the highest position on the highest court in the land.

She felt her skin begin to crawl, remembering being pregnant at sixteen, David's father demanding she have an abortion, months of fleeing and hiding to protect her unborn twins, and Ryleigh's heartfelt account of their stillbirths. It all pierced like a dagger, reopening multiple wounds in her heart.

Her body trembled as she struggled to collect herself. Pulling aside between parked cars, she pressed her head onto the wheel. *Let the shoulders fall, Sam. Inhale: one, two, three. Hold: four, five, six. Big exhale: seven, eight, nine. Repeat.* It was a well-exercised routine she used to cope with moments of panic.

She prompted her car's voice command to call Ryleigh, only to reach voicemail. "Ryleigh! Have you heard the news about Justice Wheeler? Lawrence is ready to name your fucking brother as chief justice. It's beginning to happen. My God—Aegis and your family are in the final stages of their plan to control the court. They've delivered the last three

Supreme Court justices. It's insane and can't continue. You've got to call Chandler. We need a meeting tonight. Call me back as soon as possible." Leaning back, she thought, *Buckle up, Sam. It's going to be a bumpy ride.*

Sam was turning into her parking garage as Ryleigh returned her call. "Got your message and heard the news on Wheeler. I've called Chandler. He'll be at my house by six. Catch your breath, Sam. We knew this was inevitable. We've been patient, and now our opportunity to stop them has arrived."

Sam wiped tears from her face. "Yeah, you're right. I'll be there once I have a bourbon to calm my nerves and fix dinner for Thomas." Closing the call, she felt the dark underground parking area providing momentary safe solitude as her mind wrestled with looming decisions. *Is this what I still want after all this time? Do we have enough time to stop them?*

CHAPTER 2

A Girl Scorned

Twenty-Seven Years Earlier— Raleigh, North Carolina

Jonathan Jaymes was a cartoonish but ruthless old-world plantation master serving as a one-person judge and jury over his domain. His private study reinforced his authoritarian rule with its walls of dark mahogany shelving, heavy floral drapery, plank flooring, and an expansive executive desk as his throne. It was a place of impending evil and potential harm for all who might challenge his authority. His eldest son, David, sat rigid and silent with his accuser, Samantha Mieras, out of reach.

Jonathan waited, watching them fidget in their seats as he shuffled papers on his desk. "The two of you have created a grave situation requiring an immediate remedy." He focused a disciplining stare toward David. "I cannot understand your lapse of good judgment. Your upbringing taught you better standards than lowering yourself to be with a girl of her station."

He peered over the top of his glasses as he turned to Samantha. "As for you, young woman. That you would try to entrap my son and make unfounded accusations is no surprise, considering your lack of upbringing. I will not tolerate it. You chose the wrong path to gain access to our family."

Samantha leaned forward, gripping the chair's ornate arms. She clenched her jaw, making eye contact with Jonathan. "What the hell are you saying? I didn't trap anyone." She pointed a shaking finger at David. "He invited me to his fraternity party. He kept giving me drinks until I almost passed out so he could rape me. I'm pregnant because of your goddamned son, and I'm only sixteen! My growing belly is not an unfounded accusation. It's a fact and filled with your grandchildren."

She turned to face David. "You said you loved me, then raped me while I was drunk, and now you're going to try hiding behind your father's bullshit?"

David was shaking his head as he turned toward Samantha. "Sam, we can take care of this if you listen to my father."

Jonathan's voice boomed as he slammed his fist onto the desk with the force of a judge's gavel. "Hold your tongues! I asked neither of you to speak. I'm not interested in denials or excuses. We're here so I can remedy this situation." He reached into a drawer, retrieving a bundle of currency. "Our family and the board of directors at Aegis have debated this sordid calamity and determined the best course of action."

Narrowing his eyes, he turned back to a distraught Samantha. "Your pregnancy is a disgrace, and you are not welcome here. Just look around. For God's sake, you must realize we are above your station and will not accept you or those you might carry into this family. So we have decided you must have an abortion, and it will happen as soon as possible."

Sam rose from her chair, stepping toward Jonathan. "An abortion? You pompous old bastard! I should have gone to the sheriff. I was a fool to come here believing you would help me. Believing you would care for your unborn heirs. You lied to me!"

Jonathan sat back with a smug look. "I did not lie. You misunderstood my intentions. Sit down and listen to reason. The authorities will never accept your word over ours. Your mother is a drug-addicted harlot who allows you to run wild. You are in no position to make slanderous statements and have no choice but to do as I say."

"Don't try shifting blame to my mother. David's the one who committed a crime."

"Enough!"

"How can you demand I have an abortion? I thought they violated your beliefs."

"We will never acknowledge it as being acceptable, but in this case, it is a necessity."

Pushing the money across his desk, he glared as Samantha cried into the linen shawl she'd pulled from her shoulders. "Those funds will more than cover the cost and compensate you for your silence. Do you understand your responsibilities?"

Samantha stepped back, shaking her head. "I can't believe this is happening. This isn't what you promised me if I kept quiet. You lied!"

"Silence! My decision is final. Do not make me send people to chase after you. They will find you and ensure it is done."

Raising his voice, he called for his servant. "Jackson. Take this woman out of my study and escort her off our property. David, remain seated. I will have a word with you before you leave."

Jackson gathered the money from Jonathan's desk and took Samantha's arm to escort her through the massive doors into the foyer. He whispered as they walked, "I'm sorry for you, Miss Samantha, but there is no choice. Take the money and do as Mr. Jaymes instructed. He and others will be watching. I am afraid for you. They are evil people."

Ryleigh Jaymes was just beyond the study entrance, eavesdropping on the searing encounter with her father. She stepped forward to intercede. "Thank you, Jackson. You can leave us. I will take Miss Samantha to her car."

Ryleigh wrapped her arm around Samantha's shoulder as they walked. "You don't have to do what my father ordered. Go home and wait for me. Let me talk with my father, and then I'll be home." She hugged Samantha and stormed back into the house.

CHAPTER 3

David

Ryleigh stopped to talk with Jackson as he opened the door for her. "Jackson, I have a favor to ask of you."

Jackson stood proudly, with a military posture, as he responded, "I will do whatever you ask, Ms. Ryleigh."

"I need information from my father's study. I hope it will help Samantha avoid the abortion he ordered."

"I disagree with what he has demanded of Ms. Samantha and will do whatever helps you and her. Your father will not know what we do."

"Let me finish my business with him; then I will explain what I need. Thank you, Jackson."

David's eyes were looking down as he exited Jonathan's study. He didn't see Ryleigh and Jackson talking until she pushed her hand into his chest to avoid a collision. "Huh? What are you doing here, Rye?"

"I could ask you the same question, but there's no need. I overheard the skirmish with Sam."

"Yeah, it didn't go well with her. But you haven't answered my question."

Ryleigh rolled her eyes and said, "I'm here to change Father's mind about the abortion."

"You're too late. I just finished talking with him, and we agree it's the right thing to do."

"So you're in favor of this?"

"Yes. We avoid a difficult problem for the family once Sam gets the abortion. She's the one to blame, and the burden is on her."

"Really? Or is this about David again dodging responsibility for his carelessness?"

"Don't try painting me as the villain."

"You do know she's carrying your children."

"Maybe, but it's not my problem. It's out of my hands."

"Are you admitting you're the one who got her pregnant?"

"I didn't say that. Don't try putting words in my mouth. It was a mistake she must correct without creating suspicion about me."

Ryleigh shook her head. "My God, I keep forgetting how shallow-minded you are."

David tilted his head back, sneering at Ryleigh. "Look, she's not a mother, and I'm not a father, because there are no children. There is no family if she has an abortion. How many times do I have to repeat it for you, Rye?"

"I'm standing here trying to reason with a moron."

"I am not a moron. I'm just looking out for my future."

"Well, your future may change after I talk with Father."

"Lots of luck. You've always been able to manipulate him, but it won't work. He's pissed off, and you'll be wasting your time."

"It's worth trying."

"Does he know Sam is living with you?"

"No."

"I don't think he'll be happy about it."

"It's my business, not yours or his, but I have a question before you leave."

"I'll regret asking. What's the question?"

"Why did you tell Sam you loved her and the two of you would have a future together?"

David looked down, avoiding eye contact as he flashed a smile. "I don't recall saying those things to her. She's lying if she told you that's what I said."

"You're the liar, David. Look at me and repeat your statement."

He raised his head and said, "She's always been full of fantasies, and I just let her have them. Father helped me see how she was using me. She lured me into having sex and getting pregnant to become part of our family."

"You're a pathetic excuse for a man, David. I shouldn't, but I feel sorry for you. You'll always be under someone's thumb." She started jabbing a finger into his shoulder. "And guess what? If you ever find a woman, she'll run your life just like Father."

He grabbed her hand, pushing it away. "Nice slam, Rye. Someday, you'll quit fighting us and realize swimming with the current is easier."

David had turned to leave when Ryleigh grabbed his jacket. "One last question before I go into his study. Why did you take her to the party?"

"It was what she wanted, so she could flirt like a whore. And she used sex to cloud my judgment."

"Oh, please! Stop spouting lies, David. Sam told me what happened. It was all your idea. You talked her into the party and got her drunk so you could take advantage of her."

"Well, it's her word against mine. Father will never believe her or you. No one will!"

"You bastard!" Ryleigh swung an open hand, striking David's face.

Shaking his head, he smirked. "Are you trying to defend her honor, Rye? She has no honor. Sam's a conniving little bitch who got herself knocked up, telling me she was on the pill. She's the one who lied and failed to protect herself. It's her fault, not mine."

"How could she tell you anything if she passed out from all the drinks you gave her? It was you who failed to protect her." Ryleigh pushed him aside, entering the study before he could reply to her accusation.

CHAPTER 4

Ryleigh's Petition

Jonathan was writing at his desk as Ryleigh cleared her throat to gain his attention. "Ryleigh? I didn't hear you knock. What do you need?"

"I want to talk with you about a problem."

"I'm not surprised. Today seems to be my day for solving problems. What is it?"

"I'm here about Samantha and your demand for her to have an abortion."

Jonathan's arms folded as he leaned into the back of his leather chair. "There is nothing to discuss. She will do as told, or I will have my men take care of it. Is there anything else?"

"Making her have an abortion will kill your grandchildren."

"My grandchildren? According to David, she was having sex with most of the fraternity. Any one of those boys could be the father."

"Sam didn't have sex with anyone but David. She's carrying his twins, and they are part of our family. David is lying about others having sex with her."

"Is that so? His fraternity brothers are willing to confirm his version over hers. They are upstanding young men with no reason to speak anything but the truth. She's a manipulative tart following in her mother's footsteps."

"Debating the attributes of David and his friends is not my purpose for being here. I'm asking you to reconsider your decision and have compassion for her."

Jonathan's volume increased as his face reddened. "Compassion? How can I have compassion after you told me I do not have such a capacity? Surely, you recall the accusation?"

"I do, but it was a heated emotional moment. I was angry when you demanded an end to my relationship in New York."

Jonathan started rocking in his chair. "Your infatuation with a crooked lawyer was an embarrassment for our family. Now, I'm having to resolve a similar shame for your brother. There will be no reconsideration of the abortion. We're finished talking, and you can leave."

Ryleigh began approaching Jonathan's desk. "David lied about her to benefit himself. I know she's a good person and wouldn't lie to me."

"You're believing a common girl over your brother? She runs loose without any responsible guidance."

Ryleigh's eyes closed as her voice lowered. "She doesn't run loose. Samantha's been living with me for the past six months. I've worked to provide responsible guidance. I know her heart, and I know David is the liar."

"She's living with you? How interesting, but I don't care where she lives. However, since you seem to be her guardian, I expect to hear from you she's fulfilled her responsibility. You have forty-eight hours, Ryleigh."

"We could have paternity testing done to determine if David is the biological father."

Jonathan pushed his chair back, rising to stand as his volume increased. "Anyone can falsify a test result, and it proves nothing to me."

Ryleigh responded with increased volume. "What are you afraid of, Father? Is it the truth you and David want to ignore?"

"I have had enough of your defiance." Jonathan pointed to the study doors. "I said *leave*, or must I call Jackson to escort you out?"

Shaking her head, she said, "You don't need to call Jackson. I will leave."

He was shouting after her as she opened the door to leave. "Remember, you have only forty-eight hours. Do not defy my authority, Ryleigh."

CHAPTER 5

Confidant

Ryleigh arrived home to find Sam on the couch, hugging a pillow and crying. She sat down to hold Sam's hand. "You're going to be okay, sweetie. I talked with my father, but he wouldn't listen."

"I hoped he might change his mind. What am I going to do, Rye?"

"I have a plan, but first, we must make some choices."

"Like, what choices?"

"I need to make sure you want to continue your pregnancy and deliver the twins."

Leaning back, Sam pulled her hand from Ryleigh's as her voice grew tight. "What? I can't believe you would ask that. Of course I want them. I don't need David, just them."

"Sorry—I didn't mean to upset you. I just needed to hear your confirmation one more time."

"What're the other choices?"

"There is no choice. We need to go into hiding from my father. He's sending men to find you and force the abortion. I have someone who will help us."

Sam was leaning back toward Ryleigh, asking, "Who?"

"An attorney who helps me with business matters. He's an old friend. His name is Chandler Yates."

"How can he help us, and why?"

"He has resources to keep you and the twins out of my father's reach. Chandler's willing to help because he and I have an interesting history together. I'll explain it while we fly to New York."

"Can't we stay near here instead of going to New York?"

"Staying here is too much of a risk. A big city is an easier place to disappear. Eventually, I'll move my business there and find a new home."

"But you'll be giving up this home and your friends. I don't want you to give up everything for me and my problem."

"I've wanted to make these changes for a while, and now is the perfect time."

"Are you sure it's what you want, Rye?"

"Yes. It'll be a new start for both of us. There's no family left here for you, and I'm ready to be done with mine. I know you'll have more questions, and I'll answer them as we go. Right now, time is limited. We need to be on our way by tomorrow evening. Packing and planning a new start will be a good distraction for you."

"How do we pack everything in one night?"

"We're not packing the entire house, just enough for a long trip. I have another friend who is a realtor. She will handle selling the house and arranging for movers to ship everything to New York."

"It's all happening so fast."

"I know it seems overwhelming, but we have limited choices and not much time to act." Ryleigh gave Sam a warm smile and a hug. "You'll love New York, and New York will love you. How about we get started packing for that long trip?"

"You make it sound like an adventure."

"That's a good way to think about it. Any more questions?"

"No more questions tonight. You've done so much for me, and I don't know how I'll ever repay you."

"Sam, there's nothing to repay. You're the little sister I never had, and I just want you and the twins to be safe." She grabbed Sam's shoulders, turning her to hold eye contact. "You'll become a mother in a few months, and I'll be Auntie Rye."

CHAPTER 6

Delivery

Six Months Later—New York

The labor and delivery room in the private birthing center was chilling and sterile, with clinicians consulting in hushed tones. Samantha Mieras, now seventeen, trembled on an austere medical table. She clenched the linen sheet under her body, tears streaming down her cheeks. Another contraction cascaded through her body, causing her to scream.

Reaching for Ryleigh's hand, she tried to breathe through her anguish. "Oh God, I want it to be over, Rye. I'm so scared."

Ryleigh grimaced, trying to contain tears of shared anxiety. "You can do this, sweetie. You're almost there." She patted Sam's forehead with a cool, damp cloth. Then, turning to the doctor, she whispered in a harsh tone, "For God's sake, do something before we lose her and the twins. You told me you could handle this delivery."

"We're doing our best, but her situation is more complicated than expected. She's almost there." He looked down, shaking his head, voicing a sense of urgency to those assisting him.

Another wave of staggering pain pulsed through Sam's body as she pressed her thighs into the birthing bed's leg supports. She was bearing down, almost blacking out, as the doctor eased the first child into the world. An infant's spasming cry broke the sudden interval of silence.

Sam, exhausted, barely heard the newborn's cry or a nurse's voice alerting the team, "Everyone, heads up! We have another one on the way."

Ryleigh talked with the nurses as they cleaned the twins and swaddled them in light blankets. "My associate will take the babies to a safe location as soon as they're ready."

One nurse asked, "What about Ms. Mieras?"

"As I explained to the doctor, there are men who will be here soon to try and take the babies away from her. I will tell them the twins were stillborn to get them to leave. They may ask you questions, and we need everyone to tell them the same story."

Returning to the labor and delivery room, she found Sam looking perplexed. "Where are my twins, Rye? I want to see them."

"Oh, honey, they're not here." Ryleigh was trying to catch her breath as if holding back tears. "I don't know how to tell you, but…they were stillborn, Sam."

"No, it can't be. I heard crying. What happened? Where are they?" Sam raised her voice.

"You were exhausted, hallucinating, and passed out. The medical team tried everything to save them. But the stress of hiding from David and my father caused problems the twins couldn't overcome."

"Oh God, Rye. I can't believe we lost them." Sobbing, she said, "It's not fair!"

"You did the best you could, sweetie. The months of hiding and constant harassment were too much stress."

"It's my fault for letting David get me pregnant. None of this would have happened if..."

"Listen to me, Samantha. None of this is your fault. The blame falls on David, my father, and Aegis. We'll go home soon and talk after you've rested. I've taken care of things, so you don't need to worry. Everything will be fine. You're in good hands here."

The nurse came into the room, motioning for Ryleigh to follow her. "Two gentlemen are in the doctor's office, demanding to see you."

"I'll talk with them. Can you give Samantha something to calm her? She's grieving the loss of the babies and needs to rest."

"We'll take care of Samantha while you talk with the men in Dr. Schneider's office."

Ryleigh found Jonathan's investigators in a discussion with the doctor. "I believe you wanted to talk with me?"

"Yes. I'm Joseph. This is my partner, Austin. You know we work for your father and are here to take custody of the twins."

"You're too late. They were stillborn and taken away for cremation."

"Lying to us won't work anymore, Ms. Jaymes. Dr. Schneider confirmed he delivered the babies in good health."

Ryleigh looked over Joseph's shoulder and saw the doctor raising his hands and shaking his head. "I'm sorry, Ms. Jaymes. I had to tell the truth, or they would take action to have my license suspended."

"Well, you can search the clinic, but they're gone. My associates left with the twins shortly after delivery."

Joseph looked between Ryleigh and the doctor. "I assume your associate is Mr. Yates? He seems to be the one helping you."

"My associates—meaning several people, not just one person—left with the twins. You can inform Jonathan that it's time to stop chasing. You will never be able to locate them."

The doctor added, "She's telling the truth. They left before your arrival."

Joseph and Austin looked at each other. "Jonathan wants you to contact him as soon as possible."

"Tell my father I will call him this evening."

"I'll convey your message."

CHAPTER 7

Impasse

Back home, Ryleigh was brewing tea as her phone rang. "Chandler, tell me the twins are off to their new homes."

"They're on their way. I'll have final confirmation of their safe arrival in the morning. Did Jonathan's men show up at the clinic?"

"Yes. They barged into the clinic as you and the traveling nurses went out the back door."

"What was the outcome?"

"They got to Dr. Schneider before I could talk with them. They threatened him, and he told them the twins were in good health."

"Damn it."

"I told them they'll never find the twins and to call off the chase. They said Jonathan wanted to talk with me. I'm calling him as soon as you and I finish our call."

"How is Sam doing?"

"She's sleeping. I'm hoping to bring her home in a couple of days. The delivery was harder on her than we expected. In the meantime, you and I need to talk. I've received a document you'll find to be of interest. Where can we meet to talk privately?"

"Come over to my place once you've finished with Jonathan. Call me when you're on the way, and best of luck with Jonathan."

Ryleigh opened the package Jackson had mailed to her and began reading before calling Jonathan.

"Good evening, Father. I met your man Joseph this afternoon. He said you wanted to talk."

"I've talked with him as well. Are you ready to speak truthfully, or are you going to keep creating false tales?"

"I'm ready to negotiate and have you call off your bloodhounds."

"I don't believe we have anything to negotiate, but it depends upon what you are willing to disclose, Ryleigh. Where are the twins?"

"Why do you want them?"

"They are an unpredictable risk for me and your brother now that they are alive. I must do what's necessary to protect our interests. I do not owe you any further explanation. You have defied me for too long, Ryleigh. Tell me where we can find them, and your troubles will end."

"They're on their way to adoptive families and will never know who you are. I will maintain your anonymity to avoid any risk."

"And Samantha allowed this sham adoption?"

"No. She believes the twins were stillborn. Like the twins, she will not be a risk for you if you end your persecution."

"Do you believe I will accept your word after the past six months of constant deception?"

"You have no choice. I will not reveal their location. The families have no connection with each other. You must accept that the twins are no longer a risk to your supreme plans."

"Such an interesting term, Ryleigh. It confirms my suspicion that you somehow accessed and stole my briefing file for Aegis. Am I correct?"

"I stole nothing from you. Believe what you like, Father. I want you to call off your men so Sam and I can live peacefully."

"Your impatient insistence tells me you have something to hide. The investigations will continue."

"This was a tragic ending for Samantha. Just leave her alone."

Jonathan laughed. "Your tragic ending would have been much easier if you and she had followed my orders."

"Why are you refusing to end the harassment?"

"Why? Because I know you have a hidden agenda, and I have too much to lose."

"Oh, please! You're being paranoid over nothing. What you and David do or plan to do is no longer my concern. I saved the lives of the twins. To me, they are family."

"One last time, Ryleigh. Where are they, or do we need to visit with Samantha?"

"Samantha doesn't know where the twins are. I am the only one with that knowledge. If you contact her, your precious Aegis plans will be revealed."

"Perhaps Chandler will be willing to answer my questions."

"Hah. You think Chandler would help you after what you threatened to do to his family?"

Jonathan paused, taking a slow breath before continuing. "We seem to be at an impasse."

"We're not finished, Father. Call off your dogs."

"You have no leverage to make such a demand, Ryleigh."

"You're wrong, but you're correct about my possessing your plans for David. Many people would be interested in learning about your dangerous ambitions."

"Do that, and Samantha will learn of your deception of her."

"So do we call a truce or go for nuclear destruction? I will tell Samantha the truth before you can reach her. Then I'll release the information to the press for publication."

"Damn you, girl! You have been a thorn in my side since the day you were born."

"Your pain comes from knowing I would have been a better choice for your plans than David. Your failure to recognize a woman's capabilities resulted in your choosing David, who has always been the weaker choice."

"Damn you. Against my better judgment, I will concede to a truce. Do not breach my trust, Ryleigh."

CHAPTER 8

Groundwork

Chandler was waiting for Ryleigh's arrival. *I've got to convince her to abandon the idea of hiding the twins from Sam. We'll have to tell her in the future, and now would be better for all of us.* His thoughts were interrupted by Ryleigh's frantic knocking on his door. The brisk January air swept in behind her as he opened the door.

"Jeez, Chandler, it's colder than a witch's tit out there. You could have left the door unlocked for me."

"Well, you should know better than anyone, Rye. I didn't expect you to be here this quickly. You were going to call me after talking with Jonathan."

"Well, I didn't have time to call, and I'm not amused by your witchy, backhanded comment. Offering an apology would be nice."

He snickered as he hung her coat in the entry closet. "You're right, but I couldn't resist. My apologies."

"We've got about an hour before I need to check on Sam again, but this shouldn't take much time."

"Let's go into the kitchen. I have your favorite tea and additives ready for you."

Ryleigh was pulling papers from her satchel and handing them to Chandler. She hesitated and stared at him before responding. "How can you be a jerk, making snide remarks, and then flip to being a considerate gentleman within seconds?"

"My contrasting characteristics are a constant. It's part of what drew us together when we first met. We're a perfect yin-and-yang couple, Rye."

"You're so quick with the clever lawyer's responses."

Chandler was listening as he started leafing through the notes. When he saw the cover page titled "Aegis Strategic Planning," his eyebrows rose. "How did you get this? Is it for real?"

"Jackson removed it from my father's study and gave it to me. He might be my father's servant, but his loyalties to me are stronger. So the answer to your astonished question is yes, it's his plans for Aegis and, as you'll see, my brother. Now I know why he's desperate to keep knowledge of the twins from getting out."

"Do you think the board knows you have this information?"

"No. My father doesn't want anyone to know. It was my leverage to have him stop pursuing us and the twins."

"Will he stop?"

"No. Jonathan never gives up on something he wants, but his paranoia over what I might do will add to the gray hairs on his head."

"Brilliant move, Rye. Keep him on edge, worrying about disclosures." He hesitated, then continued. "Before we go further, I have a concern. I believe we should reconsider keeping the truth about the twins from Sam. Telling her would take away any advantage for your father."

"Nothing changes, Chandler. We continue our original strategy. You and I agreed this was the best course of action."

"I know, but there's a significant risk if Sam ever discovers what we did. What if your father changes his mind about keeping quiet?"

"I'll be the one to make sure neither happens. If anything goes wrong, I'll handle it. As for my father, he doesn't want anyone to see what's in your hands. Let's stop talking in circles. Have you heard from the adoptive families?"

"Yes, the twins are safe, and I've created the funding so they will be well cared for."

"Good. Believing my father and David were the cause of the stillbirths gives Sam a focus and desire for vengeance against them. Are you still with me or looking to bail out?"

"I'm still here. You have the floor and my rapt attention, Commander."

"Damn it, Chandler! I asked you to quit being a smartass."

"Okay, okay."

"I've told Sam about our past relationship and problems with my family. Hearing how my father drove us apart helped her feel a connection with us. I didn't explain details about Aegis. I thought you would be a better choice to offer background on them."

"So she's okay with having me continue to help?"

"Yes. Sam knows how generous you've been since we arrived in New York. You've earned her trust."

Ryleigh stopped to see if Chandler had a comment before resuming. "Let me run through a quick summary of future events and timelines. Finishing high school is priority number one for Sam. Since she's living with me, we can do homeschooling. It will get her to graduation in a year. From high school, she moves on to college for a BBA. She can intern with my investment company and move into a junior partnership once she has her degree. I have confidence in her ability to thrive in private equity investing."

"You're making a lot of assumptions. What if Sam opts out of the degree or the partnership offer?"

"Way ahead of you, Chandler. I've been talking with her about this for months. She's an overachiever and a hundred percent on board." Ryleigh gave Chandler a "gotcha" grin.

"Sometimes I hate throwing kudos your way, but great work, especially keeping Sam safe during the pregnancy. I would've given millions to be there when the board learned you were helping her thwart their demand for an abortion. Getting Jonathan to back off was the final masterful touch."

"Thanks. I can manipulate him, but I don't want to overuse the advantage. David may be the heir apparent, but now he knows I would have been the better choice. Turn to page 10. It's where they spell out their major objectives." Ryleigh waited as Chandler read.

"Control of the judiciary and David being nominated for chief justice within thirty years? Who the hell do they think they are?"

"Doesn't matter. We know who they are and can wait as long as they can. When they nominate David, we go for the jugular. Over the years, they'll see us as an annoyance. The longer we wait, the more overconfident and vulnerable they'll be. Time and patience are our allies."

"I've never asked, but what's driving you in all this, Rye?"

"As you know, my father's view of women is that they are a half step above domestic help. The family taught me my role was to be an adornment at social gatherings, marry well, have children, and speak only when asked."

"You don't fit those expectations."

"I never will fit their beliefs. My father, Aegis, and my brother represent discrimination against women's rights. Protecting Sam and defying them is my contribution to stopping the injustice. It may sound like a wish list, but it's my motivation."

Chandler was setting the material aside as he looked out the window before speaking. "What if their plans fall apart or never happen? I assume you'll have an option for Sam to have some sense of justice?"

"Yes. This lays the groundwork, but we can adjust as needed. We'll be like terrorists hiding in plain sight, waiting to strike."

"I hate to repeat myself, but I need to ask again. Will we ever reveal the truth about the twins to Sam?"

"It will be a decision we'll make somewhere in the future. There will be an appropriate time to explain and perhaps reunite them."

"Okay then. I remain on board, and I like the terrorist analogy. Let's plan to meet once Sam is back home."

CHAPTER 9

Collective Vengeance

Sunshine flooded Ryleigh's kitchen as she savored her coffee while finishing her early-morning routine, recalling last week's planning with Chandler. Then, glancing at the clock, she called out to Sam. "Eight o'clock, sleepyhead. Would you like some breakfast before Chandler gets here?"

Sam shuffled into the kitchen and gazed out the window. "I'm not hungry for much. Maybe scrambled eggs and toast. When will he be here?"

"We're scheduled for nine. I can postpone if you're not up to it."

"No need to reschedule. Let's start with your breakfast offer."

They were finishing when Chandler arrived. After hanging up his coat, he walked over to hug Sam. "I'm not sure what to say other than that I'm sorry for your loss. You've been through so much, and this is not how you thought it would end."

"Thanks, Chandler. You don't need to say anything more."

Ryleigh tapped a spoon on her coffee mug to gain their attention. "Hate interrupting the feel-good moment, but we have work to do." Then, like a tour guide, she motioned for them to follow her to the dining room, where she laid out paper pads, pens, and file folders for each of them. "I thought this would work as a conference room for us."

Sam opened her folder and turned to Chandler, asking, "Why is this called Project Aegis?"

"Good opening question. Aegis and Jonathan were the source of your troubles over the past five months. They're the reason you were not allowed into the family. The demand for an abortion was their recommendation. Aegis, Ryleigh's family, and David's future intertwine."

Reaching into his briefcase, Chandler handed a thick file to Sam. "That's a complete history on them, which you can read later."

Chandler eased back into his chair and started drumming his fingers. "Here's the short history on them. Aegis was formed at the end of the Civil War by David's great-great-grandfather. The original purpose was to prevent another civil war. Good intentions initially, but corrupt political operatives gained control over the years, turning Aegis into a dangerous threat to the country's democratic foundation.

"Today, extreme political factions control Aegis. Their goal is to grow and gain control of all branches of government at the federal level. If they succeed, they will have the power to create, revise, and enforce laws based on their white-privileged ideology. It's all about gaining control through years of patient manipulation, creating a bloodless revolution, and overthrowing freedoms."

He paused briefly before continuing. "There's a parable about frogs and boiling water that will help you understand the methodology behind Aegis's ambitions. If you put a frog into a pot of tepid water and gradually increase the heat, it will remain until it dies because it does not sense the danger. Aegis began its work almost one hundred years ago. Its members have been turning up the heat slowly, knowing people wouldn't react to their slow pace until it was too late to stop them.

"We will match their strategy of patience. We wait for their ultimate move, David's nomination to be chief justice. His appointment is their final move, and we will stop it."

Chandler took a slow sip of coffee, watching Sam's bemused facial expression. "Let me elaborate on what Ryleigh told you about their actions against us. The story goes back a few years to when we met in the city and became romantic partners. Jonathan disapproved, investigated my background, and discovered I'm biracial. He threatened to destroy the reputations of my father and mother, which would have ruined their business enterprise.

"As you can understand, being biracial was unacceptable in southern social circles. To avoid public disclosure, Ryleigh and I ended our affair but have remained close friends, which enabled me to help the two of you."

Ryleigh leaned forward to interject. "Sad to say, what Chandler told you and what you'll read is the ugly truth about my family. You're not alone in wanting justice. The three of us share a collective craving for vengeance."

Sam sat looking between them, squinting. "I kept thinking it was just me until you told me what they did to you. But Chandler, I didn't think being biracial was still a problem."

"It's less of a problem today than when my parents were married in 1953. From the time I was a young child, I knew my heritage and the risk to our family's social status. My mother explained it was important to keep outsiders from knowing about it. To this day, I remain sensitive and protective of my parents as well as myself. The perceived risk of someone disclosing my secret is a reality. Call it a personality flaw."

"I understand, and I'm sorry for you." Sam turned to Ryleigh, asking, "David and your family are good with this shit?" Her face flashed red as she closed her eyes, placing a hand across her lips. "Sorry. I'm trying to improve my speaking manners, but sometimes the words jump out."

Ryleigh answered before Chandler could continue. "Sweetie. Over the past months, they've pulled David over to their side. The David you knew a year ago is gone. Now he's just another one of their bastardized minions."

"If I could finish," said Chandler. "Our plans won't come to fruition overnight. Their timetable goes out another twenty to thirty years. All of us will have vengeance, but it will take time."

Chandler watched Sam seeming to absorb his comment. "What I'm learning is that each of us has a reason for wanting justice and vengeance. Am I right?"

"Yes, Ryleigh and I have our own axes to grind."

Sam straightened her posture, looking at Ryleigh. "I don't like calling our work Project Aegis. I hate them and their name. I think we should be together as a collective team and working on the Collective Project. That name gives me focus and will remind me that I'm not in this alone."

Chandler scratched out the title on his folder and wrote "The Collective Project." He said, "I like your suggestion. What about you, Rye?"

"If it helps Sam focus, I'm good with it."

"So we have a focus, but we still do nothing for who knows how long? Where's the justice for me and my children they killed?"

Chandler answered, "We won't be sitting idle. We'll monitor what they're doing and create minor problems for them. Then, when it's appropriate, we take aggressive action. We will expose their charade when they're least likely to expect an attack. Sam, the waiting will be worth it in the end."

Sam shook her head, asking, "Why not get rid of David, Jonathan, and their other leaders now? Be done with them. Ryleigh says you have people who could make it happen. I want justice now before they can do more harm. I want something to happen now, not later!" She was raising her voice, turning red, and flailing her arms.

Chandler waited for Sam to become quiet. "It's not an eye for an eye yet. I know asking you for patience seems unfair, but it's the best course to follow."

Sam breathed deeply before speaking. "It's not fair. They're doing crap and getting away with it. Ryleigh told me it would take time. Now I'm hearing it from you. But I want them to pay now! I lost my children because of them!" Tears started rolling down her face as Ryleigh handed her a tissue.

"They will pay, Sam."

"I'm tired and pissed off. Sorry about the street talk, Rye. I need time to think and cool down. Let me read Chandler's history lesson. You can explain things I don't understand. I know I need to trust the two of you. You're all the family I have left, and we need to stick together. Promise me they won't get away with what they've done to me or the two of you."

Chandler patted Sam's hand. "I promise we will have our collective vengeance. Take your time reading, and ask questions. I'll leave so you can rest and the two of you can talk." He turned toward Ryleigh. "Call me with any questions."

He gathered items into his briefcase, exchanged hugs with the two women, and headed out, thinking, *Sam's strong, and Rye's goals for vengeance can work. I'm hesitant about continuing to hide the twins, but I'll follow her plan.*

CHAPTER 10

Attica

Twelve Years Later

The daily discussions among inmates were notorious in B yard at Attica Correctional Facility. Jack sat in with the select group, listening to Mansa, the yard's indisputable boss.

"Gallagher, there's an attorney waiting to meet with you. His name is Chandler Yates" was the gruff greeting from an approaching guard.

"Well, Chief, I don't have a lawyer and don't recall askin' for one. Ya must be lookin' for anotha crim, cuz I don't know anyone named Yates." Jack's pen lingo conveyed the surly attitude typical of Attica inmates as he broke into a grin, shaking his head and scanning the table for peer approval.

"I don't give a damn what you think, monkey mouth. You'd be a fool to turn down a meeting with Chandler Yates. I can tell him to leave, but it might upset Mansa. Mr. Yates wanted you to know Mansa arranged his visit."

Jack looked across the table to find Mansa laughing and nodding in agreement. "Is he shittin' me, Mansa? Yur doin'?"

"Yes, indeed, my friend. Don't disappoint me, Jack. You're one of my last recommendations before I leave here to breathe the fresh air of freedom."

Inmates competed to gain Mansa's approval. If he recommended doing something, you did it. He commanded respect in multiple ways. Physically, his imposing six-foot-seven stature, jet-black skin, athletic posture, and gait drew immediate attention. The graying shape-up haircut, close-cropped beard, and black eyes exuded confidence and comprehension of the complexities of his domain—no need for airs or braggadocio. Mansa used quiet, subtle methods to exert his presence and authority.

"Okay then, nottin' keepin' me here. I'll go do the talk, but only cuz you think I should."

The guard escorted Jack to the visiting area, where Jack found Chandler Yates sitting alone at a table, reviewing documents. Yates's wiry build, thinning grayish hair, and goatee reminded Jack of a movie actor playing the part of an English gentleman. His tailored gray suit and the weathered leather briefcase beside his chair completed the image.

Jack coughed lightly, gaining his attention. "You must be Yates? I was told ya wanted to meet, and one of my friends said we should talk."

Chandler looked up from his work for a first impression of Jack. "Good afternoon, Mr. Gallagher! Glad to see you took the advice of your associate. I've heard good things about you. Have a seat."

"Not sure what this is about, so gimme some details." Jack took a seat, slouching back into the chair across from Chandler. He folded his arms, squinting and sneering, waiting for an answer.

"Well, first, let's kill the gangster act. We're not in your Hell's Kitchen stomping grounds, and I'm not impressed or intimidated by false bravado. So listen closely, because my time is valuable, and I'm confident what I have to say will interest you. But of course, I'm assuming a release from this fine resort and clearing your record would be at the top of your bucket list. So do I have your attention, or should we close the discussion?" Chandler sat back, raising his chin, looking into Jack's eyes for a change of attitude.

"Whoa. Maybe we got off on the wrong foot, and I...ah, I should apologize. This place makes ya wanna shoot first and ask questions later. Know what I mean? Ya got my attention, but first, I need to throw questions your way. Like, who's paying the tab if ya represent me? What strings are you attaching? And call me Jack." He placed his hands on the table, adjusting his body to an attentive posture.

"Well, Jack. I'm here at Mansa's request. He believes you deserve a break and might be a promising associate for me if I were to arrange your release. But there are better places and times to explain what I mean by 'an associate.' Too many ears are listening here. However, I'm sure you'll find my employment offer to be legal, interesting, and lucrative.

"In answer to your first question, no one is paying me to represent you, and I expect no payment from you. My fee is your willingness to listen and consider an employment opportunity once I obtain your freedom. You'll be free to accept or decline my offer. No strings and no complications. Everything starts once you tell me to go forward with legal representation. You need to understand I can guarantee success." Chandler's head tilted to the left, his eyebrows raised. His drumming fingers disturbed the silent pause as he waited.

"So let me get things straight. Mansa set this up. You can spring me free. All I gotta do is consider workin' for ya or walk away once I'm out. No strings attached?"

"Congratulations. You've grasped the concept of straight and simple. A yes gets us started, and a no sends me away while you return to your cell for the rest of your sentence." Chandler interlaced his fingers and leaned forward, propping his elbows on the table.

Jack shook his head and smiled, extending his hand. "Damn. Okay, Yates, it's a yes."

Chandler returned the handshake, smiling. "You'll be hearing from my office. There will be papers to sign. No appearances or testimony will be necessary. We will plan to talk over lunch the day you leave here." Chandler closed his folder, placing it into the briefcase before leaving without another word. Jack sat speechless, waiting for the guard to escort him back to B yard.

He found Mansa sitting alone, watching his entourage engage in a game of basketball. "I dunno what I did ta earn a chance ta go free. Dunno how to pay ya back."

Mansa motioned for Jack to have a seat. "I selected you because you have potential, my friend. Chandler will compensate me. However, we must start some manners and proper speech lessons."

"Ya mean talkin' smooth like you."

"Yes. It's time to put your street language and attitude in the rearview mirror. I will start your rehabilitation. Chandler will finish the work once you're released. You have a unique chance to make a life-changing turn. As I said earlier, don't disappoint me, Jack."

"What 'bout you? Ya said something soundin' like ya was gettin' out too. Is Yates springin' ya like me?"

"In a way, he is. Chandler has reconnected me with an old friend from my combat days in Vietnam who needs my help in his new line of work. I almost recommended you to him, but Chandler's is a better path for you to follow."

True to his word, Chandler delivered. It took several months, but Jack was leaving Attica as a free man. He changed into street clothes and collected his belongings from the property room, along with discharge papers as the attendant sent him on his way. Jack took in a long breath of fresh air as he stepped outside the prison gate. It seemed like an impossible achievement. Striding out toward the street, he found a car and driver waiting at the curb.

"Mr. Gallagher? My name is Robert. I'll be driving you to meet Mr. Yates for lunch." He opened the door without further hesitation, inviting Jack to slide in.

Jack shook Robert's hand. "Thank you for picking me up, Robert. I'm looking forward to seeing Mr. Yates again." Jack laughed to himself and thought, *Mansa would be proud of the way I talked with Robert.* He settled into the back seat, taking in the azure blue sky, bright sun, and newness of his liberty. *Let's see what kind of future Chandler Yates has in store for me.*

CHAPTER 11
Brooklyn Heights

November 2019

Sam's anxieties over Justice Wheeler were calming down thanks to a double shot of Michter's twenty-five-year-old bourbon as she watched Thomas devour his Kitty Feast seafood dinner. "I envy you, Thomas. You have the perfect life, which explains why you're always willing to listen to my rants. We spoil each other with just the right amount of attention." Thomas jumped onto his window perch, licking his paws as he watched Sam gather her keys and leave.

Her annoyance persisted as she drove to Ryleigh's home in Brooklyn Heights. Arriving early, she found Ryleigh and Chandler engaged in conversation. "Well, so much for me always being ten minutes early and the first to arrive at events. Good to see you, Chandler. Have I missed anything important?"

Ryleigh took Sam's coat. "Chandler was updating me on his new apartment and the difficulties of moving, even if it's only a few city blocks. I told him he'd be fine once he got unpacked and settled. But we have more important things to discuss. Can I get you anything to drink, Sam? Water, tea, another bourbon?"

"Water's fine. I hit my reserve bar stock while Thomas ate. Any word from your confidential contacts at SCOTUS, Chandler?"

Chandler tapped his fingertips in front of his lips as he answered. "Everyone is anxious and remaining silent. What we've heard on the news is all I can get for now, but I'll keep asking. Something this big won't stay hidden for long. For now, Wheeler will remain on the court as long as possible, but optimism and time are not on his side. Oddsmakers say he might not see the new year."

Sam turned to Ryleigh. "Have you tried contacting your father to see if Aegis's plans have changed? After hearing about Wheeler, I'm sure they're in high gear to put the last piece of their puzzle into play."

"I talked with him after your call, but we're still on cautious talking terms. Trying to mend fences over the last two years has produced some progress. I'm going down to Raleigh for dinner and his birthday."

Sam blinked her eyes open. "Dinner at the plantation house?"

"Yes, and it's his invitation. I think he has other motives besides turning another year older. It's an opportunity to see what I can learn. He loosens up and gets more talkative after drinks and dinner."

Chandler added, "According to my White House contacts, Jonathan has been advocating to the president on multiple crucial matters for the upcoming election. He's touting that David becoming chief justice would go a long way with the party and improve Lawrence's chances for reelection."

Sam began speaking in calm, measured tones. "Good information, but more speculation than fact. I've considered giving up over the last two years. Maybe it's the years of waiting, failed attempts to derail Jonathan's ambitions, or questioning if it's worth continuing the fight. But hearing the breaking news pushed aside my doubts. The thought of David raping me, Jonathan and Aegis demanding I have an abortion, my losing my children, and the two of you being threatened always shakes my mental stability. Their privileged mindset caused all those things, encouraging them to do whatever they wished.

"We talked about catching them when they would be overconfident and vulnerable. Well, this is it. I can imagine the cheers and high fives as those bastards celebrate being close to one of their major goals. We can bring them down. Am I right? Are we still in this together?" Sam looked between them as they raised glasses in a silent toast.

She opened her portfolio, ready to make notes and take charge. "Let's go through ideas. I know you've both been working on options. We should prioritize decision-making based on clear thinking rather than allowing emotions to override sound judgment. We need to treat this as if it's another one of our investment evaluations. So sticking with our normal sequence, let's start with Chandler's counsel for handling this project."

Chandler nodded, shifting into managerial mode. "Okay, I'll start with a basic corporate structure. We need clarity on who's running the show, and I think it should be Sam. We all have scores to settle, but hers are the most important. Any objection, Ryleigh?"

"No problem for me. I prefer to operate in the background, contributing when needed."

"It's agreed—Sam's the CEO. An immediate task is to find someone to function as your field manager. We'll label that person the chief operating officer. Sam, your role is to make decisions, keep the team focused, and let the COO get the work done. Ryleigh and I will be your board of directors, advising and helping ensure your success."

Sam finished writing and added, "I want an operations person on board within two weeks. This type of search is in your wheelhouse, Chandler. I'm sure you have one or two individuals in mind. Let's hear about them."

"My main associate jumps to the top of the list, but I'll need to contact him to see if he's interested and available."

Ryleigh asked, "Is this the great Jack Gallagher, the jack-of-all-trades you always rave about?"

"Yes, he's my preferred choice, and Sam can decide if she wants to make the hire after interviewing him. However, your question seems to take issue with him. I don't know why. You've never met or worked with Jack. Correct?"

"True. I've heard a few of your clients find him troublesome. He sometimes acts independently on certain tasks. Sam needs someone who will follow her directions."

Chandler shook his head with a snide laugh. "Operating outside client requests and objectives is not in Jack's character. Clients highly rate his work. Of course, I can add names to a list of candidates, but he'll always be at the top. I want the best person for the job, and Jack's the best choice. I don't know where you get your information, Rye, but it's unreliable."

Ryleigh snapped back, "My information is reliable. Perhaps you've become lax and overlooked problems your clients have with him. I think there should be other choices beyond him."

"You don't know who my clients are, and they would never discuss his work for them with you."

"I know a lot more than you think, Chandler."

"What the hell, Ryleigh? Are you trying to…"

"Stop it, Chandler, and quit being so sensitive."

Sam raised her hands, interrupting the growing confrontation. "Whoa! No infighting, people. We need to be working together. Chandler, you're responsible for finding me a talented and reliable operations person. Get me information on your choices, and I'll conduct background checks. Then I'll do interviews. Any further objections, Rye?" Ryleigh quieted, shaking her head.

"Okay. You're up, Rye."

Ryleigh was frowning but holding back from raising further objections. "To start, our work will require the talents of more than one person. Anticipating the need for multiple associates, I've compiled a list of individuals who can help us.

"I have four candidates for us to consider and would like to explain my expectations for each of them. Of course, this list is subject to modification, since you have the final say, Sam." She stopped to let Sam and Chandler read. "I'll get fresh water while you look through their information, and I ask you to hold questions until I can fill in with my thoughts."

CHAPTER 12

Ryleigh's Selections

Sam was the first to comment as Ryleigh returned to the dining table. "An interesting collection of personalities. I have questions, but let's hear your fill-ins and see if they provide answers before I ask."

"Okay, I'll start with Ethan Brode. He's a graduate of the University of Michigan with a double major in English and communications. Ethan Brode, an investigative reporter, grew up in Ann Arbor, Michigan. His parents, who are law professors at the university, expected him to pursue a legal profession. Ethan's enthusiasm for writing won out over their desires. I would describe him as intelligent and inquisitive, with a laid-back temperament. His tendencies are to blend into a situation, observe, and formulate questions. Great attributes for a reporter.

"Ethan gives us the ability to make a head-on attack against David's nomination. He's been researching the political ambitions of Aegis. Sam and I own the *Insider*, a politics-based news source where he works. Its journalists specialize in discovering information to expose the dark-sided connection between New York's social elite and the underbelly of DC politics. Sensational political exposé is their genre. The paper's office, where it was founded, is in New York, even though they primarily target DC. The physical separation from DC allows them to strike from a safe distance."

Sam raised a hand to ask, "Have you talked with him?"

"Not directly. I've captured his attention with anonymous texts promising insider information on Aegis. Investigative reporters are eager to pursue hot leads. He's taken the bait and wants a meeting. I'm confident he'll work with us and, as you'll see, should pair well with the other candidates."

Chandler asked, "Is he aware of your ownership of the paper?"

Ryleigh replied, "I serve as the CEO, but he has no clue of my connection to the text messages."

Sam added, "While we're invested as owners, I wasn't aware of his position until now. So Rye wins my nod to bring him onto our team."

Ryleigh turned to the next set of pages. "Second on my list of prospects is Adira Tomasz. After growing up in Chicago, she moved to New York several years ago. Despite her soft-spoken nature, she can adopt a defiant tone when needed. She has good street smarts and an ability to socialize at the highest levels.

"While her background runs from a troubled childhood to work as an exotic dancer and escort to involvement in recruiting escorts, her current position is why we want her on our team." Ryleigh waited for comments.

Sam narrowed her eyes. "I'll take the bait, Rye. Who is her current employer? Your notes end at recruiting escorts, which doesn't give me a reason to bring her on board."

"I left out her current employment because it seems too good to be true. Adira is the executive assistant for David and Cynthia Jaymes."

Sam looked at Chandler, who raised his eyebrows and shoulders, waiting to let her respond to Ryleigh. "Okay, my opinion of her value to the team is changing. Keep going."

Ryleigh gave Sam a wink, continuing, "David's holier-than-thou attitude and Cynthia's hidden agendas have left her disillusioned. Adira is the perfect turncoat who can gather the inside information Ethan needs for his attacks. She will also enable us to monitor what Aegis is currently doing. Recruiting her onto our team will require some finesse."

"As I asked with Ethan, have you talked with her?"

"As with Ethan, I've taken the approach of using anonymous messaging. The results are the same. She would like to meet. Again, she has access to the information Ethan needs. Adira will also pair well with my third recommendation."

Ryleigh watched Sam and Chandler writing before continuing. "Lydia Mathers is next and presents a unique opportunity. She's married to Senator Lucas Mathers, who is the vice-chair of the Senate Judiciary Committee. He's being blackmailed by Aegis for indiscretions with an escort employed by Society, the dirty little secret sting operation run by Cynthia Jaymes. Society is how Cynthia squeezes political support from members of Congress and other political operatives."

Pausing for a moment, Ryleigh said, "Now for several twists. Lydia is thirty years younger than Lucas. I think the age spread qualifies her as a trophy wife. The escort who trapped Lucas recruited Lydia to work for Society. She's quite the independent free spirit and enjoys her newfound avocation. On top of all that, Adira and Lydia have become more than close friends. Lucas is aware of their relationship. His approval stems from a voyeuristic appetite. Safe to say, this threesome has the potential for a salacious novel."

Chandler smiled, raising a hand to pause Ryleigh's disclosures. "I see your notes give us more of the storyline, and it'll be a good read, but how do you see Lucas and Lydia working with us? And would they?"

"Yes, they'll work with us. Lydia more directly than Lucas. Both have axes to grind with Aegis and stories to share with Ethan. Remember, he's hard at work looking for a sensational story, and they can deliver enough tantalizing material to keep him writing for months.

"Through Cynthia's blackmailing scheme, Aegis believes it has control of Lucas to guarantee David's approval by the Judiciary Committee. I've talked with Lucas. He disagrees with this assessment and wants to see David's nomination fail, even if it means sacrificing his role as a senator. Both of them will help us use an aggressive strategy to defeat Aegis."

Sam clapped, saying, "Bravo, Ryleigh. I believe you've struck a vein of gold with this group. Do I work with them?"

"My first thought was to have them working with you, but now I'm thinking it should be with our yet-to-be-named operations officer. Would you agree, Chandler?"

"Yes. Sam can oversee what he does, but leave him to direct the team's activities. We can always change the dynamics later. Any additional information on your selections, Rye?"

"Here are a couple of things to know about Adira. It was my father who convinced Cynthia to give her a promotion. I'm not sure of the connection, but it's worth noting. One last twist is that Adira was the one who informed Lydia about her husband's dalliance and convinced Lydia to work for Society as a tit for tat against Lucas. She will help us recruit Adira."

Chandler burst out laughing. "My God, Ryleigh. Tit for tat?"

Now, they all were laughing. "I couldn't resist such an apropos phrase. Those are my candidates and initial ideas for utilizing them. Questions?"

Sam spoke first while Chandler listened intently. "Great work, Rye. I think all of them have a role to play. Let me read through the rest of your profiles on them and turn them over to our COO."

"Thanks for the compliment. Unless there are questions, that should round out our team."

Sam closed her file and leaned forward onto her forearms. "I have one more individual to consider for the team. His name is Roy Covington. He's a private investigator who does my background checks and other work. I've known Roy for years and trust him to help me make well-informed decisions. He will also be a good right-hand person for our COO. Your thoughts, Chandler?"

"I'm good with Rye's choices and how to use them. Like you, I've known Roy for a long time and like the idea of bringing him onto the team. I'll contact you tomorrow to review choices for a COO. Last words, Ryleigh?"

"Just a reminder, Chandler. I'm not a fan of Jack Gallagher. Sam should have multiple choices to ensure your operations candidate is right for us."

After Sam and Chandler left, Ryleigh was busy making notes and contemplating what-ifs with participants and the blueprint she envisioned. *I know Chandler will be a weasel and recommend only Jack for Sam to consider.*

CHAPTER 13

Chandler's Candidate

Gramercy Park Hotel had a reputation for being frequented by actors, artists, writers, intellectuals, and fashion designers. Chandler relished the atmosphere and the opportunity for networking with his charismatic, gregarious clientele. It was a fertile hunting ground where he could find affluent patrons seeking off-the-record legal representation to help them escape investigation for questionable activities.

Chandler arrived early for brunch with Sam. "Good morning, Martha." Shaking hands with the hostess, he pressed a hundred-dollar bill into her hand. "I need the usual seating away from curious guests for a private meeting with Ms. Mieras."

"Of course, Mr. Yates. We appreciate your patronage, and as always, I can accommodate your requests. I'll watch for Ms. Mieras and send her to join you as soon as she arrives." Martha escorted him to a back corner of the restaurant, calling a server to handle Chandler's special order of steak and eggs. "I hope you have a pleasant day, Mr. Yates. Let me know if there is anything else you need."

Striding into the Gramercy, Samantha Mieras raised her head and posture, gathering a long breath. The doorman greeted her with a familiar nod. "Good morning, Miss Mieras. I saw Mr. Yates earlier as he went into the restaurant." She returned the nod, thinking, *It's nice to be treated with respect.* No longer was she the frightened girl being scorned. Today's session was well outside a regular attorney-client discussion. Now, she was launching a plan of attack, seeking vengeance after years of patience.

Chandler was finishing his breakfast when Sam arrived. He stood to greet her, sliding a chair out for her to sit in. "Good morning, Sam. Can I order you coffee, juice, water, perhaps something to eat?" He knew her preference for ice water and black coffee but was always polite in offering alternatives. His mother had taught him to believe a gentleman never assumes a lady's desires.

"Oh, Chandler, you know my choices never change. One day, you'll learn to save the courtesies for others." Chandler gave a silent smile, nodding in agreement as he slid her chair into place. Sam took the seat, adjusting it closer to the table. She leaned forward, folding her hands under her chin with a deep sigh.

Her eyes glistened, and she spoke in a soft tone. "I thought this day would never happen. Now that it's here, I have mixed emotions, but I'm eager to hear your recommendations and suspect there will be only one, despite Ryleigh's concerns. So let's be efficient with our time and get started." Sam opened her leather portfolio, moving items on the table to create a clear business space.

Chandler shook his head. *Right to the heart of business at hand with Sam. No wasted time or effort, and she's right. I should save the chivalry for others.* He resumed his seat across from her, reaching into his briefcase to retrieve several folders prepared for their review. He paused until the server pouring Sam's coffee left. "Before we start, I should ask if you've had further conversation with Ryleigh about Jack."

Sitting back, Sam took a sip of her coffee with a grimace. "We talked for a few minutes. She continues to express concerns and doesn't believe you've vetted other candidates for my consideration. Rye sees Jack as a risk and would not hire him, but she said the final decision was up to me. So I need to hear your pitch and determine if he warrants an interview." She replaced the coffee cup on its saucer, looking for Chandler's reaction.

Chandler's voice stumbled through a frown. "Damn her and her constant attempts to manipulate. I don't know how we ever had a romantic relationship. She can't resist adding dashes of conflict, like a cook adding extra salt to every dish." He paused, beginning to drum his fingers on the table. "Sorry for the distraction. I'll mute my contempt for her interference and focus on my pitch, as you aptly called it." His face flushed as he passed a manila folder to Sam and opened the remaining one before him.

She scanned the contents without comment, examining printouts and photos as Chandler began his presentation. "Let me present Mr. Jack Gallagher. Your assumption was correct; he is my one and only candidate. As I said in our meeting, Jack and I have a long, successful history. He's handled complicated assignments for my most important clients, and his performance has always been exceptional.

"We discussed needing someone with the talent to handle various tasks, from managing people to running executive-level meetings and, if required, being a strong-armed enforcer. Jack's my number one talent and the best option for all those purposes. As for Ryleigh's concerns, I think his background and skills intimidate her, even though they've never met. As we both know, she dislikes feeling uncomfortable or challenged, but he will have limited contact with her if you hire him. Interacting with her won't intimidate him. Of course, I can still search for others if you wish."

Sam was listening but not speaking as she continued sifting through the background information. "Can you add personal information such as his family, his attitude, how you met, and why you hired him?"

"Okay. As his name implies, he's of Irish heritage and was raised in Hell's Kitchen. His father, Aidan, trained Jack and his younger brother to be hooligans with menacing reputations. The three of them, according to Jack, were competing with other family gangs, trying to be the top family gang in the Kitchen area."

"And what about his mother? Did she have any say or influence?"

Chandler smiled, nodding his head. "I can tell you Jack's a different person whenever he drifts into memories of her. Mary Gallagher was a woman with unending faith and a contradiction to his father. Despite her efforts to steer Jack away from a life of crime, Aidan ultimately prevailed in the short run. Jack's a better man today, and he believes it's because of her continuing to nudge him from above. She instilled a softer side into his personality."

"So his mom is deceased? What about Aidan?"

"His mother passed away three years after Jack and I began working together. He feels she witnessed a significant change in his life, and he finds joy in remembering that. A gang confrontation claimed the lives of Aidan and Jack's brother years back. So I've become the only person close to being family for him now."

Sam set her pen down, waiting before commenting. "You seem to have more than a business knowledge of him."

"Sam, we've been working together for over fourteen years. We've developed a brotherly relationship and learned a lot about each other. It's why I know he's the best candidate for you."

She closed the file, setting it aside. "On paper and with your personal information, he appears to be the person I need, but it's a quick observation. It prompts me to ask another question. Would you trust him with your life? After all these years of waiting, I feel like it's what I'm about to do."

Chandler was drumming his fingers on the table, wide-eyed. "I wouldn't introduce him if I didn't trust him. Yes, I would put my life in his hands."

Sam gave a warm smile, reaching out to quiet Chandler's drumming. "Calm down, counselor. My question is based on Ryleigh's hesitation. You and I have been through a lot together, but I must be able to ask questions. You also know I'll have Roy doing background checks on him. I'll make my final decision based on your information, what I discover, and how well our personalities click. Ryleigh's opinion will not come into play."

"I appreciate your willingness to look beyond Ryleigh's apprehensions."

"Let's schedule the interview. Justice Wheeler's health is declining, and time is an asset we can't waste. You'll be the first to know if I agree with you or Ryleigh."

Sam stopped talking as Chandler clenched his teeth, inhaling deeply through his nose. Waiting for a moment, she broke the silence. "The three of us have waited years for everything to come together. For the right timing. We're so close."

"You're right. Sorry if my defenses are up. It's a knee-jerk reaction when you're a guy from the South with—well, you know what I mean." He gave her a wink, squeezing her hand.

"I know who you are, Chandler. We both have complicated histories. For me, your heritage has never been an obstacle. Are we good?"

"Yes. Yes, we are." He gave a wide grin, pulling up his calendar. "Your backgrounding shouldn't take long, so how would something in the next week work?"

Sam scrolled through the calendar on her phone. "How about next Monday at 2:00 p.m.? You can give him the Soho address. It's furnished and operational. Tell him to knock when he arrives."

"Looks good. He will arrive on time."

Chandler closed his briefcase, standing to shake hands. "Let me handle updating Ryleigh and save you the grief of listening to her. You need to go into the interview with what you read in my files and learned in our conversation."

Sam smiled at Chandler's straightforward comments about Ryleigh. She watched him pull out his phone as he exited the restaurant, knowing he was calling his ace to set up the interview for her. *I hope Jack is as good as he looks on paper and in pictures.*

CHAPTER 14
Strong-Armed Enforcer

The restaurant staff recognized Jack as a familiar face after years of his meetings with Chandler. He and Chandler had developed an efficient routine for briefings on prospective clients. They would start with small talk over breakfast, followed by an exchange of folders, documents, and photographs; after that came an overview of the next assignment for consideration. Jack always had the option to accept or decline offers.

The small talk disappeared this time, leaving them to a silent morning meal. "Well, Chandler, you're being quiet and distant. How about getting your head back here with me? Your message said this client is special and requires a different approach. Time to give me the details."

Chandler reached into his trusty briefcase and handed a photo to Jack. "Sorry for not being present. My mind has been mulling over how I'll present this assignment to you. This client is a business associate, a friend, and a woman. Having a female client is a first for us. Her name is Samantha Mieras. She's a successful private equity investor who needs retribution for an injustice she experienced long ago."

Jack was listening while admiring the photo. "My first reaction is that I can't help but notice she's a helluva looker."

"She is, and she will be a client you don't have to lead or coach. Sam will know more about you and your actions than you do. With her organization and focus, she'll always be two steps ahead, expecting you to keep up. I said she's special, but *unique* or *challenging* might be a better description."

"Sounds like a powerhouse. Tell me more; I'm intrigued."

"As I mentioned, she's a close friend. We go back over twenty years. I've helped her with a variety of legal work—most of it with private equity acquisitions. We're working with another associate on a long-term personal project. It's what brought us together back in 1989. The project has reached a critical phase. I've recommended she hire you as her lead operations manager. The assignment will require skills ranging from managing tasks and people to being a strong-armed enforcer."

"Sounds like you've found another assignment made to order for me. Let's see the folder on her."

"No folder. It's different this time, Jack. Samantha will provide the details and a description of your role during an interview. It's the way she prefers to work."

Jack gave Chandler a pinched expression with his hands turning palms up. "Details, Chandler? It's how you and I work, remember? You provide information. I decide to accept or decline. We've never allowed the client to control how we function."

"Sorry, Jack. Again, no folder, no details before meeting with her."

Jack leaned toward Chandler. A crisp whisper replaced his regular voice. "Interview? What the hell? I don't do interviews. I've never done interviews. You're changing our routine without warning. This is not a good start, Chan."

Chandler was smiling and shaking his head. "C'mon, Jack. We've been at this too long to get chippy with each other. I told you that she's a special client and the assignment would differ from our norm. It's a temporary change, but there's no other path."

"Look. She might be special to you, but she's just another paying client for me."

Chandler raised a hand to stop the discussion as his phone rang. He clicked to accept the call and began wincing. "No, it's not what we agreed on. It would be best if you had some patience, Ryleigh. Yes, I'm meeting with him now. No, it'll be up to Sam. Let me call you back. Yes, got it." Closing the call, Chandler returned his attention to Jack.

"Problem, Chandler? It sounds like it might involve your associate and me."

"Ahh, no problem, but I have to call it a wrap. Are you interested in the interview?"

"Whoa, hold on. Leaving in the middle of a briefing is another unexpected change. My gut's telling me to walk away from this assignment. I don't have any details, you're booking out on me, and I have to go through an interview. I think this is where I decline the offer."

"No, Jack. Trust me: this is a job you want. Sam's a client you want to work with. Your skills are a perfect match for her. Believe me, you need to give this a shot. You can always turn it down after the interview. Does that sound acceptable?"

"My sixth sense says run, but you've stirred my curiosity, so I guess there's no harm in talking with her. If nothing else, I'll get to meet a woman who sounds tenacious and is soft on the eyes. They're somewhat rare nowadays. So yeah, I'm in for the interview. Set it up."

"The back of her photo has the location and time. Contact me with your decision after the interview. Sorry to rush out, but I have delicate work demanding my attention." Chandler gathered his papers and briefcase, leaving Jack amused at his friend's pending dilemma.

He sat there, shrugging his shoulders, sipping coffee, reminiscing about his transformation from a troubled teenager to a highly sought-after expert. It was a twisted story of a troubled kid making the best of his rough beginnings.

Waiting for the bill, he thought, *What challenges will your special client present for me, Chandler? I've got the weekend to dig for details to see who she is and what makes her tick.*

CHAPTER 15

At Odds

Chandler was pacing the curb line outside the hotel as he dialed Ryleigh's number. "Damn it, Ryleigh. I can't believe your attempted interference. So stop playing games and…" His tirade halted as Robert pulled up. "Just a minute while I get into my car."

"Stop being a damn drama queen, Chandler. You can listen and slide your ass in at the same time. We need to talk about Jack. I'm worried about what he might uncover. This isn't the time for Sam to discover the truth about the twins." Chandler was listening as he instructed Robert to drive home.

"Listen, you knew I was meeting with him to set up the interview for Sam. Interrupting my meeting was just one of your tantrums for attention."

"Sam and I talked. I knew you'd present Jack to Sam without considering other candidates. We might have big problems if Sam hires him. Let me run my short list, and then you can answer. Agreed?"

"Yes, agreed." Chandler closed his eyes as he sank into his seat.

"My primary concern is how much investigative work he'll do. I don't want him to find things you and I have kept under wraps for all these years. Am I making myself clear?"

Chandler was shaking his head, searching for a response. "I understand your anxiety. Jack's not an investigator. Sam isn't looking for him to be one. She needs a manager of people and operations. That's why we labeled it a COO position. Jack will do what Sam tells him to do. He focuses on assigned tasks and results, not the whys. I don't see him straying from his normal paradigm. So your concerns are unwarranted."

"I hope to hell you're right, Chandler. I have no choice but to ride it out. However, mark my words: I will intervene if necessary. He might be your ace, but he's disposable if he causes problems, and I'll do what's necessary to cover our asses."

"Stop with the threats. Hell, Rye, he might tank the interview with Sam or decline the job. Those possibilities would end your worrying. My process has always given him the right to turn down an offer with a client, and it's happened in the past. I'm scheduling the interview for next week. You and I need to step back and allow Sam to be in control. Can you keep your hands off the process?"

"I'll back off for the moment to see what happens."

"Thank you for cooperating. During our planning with Sam, you mentioned going to see your father. Any further thought on why he wants to meet with you?"

"Beyond that it's his birthday, I'm in the dark as much as you."

"When are you going?"

"I fly down this afternoon."

"Your concerns about Jack have raised mine about trying to determine Jonathan's motives."

"Calm your twittered nerves and enjoy the rest of your ride with Robert. We'll talk once I get back from seeing my father." Without further comment, Ryleigh clicked off as abruptly as she had jumped into the call.

Chandler was leaving a voicemail for Sam as his car arrived home. "Sam, I set the interview—one last reminder from me. Jack is who you need to hire."

CHAPTER 16

Plantation Secrets

Ryleigh stopped her rental car on the limestone driveway to watch the morning sun creating shadows through a row of trees as she drove onto Jonathan's sprawling plantation. She took her foot off the brake and eased toward the front entrance, where she saw a familiar face coming down the steps. "I was hoping to see you before anyone else, Jackson." Extending her arms, she wrapped him in a warm embrace.

"It's been too long, Ms. Ryleigh. I wanted to be the first one to welcome you back."

"Jackson, there's no need to continue with southern formalities. You and I are family. I'm just Ryleigh, okay?"

"Yes, and we will always be family, Ryleigh. Your father is waiting in his study. Do you need to freshen yourself before seeing him?"

"No, I'm fine. What kind of mood is he in today?"

"He's being quiet. I can't offer further insights. As you know, he can change as often as the wind. You'll be dining at the small table in his study. The setting might be a good omen for your visit. I hope it all goes well."

"That makes two of us." Jackson escorted her into the house, holding her hand as they walked.

He was about to knock on the massive library doors when Ryleigh stopped him. "I can handle it from here." She pushed the door open, finding her father standing at the window, surveying his domain. She spoke softly. "Father?"

He turned and smiled. "Ryleigh. I appreciate your travel here on short notice." He walked around his desk. "Please take a seat," he said, gesturing toward the table set with linens and fine china. "I thought this would be more comfortable than the formal dining area."

"You look well, Father. And I should start by wishing you a happy birthday. Will anyone else be joining us?"

"No other guests. I considered inviting your brother, but I wanted to see if we could resolve our differences and didn't think his presence would be helpful."

"I agree and wonder what led to this invitation. It has to be about more than your birthday."

"It's about repairing our relationship. The lack of frequent cordial communication is not healthy in a family. I feel the time has come for us to establish a peaceful existence." Jonathan called out for Jackson. "I need a bourbon, Jackson." He looked across the table. "Something for you, Ryleigh?"

"I'm fine with water. So this really has nothing to do with your birthday beyond the calendar date?"

Jonathan waited for Jackson to set his drink down. "You can leave us alone to talk." Ryleigh crossed her hands with an intense stare as Jackson exited the study.

"Well, I wanted a face-to-face discussion rather than a phone call. Our last conversation was a long time ago and ended on a sour note."

Ryleigh nodded, leaving Jonathan to continue. "I assume you've heard of David's pending nomination, and you know how important it is to me. Of course, assuming it results in an appointment as chief justice." Ryleigh remained silent, watching Jonathan fidget with his drink. He glanced across the table at her. "You have no comment?"

"Not yet. Please continue."

"I know you're well aware of what I and Aegis are trying to accomplish in our effort to keep radicals from destroying this great country. We have labored patiently…"

"Father, please spare me your sense of righteousness and claims of patriotism. I know what you, Aegis, and David really believe and that your agenda has no regard for anyone beyond your privileged minority."

He tilted his head forward, looking over the top of his wire-rimmed glasses. "It seems your political lean opposes mine."

"Are we going to spend our time attacking and defending political beliefs? If so, I can leave, or you can tell me why I'm here."

"All right, the truth. I want to know about Samantha's children. Who are they, and where are they?"

"That's it? What is your fixation with them?"

"They have been and continue to be a risk to our plans. I cannot allow them to suddenly appear and jeopardize David's position. You've said they would never know their relation to this family. I do not trust your word, Ryleigh. I've spent years trying to believe you've held true to your commitment, but this is a critical point in time for Aegis. I must keep this secret buried."

"I've told you this secret is well protected. I also remain steadfast in you, never having learned who they are or where they live. In your own words, there is no room for reconsideration. This subject is closed."

They sat in silence, staring at one another until Ryleigh rose from her chair and walked to the liquor cabinet. "Sit and pout like a spoiled child. I have time to sit and wait before the last flight out." She returned, swirling the ice in her vodka.

"If you allow David's nomination to go through its congressional hearing without disruption, I'm willing to reinstate our relationship and your standing in the family."

"My standing?"

"Damn it, Ryleigh. I'm trying to be civil and treat you the way your mother would if she were still with us today."

"Really? You're pulling Elizabeth from her grave to leverage me? That's rich, and you do not know what you've triggered." Ryleigh finished her drink and reached for Jonathan's glass. "I'm pouring myself another vodka and adding to your bourbon before I share a discovery I've hidden ever since she died."

Ryleigh set their drinks down and leaned her forearms on the table, watching Jonathan's eyes shift from side to side. "I've been rehearsing this in my mind for years, hoping you would die before I would have to tell you I learned the truth about us."

"Truth? For God's sake, girl, stop talking in riddles."

"I will make this as brief as possible. You need to listen. Don't try inserting denials or responses until I finish."

Jonathan reached for his glass. "You can say your piece, and I will not comment until you're done."

"Elizabeth, who I thought was my mother, made an astonishing confession to me as she was dying. She made me promise never to tell anyone, especially you, what she shared." Ryleigh looked at Jonathan as he slowly set the glass down and began rubbing his hands together. She could see the veins in his neck enlarging and pulsing as she continued.

"She told me my mother died giving birth to me and explained how you did not want to recognize me as your child. She explained how she threatened to reveal the truth if you did not accept me into the family. People would have believed her over you because they trusted her and hated you. Those are her words, not mine." She stopped to down her drink.

"I was your true firstborn, but you favored David because he was the firstborn between you and Elizabeth. I pleaded to know my mother's identity, which she did not reveal until the day of her death. She confided that her maid, whom you raped, was my birth mother. Elizabeth said you denied it happened and tried to have me aborted. She saved me from that fate, just as I saved Samantha's twins. The only existing connection I have with my birth mother today is her brother, Jackson. He doesn't know that I know he is my uncle, and I realize it's why he's always been so watchful of me."

"Are you finished?"

"Almost. Now you know why I took Samantha and prevented the abortion you demanded. You tried to destroy her twins in the same way you tried to take my life. The twins and I survived in spite of your heartless cruelty. We share a bond of survival. I also find it ironic that you threatened to shatter Chandler and his family because of his ethnicity when I, your own daughter, am biracial. I will always despise who you are and whatever you try to achieve because of your callousness. Now, I am finished."

Jonathan pushed his chair back to stand and walked to the window. "I will not deny what Elizabeth told you." He turned to face Ryleigh. "I trust this will remain between us?"

"It will unless you give me cause to make it otherwise."

"Then be warned—I cannot change the course of events that are unfolding. The conflict between you and your brother is beyond my control, and I will not intervene. This is a dangerous time, Ryleigh."

She stood to leave. "Before I leave, I ask that you continue to care for Jackson. He is unaware of my knowledge and deserves to remain in place without harm."

"There is a trust in his name that will provide a comfortable retirement. It will remain in place, and I will guarantee his safety."

"Thank you." She left the room and pulled the door closed, finding Jackson waiting.

While they walked arm in arm, as they had earlier, he explained he already knew what Elizabeth had told her. They embraced as he whispered, "My sister lives on in you, and we will be family forever."

"I appreciate your accepting me in spite of my father's vile acts."

Jackson stopped at the car, hugging Ryleigh. "There will be a day when he will be held accountable. Justice will be delivered for you and your mother. I do not know how or when. Only that it will be done."

Ryleigh could barely see the road as tears flooded her eyes. *Should I call Sam and stop everything?*

CHAPTER 17

Soho Office

Sam paced in the Soho studio. The sound of her elegant black heels reverberated against the stark white walls and oak flooring with each stride. Pacing the floor was one of her meditative methods for processing angst. She was ready to strike from the long shadows of patience and have her vengeance.

Gazing out the double window, she admired a panoramic view of the city skyline, basking in a crisp, sun-kissed Monday. It was New York at its finest, presenting larger-than-life concrete canyons of corporate offices, designer boutiques, upscale stores, and high-end art galleries. The streets below were alive with a flow of teeming masses as they seemed to dance to the unending sound of urban traffic. Sam nodded and smiled, returning to her thoughtful journey, awaiting Chandler's candidate.

She thought about David. *Twenty-seven years of hating the son of a bitch, his family, and their organization's arrogance. They felt they had too much to risk with a troubled girl. And once pregnant, I became a stigma requiring immediate removal.* Her movements quickened, raising the reverberation of her footsteps.

Pausing in the middle of the room, she took a moment to view her newly minted command center, her office of retaliatory justice. The studio presented the look of a well-appointed executive setting. A contemporary Bernhardt mahogany desk and an imported supple black leather chair nested dramatically on a hand-knotted wool-and-silk Persian rug near a small circular conference table with modern seating for guests and her ever-observant HITO wall clock. The appearance worked well to mask her malicious intent.

Jonathan would shit if he could see my domain. Thank God for Ryleigh and Chandler getting me through those dark, desperate days. David and his father's precious Aegis group underestimated me. They didn't realize what I could achieve, what I could become, and what I would do.

An almost convulsive shudder shook her body as a sharp knock interrupted her reflective considerations. She turned toward the door, glancing at her watch. *Two o'clock, as scheduled. Very punctual, Mr. Gallagher. We're off to a good start.*

She slowed her steps to gather composure. *Deep breath, Samantha. Be calm. Be powerful.* Her posture rose as she finished crossing the room to reach for the door's metallic handle.

CHAPTER 18

Interview

Sam opened the door, revealing a distinguished-looking man much taller than her petite five-five frame. She made a quick mental assessment. *Well-maintained physical stature. Salt-and-pepper hair. A manicured beard framing chiseled facial features. He looks younger than the fifty-plus years listed in his background. Sharp business casual attire and a black leather jacket complete an attractive package.* He tilted his head with raised eyebrows, waiting for her greeting. "Jack, I assume?" She smiled, extending her hand. His Sinatra-blue eyes and polite nod interrupted her thoughts again.

First impressions and appearance were critically important for Sam. The position required presenting a strong, confident executive image; an ideal candidate would be a counterpart to her strengths and skills. *So far, so good on your selection, Chandler. Let's see if he's as smooth as he looks.*

He shook her hand, finding a firm grasp matching the alert gaze in her eyes. "Since you're correct, I will assume it's Ms. Mieras I have the pleasure of meeting?" Without waiting for a response, he entered the office, carefully noting her and the environment.

"Will we be talking at your desk?" He hesitated, looking back over his broad shoulder for her response.

"Yes. Please, make yourself comfortable."

Sam crossed behind the desk as he sat, interlacing his fingers and propping his elbows on the chair's arms, with his hands resting against his chest. Opening a folder and sorting documents, she began speaking without making eye contact. "Did you have any problem locating the office?"

"None" was his smiling, cursory answer. "Finding discreet locations is a required skill in my line of work." His eyes squinted, waiting for her next question. *She's more impressive than her picture—a well-crafted business image. Crisp white blouse, black pencil skirt, heels, green eyes, pixie-cut black hair, athletic physique, all in a well-put-together package. Focus, Jack; this is a client, not a date.*

Watching her organize items, Jack inquired, "How would you like to start? Interviewing isn't my normal process when I'm engaging with new clients. Perhaps I can give you an overview of my background and why Chandler recommended me?"

Sam raised her eyes from the papers. "Well, interviews are key to my decision-making—no need for you to provide any background. However, before we continue, I have two questions. First, are you working with law enforcement or wearing a device to monitor or record our conversation?"

Samantha's head-on query didn't appear to surprise Jack. He gave a small chuckle before responding. "The answers are no and no, but it's a fair start and should allow us to talk without further fears or suspicions. Agreed?" Samantha nodded with a smirk at his answer.

"I found your background interesting," she said, leafing through the folder's contents when her voice trailed off. She looked across the desk to reconnect and assess his reaction.

"Well, from your collection of papers, it appears Chandler provided more than what you needed." Jack's full eyebrows rose as he slid back in the chair, waiting for Sam to continue.

"While Chandler made a strong recommendation, my research on you comes from multiple sources." She took a deep breath, moistening her lips, thinking, *Do not underestimate me, Jack.*

"I may know more about you than you realize. Let's see if I have it right." Now it was Sam leaning back, locking eyes with Jack. "You're intelligent, with creative communication skills and a robust appetite for new and sometimes dangerous assignments. But unfortunately, two of your weaknesses as a young man were an inability to focus and an inability to make good decisions. I believe those caused your unfortunate time as an extended guest at Attica. How am I doing so far?"

Jack chuckled quietly. "So far, so good. What else do you have?"

"I think your behavior might have disappointed your dear mother, Mary. Her faith and beliefs might have made her wish for better for her oldest son. Of course, you had a different influence from your father, Aidan, and his mobster tendencies. I would guess it was difficult to find your way with conflicting parenting." She waited for a reaction, but he remained stoic and silent.

Sam lowered her eyes, continuing to scan her notes. "Your desire to improve seems to have overcome the obstacles of your younger days. It appears you're an improved version of the rebel from Hell's Kitchen. I find your ability to make such improvements an admirable achievement, but I have mixed feelings about hiring you and would like to hear your reasoning for why I should." She straightened her shoulders and moved to the forward edge of her chair, closing the folder with a smug Cheshire-like smile.

Jack's right hand rose to his face, smoothing his lips as he looked for the right words. He leaned forward, resting his forearms on the thighs of his gray wool-and-silk blended slacks, lifting his head. "Nice work on my history. I'm not surprised by what you think of me. I would have expected nothing less based on the research I completed on you." He stared into her eyes.

"After hearing what you said, the old version of Jack Gallagher would have ended this meeting by walking out in search of something or someone to destroy. Those days of impulsive behavior are gone. As you stated, I've identified and corrected many of my faults. Thanks to Chandler's coaching over the past years, I've broken free from the influences of my father. How am I doing, Samantha?"

She gave him a demure smile and a slight nod. "So far, so good. Keep going, Jack."

He took a breath and squared his shoulders to match hers. "You and I are very similar. Both of us are strong-willed, assertive people who excel at business and life. You need to hire me for many reasons. First, it would be a mistake if you didn't, and you don't make mistakes. Second, you need to hire me because I have the talents and street smarts to accomplish whatever your objectives are. Third, I will exceed your expectations. Reasons four and five: I'm your best choice, and I want the job."

Jack placed his hands on the edge of the desk as he slid to the edge of his chair, speaking in a soft, confident Irish brogue. "So, Ms. Mieras, as my ancestors would say, tell me your story, bean, and let's be gettin' on with the details of what ya need done." Then, giving Sam a wink, he slid back.

She stifled a laugh, shaking her head at Jack's reference to his heritage, and responded, "Okay, Jack, I appreciate your candor and agree with your assessment of our commonalities. You just won me over. The job is yours, and from here on, ya kin be knowin' me as just Sam."

Jack smiled, thinking, *I may have found an equal; this time, it's dressed in heels and a skirt. Who would've thought?*

Sam pushed her research files aside. "You need to understand. I like straightforward communication, Jack. No false formalities. It'll make our work less complicated."

Jack remained relaxed in his chair. "I'll second the motion. On that note, Chandler said you have an unsettled grievance needing closure, but he didn't provide further information. I know there's more to it, so I'll let you provide the specifics." Jack took a long breath, moving his hands back to his chest. "The stage is all yours, Sam."

Sam sighed, maintaining eye contact as she explained her need for vengeance after being treated like trash years ago. She spoke with calmness and deliberation, delivering a detailed recollection of events. An eyewitness account told from the victim's perspective. "Their demands and abandonment ripped away so much from me. Now, we're at an eye-for-an-eye moment years in the making. It's my turn to rip their desires to shreds." Her hands clenched into fists as she asked, "Do you understand my anger and anguish?"

Jack stared without blinking as he absorbed her story. He let her testimony linger as he worked through thoughts to respond without judgment. *She has the forlorn look of my mum when she was holding steadfast despite how my old man treated her.*

"I appreciate your willingness to share painful memories. And yes, I understand your distress." He shifted his forearms out to the arms of the chair. "Time for a few questions. What are you expecting me to do, who is the primary target, and what's the final objective?"

"Good questions. As my operations manager, you'll be assembling a team and coordinating everyone's assignments to ensure we stop David Jaymes from becoming chief justice."

Sam edged forward, placing her elbows on the desk with her interlaced fingers propped under her chin. "You asked about a primary target. There are three. David Jaymes; his father, Jonathan; and Aegis. They are the offending parties who collaborated to demand the abortion and caused the twins to be stillborn. I'm sure it's obvious, but I want the connection to be clear. My hatred for them often rises beyond rational control. One aspect of your responsibilities will be to temper my fits of rage and keep us on track."

She paused, easing into the back of her chair as she raised one finger to keep Jack from responding. "Placing this level of trust in another person is outside my comfort zone. Your performance will earn or destroy my ability to trust you. I'll know where we're at by the end of your first assignment. From there, we will continue or part ways."

Jack displayed his self-assured smile as he cleared his throat. "I know you're moving outside your comfort zone, and I'm sure we will continue far beyond the first assignment. Have you given thought to what tools I might use? I can accomplish your objective through persuasion, intimidation, physical harm, termination, or all of the above. Your preferences, if any?"

"All the elements you've mentioned are on the table. My decisions on what is necessary and appropriate will be a work in progress. I haven't made any final decisions yet."

Jack sensed an intensity in Sam's posture as she spoke. He took another breath. "Well, Sam, I'm willing to take on the work. As for compensation, I'll leave that discussion between you and Chandler. There are no written contracts. You and I operate on a verbal agreement and handshake. I'm available to start now." Jack never changed his posture or lost eye contact.

Sam raised her head and eyes upward, following the slow-moving ceiling fan as it watched with constant, non-judgmental revolutions. "One last condition. I maintain final approval for major decisions—no unilateral or rogue actions on your part. You and I work as a unified team."

They stood to shake hands. "I'm here to follow your orders, Sam."

CHAPTER 19

The Collective Project

Sam swiveled her chair to retrieve a small box from the credenza and pushed it across the desktop for Jack. "Since we agree on keeping things simple, I'm confident how we work and communicate will satisfy you. This office is our base of operation. It's available for your use as you find necessary." Jack listened, gathering the box to set it on the floor without inspection.

"You'll find a phone in the box, along with the code for access to the office. The phone is for emergency text messages between us. You'll know a text is from me when it displays my ID as J93. We'll use our personal phones for voice calls."

Jack interrupted. "What's the significance of your phone ID?"

Sam hesitated. "My twins were stillborn in January 1993. It's a reminder and keeps me focused. May I continue?" She tilted her head, squinting her eyes and wrinkling her nose.

"Sorry for the interruption."

"Apology accepted. We will meet whenever you or I feel it's necessary to provide updates and discuss assignments. Our meetings can be here or at another location that suits the reason and urgency for talking. The only person you need to communicate with is me. Chandler is the exception since we both have a shared level of trust in him." She watched

Jack make mental notes like a seasoned waiter taking dinner orders without pen or paper. "Questions so far?"

"No immediate questions. I'm ready to make things happen. So let's see how interesting your work is and if it will be dangerous."

Sam acknowledged Jack's comment with an affirmative nod before continuing. "Back to David Jaymes. He's a US Court of Appeals justice for the Second District in New York. His family founded Aegis. Today, Aegis is a powerful entity, influencing appointments at many levels of the judiciary. Its influence and power result from calculated efforts over many decades. In the box, you'll find a USB drive with an extensive history of David, Aegis, and Aegis's activities stretching from the end of the Civil War to the present.

"David is at the top of the president's list of possible nominees for the position of chief justice on the Supreme Court. The nomination could happen anytime because of the hospitalization of the current chief justice. Our targets are vulnerable now because they're arrogant and believe they cannot fail. In essence, they won't see us coming for them." Sam looked to see if Jack displayed any recognition of Aegis or David. "Aegis has controlled the last three appointments to the Supreme Court. David is the last piece of the puzzle to put in place. Once he's there, nothing can prevent Aegis from achieving its goal of making divisive revisions to landmark decisions."

He remained reserved and attentive, allowing Sam to continue. "The Collective Project was born when my twins were stillborn. Our team has been methodical in creating annoying obstacles for Aegis over the years. Nothing drastic, just enough to be an ongoing pain in the ass. Now, with the pending nomination, we need to take more aggressive steps to achieve our goal of stopping them."

Raising his hand, Jack interrupted. "You seem to imply your project involves more than you. Who else is involved?"

"I, Chandler, and a third person, Ryleigh Jaymes, are the core participants on the project."

"Wait a minute; you said Ryleigh Jaymes? Is she related to David?"

"Yes. She's David's older sister and estranged from the family because she took me in as an emancipated minor before my pregnancy. Ryleigh helped me avoid having the abortion demanded by her father. David's spiteful influence led to the family's further alienation of his sister. She maintains as much hatred for her brother as I do."

"Okay, I get her reason to be involved. What brought Chandler into working with you and Ryleigh?"

"I don't think Chandler's ever shared this part with you. David's father discovered Chandler was biracial when he and Ryleigh became involved in a relationship. He blackmailed Chandler and his family, threatening public disclosure, and ended the romantic connection. As you can see, Chandler also has scores to settle. There's more detail on the USB drive for you to study."

Jack looked aside, processing the new revelations. Then, returning his attention to Sam, he asked, "Will I be working with all three of you?"

"No, you'll work with me to avoid conflicts. And in Ryleigh's case, it's for the best, since she's not a Jack Gallagher fan."

"Yeah, I'm not surprised after Chandler took a call from her. I can accomplish what you want if we limit who is directing me."

Sam gave a nod of agreement. "I agree on limiting direction and keeping our common purpose to inflicting serious damage on Aegis, destroying David's reputation, and stopping his rise to power. As much as I would like to damage him physically, it's not in our best interest."

"There would be serious consequences if you were to harm a pending chief justice."

"Would it be a problem for you if I felt it was necessary, Jack?"

"No problem. I follow your lead. So the three of you are the major stakeholders. Are there more players?"

"Not yet, but soon. Two potential associates will be the focus of your first assignment tomorrow. Beyond those two, we have three more. As our operations officer, you're the decision-maker. It's your team to build. From my perspective, you're the most important player. Additional people will work directly for you."

"Sounds like things are going to happen at a fast clip. Where do I start earning my keep?"

Sam retrieved several folders from the desk drawer as one of the city's constant emergency sirens raced past on the street below. "Let's move to the table to review your first assignment and potential team members."

CHAPTER 20

First Assignment

Taking a seat, Sam placed the folders on the table. "I like your enthusiasm and agree about a fast pace." She withdrew an envelope from one folder. Jack watched her movements in silence as she placed a collection of photos in front of him. He began sorting through the images.

"These are surveillance photos of Ethan Brode and Adira Tomasz. They will be your first two prospects. Ryleigh and Chandler have recommended recruiting them. I agree with the reasons for their selection, but your assessment will drive the final decision. Do you know or recognize either of them?" She paused, searching Jack's eyes and expression for recognition.

"Never met or had contact with either." Jack's head rose. "What's their backstory?"

Sam slid a file marked "Ethan Brode" over to Jack. "This is an in-depth rundown on Ethan and our plan for his involvement. He's a young investigative reporter, headstrong, with good street smarts. I would label Ethan as determined and practical. I see him as the point of the spear for our attack on David and Aegis. We can arm him with knowledge and evidence to write news articles exposing their agenda."

Turning the pages, Jack stopped at a group of news clippings as Sam continued. "Ryleigh has been sending him anonymous messages related to his probing of Aegis. The texts have told him we can provide insider information. We've scheduled a face-to-face appointment for you and Ethan tomorrow afternoon. You will present yourself as the message sender. He'll be at the Bluestone Coffee Shop in Bryant Park at one o'clock, looking for a person reading the *Times* on a park bench outside the shop."

Jack pressed a finger to his cheek. "This sounds like a spy gig. Do you have copies of the messages? I should review them to sound authentic and up to speed when I talk with him."

Sam handed another folder to Jack. "You'll find them in this file. There's plenty of homework to read and study this evening.

"Let's continue with the background on the second prospect, Adira, and then see what questions you might have about her."

"I'm listening."

"Her real name is Dora Tomasz, Adira being a professional alias she used as an exotic dancer and high-class escort. Currently, she's the executive assistant for David and Cynthia Jaymes. As you will learn, she also manages the seamy side of Aegis called Society." Sam paused as she handed over a folder labeled "Adira."

"Her character traits are like Ethan's. She has good street smarts, is headstrong, and desires success. She has a quick wit and temper. While Ethan might be on the reserved side, Adira can be right up front, in your face—no pretenses. She might be resistant to your first encounter with her, but I think you can coax her into working with us. As you can see from the photos, she fits the description of eye candy. Her image disguises a sharp intellect with a lethal sting if you mistake her for someone who is feebleminded. So don't underestimate her."

Sam hesitated, expecting a comment as Jack studied the photographs and information in her file. "According to Ryleigh, Adira has been questioning her involvement with Aegis. Her willingness to meet is an opportunity for us. Working as an executive assistant means she has access to vital information we can use. If you convince her to work with us, she will be invaluable. We plan to draw Ethan and Adira into a working alliance with you and the third prospect."

Jack shifted his attention, which had been absorbed by the files. "Since I'm doing an interview with Ethan at noon tomorrow, when and where will I see Adira?"

"Tomorrow at four o'clock in the Algonquin Hotel restaurant on West Forty-Fourth Street." Raising a hand, Sam gestured for Jack to talk.

"Well, thanks to your scheduling, I'll be plenty busy." He gathered the photos and files off to the side. "You said there were more players to consider. Who are they, and when do I have contact with them?"

Sam pushed two more files across to Jack. "There are two additions, Senator Lucas Mathers and his young wife, Lydia. Their backstories are in those files. You will have more contact with Lydia than the senator. I believe you'll find them to be more than interesting. They will be your second assignment, and we'll discuss their potential involvement once you've met with Ethan and Adira. As for when? We need to keep moving as fast as possible."

Now, it was Sam being the attentive listener as Jack asked, "Sounds like Ryleigh is the only one who's had direct contact with Ethan and Adira. Am I correct?"

"Yes."

"Tell me what you expect from my first assignment. I want to ensure I don't give you any reason to part ways with me."

"As for my expectations for tomorrow? First, you need to determine if they can benefit us. Second, can you get them to work with you? They will not have contact with Chandler or me unless you feel it's needed. Possible contact with Ryleigh will be based on their previous relationship with her."

"Can I discuss her recommending they work for us?"

"No. I want them to believe you're the one sending anonymous messages. I'm sure they may have questions about who you're working with, but for now, all they need to know is you and what you want from them."

Jack was leafing through the copies of messages Ryleigh had sent. "I think I've got the picture. I'm the front man. You, Ryleigh, and Chandler are the silent partners?"

"So far, so good, Jack."

"Do they know one another?"

"Ethan and Adira have never met. As you'll discover, Lydia and Adira are quite familiar with each other. More questions, Jack?"

"Just one, but it's more of a request than a question. I'd like to add an associate I know and trust."

"It depends on who it is and what you need this person to do."

Jack shifted his weight in his chair, hands leaning into his thighs, squinting at Sam. "His name is Roy Covington. An old friend and retired Vietnam photojournalist. He does various investigative work and would be a great wingman for me."

Sam raised her hands, laughing. "Roy Covington? Really?"

"Not sure why his name amuses you, but yes, he's the guy I would trust working with me."

She was still laughing and replied, "Roy's the one who did the background investigation on you and all the others. The surveillance photos are also his work. So of course you can bring him on board. I was considering recommending him if you didn't have an immediate prospect. I'm sure he'll laugh when you contact him."

Jack moved back in his chair. "Hell, what a small world. Roy and I've worked together for many clients over the years. I know he'll join. And since he's already up to speed on the others, he can give me additional insight after I meet them."

"We seem to think alike and are off to a good start, Jack."

"I'll agree with that one. I have all the information I need to complete my first assignment. I'll contact you once I've finished the interviews and talked with Roy." He stood and extended his hand before gathering folders, photos, and the box.

Sam provided another firm handshake. "I look forward to our work and success together." Then, after watching him turn to leave, she returned to her desk, shaking her head and laughing to herself. *Chandler was right. Jack was a good choice. He makes me wish I had known him sooner, for other reasons.*

Hailing a cab outside Sam's office, Jack gave directions for an intermediate stop, telling the driver, "Drop me at Bryant Park."

He started planning the next day as he gazed out the cab window. *The coffee shop for Ethan's interview is in the park, and the Algonquin is a few blocks from there. Checking out both locations and walking will allow me to think.*

CHAPTER 21

Backgrounding

Jack was ordering a coffee when his phone buzzed with a call from Chandler. "Hey, I was getting ready to call and update you on my interview with Sam."

"Where are you now, and can you talk?"

"I'm at Bluestone Coffee Shop in Bryant Park, checking out my assignments for tomorrow. Hold on while I find a quiet area so we can chat."

Jack paid for his beverage and settled onto an empty park bench. "Let me say the meeting with Sam went better than I thought. I've agreed to take the job and have a few questions about her, Ryleigh, and your involvement with them on the project." Jack waited through several moments of silence before asking, "Chandler, you still there, or did I lose you?"

"I'm here. Just trying to imagine what questions you'll ask."

"Well, let's whittle it down to one key question. Who's calling the shots on the project? I feel it's Sam, with you acting like a big brother. You offer advice when asked, and she decides what to do. The question mark is Ryleigh. Does she override Sam? What's the actual picture, Chandler?"

"Sam's the one calling the shots, and you've nailed how she and I will coordinate. She'll follow my advice but often makes adjustments, which usually turn out to be good improvements. As I'm sure she explained, we've been at this for many years with methodical patience. We've known Aegis's plan for David's future and waited to strike at its high point of overconfidence. Our time has arrived with David's pending nomination, so we're hiring you to gather a group of associates and stop him.

"Ryleigh's the wild card for all of us. She doesn't override Sam's decisions, but she's a powerful influencer. I've known Ryleigh for a long time. We were romantic partners at one time, but I underestimated her family's capacity to destroy anything outside its accepted paradigms. It was enough to create a wedge in our relationship, but we salvaged a tolerable friendship.

"Sam desires vengeance, but time has mitigated the malice factor for her. However, with Ryleigh, the desire for malice has intensified tenfold. Ryleigh will try to manipulate actions and events to get what she wants. Sorry for the long answer, but it paints an accurate picture."

Jack took a long sip of coffee before answering. "It makes sense. Sam came across as having a strong lean toward whatever is necessary to stop David, even to the point of violence or taking him out. But you say she's softened. If so, what's her current desire?"

"Not to sound like a lawyer and dodge the question, but it's a bit of both. When she's talking with Ryleigh, her mindset is more hostile, and less so when she's away from Ryleigh's persuasions. Let me use a stronger descriptor for Ryleigh instead of a wild card. Ryleigh could become problematic for Sam, the project, and you. She has been adamant Sam should not hire you. She feels you will place our goals at risk by making bad, unilateral decisions. So be careful, Jack. Ryleigh could become a serious potential obstacle. Your involvement with her should be minimal. However, if you can win her over, she will be a powerful ally."

Jack chuckled into the phone. "I'm hearing you loud and clear. You know I've handled worse with previous clients and still exceeded expectations."

"I wouldn't have recommended you if I had doubts about your capabilities. From here on, you're working for Sam, not Chandler Yates. If needed, I will follow Sam's lead for any further involvement."

"Thanks for the vote of confidence. I'll try to play by the rules." Ending the call, Jack relaxed in the late fall sunshine. *No need to check out the Algonquin. It's been there forever and hasn't changed. I need to head home and study Sam's files. Tomorrow will be busy and demanding.*

CHAPTER 22

Chance Encounter

The city was alive with its surge of office workers, scurrying executives, and wandering souls covering the thoroughfares like an all-consuming lava flow. Ethan was running late for the interview with his anonymous source. After months of research, he felt this could be his big break.

The tipster had said he or she could deliver inside information. Cautioning thoughts sped through his mind. *This is what reporters dream about, Ethan. Don't be overoptimistic. It's not Watergate, and the source is not Deep Throat. You need to know who's sending the messages and if you can believe this person. Make an offer to keep the source's identity confidential—off the record. Yeah, emphasize how we need each other. Don't let the source have the upper hand.*

As he jogged and weaved through the sea of humanity, his eyes darted back and forth, looking for openings. He was feeling like the white rabbit in Alice's adventures. The moment when he had that distracting thought was when it happened. Bam! It was like two cars colliding, unable to avoid each other.

"Oh shit" was the involuntary vocalization leaping from his startled brain. He never saw her in his path as he dodged left. She was in front of him in the blink of an eye. The impact was unavoidable, as their shoulders caught, spilling her and the contents of her bag to the ground. His instincts were going into alarm mode. *Oh God, I don't have time for this.* He knew he couldn't let it be a hit-and-run. He had to stop and offer help. But his mind was screaming to get to the interview as she glared at him from the sidewalk.

"Nice move, asshole. Next time, you might try 'Excuse me' or 'I'm sorry' instead of 'Oh shit.'" Her rebuke stung his senses as he reached down to help her. He tried to find words, but her verbal attack and fiery scowl brought his response skills to a silent standstill.

As if he were a deer caught in bright headlights, her piercing eyes froze Ethan as a powerful sense of familiarity overwhelmed him, turning loose a surging wave of questions. *Who is she? Do I know her? Can she hear my mind crying out to reconnect?*

Ethan shook his head to stop the cascading queries. With a deep breath, he spoke politely. "Yes, of course, I'm sorry, miss. Are you okay? Let me help you." He was searching for the right words but felt inept and vulnerable.

Her response was as bitter as her first reaction. "I'm fine, you clumsy ass. Pay attention to where you're going, and next time, find someone else to run over." Ethan continued offering his hand, watching as she retrieved her belongings. Muttering obscenities, she brushed his hand away, returning to her feet. Then, like a whirling dervish, she was gone.

Finding answers to his confounding thoughts would have to wait, perhaps forever, as he watched her disappear into the bustling crowd. Standing alone, he shook his head, needing to get on with business, hoping his interview would still be there waiting for him.

CHAPTER 23

Bryant Park

Ethan was out of breath when he reached Bryant Park. Squeezing into the crowded coffee shop, he bumped into another customer as he started scanning the park for someone reading the *Times*, but without luck. *I hope I haven't missed my source.*

Waiting for his order, Ethan savored the aromas of freshly baked pastries and roasted coffee beans. He was stepping out the door to continue searching for his contact when he felt a tap on the shoulder. Turning around, he found himself facing the stranger he had jostled inside the shop.

"Hello, Ethan. No need to look for me reading the paper on a bench."

"Ah...Yes, I'm Ethan, and I should apologize. Seems to be my day for trying to run over people." Ethan was making a quick visual assessment of Jack. *So this is my tipster? I wasn't sure if it would be a man or a woman, but now I have a face to connect with the messages.* "Let's find a seat away from eavesdropping people." Ethan took the lead in locating unoccupied seating.

"Good idea—my preference as well." Now, Jack was assessing Ethan. *A little taller than I expected and seems to be a bit nervous. I'm sure he's brimming with questions. I'll let him guide the initial conversation.*

They crossed the park, Ethan talking as they walked. "Your messages have been helpful in my research for my planned series about Aegis. I have a lot of questions, but first, I'd like to get some background information."

Ethan began drinking his coffee while Jack seated himself before speaking. "Since you're the reporter, anyplace you want to start is good with me." Jack sat sideways on the park bench, facing Ethan with a squinting look, waiting for the interview to begin.

Ethan pulled out a notepad and pen, looking up once, ready. "You know my name, and I'd like to know yours unless you prefer remaining anonymous. Our discussions will be off the record, and I will maintain your confidentiality." He was expecting an immediate response from Jack, who was nodding, taking time before answering.

"Jack's the name, and to save you a question, it's my real name. My last name is unnecessary, so we'll leave it at Jack."

"Okay, Jack. Why did you pick me to share information about Aegis with?" Ethan started tapping his pen on the paper, ready to document whatever was said. Jack raised a hand, rubbing his chin and placing one finger on his closed smile. Ethan's posture started shifting, and he finally added, "The question has no bearing on my story. However, knowing why will satisfy my curiosity."

"Let me answer, and then I have a question for you." Jack leaned forward, pointing a finger at Ethan. "The obvious reason for selecting you is because of what you do. You're an investigative reporter. Who would be a better choice to dig into a political scandal than someone like you?" Jack leaned back. "I'm curious to hear about your progress. Knowing where you are in your explorations will tell me if continuing our discussion is worthwhile." Jack folded his arms, raising his chin.

"Fair enough; since your messages pointed me in the right direction, I can share some of my progress." Ethan set the pen down, retrieving a folder from his backpack. Jack placed an outstretched arm on the back of the park bench as Ethan shuffled through papers.

"Your first message in October asked if I was interested in information about clandestine politics. You told me to respond with a yes if I was interested, and I did. From there, it was a matter of following your subsequent trail of leads. Sometimes, I felt you were looking over my shoulder, helping me correct wrong turns." Ethan closed the folder, pressing the tip of his tongue against his upper lip.

"I could go into the details of our exchanges, but you already know what you sent. Right, Jack? Maybe I should ask you to describe the information we've shared to verify you are the messenger. Your last one hinted at providing substantial proof of some of my suspicions and discoveries. Tell me, Jack, are you my anonymous messenger? I have a hunch you're not." He placed the folder and notepad back into his computer case, looking at Jack.

Jack laughed. "Okay, I'll play the game, Ethan. You've received forty-three messages. They've provided some information you would never have found on your own. Am I your messenger? No, but I am responsible for an effort intending to expose the dark side of Aegis and end its attempt to control the judiciary system and the Supreme Court.

"I'm here to see if you want to write investigative stories that could be bigger than Watergate. It's an offer for more than a front-row seat to a once-in-a-generation opportunity. We'd like to have you involved. Your stories would be from a first-person perspective. I should emphasize this is an all-in or all-out proposition. If you accept our offer, we'll continue providing credible leads, contacts, and insider information."

"So you provide the paths for content, and I write the stories?"

"Yes, but with one condition. You'll provide copy for our review and approval before publication. Your cooperation ensures we create an escalating level of paranoia so those who control Aegis stumble and incriminate themselves. This will be like a chess match, requiring nerve, patience, and timing. And one last item—it could become dangerous." Jack could see the growing interest as Ethan locked eyes with him. "Are you in or out?"

Ethan closed his eyes, raising a hand for Jack to pause. "You've brought me to the edge of accepting, but I need to clear this with my editor."

"What if I told you we were disclosing this offer to your editor as you and I are talking?"

"No way. I think you're playing a bluff poker hand. So I'll call your bluff and contact my office."

"Go ahead. Pick up the phone and call your editor. You can move and have a private conversation. I'll be here waiting."

Ethan pulled his phone from his bag, stepping away as he dialed. Jack watched him pace, gesturing with his free hand. Once the call ended, he stood looking across the park's expanse before returning to Jack. "I don't know who you are or how you got to my editor, but we will agree to your conditions."

Jack reached out to shake hands, saying, "All I can say is things above your pay grade are unfolding. Don't get me wrong. You are now one of the most important parts of making this work. Sometimes, going with the flow is easier than trying to make sense of what's happening."

Jack reached into the breast pocket of his coat for an envelope and handed it to Ethan. "The name is Jack Gallagher, but I still prefer Jack. You'll find my contact information, details for your next lead, and a story we'd like to see in your paper one week from today."

Ethan was speed-reading, turning pages. "Senator Mathers? And his wife? Escorts and blackmailing members of Congress? They are expecting me to contact them? Are you sure about this?"

"Yes—everything we give or tell you will be vetted for accuracy. They're expecting to hear from you and will be cooperative. Lydia, the senator's wife, will be your verification source for what he tells you.

"I'll look for a draft of your story to approve before publication. We're going to make a great team, Ethan." Standing to leave, Jack smiled, reaching to shake Ethan's hand. "Welcome aboard the Collective Project."

Ethan said as he was turning to leave, "Thanks for the opportunity, Jack. I won't disappoint you."

Looking at his watch, Jack headed for the Algonquin Hotel and his next interview.

CHAPTER 24

Ethan Brode, Reporter

Ethan left Bryant Park energized, wanting to stop and re-read Jack's instructions. He also knew his editor was waiting and eager to read what was in Jack's letter. He paused at the subway entrance, thoughts racing. There was no time for trains. He walked to the curb and hailed a cab. The opportunity Jack had provided was exciting beyond his wildest imagination.

Settling into the cab, he recalled how good fortune had landed him in New York. A college friend had introduced him to Ed Bradford, managing editor of the *Insider*, who had made Ethan an offer his inquisitive heart couldn't refuse: a position as an investigative reporter with the potential to make it big in the Big Apple.

Ethan's parents were concerned about expenses and living in New York but had allowed him to pursue the opportunity thanks to an offer from a wealthy family friend. They had known Ryleigh Jaymes since before Ethan was born, and she assured them he would be safe under her watchful eye. They knew her as the CEO of a successful private equity firm that sponsored and supported recent college graduates daring to chase their dreams.

Arriving at the office, he checked in with the receptionist, who told him Ed was waiting for his return. He walked into Ed's office, saying, "I figured you'd want to see me right away."

"Close my door. I'm unsure what's happening or who you're involved with in this story, but they pull powerful strings. Just before you called, I was on the phone with our chairperson. She told me you'd be calling and that we needed to agree to whatever your informant was offering. No details from her other than that this would be a once-in-a-generation opportunity. And then you called, using the same phrase. What the hell's going on?"

Ethan gave Ed a rundown on the anonymous messages, how they provided information on Aegis, and how all the previous tips were reliable. "Thanks to their information, I've started cracking the seal of secrecy on Aegis." He explained about meeting Jack, hearing his offer, and receiving the envelope with information to help him write the first in a series of articles for one of next week's editions. His heart was sprinting as he tried to catch his breath.

"Let me see what this Jack guy gave you." Ethan handed Ed the envelope and sat while Ed read. Ed looked up at Ethan, asking, "Lucas Mathers blackmailed after a fling with an escort, and his wife will confirm it?"

"Yeah, and Jack assured me everything was accurate and vetted. Until now, that's been the situation. His condition is that he gets final approval on the stories before we publish them. I don't know if our chairperson knows his requirement or if she'll agree to it."

"Oh, I'm sure she's aware of it. Board members tell me Ryleigh James doesn't make decisions without full details."

Ethan pulled his head back, giving Ed a startled look. "Who? I thought I heard you say Ryleigh Jaymes."

"Yes. She's the chairperson of the private equity firm that bought the paper about a year before you arrived. I don't have much interaction with her. She lets us do our work without interference, and until now, she's never told me what to do."

"Ed, she's a close friend of my family. She's the one who convinced my parents to let me take this job."

"Well, kid, you've got a powerful friend in high places. My job is to make sure we do what she wants and whatever Gallagher asks. Contact the senator and his wife, write the story, and get approval so we can go to press on it. I feel this is just the start, and it will get big."

Ethan was quiet, thinking. *I need to call Ryleigh tonight.*

CHAPTER 25

Adira Tomasz— Executive Assistant

As Adira enjoyed the fall weather and maneuvered along the crowded sidewalks, her momentary gaze at the sky was interrupted by a sudden body-slamming impact that sent her sprawling to the pavement. Adira never saw him weaving through the swarm. His immediate reaction to their collision was a pathetic "Oh shit."

Adira's reaction was a reflexive outburst at the sudden intruder as expletive-laden thoughts ranted in her head. *He's just standing there like a jerk, looking at me, and all I get is an "Oh shit"? I'm down on my ass, needing to retrieve my stuff off the pavement. Watch out, dude; I'm pissed.*

His offer to help reignited her rage. Stuffing belongings back into her bag, she gave him a drop-dead leer. With a cutting tone, she fired, "Pay attention to where you're going, and next time, find someone else to run over." Rising to her feet, she spun away, leaving him bewildered at their encounter.

She headed for her 1:30 massage appointment, which she knew would soothe her frayed nerves. Adira's mind wandered back to her early years in one of Chicago's ethnic neighborhoods, where she had struck out on her own, a runaway child of the street at age seventeen, using her model-like figure and gorgeous looks to earn a living dancing in strip clubs before moving to New York.

Other dancers called her street smart, watching her work in some of the upper-echelon clubs while avoiding the lure of drug and alcohol addictions. A friend introduced her to the lucrative opportunities as a highly paid escort for the city's wealthy and their political allies from DC.

She met Cynthia Jaymes at a private social event in the city. Their personalities clicked, and Cynthia convinced Adira to work for her unique escort agency, Society, which catered to the influential figures from DC with whom Adira was familiar.

Cynthia treated Adira well, promoting her to be the executive assistant for her and her husband, David. The position provided Adira with firsthand knowledge of Aegis and its hidden agenda.

David's arrogance and sense of privilege created a growing sense of disillusion in her. Recent anonymous messages had brought her to a decisive crossroads. She hoped her upcoming appointment at the Algonquin would provide an opportunity for change.

Leaving the spa, she wondered, *Who is the person sending me messages? Is it a scam or someone I can trust? I'll call Lydia tonight for advice.*

CHAPTER 26

The Algonquin

Adira arrived early for her interview at the Algonquin. She was familiar with its notable standing as a distinguished literary hotel. Stories of the Round Table's daily gathering of journalists, authors, and theatrical greats often left her wishing she could have lived in that era and taken part in their discussions. For Adira, it was a desire for a lost time of elegance dissimilar to today's chaotic social environment.

The bellman opened the door, welcoming her and wishing her a good day. She loved the environment. The hotel's old, dark decor felt warm and comforting in the way an old pair of shoes felt good on her feet, even if they'd gone out of style.

She stopped at the desk, asking if Hamlet was available. Throughout its history, the Algonquin had always had a lobby cat, the original having been named Rusty. The current resident feline was Hamlet, a rescue from a cat colony on Long Island. The desk clerk pointed to a padded perch on the left side of the desk. There he was, showing a persnickety personality, overseeing his kingdom like a diligent hotelier.

"Hamlet, it's Adira. I've come back to see you." Being ignored by Hamlet, she walked into the dining area. "Table for two, and off to the side, please. I'd appreciate space for quiet conversation. I'm expecting a guest who will ask for me.

Please send this person to my table." After ordering a light lunch, she began reviewing her messages and email.

She was on the phone while finishing a salad when a distinguished-looking man walked up to her table, stooping over and cocking his head to gain her attention. "Excuse me, Adira?" His polite greeting resulted in a look of pleasant surprise from her.

"Ah, yes. Please have a seat while I finish my call. I'll only be a moment." Adira raised her chin and eyes, giving him a quick once-over as he settled across from her. "I'll have to call you back. My appointment is here. Yes, we can talk once I get home. Not sure what time, but not late."

Jack was making a visual assessment as she finished. *She's as much of a knockout as her pictures. Soft on the eyes, as an old Irish friend would say.* He placed his folded hands on the table and ordered coffee and water.

"Sorry to be on the phone. I was tidying up communications until your arrival. Since you know my name, you must be my scheduled appointment." Casting a whimsical expression his way, she waited for confirmation.

"Yes, I am." He couldn't help but stare at her as she reached across the table with a firm handshake and a familiar piercing look in her eyes. "My name is Jack, and I appreciate your willingness to meet." The server interrupted, delivering his coffee, asking if there would be anything else. "Nothing for me. Perhaps for the lady?" He nodded in deference to Adira.

Adira locked into a visual assessment of her guest, responding, "I'm fine for now, thank you." Her thoughts worked through the mental checklist she used when evaluating strangers. *He provides a gentle persona and sophisticated appearance. Looks like he stepped out from the cover of* GQ. *Is he my anonymous messenger, or did the messenger send him?*

"Well, Jack, are we going to be polite and ask about each other's backgrounds? I'd like to skip the polite, conventional banter. My preference is for asking straightforward questions. Like, who sent you here? Because I feel you're not the one sending messages to me. Just a woman's intuition, but am I correct?" She gave him a teasing look, winking and nodding, thinking, *Come on, Jack or whoever you are—let's play a little game of chess to see what's going on.*

Adira had a passion for playing chess. It was a game many men preferred, but she relished defeating them at their own game. Her trademark moves for winning were strong opening gambits and distraction. Wielding her intriguing personality and tempting looks to throw opponents off their game plans was a well-honed skill. She gave Jack a flirtatious smile, thinking, *Men can't keep their dicks from overriding their brains. It's so easy and so much fun to crush them.*

Jack threw his head back, expelling a rush of air through his lips, trying to avoid her ploy. His hands changed position as he placed one over the other. He was processing words to make the correct tactical reply. *She thinks she can gain the upper hand. Another strong woman like Sam—two in two days. Okay, Adira, game on.*

She glanced around the room, avoiding eye contact. "It's your move, Jack. You won't hear a peep from me until you answer. I have lots of patience and time to dance, honey."

Jack shifted in his chair, resting his forearms on the table and drawing a full breath to regain his equilibrium. "What would you like to know?" He scanned her facial expression, finding a deft poker player's look.

"Well, let's start with who sent you. What are we trying to achieve here? Try keeping it to the truth—I hate bullshit and clever, fast talk. Take your time, sweetie; no game clock to pressure you into a dangerous move. I'm here for at least another hour, or I can walk out now." Adira sat upright and tall, spreading her hands flat on the table's surface.

"Okay. Jack Gallagher is my real name—no need for disguise, pretense, or, as you stated, fast-talking bullshit. You could classify me as a freelancer specializing in the persuasive arts."

He gave a snickering grin before continuing. "Your intuition is spot on. I'm not the person messaging you about Aegis, Society, David, or Cynthia."

He saw her eyes flash at the mention of her employers. *Hah, struck a nerve. I'll let my mention of Society shake her bravado so I can find another weak spot.* Jack was moving on from defense, ready to make offensive strikes. His instincts flashed back to following his adolescent lessons under Aidan's fighting creed. Strike a blow and then strike another before your opponent can recover.

"You seem surprised at my mention of Society. I'm aware of your growing doubts about working for David and Cynthia, and Aegis. I believe those concerns brought you here to find out more. How am I doing?"

Adira sat stone-faced, leaving Jack to continue. "I know your history as a high-class escort, snaring politicians and wealthy business executives using sex and fetish desires as bait. You worked your way up the ladder, recruiting other women to work as escorts for Society. It plays like a sequel to the old movie *Sex, Lies, and Videotapes*." Jack paused, raising his posture, trying to gain a position of dominance in their exchange.

After the first startle, Adira remained devoid of emotion. Sensing an opening in Jack's pause, she leaned forward, whispering across the table with a look of pleasure, "Honey, my only surprise is you had the balls to try to intimidate me with your little speech. I think you meant to embarrass or shock me. Right, Jack? Well, it sure as hell didn't work." Adira's eyebrows lowered, pinching together as she pushed back into her chair.

Cornered and feeling back on defense, Jack shifted his thoughts to a higher gear. *She was waiting for me to overplay my hand. Damn it—I underestimated her. It's too late to recover the lost ground. Sam was right. This one is a challenge.*

Jack shook his head, clearing the mental confusion. "You wanted to know the endgame for today? My assignment is to convince you to work with a team of specialists in bringing down Aegis, Society, and David Jaymes. I know his arrogance and disregard for women piss you off, and Cynthia enables him in order to mask her own litany of faults. These are dangerous people, and you are at risk. We can help you escape, and you can help us succeed."

Adira pushed her chair away from the table to stand. Staring down at Jack, she raised her hand, motioning him to remain seated. "Look, Jack, I'm aware of the risks and types of people I associate with in my line of work. I need time to think and talk with someone before deciding which team to play for, if any. Text me your personal number, and I'll contact you with my decision within the next day or so."

Adira sauntered through the lobby, thinking, *It's time to go home, have a glass of wine, and call Lydia.*

CHAPTER 27

Advisors

Later that evening, in her apartment, Adira was about to pour a glass of wine when her phone vibrated with a call from Lydia. "Hey, girl. I wish you were up from DC and we could have a drink together. I've had a bizarro day and need some girl time to get clear-headed advice."

Lydia said, "You're in luck. I'm up at our townhouse alone for a few weeks to socialize, shop, and spend time with you. Lucas is stuck working in DC over Thanksgiving. Catch a cab, and I'll have some merlot waiting for you."

"You're awesome. I'll be there shortly."

Adira rang the bell at the townhouse. Lydia opened the door and embraced her. "You, sweetie, are a gorgeous sight to behold."

"Oh my God. I can't believe you're here just when I need you."

"Well, your timing was fortunate. I'm ready to hear about your bizarro day after I fill some wine glasses."

Adira recapped her collision with a strange yet familiar guy. "I keep having a feeling of having met him before, but he probably just looks like someone I know. Poor bastard. My raging temper overwhelmed him to the point he could hardly speak."

"Oh, honey, a man's mind freezes anytime a woman makes an intense confrontation. I can win any argument with

Lucas, whether right or wrong, by waving my hands, stomping around, and going on a bitching tirade." They laughed, clinking glasses in a toast before Lydia continued, "Sounded like your day had more than one bump in the road. What else happened?"

"I met with a man who's involved with anonymous messages I've been receiving about Society and Aegis. It's been going on for about a month."

"Is he a freak or stalker type?"

"No, not either of those. He knew a lot about me, my history, and my working for Cynthia. He said he's part of a team or some kind of group working to go after Aegis and David. He wants me to help them stop David's nomination and expose Aegis for what it is."

Lydia asked, "Wait a minute. Did you get his name?"

"He said his name is Jack Gallagher. Why?"

"I think he was telling you the truth, that he's recruiting, and believe I'm next on his list. Ryleigh gave me a heads-up to expect a call from him. It has to be the same guy. She said he would schedule a talk with me, but she didn't explain why."

"Are you going to meet with him?"

"Well, was he good-looking?"

"Hey, you're with me."

"Sorry. I was teasing, sweetie. Of course, if he calls, I'll meet with him. Ryleigh said it would be a good move for Lucas and me. Are you considering working with him?"

"I told him I needed to think and talk with a friend before giving him an answer. I was going to get Ryleigh's opinion, but I trust you more than her."

"Well, my advice is to tell him yes. I know how upset you've become over David's attitude. He's such an arrogant prick. And I can see we're heading for problems with Cynthia, with how she's trying to manipulate us. She doesn't give a damn about anyone but Cynthia."

Lydia lowered her tone. "Maybe this group can get us out of her clutches. We need to be cautious and not let Cynthia know about Jack or what he might ask of us."

"Good advice. Talking with you and having a little wine is calming my nerves."

Lydia smiled as she began smoothing Adira's arm. "I know what we need, and it'll be more fun than the day you've encountered. Stay with me tonight. I'll draw a hot bath in the soaking tub. There's room for both of us. A girl-on-girl night will be good fun." She leaned forward, caressing Adira's head, gently kissing the taste of wine on her lips.

Adira returned the kiss as they stood from the couch. "Go fill the bath and light some candles, and I'll pour more wine. I can contact Mr. Gallagher in the morning. You and I have more important and delicious things to do tonight."

Ethan was kicking back at home after a long day preparing for his upcoming interviews. His thoughts kept returning to the encounter with Jack—he wondered why Ryleigh had never told him about owning the paper. *Okay, Ethan. Time to call her and get things out in the open.*

Ryleigh answered on the second ring. "Ethan, I thought you would have called sooner. Your head must be ready to explode with questions."

"Now, there's an understatement. My first question is, why didn't you tell me about your involvement in the paper? The second one is, is Jack working for you, or is it a coincidence?" He knew his tone was coming across as accusatory, but it didn't matter. Ethan wanted straight answers.

"Well-stated questions, Ethan. I wanted you to work for the paper because I know your passion for investigative journalism. You and the *Insider* are a good match, and I didn't want my ownership to get in the way of you making your own decision. I would have told you sooner, but the right time wasn't there. It was in the best interests of the paper and your future.

"I assume you told Ed about my relationship with your family. If so, it brings him into our circle of friendship and awareness. He'll maintain confidentiality for us and continue to be an excellent resource for you."

After a few minutes of thoughtful silence, Ethan said, "I wish I had known sooner, but I understand. However, you didn't answer my question about Jack."

"Jack's managing the project for a group of us concerned about Aegis manipulating the course of governance in the country. I know your research has raised your awareness and similar concerns. My colleagues selected Jack, and he works under their supervision. Do you have any concerns about him?"

"No concerns. He seems focused and friendly. I think he's someone I can work with on my stories. I'll reach out to you if my feelings change. For now, I'm excited about being part of your project. Outside of Ed, I'll keep our connection to myself."

"I agree. It's best for everyone and will let you focus on your assignments. We can always talk one on one as things progress. Say hello to your mom and dad for me next time you talk with them."

CHAPTER 28

Debriefing

Early the next morning, Jack arrived at the Soho office well before Sam and placed a notebook on the table before heading for the Keurig to make a fresh coffee. He scanned the studio with his eyes, admiring the professional appearance and comfortable feeling. He briefly considered sitting at Sam's desk but immediately discarded the idea. His experiences had taught him the value of respect and knowing one's place in a working relationship and never overstepping boundaries. "Respect earns respect" was a life lesson ingrained from his mother. The recollection guided him to a proper seat at the circular table.

His phone buzzed with an incoming call. The screen let him know it was from Roy Covington. "Roy, how the hell are you, man? Thanks for returning my call." Looking up at the slow-moving ceiling fan, he rocked the chair onto its back legs.

Roy asked why Jack was calling, remarking it'd been over two years since they'd last talked. Jack agreed. "Yeah, it's been a while. I'm about to start a meeting and don't have much time to talk. How about getting together for a drink? I have need of your talents. I think it's something you'll want in on."

Being a man of few words, Roy said, "Sounds fine. Where and when?"

"Let's try the Blue Bar at the Algonquin. I was just there for lunch but haven't been to their bar in ages. Can you meet this Friday at one o'clock? Hell, I'll even buy the first round." Jack was glancing at the wall clock and watching the door. He wanted to close the call before Sam arrived. "Great, I'll see you there." He heard the door opening just as he placed his phone on the table.

Surprised at finding the office lights on, Sam opened the door with a sense of caution. Halting to scan the room, she discovered Jack sitting at the table sipping coffee. She straightened her posture, clearing her throat to draw his attention. "Good morning, Jack. I'm not accustomed to people arriving ahead of me. A bit of a surprise, but in a pleasant way." Sam was still doing a visual survey, heading for her desk.

Jack set his cup on the table, standing to greet her. "I'll take it as a compliment, Sam. Like you, I prefer to be early and never later than on time. It gave me a few minutes to review points for our discussion. Can I make a coffee for you?" He started for the cupboard before she could answer, assuming she'd accept his offer.

"That would be nice. You'll find half-caff pods in the cupboard, which is what I prefer. Limiting caffeine works best for me, even in the morning." Sam set her briefcase by the desk and sat in the chair next to his at the table. She was eyeing his notebook, eager to hear what he would disclose from yesterday's contacts with Ethan and Adira. She looked up as he returned with her half-caff request.

"Thanks for being the barista. I'm not accustomed to a man catering to my morning requests." Sipping the coffee allowed her to quiet her desire to take charge. *Patience, Sam. Enjoy the attention and company.*

Jack pulled his chair up while opening the notebook. Sam was trying to hide an admiring look of pleasure as she held the cup with both hands near her face, waiting for Jack's briefing. "I shouldn't need my notes. I'll leave them for your review later. Both meetings produced the results you expected. One subject was friendly and willing to cooperate; the other was testy."

He paused, looking at Sam for a reactive comment, finding her sitting with a pleasant smile. She was nodding, studying him, thinking as her face flushed, *It's not a social date, so stop ogling the view and pay attention to what he's saying.*

"I'll start with Ethan. He expected to be interviewing me. Without question, the anonymous messages piqued his interest." A momentary pause enabled him to monitor Sam, trying to assess her mood and reactions.

"So right out of the gate, he guessed I wasn't the mystery tipster. I gave him the pitch about having a Watergate opportunity. He might be a junior reporter, but Watergate rang his bell. I stuck with the talking points Ryleigh provided. My one hesitation was telling him to call his editor. I'm glad I stuck to the script because we ended up with Ethan and his editor agreeing to work with us."

Sam added, "It was Ryleigh's doing. Our equity firm owns the paper, with her as the chairperson. She talked with the editor as you were talking with Ethan. Sometimes, adhering to timing in a schedule has benefits, and Ryleigh is a wizard at planning and execution."

"I'm impressed and have a hunch it won't be the last time."

Setting her cup down, Sam folded her arms. "What's your overall impression of Ethan?"

"Well, he's an energetic young man. I think we connected well. Like all good reporters and anglers, he wasn't about to let this catch get away. They'll publish the first story next week. He'll provide an advance copy for us to review and edit before printing. Any thoughts?"

"We need to encourage him to keep making probing inquiries to irritate David and Cynthia. They're a suspicious pair, always worrying about someone plotting against them. I know they're aware of and monitoring Ethan's activities." Sam made one of her familiar pauses with deep breathing. Jack knew he needed to let her continue without interruption.

Sensing she still had the floor, Sam said, "As we've discussed, eventually, we'll bring Ethan and Adira together. I'm confident they'll see the advantages. Tell me about your testy encounter with her."

"As you warned me, she's confrontational, coming right at me without hesitation. Like Ethan, she doubted I was the person sending messages. I'm not sure how they made their deductions, but it doesn't matter. Adira has a strong energy. No mincing words or hiding contempt for my attempted intimidation. Her personality is like Ethan's, but with a punch." He paused before continuing, seeming to weigh more thoughts. "It's obvious why she's successful. The fashion model's looks and soft, sensual voice create a distraction from what lies below the surface. You told me not to underestimate her, but I did. No long-term harm, though."

"I tried to warn you, Jack."

Jack gave a quiet laugh, shaking his head. "I have to say, you and Adira went to the same school for passive-aggressive training. Please don't take that wrong. I admire strong women and mean it as a compliment. To top it off, she has the skills to go from being harmless to making a vicious strike in the blink of an eye. Few people can command that tactic as well as I witnessed."

He moved back into his chair, continuing, "I'll know her decision in a day or two. If she accepts, I agree with you about her and Ethan being a good team. He's more laid back, but both seem to have a good work ethic, and I like that in associates. Whatever we have in mind for them, they will accomplish it." Jack exhaled, closing his notebook.

"Am I still on the team, and where do we go from here?"

CHAPTER 29
Assignment Lydia

"Yes, you're still on the team and here to stay. I don't need to make any further assessments of you. You handled the first assignment well. We have much to accomplish and, perhaps, not enough time. Let me get some notes and files from my desk so we can discuss interviewing your next prospect, Lydia Mathers."

Jack watched as she walked across the office and bent over to retrieve items from her credenza. He smiled, thinking, *Sam might be older, but she's as hot as Adira. This job is going to require dodging wandering thoughts.* He let out a short laugh as Sam returned.

"Did I do something to trigger your humor?"

"Nope. Just a stray thought and my growing interest in working with you."

Jack's subtle innuendo escaped Sam's notice, as she was leafing through papers. "I know you've read through Ryleigh's plan, but we might start considering modifications with Lydia."

Jack's phone buzzed on the table with an incoming text. Glancing at the screen, he said, "It's from Adira."

"What's she saying?"

Jack scrolled the message as he read. "'I've talked with my friend, Lydia Mathers. I believe you'll be meeting with her soon. She's talked with Ryleigh Jaymes about your plans.

Lydia and I feel it's in our best interest to work with you. I'll join the team if she does.'" Raising his eyebrows, he looked at Sam for comment.

"Hmm. I'm not surprised. I forgot to tell you that Ryleigh, Adira, and Lydia are friends. More about their relationships in a minute. We need to stay on top of Ethan and his interviews with Senator Mathers and Lydia. His first story needs to hit next week. Second, bring Roy Covington on board as soon as possible. While his role isn't in Ryleigh's plan, I agree with you about needing a trusted partner in the field."

Jack said, "I'll talk with Ethan today. I've already contacted Roy. He and I are planning to meet on Friday."

Sam pushed her notes to the side. "Lydia presents a dilemma for me." She paused and folded her arms, looking at Jack with squinted eyes.

Jack wanted to ask but waited, thinking, *What's troubling her about Lydia?* After several moments, he ended the silence. "Sam. Whatever your problem is, bring it out in the open. You and I need to talk without obstacles. I recall your preference for straightforward communication, no formalities, and how that will make our work less complicated. Well, this is the time to talk straight."

Sam nodded in agreement. "Yes, I remember saying that. So here it comes. Ryleigh's recommendation to use Lydia is valid, but I think there's a conflict of interest. At least, it's the way I feel about their relationship. Lydia is Lucas's young, promiscuous wife. They're a secret swinger couple, and now she's functioning as a political hooker for Society. Ryleigh may be comfortable with her, but I'm not there yet."

"If you have those concerns, why are we recruiting her?"

"She and Adira can corroborate information and provide Ethan with sensational tales of illicit affairs and blackmail schemes for political gain. She knows how Aegis and Society interact. The same is true for Adira. Between them, Ethan has a pot of gold. It's a story his paper dreams of having at its disposal. She and Adira can deliver lethal information for us to use to expose Aegis and David."

"Okay, I'm hearing that Lydia's valuable but working with her might bring some risk. I think you're telling me to be careful with her. Am I on the right track?"

Sam was searching through her thoughts before responding. "Yes. Very careful. I recommend doing the initial interview here. It puts her on our turf and allows you to be in control, which is difficult in a restaurant or other locations."

"Okay, I'll try to schedule with her for Friday morning. As you said, time is limited, and I need to keep moving forward. Anything else for discussion?"

"I think we're done for today. Be on guard with Lydia. I wouldn't want you getting bitten by a snake." Sam gave him a wink and a sly smile.

Jack grinned, saying, "I'll text you the time for my meeting with her so we don't all end up here simultaneously."

"Sounds like a plan. I'll look forward to hearing from you about Lydia and Roy. Good luck, Jack."

Jack left the office with questioning thoughts. *Is Sam concerned for my safety, or is she feeling threatened by Lydia? First things first. Call Ethan and get him to interview Lucas and Lydia.*

CHAPTER 30

Lucas Mathers, Senator

Jack provided Ethan with a private cell number for Senator Mathers so they could connect without interference from his Senate staff. Ryleigh, having a personal connection with Lucas, made the initial contact, explaining she had a reporter working on a series of stories to expose Aegis. The senator told her he was more than willing to talk to Ethan.

"Senator Mathers, this is Ethan Brode, and thanks for taking my call on a Thanksgiving morning. Ryleigh Jaymes said I wouldn't be disturbing any holiday plans."

"I've been expecting your call after talking to your chairperson. I don't have a lot of time, Ethan. While others enjoy the holiday, my work obligations persist without breaks. So make your questions short, and I'll do my best to provide useful answers. And you can just call me Lucas."

"Thank you, Lucas. I'll be as brief as possible since you've been gracious enough to speak with me. I want you to be aware this conversation will be off the record. Any part of our discussion in my story will state the information was obtained from an anonymous but reliable source, and I will not disclose your identity."

"Good. There will be a time when I may be ready to step forward, but not yet."

"My first question is, are you being blackmailed by an organization because of an encounter with an escort?"

"Way to lead off with a ballbuster question, Ethan. *Blackmail* might be a bit of a misnomer; I prefer calling it coercion."

"Was it over a sexual encounter with an escort? And did the organization threaten to tell your wife?"

"Let me make this simple and keep us from doing a round of ninety-nine investigative questions. You can write while I tell my story. You can even turn on a recording device to keep up with me. Just keep my name out of it. Are you good with me talking and you listening?"

"My phone is recording, and my pen and paper are waiting, Lucas."

"I'm sure you've done background work on me and heard the rumors about me being a sugar daddy for my trophy wife, along with our being part of a swinger's group. I don't care about the labels people try to slap on my ass, but Lydia should be off limits, and our private lives are not anyone's concern. Do we enjoy the company of people outside our marriage? Yes. I believe it's known as having an open relationship. It may rub people the wrong way, but I don't give a rat's ass about what anyone thinks. Am I being too blunt for you, Ethan?"

"No, sir, you can paint vivid pictures without offending me."

"Good. Lydia and I have an arrangement of convenience. Hell, she's thirty years younger than me and often left alone while I'm out conducting congressional business. So your question is, did they threaten to tell her? Damn right they did, but I beat 'em to the punch. I told Lydia everything and took the wind out of their sails.

"Hell, Lydia already knew most of it. And topping it off, now she's working with the escort who snagged me. They're out hunting other senators and representatives. Finally, the girls have had enough of Cynthia and David Jaymes and are ready to turn the tables on them. You might not understand it, son, but this is sweet justice coming around to bite 'em in the ass, and they don't see it coming. Hold on while I answer another call."

Lucas switched him to hold, leaving Ethan thinking, *He lives up to his reputation of being a barn burner.*

"Sorry for the interruption. Where was I?"

"You answered another call just after saying sweet justice is about to…"

"Okay, okay, got it. I hope the girls catch a lot of my two-faced chickenshit colleagues. The bastards deserve a healthy dose of coercion for looking down on me and Lydia. Yeah. It'll happen, and it doesn't matter whether you call it revenge, vengeance, or sweet justice. In my book, it's all about how what goes around comes back around." Lucas let out a bellowing laugh, loud enough to make Ethan hold the phone away from his ear.

Ethan jumped in with several questions as the senator settled down. "Is Aegis the organization threatening you? What proof do they have, and what are they demanding?"

"Slow down, son. Their proof is a video recording of the encounter. A celebrity might survive such a disclosure. A senator can't. Constituents don't enjoy voting for philanderers. Cynthia Jaymes, Aegis's new leader, is demanding I give her husband a free pass on his nomination, or they go public against me. Rumors are easy to dismiss as political attacks and lies. Video doesn't leave room for maneuvering. Someone with a lot of power and influence is orchestrating all this. Is it Aegis? Hell yes, along with that son of a bitch Jonathan Jaymes, but it would be my word against theirs.

"My career is winding down, and I'd like to leave office on my terms and timetable. The people you're working with told me they could bring Aegis and David Jaymes down and explained how my role on the Judiciary Committee could help. However, if Aegis learns I'm working against them, they'll fight like hell to remove me from my chair position, and David Jaymes will have a clear path to become the next chief justice. My aim is to prevent it from happening. Now you know why I must remain anonymous until later in the game."

Ethan was making notes to supplement the audio recording. "I fully understand your predicament and will guard your anonymity with my life."

"Let's hope such a need doesn't occur, Ethan. Aegis has taken similar coercive actions with other political figures, which will cloud their assumptions about where your information is coming from. I plan to continue my work until Aegis is defeated. Then, I will resign and sail into the Louisiana sunset. Do you have enough for your story?"

Ethan thought before answering. "You've been helpful, Senator. One last question. Can I contact you if I need a follow-up after talking with others?"

"You have my number and can call me on an as-needed basis. I need to get back to work, even though it's Thanksgiving. Lydia is in New York. So I'm batching it. I would guess she's on your list for an interview. If not, she should be. Lydia can provide details on Aegis and how they work. She'll be just as frank and colorful as I am in answering questions. She can also verify facts from our discussion. So you have my permission to contact her. Tell your group to make sure they succeed. I'm counting on them."

"I'll make sure our group is aware of your support for our success. I have an interview with your wife later this afternoon, and I appreciate you allowing me to talk with her."

CHAPTER 31

Ethan and Lydia

Lydia was in New York when Ethan reached her. She was agreeable and accommodating, suggesting talking with him at her townhouse at 4:00 p.m. Not sure of what to expect, Ethan was nervous as he rang the doorbell. The senator's description of her as being frank and colorful set the stage for uncharted waters.

Ethan's eyes widened as the door opened, revealing a stunning woman in a sports bra and leggings. She was taller than he had imagined, with platinum blond cropped hair and brilliant blue eyes.

"Sorry for the sporty look, Ethan. I got into a longer Peloton workout than I had planned. I can change if you'd be more comfortable?"

Ethan was floundering through the momentary distraction for a reply. "No need to change, Mrs. Mathers."

"Oh, honey, the name is Lydia. Mrs. Mathers is for the stick-up-their-ass DC crowd. You and I will get along better if we just use first names. So come in, Ethan, and let's get comfortable."

He took in the well-appointed home as Lydia escorted him to a spacious living room with cathedral ceilings and ample cushioned seating. *It looks like a playpen for adults* was his first thought, but he kept it to himself. "Thank you for making time for an interview, Mrs.—I mean, Lydia. I spoke with your husband earlier, and he said it was acceptable for me to talk with you."

"Thanks for being upfront, but Lucas already called, asking me to cooperate and provide whatever information you need. I have more to share than you have time for today, but you'll get enough to use in your initial story, which I hope will shake up Cynthia and her group. Before you leave, I'll also provide you with reference material for reading and research.

"Like Lucas, I have to ask you to keep my identity anonymous. You should understand Cynthia Jaymes is a paranoid bitch and will question Adira Tomasz and me as the sources of the information leaked to you. Keeping our names out of your stories will send them scrambling like cockroaches, allowing us to keep collecting information. Enough of setting up parameters. Where would you like to start?"

"You mentioned Adira Tomasz. I don't have her on my interview list, but I believe she's the executive assistant to Cynthia and David Jaymes?"

"That's right. You should know who Adira is and plan to contact her. She's another confirming source for what I'll share with you. Lucas said he shared how the three of us came to be involved with one another."

"Yes, he explained the connection between the three of you and Society. From what I understand, it's a high-class escort service operated by Aegis, catering to political figures. Escorts secretly take photos or videos of sexual encounters with politicians and wealthy political influencers and turn over their evidence to Aegis, which demands funds and cooperation to maintain confidentiality. Have I made an accurate assessment?"

"Well done, Ethan. Society was the brainchild of Cynthia Jaymes and enabled her to become the chairperson for Aegis because her idea became the goose, laying eggs of gold for Aegis and creating leverage to gain whatever political favors the organization wanted. It's a sweetheart operation of sex, coercion, and influence or control."

Ethan was finishing notes and scanning his list of questions for Lydia. "Why are you working for Society? You're not a fan of Aegis, and they're trying to blackmail your husband. Working for them seems to contradict not being a fan."

"There are several reasons I work for them, and hope I can be frank in my statements?"

"Lucas said you would be. I don't think you'll make me uncomfortable. The more descriptive, the better."

"Hah, of course Lucas told you I wouldn't hold back in talking with you." Lydia paused a moment. "I'm going to have a little wine to loosen up as we talk. Care for any, Ethan, or would it be against your work ethic?"

"Thanks, but I'll pass on the offer, Lydia." Ethan watched her saunter across the room, thinking, *She matches the image of a trophy wife, no matter who her husband is or any age difference.*

She rejoined him with her wineglass in hand. "Not sure if Lucas explained: I love sex, and so does he. It's what brought us together and still works well. We have this New York location for hosting swinger parties. It's better to be away from the prying eyes and ears of DC.

"As for working with Aegis, I enjoy myself even though their clients are narcissistic, misogynist, fat-bellied assholes. Most of them haven't seen their dicks in years. Catching Aegis clients makes me feel powerful as I watch their moral judgment overridden by their desires."

Ethan raised a hand to pause Lydia with a question. "I have a basic understanding of what happens, but how does it happen?"

"It's a simple catch-and-kill process. Aegis controls the hotel rooms, with multiple cameras documenting every word and movement. Once I've collected my upfront fee and given blow jobs and a great ride, I get dressed while making small talk. Then, I spring the trap, which is where the fun begins. When I inform clients that the encounter has been recorded on video and that they will be contacted with further instructions for payments, it gives me an orgasmic high."

"What's their reaction?"

"Oh my God, you should see how they fly into a rage, plead, and almost piss their pants as I strut out of the room and close the door behind me. A few have chased me down the hall, pleading as I enter the elevator while blowing them a kiss." Lydia slowly sipped her wine, looking over the glass at Ethan, thinking, *He's cute, but I don't do beginners.*

"How did Aegis convince you to work for them?"

Lydia gave him a devious smile. "Adira recruited me. You need a little more background to understand my relationship with her. Society is more than an escort service. It's also a social organization for people with the right connections to add spice to their lives. Lucas and I first met Adira at one of Society's parties, where she lured him into a rendezvous without me. After snaring Lucas, she convinced me to join her in capturing other politicians. It was an opportunity too good to pass up—for revenge against those who've criticized Lucas and me. And now, Adira and I have become an intimate twosome. We can get it on with or without male accompaniment, and Lucas loves to watch and jump in whenever we let him."

Ethan's face flushed as he wrote; he tried to stay focused on his questions. "I assume David and Cynthia Jaymes are at the top of your revenge list?"

"Oh, hell yes. Aegis screwed up, going after Lucas before the nomination and failing to realize he could defeat their ambitious plans. Justice Wheeler's diagnosis and hospitalization came out of the blue, surprising everyone. This may be the best chance for Jack's team to upset their apple cart.

"Cynthia is furious about Lucas being threatened without her approval. She's obsessive about control, and it slipped through her fingers. Since the news of David's pending nomination, her advisors have been trying to convince her they have Lucas cornered, with no choice but to usher through David's nomination."

"But Lucas told me he isn't going to let them sweep through David's nomination."

"That's right. Cynthia Jaymes and Aegis made a wrong assumption and underestimated Lucas. He isn't worried about a sexual scandal. Damn, Ethan. We're from Louisiana. It's a place with a rich history of political scandals." Lydia broke into a raucous laugh, one similar to what Ethan had experienced with the senator.

"Lucas is ready to be done with DC and all its bullshit, but not until he settles his score with Aegis and Jonathan. Your work and Jack's team's work give Lucas the leverage to blindside them. Your articles will be the key to making it happen, but you need to be patient and leak information in small doses, quoting vetted, anonymous sources. Let me get the information I have for you to safeguard and use."

Lydia rose from the couch and crossed the room. Walking back to Ethan, she handed him an accordion file organizer. "In here, you'll find printouts of my Society clients, dates of encounters, and memory cards. The cards contain video files. I'm giving it all to you for safekeeping and future use in case Aegis comes after me. They're dangerous and will become desperate to stop you, the people you're working with,

Adira, and me. So this is your research information. Guard it with great care."

Ethan was looking up at Lydia as she continued, "You should have enough kindling and firewood to create fiery and entertaining stories. You can contact me anytime for clarifications. Right now, it's time for us to end the interview. The wine, our discussion, and your choirboy look make me want to have you between my legs, but we'll save the possibility of a rodeo ride for another time."

Ethan's face flushed again as he stood and cleared his throat. "I appreciate the time, and as promised, you've been informative and colorful. I'm sure we'll talk again."

Lydia reached out, caressing his face to pull it close, delivering a deep-throated kiss. She pulled away slowly, licking her lips and rubbing the front of his slacks, saying, "Enjoy the tingling rise in your pants, Ethan. It's been fun meeting with you."

As he left Lydia's townhouse, his head and emotions were spinning. *I should be writing a book about Lydia and Lucas instead of a news article. I wonder if Jack is going to be recruiting her.*

CHAPTER 32
Illicit Enticements

Lydia knocked on the door to the Soho office as Jack set up for her interview. Opening the door, he extended his hand. "Good morning, Lydia. Can I offer coffee, or would you prefer water?"

"Water is fine." She gave the office a thorough once-over as Jack slid a chair out for her. "I like the office. A crisp, professional look, obviously done with a woman's touch. No offense, but you don't appear to be the decorating type."

Jack returned to the conference table, placing a water glass for her. "No offense taken. I'm a man of many talents but short on those skills."

Lydia slowly stroked the side of the water glass as she tilted her head for a different view of him. "I'm sure you have interesting talents, but we'll stay on the business side for now." She paused to see if he would respond to her opening flirtation but only found him waiting for her to continue. "I met with your young reporter yesterday. Cute kid. I handed him a treasure trove of information most reporters would kill to access. I hope he follows my advice for using it."

Jack looked across the table. "I talked with him last evening, and he knows the value of what you handed over to him. We talked about exercising restraint—not rushing out with too much too fast. He said you told him a lot of it was for future use in case Aegis comes after you. Do you think they will?"

"Do I think they'll come after me? I know they will once Ethan releases stories about them. Cynthia Jaymes will go ballistic. She'll be out to stop attacks against Aegis and the almighty justice David Jaymes. Mark my words; she'll do whatever she feels is necessary to protect her turf. Everyone involved with you, everyone trying to stop David's nomination, will be at risk."

"Everyone? Who else do you think will be working with me besides you, Adira, and Ethan?"

"Come on, Jack. Don't play coy with me. I'm willing to work with you if we can be honest with each other. Who do I think is involved? Let's see. Your team includes Ryleigh, Samantha, Chandler, Ethan, Adira, Lucas, and me. Ryleigh brought me up to date after convincing Lucas and me to consider working with you. I'm the one who convinced Adira to join your team. How am I doing, Jack? Did I miss anyone, sweetie?"

"Not bad. You have the key players identified. Given your familiarity with the team and our objective of derailing David Jaymes, I think we can move on to specific tasks or assignments for you to consider."

"What do you have in mind? I'm hoping it goes beyond a business relationship."

Jack was trying to avoid Lydia's lure. "We need to distract Cynthia from going after Ethan once he publishes his first story. Are you willing to be a double agent?"

"Maybe, but I need to know more before agreeing to play the role."

Jack sat back in his chair, tapping his pen on the table. "Cynthia needs to see you as being on her side. You could tell her you're upset about her people feeling Lucas has a conflict of interest in overseeing David's nomination. Convince her they're wrong about him. Assure her he will support David's nomination.

"Right now, Cynthia trusts you and Adira. The two of you need to keep her trust for as long as possible."

"So Adira and I will be your double agents or moles?"

"Yes. Eventually, her fears and paranoia will focus on the two of you, which is when we need to pull you back for protection. The more Ethan writes, the greater the risk. Am I making sense?"

"Perfect sense. It's an interesting cloak-and-dagger operation. I understand the dangers, but it's also exciting, and I love excitement. So yes, I'm willing to be your double agent. Is Adira aware of what you want us to do?"

"Not yet. I plan to talk with her about you and her working with Ethan as his inside source of current information. His stories should throw them off balance, panic them into making mistakes. We'll have the three of you and one additional player coordinating plans once Ethan's first story hits the street."

Lydia turned her head at the mention of an additional person. "Sounds like you have someone I'm not aware of. Mind if I ask who the mystery person is, or do I have to wait like a good little girl? I don't appreciate being kept in the dark unless it involves time between the sheets." She tilted her head and touched her lips as she winked at Jack.

Jack returned the smile, staying on task. "No need for secrecy. His name is Roy Covington. I don't think you know him, but he will be invaluable to us."

"Hmm. You're right; I don't know him, but I'll look forward to meeting him. Is there more instruction today, or are we ready to close?"

"I think we're good for today. I'll be scheduling a briefing for everyone within the next week. So look to hear from me soon." He handed her a card with his cell number, saying,

"Call me anytime you have an idea or need help. Do you have any other questions?"

"Just one. I have to ask if the office has a restroom. My morning coffee and the water have exceeded my maximum capacity."

"It's to the left of the kitchen area." Jack watched Lydia as she walked across the office, thinking, *Another hot looker. Jeez, this job has them jumping out of the woodwork. The upside is that she's more cooperative than I expected.* He was lost in thought when Lydia returned. He looked up to see the top two buttons of her blouse undone, revealing a titillating view.

Lydia licked her lips, pointing a finger at Jack. "All the talk about being a double agent and political dangers has me aroused, Jack. I'm feeling restless and need some enjoyable diversion."

Lydia leaned in, her blouse on the verge of losing its ability to contain her breasts. "Hope you're enjoying the view, Jack. My girls are aching to have you nuzzle and pleasure them. I was thinking of a few drinks and some time together. We could get to know each other better, if you catch my drift. I don't bite, and I can put a satisfied smile on your face." She moved closer. "I have a gift for you."

She smoothed his hand with a pair of silk panties before placing them into his shirt pocket. "It's an invitation, Jack." He sat wide-eyed, feeling a rising excitement. "Hah. You're speechless; how adorable, sweetie. Does the proverbial cat have your tongue? I hope not, because I have fantasies about what you can do for me with it." She bent over to kiss his cheek and whispered in his ear, "Drinks and playtime at my place or yours, Jack? And just so my intentions are clear, I'm one hell of a fuck."

Jack leaned as far back as the chair would allow. "You're a tempting offer, Lydia, but our relationship needs to focus on business." He pulled the panties from his pocket, handing them back to her. "I have to say, I've never experienced an invitation quite like this, and I'm flattered."

She pushed his hand away. "Keep them, Jack. Maybe you can return them to me later. I'm sure I'll think of a reason to call and need your help with something." She turned, patting her ass as she looked over her shoulder, and blew Jack a kiss before going out the door.

Jack shook his head, walked to the kitchen to rinse his coffee cup, and began talking out loud to himself. "Damn, Jack. Since when do you pass on a hot piece of ass ready to go a few rounds? Get your shit together, man, and keep her at arm's length. There'd be a hell of a catfight if Sam were here. She had good reasons to warn me about Lydia."

As he locked the office door, his thoughts turned to his next meeting. *I need to head for the Algonquin to meet with Roy. I damn sure need a drink.*

CHAPTER 33

Roy Covington

Jack found Roy at the Algonquin Blue Bar with a bourbon in hand and one waiting. "Roy, thanks for ordering my drink, but I said I'd buy the first round."

"Hey, I only did the ordering. The tab is still on you, bud."

Jack reached out for a handshake. "Great to see you again."

"Same here. You're still looking good, Jack. I'm sure New York's finest women are still chasing after you. Are you still working with Chandler?"

"Yeah, he calls me his strong-armed ace agent and has a constant lineup of clients needing my help at whatever price we choose to charge. But rather than reviewing past clients, I want to talk with you about my current one, Samantha Mieras."

Roy flashed a grin, nodding. "I can start by saying she's a dynamo, and it's been great working with her. Drop-dead gorgeous looks and a killer instinct for achievement. I'm guessing her project involves the surveillance and background investigations she's had me doing. You were part of the group I investigated, although I didn't tell her I already knew you. Tell me what else you'd like to know."

"No additional details about her. It's about the project she hired me to manage. The individuals you investigated are being brought together as a team, and I need someone to help run the operation. That's why I called you."

"Is she okay with you bringing me onto the project?"

"Yeah, no problem there." Jack was savoring the bourbon Roy had ordered. Setting the glass down, he said, "She was going to recommend I consider bringing you on board before I asked. We laughed over having the same thought of who could help me manage things. Are you available and up for working together again?"

"Tell me what you expect my role to be before I answer."

Jack looked around to make sure no one was eavesdropping on their conversation. "The project will be risky because of the organization and people we're up against. This will demand your best skills. I need someone who will protect my backside to keep me from being blindsided. If you're interested, we can discuss the details and lay out strategies at my place. Bars and restaurants have too many curious eyes and ears. What do you think?"

"You have me at ninety percent yes with 'risky' and covering your backside. Tell me the names of the other team members."

"I'll use first names since you know them better than I do now. We've got Ethan, Adira, Lucas, and Lydia. Sam also has Chandler available. There's one more, Ryleigh Jaymes, but I don't think you're familiar with her."

Roy was nodding with each name until Jack mentioned Ryleigh. "You've got an interesting cast of characters, Jack. The last one is someone I don't have much information on, but I suspect she has an association with David and Cynthia James. Sam has me currently looking into them and their organization. Am I right about Ryleigh's connection?"

"Bingo. And you're well into the work I saw as your initial assignments. A personal note on Ryleigh. She's not fond of me, but I don't have a clue why she feels that way. Maybe you can figure it out."

"Maybe. Last question before I commit. Is the work on Chandler's dime or yours?"

"You'd be working for Sam; it's her dime."

"That's all the answers I need for now, and I'd be happy to sign up." They raised their glasses in a toast.

"Hey, before we head for my place to iron out details, tell me what else you've been doing besides working with Sam."

Roy hesitated before answering. "Nothing special, just investigative work and special projects. Background investigations are how I find the special things to do. You know me and my preference for being a freelancer. I show up where the work is available. Right now, it's with you."

"Hey, let me know if you ever need help. Once this job is complete, I think I might be ready to try freelancing."

"I'll keep you in mind and might recruit you for something special down the road. Let's move on to your place."

Jack set his empty glass down and reached to shake Roy's hand. "Glad to have you on board, Roy. I have a meeting with Sam tomorrow morning to update her on my results from today, and she'll be happy to know that you're with us."

CHAPTER 34

Lydia Outcome

The next morning, Sam arrived well ahead of her eight o'clock update with Jack. She linked her laptop to the storage drive on the HITO wall clock to download the video of Jack's meeting with Lydia. Making a quick cup of coffee, she watched the computer screen as the video played. *The picture quality and sound are like I'm at the table with them. Let's see how Jack did.*

Sam remained calm until the she reached the part where Lydia returned from the restroom. "You slut! I knew damn well you'd be trying to hit on Jack. Hands off, you bitch." Her angered stress subsided as she watched Jack's rebuff of Lydia's advances. "Nice work, Jack. I knew there were multiple reasons for feeling attracted to you."

She finished the video and started a cup of coffee for Jack as he arrived ten minutes early. "Morning, Jack. Your coffee's almost ready. Have a seat at the table, and I'll be right there." She smiled as she placed a cup for Jack and sat near him. "I'm eager to hear how your day went and if we have a full complement of associates to move forward."

"Thanks for returning the barista service. Like you, I'm unaccustomed to having personalized coffee in the morning."

He placed both hands on the table. "I'll start with Roy. He's on board and forging ahead with your requests for current information on David and Aegis. I guess I should thank you for starting him down those paths. The combination of knowledge from Ethan, Adira, and Lydia will develop into a complete picture of what we're up against once Roy adds what he uncovers. I gave him one more investigation to add to his list."

"Who did you add?"

"I wanted more information on Ryleigh. While you and Chandler know her well, I want an outsider's view. Roy doesn't know her, and his input will be unbiased. I hope my additional request passes muster with you. If not, I'll have him back off on her."

"No problem, Jack. Given that she questioned your hiring, I think it's a good move. It fits with a saying from Sun Tzu's book *The Art of War*. 'Know thy enemy, and you will never be defeated in a hundred battles.'"

"I'm not surprised you're familiar with the book. I've read it a few times after a friend named Mansa gave me a copy to help me survive the environment at Attica."

Sam pursed her lips. "Seems like unusual reading material for a prison setting, but no matter. It's fascinating how we keep uncovering more similarities between us. Tzu's reference shows why Roy's work is critical in supplementing what our team members reveal about the other side. Knowledge is one of our best assets."

Jack was ready to review his encounter with Lydia. "That brings us to Lydia. You called her dangerous. I didn't realize the term would have a double meaning."

Sam nodded, asking, "What do you mean by 'a double meaning'? I meant she could be dangerous for our project by focusing on her personal agenda rather than ours." Her lips parted in a sly smile as she waited to hear Jack continue recapping the interview. *Let's see how transparent you're willing to be, Jack.*

"I understood the risk to the project. The background report showed she was a vixen with a strong sexual appetite, and that was the hidden danger. Some of the best working girls have tried hustling me in the past, but I was caught off guard by…let's say I wasn't expecting an offer to get laid here, there, or anywhere." Jack stifled a laugh, adding, "I know I can be frank with you. Lydia damn near bared her tits and rubbed them in my face. I think she would have done me on your Persian rug."

Sam was chuckling at Jack's attempt to describe the situation. "I've heard she's an in-your-face girl, and your statement seems to confirm the billing."

"Don't get me wrong. Lydia may be up there on the temptation scale, but you outshine her in class and looks. I'm sorry—that might have sounded inappropriate, but I didn't mean to be out of line." Jack's face showed a tinge of red as he tried dancing around his comment. "I mean, regarding our working relationship." He rubbed his chin, closing his eyes.

"I'm feeling flattered. I also appreciate how you didn't fall prey to her approach. It's her nature to come on to men, but it sounded more assertive than I expected. Lydia uses her looks and sex as power elements and is damn good at wielding them. I need to offer a confession and be transparent with you. The office is on security surveillance, which means I have a video of the meeting."

"Have you watched the video?"

Sam bit the inside of her lip. "Not yet. Should I?"

"Watching it is up to you. If you do, you'll find my explanation was accurate. And for the record, Lydia's a little indelicate for my appetite."

Sam reached out to pat Jack's hand. "I don't need to watch the video. I believe you and know I can trust you. With relationships, I tend to be cautious. They've been very few for me. I like what I see and feel when I'm with you, but we need to keep concentrating on our project's objectives for now. Anything else between us can be a work in progress. Am I being too direct or expressing something different from your feelings?"

Jack gently squeezed Sam's hand, trying to decipher her meaning. "My emotions tell me we have a good connection. However, business needs to take priority. We'll play it by ear and see what happens."

"Can you avoid her approaches and keep her focused on our objectives? I guess I'm asking, do we still want her on our team, and can we trust her?"

"Yeah, I still want her on our team. I think she's the key to keeping Adira with us, and they can watch out for each other. Adira will help make sure Lydia stays focused and that we can trust her. I see the plan working better with them as a pair rather than with only one. Do you agree?"

"I have to agree with your assessment. And as for Lydia's sexual overtures? I trust you, Jack."

"Sam, for me, relationships are more than quick flings. You can stop worrying about Lydia drawing me in. Does that make sense?"

"Loud and clear, and I like the message. Okay, Lydia and Roy complete the team. From here on, you and I communicate when we have questions or updates. I want to stay informed about what's happening, but I don't want to micromanage your style. Oh, one last question. When is Ethan's article being published?"

"I should have a copy for us to review by Monday, with publication Tuesday."

"The reaction from the other side will tell us what we're up against."

CHAPTER 35

First Strike

Ethan wrote the first article with Jack's advice ringing in his mind. "Your first strike starts the fight. The follow-up needs to continue making hits to keep them back on their heels. Rule number one: strike the first blow hard, without warning. Second, never admit you're wrong or show any sign of weakness. Third, hit harder, again and again. It's called relentless intimidation, Ethan. We have the element of surprise on our side and a fistful of reliable information to continue striking them with. Make us proud, son."

The *Insider*'s front-page headline caught the attention of politicians and political operatives. It was a hard strike, made without warning. Ethan was about to gain fame and notoriety with his byline and story angle, as they set off alarms from New York down to Raleigh, North Carolina. Little did he know the repercussions of the vortex he was setting into motion. Jonathan Jaymes fumed reading the story online.

UNMASKING A HIDDEN THREAT

By Ethan Brode, investigative reporter for the *Insider*
When considering judiciary selections, one should not commingle coercion, blackmail, illicit encounters, and a list of senators, representatives, and political influencers. The *Insider* has been investigating an organization

influencing federal elections and judicial appointments by blending those elements to serve clandestine motives to control the federal judiciary. In this initial story, we will use the name Organization A to refer to the entity.

The scheme has been brewing secretively for decades. It's an almost mythical tale of an organization that had good intentions after the Civil War but was seized by corrupt political actors seeking to manipulate governance for personal gains.

The organization originated from a blending of two opposing groups. One side espoused scholarly discourse and vigorous policy debate, leaning toward the political right. The other side created alternative, opposing views through increased civil discussion. The discontentment of radical political factions on both sides has led to a mindset of entitlement without regard for the rights of the general populace.

Operating under the cover of anonymity, the organization has strategically built formidable influence and persuasion within the federal government's legislative and executive branches.

The recent announcement of Supreme Court chief justice Wheeler's health issues presents the opportunity Organization A has waited decades to see happen. President Lawrence, long an advocate of Supreme Court control by his party, has set the aspirations of Organization A on the threshold of success with his recent pending nomination for chief justice.

President Lawrence's top-rated nominee is David Jaymes. He is the current chief judge on the Second Circuit Court of Appeals in New York. Appointing Jaymes would create an unstoppable supermajority, placing decisions on citizens' rights and other hot-button issues in the lethal crosshairs of revisionists.

What is Organization A? Follow the *Insider* as our continuing investigation reveals its secrets and primary operatives.

Like the wizard from Oz hiding behind a curtain, Organization A has created illusions to mask its identity and worked to seize control of the country's cornerstone, democracy. Is it fact or fiction?

We will continue to update this developing story.

CHAPTER 36

Reaction

Dawn was breaking in North Carolina, and a storm of exasperation was building for Jonathan Jaymes as he read the online version of Ethan's story. Red-faced and shouting obscenities, he closed the computer's connection. "Jackson, get me a glass of Old Camp, and bring it into my study damn quick." From the angry timbre of Jonathan's demand, Jackson knew it required immediate attention and delivery without question. Setting the whiskey on the desk, he promptly exited, closing the massive mahogany doors behind him.

Jonathan Jaymes rummaged through papers, searching for a pen, as he dialed David's number and became more irritated with each unanswered ring. "David, have you seen this outrageous piece in the *Insider*?"

"I've read it, and we will handle it from here. There's nothing for you to do or be concerned about."

"Where is Cynthia, our illustrious chairperson, and what the hell is she doing about it?"

"Calm down, Father, or you'll stroke out. Cynthia's already working the phones, assembling a group of our best associates with the skills to put a stop to this reporter. He's been snooping for months. We know who he is and where to find him."

"You're damn right. You need to find him! Do you hear me? I want to know who put him up to this nonsense. I don't care if Cynthia has to buy and shutter the paper. We are at a precarious point, David."

"I know the stakes, and Cynthia will quiet the story."

"I want something done now. I do not want to hear about or read any more public accusations. Stories like this can flush away your nomination and years of patience if they get their hands on the right information."

David was trying to stifle a response. "Things work differently today than in your heyday. We have subtle methods to persuade people to see things our way. We will convince them to stop any further attacks."

"Cut the double-talk, David. In my day, a rope and a tree were the only persuasions needed, and they convinced people to do as we demanded."

"Ropes and trees are unacceptable today. So unless you have something constructive to add, I need to see what Cynthia has accomplished."

Jonathan hesitated as he listened, savoring the last drops of his favorite whiskey. "You do that, David. Then tell Cynthia I'm calling an emergency meeting of the board. We'll be gathering in my study this Thursday morning at eight. You stay in New York. I want her here."

"I don't think…"

"Oh, shut up, David. What you think isn't worth a tinker's damn. We need to ensure this paper and its reporter know what they've started and feel a painful return volley. Charter a flight, and make sure her ass is here for the board's discussion." Jonathan closed the call and swiveled his chair to look at the morning sun as he called for Jackson to bring another whiskey.

CHAPTER 37

Call to Action

Nine trustees and Jonathan were finishing a light breakfast and waiting to have the conference table cleared for business. Cynthia handed out a printed copy of Ethan's article as she called the meeting to order.

Jonathan stood to speak. "I want to remind everyone how close we are to achieving one of our most important objectives. This open attack, disguised as a news story, is an unacceptable personal affront to who we are and what we have worked to accomplish. Decades of planning, patience, and strategic maneuvers are at risk. I will turn the meeting over to Cynthia to define our direction and responses. Cynthia?"

"Thank you for the reminder and for setting the tone, Jonathan. Gentlemen, we are now at war with an unknown enemy. Ethan Brode may have written the article, but he is just one piece of the puzzle. I have initiated steps to gain his cooperation and stop further harassment. I have also instructed some of our best analysts to identify who is behind him and what those people's future objectives may be."

Jonathan raised a hand to stop Cynthia and asked, "Who owns the paper? Can we buy it and close the shop? It might be the most practical way to avoid further escalation."

"As for ownership, it's a private corporation out of Delaware. Our investigators found it's one of several nested shell companies created to hide the actual owners. We're working to peel the layers back, but it will take time. Forcing a buyout and shutting the paper down is not an option. As we all know, its reputation is for digging into scandalous, sometimes questionable rumors and fanning public outrage. We are simply one of its current targets. Closing it down would just add fuel to the fire this piece has started. Oliver, do you have a question or comment?"

"Yes. Several of us have been trying to imagine who might be handing information to this reporter and trying to assail Aegis and David. We think you should look at Senator Mathers. You know how furious he was after being leveraged into favoring David's nomination. Our sources believe he might look to double-cross us. There could be others, but he's the most recent and important regarding the nomination."

Cynthia was jotting a note on Oliver's concern and said, "While I appreciate the suggestion, I'm confident he is not the root of our problem. We have more than one pressure point with him, but I will have it looked into. We have other suspects on our list to research."

Jonathan perked up at the mention of additional culprits. "Who's on your list?"

"First name is Samantha Mieras, a venture capitalist from New York. I'm unsure of her motives, but we're working on it."

Jonathan interrupted with an explanation. "I can tell you why she would be a person of interest. It goes back some twenty-seven years or more. Long before you knew David, he impregnated her when she was sixteen. The existing board and I ordered her to have an abortion and paid a handsome sum to make the pregnancy and her disappear. She took the money and never went through with the abortion. I had a feeling she might be involved and pulled an old file from my archives."

Jonathan gathered a folder marked "1992," handing it to Cynthia. "This is the background on Ms. Mieras and how she evaded our directive to have an abortion. She had two people assisting her. One was my daughter, Ryleigh. The other was Chandler Yates, a romantic partner of Ryleigh's. You will also find ample background information on him in the file. It was all a rebellious action by Ryleigh and Chandler against me and the board for ending their relationship. I hired investigators to follow up on the situation. Their reports are in the file and should be of interest, considering you suspect Ms. Mieras to be the source of our current problem. I will provide you with additional information after this meeting."

"Well, based on what you've said and what I think will be in the reports, I'm confident we've identified the source of our problem."

Jonathan tilted his head. "I assume you know her business partner is Ryleigh." An audible gasp silenced the room. Jonathan continued in defense of his daughter. "Ryleigh may be a business partner. However, that fact does not confirm she is an accomplice. I will talk with her to find out what's happening."

"Yes, I am aware that Ms. Mieras and Ryleigh are business partners. At this time, I would rather you not talk with Ryleigh. I will put my resources to work on this and get back to you with their results."

Cynthia was smiling, knowing she had the upper hand. "Let's put this to a vote. Those who favor having an in-depth look at Ms. Mieras, Ryleigh, and Chandler Yates, raise your hands." All but Jonathan voted in favor. "And those opposing Jonathan's speaking with Ryleigh before I've completed inquiries?" Again, the vote was nearly unanimous. "We have a nine-to-one vote on each motion, Jonathan. Do you want to override the consensus?"

"I will not override."

Cynthia felt her position as chairperson strengthening with the majority vote from the board. "Regarding silencing the reporter. Our associates will complete their work with Mr. Brode before I return to New York this evening."

One board member asked, "Can you assure us you can avoid physical violence? I would hope we are not that desperate yet."

Cynthia screened the room for reactions to the question before responding. "Mr. Fredericks, I opened this meeting with the statement that Aegis is at war with an unknown enemy. Our timetable is precarious and hangs on the current chief justice's declining health. We will be as cautious as possible but also as aggressive as necessary to avoid a perception of weakness. Our chief of security, Charles Abbott, and I will make appropriate decisions. My role is to safeguard our mission and achieve our objectives, no matter what they require. Am I providing a clear enough answer?"

Jonathan added, "I feel Cynthia has the situation in hand and trust her judgment. Speak now if you feel otherwise." The room fell silent, leaving Jonathan to adjourn the meeting.

As the other board members left, Cynthia remained seated, poring over the documentation Jonathan had provided. He didn't appreciate Ryleigh's being suspected, but he supported Cynthia's commitment to investigating all possibilities.

"I realize that I must set aside fatherly concerns and accept your efforts to ensure our success. I will move to my study while you read. We will discuss more details over bourbon or whiskey once you're ready. Understand one important fact. No one has seen what you'll find in the file. Not Ryleigh, David, or any other member of the board."

Cynthia spent most of the afternoon reviewing the extensive file and making notes. She found Jonathan in his study, reading a favorite Hemingway novel, *For Whom the Bell Tolls*. Cynthia spoke softly. "Is this a convenient time to interrupt and have our discussion?"

Turning his chair, Jonathan set the book aside, folding his hands on his desk. "Of course, my dear." He motioned for her to sit and called out to Jackson. "Two bourbons, neat, with water on the side for Cynthia." To Cynthia, he said, "I've been waiting for years to talk with someone about what I gave you. And before we start, it now belongs to you. We will talk, and then you decide what to do."

Taking a seat in front of Jonathan's desk, she waited for Jackson to leave. "One question, Jonathan. Your investigators ended their report without explaining what had happened to the infants. The report stated that someone took the infants and raised them without informing Samantha. Apparently, Ryleigh lied to her, saying they were stillborn. Have you confronted Ryleigh about knowing what happened to them?"

"She and I had a confrontation and reached an unsettling impasse. However, it has remained a private matter between the two of us. My investigators continued searching, to no avail, for almost eighteen years."

Jonathan and Cynthia talked for hours, exchanging views and possibilities in an attempt to solve the predicament of how to conquer the obstacles impeding David's nomination. "I have faith in you and your abilities, Cynthia. I do not have the same level of faith in David. You have my support to take whatever actions you deem necessary to ensure our success with the next court appointment. It may come down to removing David as the nominee and using an alternative candidate. Would that be problematic for you as the chair of Aegis?"

Cynthia folded her hands under her chin, closing her eyes. "I've been concerned about David's attitude and capabilities over the last two years but was hesitant to discuss my concerns with you. As the chair of Aegis, I know it might be beneficial for us to have the president select a replacement for David. I will have a better feel for a decision once I return home and see how he handles the current dilemma."

Jonathan rose from his chair to look out the window and began speaking as if he were addressing the plantation's sprawling landscape. "I will follow up with the board to ensure you have their commitment." Slowly, he turned to face Cynthia. "I'm placing great trust in you; do not allow David to distract your judgment. Your challenge will be to decide outside the bounds of marital partnership. Our business holds greater importance than your relationship with him. If you were to make the wrong decisions, it would be a disappointment to me."

The chartered return flight home was lonely and restless. Cynthia's thoughts went from Jonathan's file and her discussion with him to the young reporter. *How much information does he have, and where is it coming from?*

CHAPTER 38

A Shot across the Bow

The doorman greeted Ethan, telling him he might have guests awaiting his return. Exiting the elevator, Ethan noticed his door was slightly ajar. He pushed it open with caution and discovered his apartment looked like an Oklahoma twister had torn through it.

Closing the door behind him, Ethan found a strange man seated on his couch, watching a soccer match on ESPN. The man stood, shut off the television, and turned to Ethan. "Damn, you work late, newsboy. I've been wondering when you'd come home."

Ethan's reporting skills had him making mental notes of the man he was encountering. He had broad shoulders and a muscle builder's physique; he was at least six-two, with dark, slicked-back hair, a scar on the left side of his face, coal-black eyes, and a sneer for an expression. This was a man he would not forget.

"Who are you, and what have you done to my home?"

"Who I am is not important. However, the name is Charles. Sorry about the mess, but my associates were looking for something and failed to tidy up when they left."

"What were you looking for?"

"Something that might tell me who put you up to writing a nasty story and lying about my friends."

Ethan's respiratory rate increased as the stranger moved toward him, tightening his black leather gloves. "This is gonna hurt, newsboy, but I need your attention and some answers." Without further warning, Charles impacted Ethan's chin with a vicious left cross, sending him to the floor.

Shaking his head and staring up, Ethan shouted, "Man, you didn't have to smash me in the mouth."

"Oh, but I did. Pick your ass up off the floor and pay attention. The people I work for are very concerned with what you've written. Oh, let me be frank with you. They're pissed off. You seem to have information they don't want to appear in the paper or anywhere. So first question. Who is your source?"

"It's none of your business. Besides, my sources are anonymous. As a responsible member of the press, I've promised to maintain their confidentiality."

Grabbing Ethan's collar, Charles lifted him up, slamming him against the wall. "Not a good answer, newsboy. Let's try it again. Who is your goddamned source?" He turned Ethan loose, stepping back. "Don't make me hurt you again. I'll give you a three count. One, two…"

"Stop. You don't have to hit me again. I want to know who sent you here." Ethan's eyes were wide as blood oozed from his lip and chin.

"No, no, no. You don't get to ask questions, newsboy." With that, Charles delivered a right-handed blow, causing Ethan's head to bounce off the wall. "Listen to me. This is how it works. I ask questions. You provide answers. If you don't provide answers, I'm unhappy, and you don't want to keep making me unhappy because I will keep hurting you. And I really enjoy hurting people."

Ethan's face was numb, his mind spinning like a wobbly top, trying to think defensively. Charles made a backhanded strike with his left hand. "Damn it. You can't beat it out of me. I have integrity as a reporter and won't tell you who." Sensing a pause, Ethan tried to hit back, but Charles grabbed his arm midstrike, grinning like a superior gladiator.

"Oh, Ethan. You're a weak little newsboy, not a fighter. I don't have time to pound it out of you. So let's try another level of persuasion." Charles laughed as he stepped back, drawing a pistol from his coat pocket and placing the barrel against Ethan's forehead. "Say a quick prayer, Ethan. It's been nice meeting you."

"Oh, God. Don't kill me." Ethan could feel his heart flutter as he shut his eyes and heard the gun click without firing.

"You almost pissed your pants, Ethan. Most men do when death comes so close. I will not kill you yet. Listen carefully. Your days of writing nasty stories about my friends are over. I don't want to see anything written about my friends by you or anyone else at your two-bit news organization. Follow my instructions, and we will never see each other again."

Charles took a deep breath, turning his head as if to survey the room before continuing. "Failure to be obedient will bring me hunting for you. There will not be a happy ending because I love to kill whenever I hunt."

Lowering the gun, he said, "One more thing, Ethan. Tell whoever put you up to this they're on my list. It's not a warning. It's a statement of fact. Once I know who they are, I will be out hunting." Without further discussion, he turned and left.

Ethan's heart was pounding as he tried gaining his wits. *Two calls to make. Ryleigh and Jack. Rinse my face, calm down, and make notes about everything he said and did. This is not what I signed up for, Jack.*

He began picking up his belongings to restore order to the apartment as he dialed Ryleigh's number.

CHAPTER 39

Mayday

Ryleigh's phone went to voicemail. Debating leaving a message, Ethan decided calling Jack was better than leaving an alarming message for Ryleigh. He closed his eyes, recalling a relaxation method a friend had taught him. "Let the shoulders fall. No tension in the muscles. Inhale: one, two, three. Hold: four, five, six. Big exhale: seven, eight, nine. Repeat."

It surprised Ethan when Jack picked up the phone right away. "Jack, it's Ethan. I...ahh...I have a problem."

"You sound rattled. What's going on?"

"I returned home from work and found a stranger waiting for me in my apartment. I don't know how he got in, but the place was in shambles. His name was Charles. At least, that's what he said it was. He roughed me up, made threats, and put a gun to my head." Ethan was gasping between words, trying to breathe. "Jack, nothing like this has ever happened to me. What should I do?"

"Okay, you can give me details later. We need to act fast. Gather what you need to be gone for a few days. You're going to be staying at my place for a while. We can have someone clean up your apartment later. I'll be there in ten minutes to pick you up. Wait for my text before you come down to the street. Do not tell anyone what happened or where you're going until we talk. Got it, Ethan?"

"Yes, and thanks, Jack. I wasn't ready for this." He gathered clothes and essentials, thinking, *It's a good thing I left my computer and external drives at the office.* Ed's advice to store all Lydia's information in a safe-deposit box had been a brilliant suggestion on his part. There was nothing here for Charles to take.

Jack was in his car, navigating through evening traffic, thinking, *Son of a bitch. I should have expected a reprisal. They've moved quicker than we expected. Okay, it's time for changes. We need to rethink things.* He pulled up in front of Ethan's building and sent a text. Then he dialed Sam, hoping she'd answer.

"Sam, we need to change tactics and make modifications to your operations plan. Can you be at my place as soon as possible?"

"What do you mean by modifications?"

"Thugs from Aegis went after Ethan, roughed him up, and made serious threats. He's all right but a little rattled. I'm picking him up and will have him staying at my place for now."

"What did they do to him?"

"I think it's better if you hear it from Ethan. I'm also contacting Roy to have him join us. We need to huddle up, starting with the three of us sitting with Ethan. Gotta go—he's coming out of the building."

"Okay, I'll be there as soon as I fix Thomas his dinner."

"Thomas? I didn't know you had a roommate."

"He's my cat and no threat to you. Focus on taking care of Ethan. I'll be there soon."

Jack was dialing Roy's number as Ethan threw a duffel bag behind the seat. "Hop in, Ethan. We'll make sure no one is tailing us and then head for my house." Roy answered his phone, and Jack told him he was calling an emergency meeting, explaining that Sam would join them. "Don't have time for details, Roy. See you at my house." He closed the call, handing his phone to Ethan as they pulled out to leave. Jack started scanning his rearview mirror for intruders. A black Audi with heavily tinted windows swung out to follow them.

Jack reached into his coat, passing a Glock to Ethan. "Hang on to it and be ready to hand it to me if things get feisty. I had a hunch they were watching your place. Okay, it's time to buckle in and sit back. We're going to violate a few traffic laws."

Jack was power shifting his vintage TR6, torquing up its Ford 302 V-8 conversion engine, weaving between cars, and racing down the street. Running the first red light didn't shake whoever was behind them. The Audi was closing fast as Jack looked for a way to ditch the pursuit.

He was coming up on a delivery truck with its lights flashing, seeming to have the road blocked down to a tight lane. He knew his Triumph was narrower than the Audi chasing them. Jack punched the accelerator, darting through the gap between the truck and parked cars as the pursuers screeched sideways, skidding into the back of the truck. "Are you doing okay over there, Ethan?" Jack laughed as he spoke, seeing Ethan grimacing with his eyes closed.

"Yeah. You didn't tell me you were a stunt driver." Ethan was working on his relaxation routine for a second time in one night.

"Acquired and sometimes necessary skills in my profession."

Jack was searching the traffic behind them to ensure the Audi was gone and there was no replacement. "Let me give you a quick heads-up on what's about to happen and who will join us. Samantha Mieras will be there, along with Roy

Covington. Sam's my boss and running the show for what we're trying to do. Roy's my wingman. He has experience in combat situations—not as a soldier, but he knows a lot about military tactics and is cool under fire. Because of the fiery response to your article, we need him to help control the situation. Seems like you caught the attention of some dangerous people, Ethan."

He was taking a circuitous route home to ensure no one picked up the trail. "You're about to learn more than we planned to tell you this early in the game. As we determine changes to our original plan, we'll pull the curtain back for you. This is the front-row seat I mentioned when we met at Bryant Park."

Ethan was muddling through conflicting thoughts as they drove to Jack's place. *This is like scenes out of a Bond movie. Phew. Maybe this is more than I can handle. Maybe Jack and his friends need someone with more experience. Who are they?*

CHAPTER 40

Modifications

Jack was pulling into his parking garage, knowing Roy and Sam would arrive soon. "Grab your bag, Ethan. My place is down the street, about half a block from here. Unless you've eaten already, we'll have time to whip up a few snacks."

"Yeah, I could use something to eat. But don't go to any trouble; I'm not a picky eater, so anything light will do." Ethan was noting the neighborhood as they walked up the steps to Jack's front door. "Nice-looking digs, Jack."

Jack looked over his shoulder as he unlocked the door. "It's been a progressing project over the last seven years. The outside was challenging to restore its original 1910 luster, but it was worth every penny since it matches the revitalized neighborhood. I think you'll be safe and comfortable here."

Ethan tried to take in the towering open foyer with its deep, direct view of an open garden and seating area next to an expansive kitchen. Looking at a series of floating stairs making an endless rise upward, he asked, "How many floors are there?"

"Four, counting the rooftop deck. I'll head for the kitchen while you pick out a guest bedroom on the second floor. There are two to choose from, each with a private bath. So pick what looks good. It's yours for as long as needed. You'll also find an office area between them for working, and the

Wi-Fi password is 1972TR6. Take your time getting settled, and maybe call your editor to update him on your day; talking about it will help calm your nerves."

The front door chimes rang as Ethan reached the guest bedroom level, still taking in the spacious contemporary setting and an eclectic collection of noteworthy artworks. He sat on the edge of a bed, taking Jack's advice and dialing Ed.

Sam received a surprise hug from Jack as he welcomed her into his home. "Thanks for coming over on short notice. Ethan is upstairs collecting his wits, and Roy will be here shortly. I'm putting appetizers together in the kitchen. I'll show you where drinks are and let you handle the bartending."

She was smiling and taking in the environment. "Well, Jack, this place is more than I expected from an unattached man's home. I assumed the 'unattached' part and apologize if I crossed a privacy line."

"No problem, Sam. I'm as unattached as you, except I don't have a Thomas. I can compete with a cat, but there's no one…" Jack was fumbling for words, which was becoming a regular occurrence whenever he was near Sam.

"Were you going to tell me I have no competition?" Sam's eyes twinkled at the chance to get a flirty dig in with Jack.

"Yeah…something like that, but my mind freezes around you. Gotta work on getting it under control."

"Please don't change. I think it's an attractive trait. And the lack of competition is a nice tidbit for me to know." She followed him into the kitchen, noting the adjoining living area with its massive fireplace warming the chilly December air. "I am very impressed, Mr. Gallagher, and…I…ah…never mind. I was beginning to ramble."

"What's the matter, Sam? Catching my disease of tumbling over words? Maybe we can carry on with this discussion when business isn't in our way."

"I would like that. So you were going to put me to work fixing refreshments. Where does the bartending happen?"

Jack reached over her head, opening a double-door cabinet containing an ample liquor selection. "Glasses are off to the left. The fridge has ice, limes, lemons, and softer selections for anyone not imbibing with us. Wines are in the island's lower racks, if you prefer vineyard selections." He was multitasking, talking and finishing a charcuterie board, watching her reactions from the corner of his vision.

"I'm not sure what's more impressive, the environment or your culinary skills. Tell me the chef's preference for liquid enjoyment."

"Double bourbon on the rocks, please. There are several brands. I like them all, so pick one for me."

"I like a man who enjoys his bourbon and will join you. Umm…how about the Yellowstone Select? It's one of my favorites."

"One of mine as well. It's why I have several bottles of it. A well-stocked cupboard can never have too much bourbon."

Sam was getting ice as the entry chimes rang again. "That should be Roy. I'll get the door, and you can pour another double for him." Jack returned with Roy in tow as Sam handed out the freshly poured glasses, raising hers.

"Here's to us, gentlemen. May success be our good fortune."

Roy and Sam were talking near the fireplace as Ethan walked into the kitchen. Jack raised his eyes from the culinary work, asking, "Would you like to join us in a round of bourbon, or do you have another preference?"

"I should probably stick with water for now."

"Were you able to reach your editor and talk?"

"Yes. He helped me calm down from my run-in with Charles and the thrill ride with you." He broke into a grin as Jack laughed at the driving comment.

"Sorry my driving added to the intensity of your evening; let me get your water and introduce you to our boss lady and my wingman." Jack made introductions and returned to the kitchen, retrieving the charcuterie before excusing himself. "I need to make a quick call and will let Ethan fill you in on his encounter with a hired gun from Aegis." Jack left the room, dialing Chandler's number.

Jack returned to his guests as Ethan was wrapping up his story. "I've talked with Ed Graves, my editor. In his opinion, this is a case of powerful intimidation, suggesting that we've struck a sensitive nerve. He liked the idea of my being away from my apartment for a while, seemed comfortable with who you are, and told me I could trust you. But I still have questions."

He surveyed the group. "Hate to sound like a nosy reporter, but who are you people? What's your objective and the story behind it all? Sorry for all the questions, but after today, I need answers to keep me in the game. And on second thought, maybe it's time I tried some bourbon to fit in. Am I making sense?"

Jack jumped in to answer first. "You're making sense, Ethan, and you deserve answers. I'll get your drink while Sam explains who we are, our objectives, and the backstory." Sam went through her history and added background on Aegis that Ethan had yet to uncover in his investigations.

"I appreciate your explanation, Samantha. The reporter in me works better with insights. One more question. Is Ryleigh Jaymes on your team? If she is, why isn't she here?"

Sam hesitated, looking between Jack and Roy before answering. "Yes, Ryleigh is on the team. She and I are partners in an investment company which, among other holdings, owns your paper."

"I'm aware of the ownership and discussed it with Ryleigh after my first meeting with Jack, but you didn't explain why she's not here."

Jack took over the conversation to save Sam from doing a precarious balancing act. "I'm the reason she's not here tonight. Ryleigh and I are not on the best of terms yet. She expressed reservations about hiring me but left the final decision to Sam. Eventually, Ryleigh and I will find common ground and work well together." Jack looked at Sam for comment.

"What Jack is trying to say is, he and Ryleigh need time to know each other better."

Jack jumped back in, saying, "Sometimes, it's better to limit conflict to achieve a project's objectives. You should also know she's not the only one absent this evening. Chandler Yates, the attorney Sam mentioned in her backstory, is not here, but you'll meet him soon. He and Ryleigh play essential roles and will be visible when needed. Discuss what I've said with Ryleigh. I'm sure she'll confirm the accuracy of my statements."

"Okay, I'll talk with her, and thanks for the clarification."

Roy, having sat silently, finally spoke up. "I believe we're here to discuss changing our original plans, since Aegis appears to be raising the stakes. What have you got in mind, Jack?"

"I'll share my ideas but leave final decisions to Sam." Jack looked in her direction to see if she wanted to comment.

"Don't wait on me. I'm as curious as Roy and Ethan to hear what you see as new ideas."

Jack began, "Well, the biggest change is with Sam. Our original plan had you staying in the background, letting me run the ground game. I think you need to be in the mix with Adira, Lydia, and Ethan. We don't know how much time we have, and having multiple levels of communication limits how fast we can act or react to what's happening."

Ethan interrupted. "You mentioned Lydia and Adira. I assume Lydia's the senator's wife, but Adira is a mystery person for me—I just know her name and that she's a close friend of Lydia's."

Jack responded to Ethan's inquiries. "Okay, you're right on Lydia being the senator's wife. Adira is the executive assistant to David and Cynthia Jaymes. Lydia and Adira will be your inside sources for information on Aegis. Our plan was to connect you with them next week. Roy and I feel it's better to make the connection sooner and rescheduled the introductions for tomorrow morning."

Roy reached into a weathered leather briefcase and handed Ethan two files. "It's a summary of my background investigation on your new partners and will give you a good feel for who they are and why they're essential to our plans. I thought you'd appreciate reading what I discovered about them. They can monitor the pulse of what Aegis is doing and planning. As you've learned, inside information is tough to come by. You'll now have a direct feed through the two of them."

"I've interviewed Lydia, and she's...well, I'll say she's interesting, with a strong erotic personality. I hope this comment doesn't offend you, Sam, but I was lucky to avoid being raped when talking with her at her townhouse." Ethan's face turned red as he made the statement.

Sam laughed, telling Ethan, "You and Jack share a similar experience with her, and I'm not offended by your assessment. All of us are free to speak in honest terms. Sometimes, it's the best method for conveying feelings. So never hold back with this group."

Ethan opened Adira's profile, going wide-eyed at the photos of her. "Oh my God. I ran into her on the street. I mean, I literally crashed into her and sent her tumbling onto the sidewalk when I was hurrying to meet Jack at Bryant Park. Wow, she was angry, and I'm putting it mildly. It might take some effort to get her to work with me." He was shaking his head and laughing to himself. "I'll never forget her. She's gorgeous, with a quick temper."

Jack raised his eyebrows, saying, "Sounds like you may have made an impression on her, Ethan. We can help smooth out the wrinkles for you."

"Hope you're right. I'll be reading her background with special interest and may want more information if you have it, Roy."

"Are you looking for anything specific?"

"I'm not sure. It's hard to explain, but my head keeps telling me we've met before. I've been racking my brain, but it keeps coming up empty. It was like her eyes were trying to communicate with me. I'm probably sounding crazy, but I know there's a connection." Roy was making notes and told Ethan he'd look for additional information.

Jack was looking at his watch. "I hate to bring this huddle to a halt, but I told Lydia and Adira to meet us at 7:00 tomorrow morning, which is a little over six hours from now. To recap my major change, Sam's coming off the bench to play first-string status. Tomorrow, we map out our next actions. Everyone good?"

Roy and Sam told Ethan he was making the right decision in working with them and that they'd ensure his safety. He headed up to the guest room, thinking, *They seem like good people, and Ed says I'm making the right choice to be with them. I hope Adira can look past our first meeting.*

Sam drove home at a slow, pondering pace. As usual, Thomas awaited her return, purring for attention and a late snack. "Okay, buddy, you win. Besides, I need to talk and see what wisdom you'll provide. Jack wants me to do more than work from the sidelines." Thomas looked up from his finished treat, tilting his head as if he wanted to hear more.

"This might become more difficult than we thought. Aegis is going to come after us. I hope we can keep everyone safe." Thomas jumped into her lap, curling up to see what else was bothering her.

"On another note, I need to control my jealousy over Lydia. She'd better be on good behavior. I may not own Jack, but I have first-claim rights." Thomas looked up at the mention of Jack's name. "Don't get worried, Thomas. You're still the man of the house, but you might need to make room for a less-than-monogamous relationship with me. I hope the two of you will like each other. Let's get a few winks in before the alarm goes off."

CHAPTER 41

Morning Encounter

Sam was still trying to stir her energies from the quick night's rest as she unlocked the office door, finding Jack brewing coffee. "Why am I not surprised you're here already?"

"Good morning, Sam. Can I make you a cup of your favorite half caff?" His bright smile and chipper attitude were a startling but welcome beginning to her day.

"I would appreciate it. Is Ethan here with you?"

"Not yet. Roy picked him up earlier so they could talk with his editor again. The kid needs more confirmation, and Ed will come through for us."

"You sound pretty confident about Ed."

"I am after we talked on the phone."

"What did you tell him?"

"Enough to satisfy his curiosity about who his paper and Ethan were pairing up with against Aegis. Sometimes, it pays to have well-informed substitute players in case they're needed later in the game. Any problem with what I've done?"

"No, no problem. I think it was a good move for us and Ethan." Sam set her case beside the desk and walked up to Jack with a questioning look, biting her lower lip. Jack backed up against the kitchenette counter as she crowded into him. "We agreed on straight talk as we work together. No hidden meanings between the lines, and no BS. Right?"

"Yes, we did. So is there a problem, Sam?"

"Lydia Mathers. She's my problem, and I don't want her to be a problem for us."

"She won't be a problem and will work well with Adira and Ethan."

"C'mon, Jack. I know her value to the team. That's not what I'm talking about. I don't want her thinking she can come on to you. You and I have started with a good working relationship. And…this is the straightforward part, no beating around the bush. You stirred things inside me from the minute you shook my hand and walked into the office for your interview. I've avoided feelings like that because I don't trust people, especially men. I think about you and don't want to avoid anything with you."

Grabbing his collar, she surprised Jack as she pulled his face close and planted a firm, moist kiss on his lips. He let his hands brush across her cheeks, cradling her head, extending the moment.

Sam backed away, locking eyes with him. "I'm not a Lydia Mathers, but I like what's started between us. Is there room for a personal and business relationship, or will it complicate things?"

Jack grasped her shoulders, searching her dark eyes. "Nothing's too complicated for me," he said confidently. "You caught my interest before the interview. As for Lydia, I've told you that you can set your concerns aside. As Ethan said, she's overwhelming. She might try to compete with you, but you have nothing to fear. If she flirts or makes moves, you can smile confidently, knowing it gets no traction with me."

"Might be easier said than done."

"I understand; it's a woman's prerogative to be possessive. We can see what develops between us, but we have to keep the project's objectives in the forefront."

He returned to the Keurig, retrieving her coffee, saying, "No woman has ever used your head-on approach with me. Well, Lydia sort of tried, but it didn't work." Flashing a smile, he tilted his head, waiting for her reply.

"Well, I've never been so direct with a man. I guess we need to save those thoughts for later and prepare for pulling the team together." They began pulling chairs around the conference table as Roy knocked on the door.

He opened the door slowly. "Hope we're not disturbing anything."

Jack raised his hands as if to surrender. "Caught by my wingman and guilty of preparing for a meeting without your help. I'd suggest making some coffee, but you and Ethan appear to have taken care of yourselves."

Roy gave Jack an assuring nod. "We did, and the morning's off to a great start."

Ethan followed Roy into the office, thinking, *I don't see Adira. Remember Ed's advice. Relax, fit in, and remember as much as you can. Roy assured me it was good advice.*

CHAPTER 42

Orientation

Lydia and Adira were laughing as they walked into the office. "Greetings, everyone. We would have knocked but didn't think it was necessary."

Sam stepped forward. "Welcome to our team orientation, ladies." She extended a firm handshake to each of them, locking eyes with Lydia. "Let me introduce you to the rest of your associates." Sam played the guarded hostess, establishing her territory.

Adira's eyebrows rose as she shook hands with Ethan. "You?" Still grasping Ethan's hand, she turned to Lydia. "Oh my God, this is the clown who put me on my ass near Bryant Park." Shaking her head, she turned back to Ethan. "Sorry about the clown remark, but you did bowl me over in the middle of a crowd."

"I'm so sorry that happened. It was all my fault. Calling me a clown was a kinder description than you shouted at me that day."

"Thanks for the apology. Lydia told me about her interview with you and said you seemed likable. Let's put the run-in behind us if it's okay with you."

"Yes, I'd like to get past it."

Jack invited everyone to take a seat. "Thanks for making time to be here. I think the best place to start is with Sam providing the background on the Collective Project. Ethan,

Roy, and I have heard this before, but a refresher won't hurt. Sam?"

Sam related her story, going back twenty-seven years, explaining Ryleigh's and Chandler's roles and the goal of blocking the ambitious plans of Aegis and David Jaymes. "With everyone up to speed, I'll give Ethan a chance to explain what happened to him last evening."

Ethan's cheeks flushed with embarrassment. He described the confrontation with Charles, as well as Charles's substantial threats to silence further articles. "I'm not accustomed to physical intimidation, but I'm also not ready to abandon writing articles." He motioned for Jack to continue.

Lydia seized the transition to speak. "Before Jack begins, I'd like to ask some questions."

Sam sat back in her chair, motioning with her hand for Lydia to proceed.

"Maybe it's just one question. We understand the project, you, and Jack, but no one offered information about Roy. He sits silently, watching us and writing notes like a shrink analyzing patients." Her eyes squinted as she turned toward Roy. "Who are you, and why are you here, Roy?"

Roy stretched his arms, folding his hands on the table. "Guess it's my turn to speak and remove the mystery. I'll start with a quick reveal on Roy Covington. I'm not a shrink. I'm an original good guy, a photojournalist by trade who cut his teeth covering combat activities in Vietnam. All I carried was a pair of Nikon cameras, lenses, and notebooks, trying to provide an accurate picture of what was happening. After returning to the States, I worked through decades of freelance assignments and started doing investigative work for clients like Sam and her investment firm. The investigative sideline, along with other interests, became a full-time occupation. Having done extensive background checks for

Sam, I'm very familiar with each one of you. Does that satisfy your curiosity?"

Lydia leaned forward, continuing to probe. "Almost, but what's your role going forward?"

"My current role is to be Jack's wingman. In simple terms, I'll try to keep him from being blindsided and to furnish whatever support he needs. Actually, I'll be providing support for each of you."

Lydia was smiling and nodding as Roy talked. "Okay, questions answered, and I'm glad you're here to cover everyone's asses, Roy. Guess it's back to you, Jack."

Jack handed out packets. "What you'll find inside is a listing of initial assignments for you and the rest of the team. You need to be familiar with everyone's assigned tasks so you can fill in for a teammate if necessary."

Ethan raised his hand, asking, "You make it sound like some of us might be injured and unable to do our work."

"It could happen. Hopefully not, but I like to be prepared."

Jack turned past the title page to continue. "I'll start with Adira and Lydia. Your initial work will be risky—you'll be trying to gather all the information you can from David and Cynthia. It'll be a combination of asking discreet questions and downloading sensitive data from their computer system. Completing those tasks needs to happen quickly because they'll become suspicious, and then the risk factor increases significantly."

Lydia laughed, saying, "Being nosy is my best skill. Cynthia loves to gossip and believes I'm out to burn Lucas for his fun time with Adira. I can get her to tell me what's happening and bothering her. Playing the close friend worried about her stress levels will be easy."

Adira reached over to high-five Lydia. "She's right about gossiping with Cynthia, especially when Cyn feels threatened. Paranoia is her weakness. The more paranoid she gets, the more she talks. While Lydia distracts her, I can download contacts, communication documents, and financial information. They've become lax with watching what I do and have access to."

Jack was making notes before speaking. "I appreciate your confidence level, but caution and awareness need to be a priority. I believe Cynthia flew down to Raleigh for a meeting with Jonathan and the Aegis board. I'm sure they told her to end further public exposure for David and Aegis. So watch for changes in attitude with them. Your secondary assignment, for now, will be to help Ethan sort through things to use in future stories."

Roy handed business cards to Lydia and Adira, adding, "Contact me with the information you collect. Limit your contact with Ethan to phone, email, or texting. Aegis will have people watching him, and seeing the two of you in direct contact will raise a red flag."

Jack nodded and watched as Lydia's and Adira's demeanors appeared to become more serious. He turned to Ethan. "Your role is to keep churning out stories for publication. The next one needs to go out next Tuesday. Keep sifting through the trove of information Lydia gave you during her interview. We'll get you fresh information from the girls and see if it adds to what you already have."

Lydia stiffened her posture and glared at Jack. "*Girls*, really, Jack? Should we now be referring to the men as boys? How about *ladies* rather than *girls*?" Adira put her hand on Lydia's shoulder as if to hold her down in her chair.

Sam raised her hands. "Hey, we need to work as a team. Insulting or going after one another is counterproductive. Jack, I agree with Lydia. Your comment was inappropriate."

"Okay, okay. Sorry, ladies. I'll work on my word choices and behavior. Does that help settle the dust, Lydia?"

"A little, for right now."

"I think we're done with assigning tasks. Roy, Sam, and I will work to identify where Aegis might have additional weaknesses we can exploit. The next item isn't in your assignments, but I feel Ethan's encounter with Charles warrants discussing security or protection for all of us. I'd like to hear your opinions. Do we need protection or not?"

Lydia leaned back in her chair and said, "I don't like being watched by people I don't know or might know. Adira can stay at my place, and we can watch out for each other." Adira was nodding in agreement with Lydia.

Ethan raised a hand. "No need to protect me either. I'll take up an offer from my editor to stay with him while all this unfolds. Any problem with me moving from your place, Jack?"

"No problem with moving, but all of you should be aware of your surroundings. Contact me or Roy if you're feeling uneasy. Between us, we can muster people to keep you safe. Any thoughts or further questions before we leave?" He turned to see Sam fidgeting in her chair. "Sam, is there anything you would like to add?"

"Only to express my appreciation to all of you for helping me hold David and Aegis accountable." She stood to shake hands with Lydia, saying, "You and Adira need to be careful and contact Jack, Roy, or me if you sense things becoming uncomfortable."

"Thanks for the concern, Sam. We'll be fine."

Roy began collecting coffee cups, saying, "I look forward to hearing from the ladies and contacting you with their results, Ethan."

Sam was quietly watching as Lydia, Adira, and Ethan left. "Well, Jack, now that the foot soldiers are gone, what are the assignments for the three of us?"

"Nothing new other than contacting Ryleigh and having her see if she can learn anything from her father. I have a hunch he's aware of her involvement with us. If so, he might dodge and block her out, but it will tell us where they're at."

"I talked with her on the way into the office this morning. The chances of getting information from Jonathan died just before we hired you. Ryleigh went to see him, and it didn't go well. She says it's a lost cause to try. Jonathan has shut her out, perhaps forever."

"Okay, that source of information is no longer available. Roy?"

Roy was closing his case, preparing to exit. "I'm going to leave the two of you to discuss activities since I have my hands full looking for chinks in the enemy's armor and need to address some unfinished business. I'll also explore security options. Better to be prepared for the worst than to be caught short."

Sam tapped her pen on the table, asking, "Any immediate ideas or prospects for protection if we need it?"

"Yeah. I have an old friend, Washington Jeffries, from my days in Vietnam. He and I do some special assignments together. He has available resources and skills that can handle security issues for us."

The mention of Washington Jeffries made Jack's eyes widen. "Wait a minute. I had a friend back at Attica with that name, but he preferred being called Mansa. He's the one who set me up with Chandler. Are we talking about the same guy?"

Roy started grinning. "Apparently—or as Mansa would say, indeed we are, my friend."

"You never told me you knew him."

"You never asked. Hey, even if you did, I couldn't provide any further information beyond that he's an option for dealing with security."

Sam interrupted their exchange. "Check with Mansa and see if he can be available on standby. My intuition tells me we will need his services."

"Will do, Sam, and I'll tell Mansa you said hi, Jack. Unless there are more questions, I'll be on my way."

Jack leaned back in his chair, watching Roy depart. "It's a small world, Sam. I can't believe Mansa is resurfacing in my life."

"Is that a problem?"

"No, but I'll be taking Roy up on the offer of a drink and getting the rest of the story. I trust both of them, so there's no problem."

Roy stood at the curb, hailing a cab and thinking, *Phew, dodged that one. You need to call Mansa and then return the call from Cynthia Jaymes.*

CHAPTER 43

Defensive Preparation

David was pouring coffee as Cynthia walked into the kitchen. "What time did you get back from Raleigh? I fell asleep around midnight and didn't hear you come in."

"It was just before two. I caught a quick nap on the flight after talking with Charles about his visit with the reporter."

"Well, fill me in on the board meeting and the results from Charles."

"Let me get my files and notes. Pour a cup for me, and we'll talk in my office."

David followed her as she pulled files from her travel case. She sat on the forward edge of her chair, squinting at David with a sneering eye. "Before we begin, I'd like some information."

"Like what?"

"Does the name Samantha Mieras ring any bells for you?"

"Samantha Mieras? What does she have to do with your meeting?"

"Jonathan and I were trying to identify a likely source for the story in the *Insider*. It has to be someone with a score to settle with you. We think she's behind it and working with your damned sister. He gave me some background about her and told me to ask you for your version. So here's your chance to come clean with me. I don't like being blindsided, David."

"Jesus, Cyn. You're acting like it's a recent incident. I'd appreciate a little gentler attitude."

"How's this for gentler, Your Honor? Tell me what the fuck happened with her."

"Shit. It goes back to when I was in law school. She turned up pregnant and tried to accuse me of raping her. My father sent her off and paid for an abortion. I never saw or heard from her again. End of story."

"Did you rape her?"

"Hell no, it was consensual sex. Besides, it doesn't matter. I didn't rape her."

"Every guilty man says the same thing, David. How old was she?"

"I'm not sure, maybe sixteen. It doesn't matter, Cyn, because I didn't rape her."

"So the nominee for chief justice of the Supreme Court raped a sixteen-year-old girl when he was…what, twenty-four or twenty-five? Sounds like rape of a minor by an adult who should have known better."

"You make it sound like a criminal act. It was a fraternity party. I probably wasn't the only one screwing her brains out. Besides, there were no witnesses to back up her accusation that I raped her."

"No witnesses? People who attend parties see and hear things, and they have great recall when questioned by a congressional committee and the press."

"It won't happen, Cyn."

"Really? If it does, people will feel sorry and believe her over you. You're digging a deeper, darker hole every time you open your mouth. This is the kind of shit the reporter and his paper would love to put into print. I can see the headline now. 'Chief Justice Nominee David Jaymes and His Fraternity Brothers Gangbanged a Minor Before Sending Her Off for an

Abortion.' I'm sure President Lawrence and his supporters will continue backing you after reading a headline like that." Cynthia gave a sarcastic cackle, shaking her head.

"The solution is simple. We need to take out the reporter and whoever's involved with him."

"Well, before you go off the deep end, this is where the story has an interesting twist. Your little honeypot is now a senior partner in Ryleigh's investment firm. Your father doesn't want to believe your sister is involved. I'm convinced that she is and the two of them are directing an effort to stop your nomination and expose Aegis and Society."

"Is this something you're imagining, or do you have proof?"

"No proof yet, but we're going to investigate. The board voted to look into Ryleigh, her firm, Samantha, and anyone else we think might be involved. On the flight home, I added Chandler Yates to the list of suspects. How's that for another name out of your dark past? He and Ryleigh maintained close contact despite your family's efforts to end their relationship."

"Why do they want to do this to me after all these years?"

"Why? Let's see. You told your father Samantha was gangbanging the entire fraternity. Then Aegis, you, and your father ordered Sam to have an abortion. He pursued and harassed her and Ryleigh for years. Jonathan pushed Ryleigh aside once you were born and bestowed firstborn privileges on you over her. You and your father ruined a relationship between Ryleigh and Chandler, threatening to destroy him and his family by disclosing the secret of his biracial ancestry. Oh my God, I could go on and on. Do you need to hear more, David? The three of them have a multitude of reasons to destroy your career, Aegis, and your father."

"It's all hearsay. There's no trail of documents or any other type of proof. I will say the abortion was her idea and I tried to stop her. I will deny everything. It's her word against mine."

"Oh hell, hang on to your britches, David. It turns out she never had an abortion. Somewhere out there, your fucking sister has hidden a set of twins that belong to you. I don't know her motive, but DNA testing can put you at the scene of the rape."

"Goddamn it—stop saying I did that. I do not have any children or a family. It's all lies."

"I'm done arguing with you. I will see what Charles can do to stop them."

"What are our options if it's them and they refuse to stop?"

"I'm not sure, but all options are on the table. We will be as forceful as necessary. We're good at coercive pressure, and I'll put it to use. I've talked with Charles regarding stronger levels of persuasion."

David paced the floor, flailing his arms. "Don't tell me what he and his thugs will do. Just have them do it. Did he get any information from the reporter or get him to agree not to write more stories?"

"Charles said he put the fear of God into him. They were starting surveillance to track his movements and discover who his accomplices were, but he fled with someone, and they lost them in traffic."

"Did they get a license plate number to track them down with?"

"The plate was covered. Whoever helped him is clever, thinking one or two moves ahead of us."

David stopped pacing to place both hands on the desk. He leaned forward, glaring at her. "Is the board willing to let you take whatever actions you feel are necessary?"

"I have a unanimous and unlimited green light from the board and your father."

"Good. Start more aggressive action without waiting for investigations. We silence whoever is causing problems before they make another attack. Hit the reporter again and anyone else we suspect."

"It's not that simple. Going after innocent people can cause nasty and unnecessary publicity. Our investigators will have names for us in a few days. It's better to wait and go after the correct targets."

"Bullshit, Cyn. I need this shut down as soon as possible. Quit worrying about hurting innocent people. This is a war, and bad things happen in wars. Sometimes innocent people get caught in crossfire. I am not concerned with who gets hurt. I'm concerned about David Jaymes. Period!" He raised his hands from Cynthia's desk as his eyes bulged and his face reddened.

"Calm down, or you'll have a stroke."

He slammed a fist back onto her desk. "Don't you dare tell me to calm down. It's not your career at stake, Cynthia. Goddamn it—if they uncover the demanded abortion and your use of Society to blackmail elected officials, my chance of becoming chief justice is over. I'm done with you and my father deciding what's politically correct. Turn Charles loose!"

Cynthia raised a hand, gesturing for David to stop talking. "Okay, I'll send Charles on another mission."

"What are you planning for him to do?"

"You said you didn't want to know his plans. It's better to exclude you in case you have to answer congressional inquiries about anything Charles does. You need to focus on winning over the press and congressional leaders. Work on gaining their support and help in deflecting accusations. I'll have our lobbyists and spin specialists work on strategies with you."

"I don't need your overpaid specialists. You stick to putting pressure on the reporter and his backers. I'll handle the public front. Just tell my father to back off."

"I'll talk with Jonathan. We also need to keep the president behind your nomination. I'll leave that one to you. You must convince him false information and rumors are being spread to slander you. He's faced those problems and knows what it's like. It's time he returned favors for the work Aegis has done defending him in the past."

David stepped back from Cynthia's desk with a smug look, nodding in agreement. "Yes, you're right. He can't afford to bail on us. I'll work to ensure confirmation votes are ready once Wheeler's out of the way. Damn, it'd be convenient if the bastard suddenly resigned or croaked in his bed. Maybe something Charles can expedite?"

Cynthia grimaced at the suggestion. "Rushing his demise is not a consideration. His cancer will take him out, not us."

Her phone began to chirp as David made a parting response: "Well, his cancer better step it up before I lose my patience."

Cynthia looked at the caller ID as David stormed out. She gathered herself, switching on her cordial tone. "Charles, thank you for calling. I've been talking with David. Let's make another persuasive visit. You can start this evening. The first target will be Samantha. Yes, as we discussed. There will be a new task to discuss once you're done with her."

Cynthia ended the call and scrolled through her contacts until she reached Roy Covington's number and dialed. "Roy, Cynthia Jaymes. I know last evening's message was late, and I wanted to follow up to ensure it went through. Let's have a conversation about working together."

CHAPTER 44

Ominous Encounter

When Sam returned home after the team briefing and trying to catch up on prospective investment opportunities for the firm, she found her front door ajar. She hesitated, slowly pushing the door open to survey the house.

Her eyes went wild, trying to comprehend the chaos of her household. Closets and drawers were open, their contents strewn across the floor. Her heart raced as she called for Thomas, who would typically run into the room expecting dinner. Thomas did not appear.

Walking through the house toward the kitchen, she dialed Jack's number. The phone seemed to ring forever before he answered. "Jack, someone broke in and turned my house upside down. I can't find Thomas. This is like what happened to Ethan."

"Sam, I'll be there as fast as possible. Get to where you feel safe in the house, and stay put. I'll call once I'm there, and we'll find Thomas." There was no response. Then Jack heard a man's voice addressing Sam.

"Good evening, Samantha. Sorry to have made a terrible mess of your home, but we were in a hurry and looking for things. My associates took what they thought appropriate and left a gift package. I was lingering until you arrived so I could deliver a personal message."

"Who the hell are you, and what are you doing in my home?"

"Oh my, pardon my lack of manners. The name is Charles. Charles Abbott. I'm sure Ethan told you about my recent chat with him. Nice young man, but not much of a fighter."

He tilted his head, pointing a finger at Sam's phone as it hung in her hand at her side. "You can disconnect the call, sweetheart. I'm sure Jack has heard enough of our conversation and will be here shortly in his speedy little red sports car with the masked license plate to rescue you."

Sam's eyes blinked as she screamed, "You son of a bitch. Get the fuck out of my house."

"My, my. Such a dirty mouth for a professional woman of your stature. Happy to oblige and depart, but I thought you'd want to know what happened to your precious Thomas. He was such a friendly feline. You should have warned him about stranger danger."

Charles rose from his chair and walked past Sam as she stood frozen in the kitchen. "Perhaps it's better for you to believe Thomas is safe somewhere. In the meantime, please convince Ethan to stop writing nasty lies about my friends. And tell the rest of your merry band it will become exceedingly dangerous if they continue helping you to be an obstacle for David Jaymes."

Sam turned as Charles sauntered through the house. "Where the hell is Thomas, you bastard?"

Charles stopped and turned his head, giving her a wink. "Toodles to you, Sam. People say that cats have nine lives. Who knows—Thomas may have at least eight more left."

Sam watched Charles go out the front door; he whistled and disappeared into the night. She slumped into a chair, shaking her head as tears welled up and ran down her cheeks. "Thomas, I'm so sorry. What have we started? Where are you, Jack? I need you."

After a few minutes, she looked out the door to see Jack charging up the stairs with Thomas nestled under one arm.

"Jack, oh my God—you have Thomas."

"Yeah, I figured it was him. I was getting out of my car when a guy walked up and pushed him into my chest. He said it was a gift from Charles; then, in a blink, he was gone before I could stop him."

Sam rushed to hug Jack and Thomas. "Come in, come in. You won't believe what they've done to my home. Charles was here waiting to taunt me about Thomas. He's the bastard who roughed up Ethan." She scooped Thomas out of Jack's arms and headed for the kitchen. "Momma was so worried about you. We need to talk about hiding from strangers."

Jack was surveying the mess left by Charles and his thugs. "Let's get Thomas some dinner. I'll help you straighten things up, and then the two of you are coming to stay at my house."

"We'll be fine here once I restore some order." Her eyes were tearing up again as she trembled, trying to take measure of what had happened. "Your house may not be any safer than mine or Ethan's."

"You and I were having the same concern. On my way here, I called Roy and told him to have Mansa secure my house."

"I don't know, Jack. Thomas and I will be fine. Have Roy and Mansa secure my house along with yours. I don't think Charles will return tonight."

Jack wrapped his arms around her. "I'm not leaving without you and Thomas." He stepped back, placing his hands on Sam's shoulders, locking eyes with her. "If it makes you feel better, we'll stay here, and you can pack in the morning.

Then, the three of us make the move to my place. Sorry to throw orders at my boss, but you hired me to handle this kind of situation. We can set my place up as a command center to operate from."

"Okay, you win. I'll feed Thomas, pack, and go with you. I can call my cleaning lady to be here tomorrow."

"That's a good idea. You can tell her you and Thomas will be spending time at my house."

"I don't want to impose on you."

"Look, Sam, things are getting bumpy. I want you to be safe, meaning you'll stay with me as long as necessary. And it will be my pleasure to have you and Thomas sharing space with me. Sometimes a bachelor needs houseguests." Jack was smiling and giving a nod to Thomas as he tried to calm Sam with a moment of levity.

Sam gave a small laugh, picking up on Jack's lighter tone. "Do I need protection from you?"

Jack roared with laughter as he blushed. "Oh my, I like how you think, and it's good to see you recovering with a bit of return kidding. However, this will be more business than socially oriented."

"Thank you for being more than a strong-armed enforcer. I didn't see this level of trouble happening so soon. A bourbon and talking by your fireplace would be a welcome distraction."

"Yeah, ya can be tellin' me what needs doin', Ms. Mieras."

"Well, I'd like a wee bit better start for a date, Mr. Gallagher."

"I would agree, bean." Thomas was purring and rubbing against Jack's ankles. "Guess he doesn't like being ignored. I'll feed him while you pack. Where do I find his food?"

"You'll find cans of Kitty Feast in the cupboard above the sink." Jack fed Thomas and began packing cat toys, the litter box, and the remaining cans of Kitty Feast, thinking, *Look at me—the guy who doesn't have pets and prefers his quiet solitude is now jumping into the deep end of the pool.*

He was tidying up some of the mess in the kitchen as Sam reappeared with two suitcases in hand. "I'm as ready as possible and thought we should call Roy to update him."

"Again, our minds were on the same wavelength. I tried reaching him but had to leave a message. He's probably on the phone with Mansa."

CHAPTER 45

Lines in the Sand

Finished with his call to Mansa to secure Jack's house, Roy sat at his desk, debating whether to return Cynthia's call, before dialing her number. "Cynthia, it's Roy. Long time since we've talked."

"Yes, it's been a while. Our last engagement was having you do background for my security director, Charles Abbott."

"And the reason for this call?"

Cynthia laughed, sliding forward in her chair. "You haven't changed your inclination for short, direct conversations."

"No need to change what works."

Cynthia's eyes were darting back and forth as she reached for her pen and a blank notepad. "Guess I'll follow your lead and be direct. Your previous work for me was outstanding. I was told you were the only one who could do backgrounding on anyone anywhere in the world, and you delivered. I should tell you I hired him over your hesitations, and he's been worth the money."

"Good to know, but it doesn't explain this call."

"I have another opportunity for you if you're available and interested."

Roy blew out a slow breath. "I'm involved in an assignment but can always consider additional work. It depends on the scope of your request. What do you have in mind?"

"I need background checks on several individuals and their relationships with one another."

"And the purpose of the investigations?"

"I never explained before that I'm the CEO of an organization called Aegis. We've become the target of false accusations, and I'm trying to identify who is behind the defamatory statements. We're working with the president to fill a position on the Supreme Court and can't afford adverse publicity. Let's just say we need the rumors to stop, which requires identifying the sources."

Roy felt the hairs rise on the back of his neck at the mention of Aegis, thinking, *Ask questions and stall.* "Seems like working with the president should provide you with far better resources than me for doing backgrounds on people."

"We need to keep the inquiries out of official channels."

"Okay, I have a few questions to understand the scope of the assignment, if you don't mind my asking."

"I'm okay with a few questions."

"Who are the individuals you'd want me to investigate, and how will you stop their accusations?"

"Hmm, the last time I engaged your services, you just needed to know the timeline and how much I was willing to pay."

"My current engagement requires me to ask clarifying questions. So who..."

"You don't have to repeat the questions, Roy." Cynthia stretched her neck, shaking her head before continuing. "Aegis is a political group supporting my husband's possible Supreme Court nomination. Individuals are making false accusations to derail his nomination and appointment. I need to know who's making the attacks. Your work doesn't require knowledge of how we will stop them."

Roy closed his eyes, thinking. *Time to let her think she's controlling the call so I can see what options might be available.*

Cynthia interrupted his thoughts. "Do we have a problem, Roy? My sixth sense suspects a conflict. Are you still there?"

"Yeah, still here. Just pondering questions to ask. How many individuals, and who are they?"

"Probably three to start and more to follow. I need information on David's sister, Ryleigh; her business partner, Samantha Mieras; and a rogue New York attorney named Chandler Yates. There will probably be more. It depends upon what you discover and how many more are involved."

"What's your time frame?"

"I need results as fast as you can deliver." Cynthia laughed, saying, "Yesterday would have worked best."

"You dodged my question about how you'd stop their actions. I don't want to put people's lives at risk."

"Now you're asking too many questions, which makes me ask who your current client is, Roy. Are you working for the people trying to attack David? I don't have time to waste playing games. I want a yes or no."

"Yes, we have a conflict for doing investigations. Maybe we can find another way to work together, or I can end our call. Your choice, Cynthia."

Cynthia's mind was racing as her emotions rebounded from anger to scheming. "Hold on, Roy. You're right—maybe we can find a way to work together. Of course, I'm assuming you're working for, let's say, the competition?"

"Still here and listening."

"My aim is to keep events from escalating to where people get seriously hurt. Perhaps we could arrange a way to find a peaceful solution. You could be an intermediary and help negotiate a truce. It's a role that fits you as well, as being an investigator does. Do you feel there's a possibility for considering being an arbitrator?"

Roy exhaled. "That's an acceptable option. Would you be willing to call a temporary pause until I can get back to you?"

"Not unless the competition will do the same. I have people executing plans as we speak, but I can call them off if I have assurances there will be no more news articles or damning accusations."

"What assurances do you need?"

Cynthia laughed. "Come on, Roy. Don't play dumbass with me. They need to allow David's nomination to go through a congressional hearing. Hell, there's a chance Congress won't approve him for the position. Beyond those requests, I want a face-to-face meeting to stop further escalation."

"Okay, I'll try, but I'm unsure how fast things can happen."

"Look, Roy, nothing pauses on our side until they're willing to back off. It's never too late to stop a war, but it takes two to reach peace. You have until next week to tell me whether we can pause and meet. So talk it over with them and call me."

Cynthia ended the call and searched her phone for two old contacts, Chandler Yates and Ryleigh Jaymes.

CHAPTER 46

Scheming

Chandler's phone went to voicemail. "Chandler, Cynthia Jaymes. I'm calling with a proposal that should be of great interest to you and your family. Contact me for details." She ended the call and was walking out of her office when her phone chirped, showing Chandler returning her call.

"Chandler, thanks for the prompt response. I hope you're doing well."

"As always, I'm fine and surprised to hear from you."

Cynthia was reviewing a mental list of what to offer Chandler as she returned to her desk. "I'm calling with an offer to settle differences between you and Jonathan."

"I doubt you could achieve such a lofty goal, but I'm listening."

"It involves guaranteed secrecy of your family's lineage for you and your parents, significant monetary compensation, and an apology from the family. Am I generating interest?" Chandler couldn't help but laugh at what Cynthia said. "I'm glad you're amused, Chandler, but I'm serious about all of it."

"Sorry to laugh, but I can't believe Jonathan would ever agree to such an offer."

Cynthia was back in her seat, writing as she talked. "Things have changed, and I have more influence than you can imagine. The question is, have I piqued your interest?"

"Sure, I'm interested. Secrecy and protection for my family rings in as a desirable outcome. I imagine there's a robust price for such a prize. Tell me what you need from me to grant these magnanimous rewards."

"Cooperation and a change of allegiance."

"Can you provide some context?"

"I believe…no, I'm convinced you're involved with Ryleigh and whoever her associates are in trying to discredit David's nomination as chief justice. Am I on the right track?"

"Perhaps…"

"Oh, please, Chandler, spare me the evasive lawyer's responses. I don't have the patience for delaying tactics. Besides, it just confirms you're working with them." Chandler was drumming his fingers on his desk, wanting to respond but delaying so Cynthia could finish her pitch.

"Let me be more direct and complete with my proposition. I'm willing to do whatever it takes to convince you to work with us."

"What if I decline your offer?"

"If you refuse, we will destroy you and your family. Just to be clear, my offers and coercion are firm. With or without your help, I will stop the political interference."

Chandler's mind was struggling with conflicting interests, torn between family and associates. "Is there middle ground or room for compromise?"

"Zero chances. Which side will you choose, Chandler?"

"I need time to consider and talk with my family. Playing the role of Benedict Arnold is not enticing, but neither is the thought of peril for my parents."

"You have choices to make. I'm sure you're familiar with the phrase 'Blood is thicker than water.' So think hard and talk with whomever. And to help you, I'll provide your mother and father with the terms of my offer. I'm sure they will place a high value on maintaining privacy and protecting their business enterprise. I need an answer by next week. Don't make the wrong choice, Chandler." She clicked off before Chandler could respond.

Cynthia's next call was to Ryleigh. "Ryleigh I wasn't sure if I'd be able to reach you and thought an evening call might have the best success."

"Well, it worked. Wait a minute—I have another call coming in." Ryleigh put their call on hold. After ten minutes, Cynthia hung up, deciding to let Ryleigh call her back.

After another twenty minutes, the return call came. "Sorry about the lengthy pause. It was a call requiring my immediate attention."

"Of course. I understand, and there's no need to hide who called you. I'm sure Chandler was filling you in on our discussion earlier this evening."

"Good guess, Cynthia. He gave me the details of your offer. Kind of a desperate, ballsy move, even for you. So what scheme will you be throwing at me?"

Cynthia turned the pages of her notes on the proposal terms to Chandler. "My reason for calling you is the same as with Chandler. I want an end to your attempts to derail David's nomination."

"Not gonna happen, Cynthia."

"Don't be too hasty in deciding, Ryleigh. I have information and an offer you need to consider. Of course, if you're not interested, we can end the call here."

"Oh God. You're such a manipulative bitch. Curiosity begs me to hear what I'll decline to accept."

"Let me start with what Jonathan shared with me from years ago and has held in confidence. He will overlook your past actions, but going after David crosses the line." Cynthia paused while writing notes to address with Ryleigh.

Rolling her eyes, Ryleigh pulled in a deep breath. "You're a conniving bitch, but I'm still here. I know you're dying to throw me off guard with a shocking revelation. So tell me your offer I shouldn't be able to refuse."

"Here are the facts. I know you protected Samantha during her pregnancy until she gave birth. You lied to her about the stillbirths and sent her babies to who knows where. I also know Chandler Yates worked with you and still does. How's the accuracy of my—as you call it—revelation?"

"It's an interesting story, Cynthia. What proof do you have?"

"How about signed statements from the doctor and his staff, as well as certificates of live birth?"

"You're bluffing. You do not have any documentation."

"Wrong. Jonathan gave me copies of what his investigators got."

Ryleigh rolled her eyes, asking, "So what's the enticing offer for me to consider cooperating with you?"

"It's simple. Let David's nomination take its natural course, and stop the accusations in the press. In return, your father will restore his relationship with you and grant you priority rights to his estate when he dies. In his eyes, this will return your firstborn privileges."

"My last conversation with my father severed all ties. I don't believe he's aware of what you're trying to do. You have no clue about my last encounter with him. He would never agree to such an offer after he learned of what I knew from the past."

"As I am CEO of Aegis, he will abide by my decisions."

"And what's the threat or consequences when I turn you down?"

"If you don't cooperate, we'll destroy your reputation, bankrupt your investment firm, and start lengthy legal battles that will leave you penniless."

Cynthia went silent as Ryleigh mulled over several answers before speaking. "Bravo, Cynthia. You've mastered the Aegis skills of coercion well. My answer is like Chandler's. I need to have a conversation with other people. I can't unilaterally decide to pause our actions. And put in your notes that I have no interest in accepting your offer. I am willing only to deliver your message, asking for a pause in attacks on each other."

"Okay, I'll expect to hear from you soon. And you need to know Jonathan will not talk with you until you've agreed to the proposed terms, so there is no need to try negotiating with him."

"You can tell my father I have no intention of ever speaking with him again."

"Fine. I look forward to your call." As with Chandler, Cynthia clicked off the call before Ryleigh could respond.

CHAPTER 47

Connecting

Getting Sam, Thomas, and their assorted belongings up from Jack's parking garage took multiple trips. "Why don't I set Thomas up with his bed in the kitchen and litter box in the laundry room, so it's like his setup at your house?"

"I can set him up once you show me where to put my suitcases."

"Well, let me carry your cases up to the second floor. There are two guest rooms. You can pick what feels comfortable."

"Where's your room?"

Jack was off, raising his volume and continuing to talk over his shoulder as he climbed the stairs. "Third floor with my office and workout room. I'll be right back down."

Sam was feeling better and thinking, *I wonder if the bachelor can handle long-term guests.* She was setting up Thomas in his new environment as Jack returned.

"I can rustle up some dinner. I know you didn't get that far at home."

"I'm not starving, but some snacks would work, with a drink and conversation."

"Okay. Tell you what. You've had a tough day, so go settle into a room, get a relaxing shower, slip into some comfortable clothes, and come down when you're ready. I'll fix us some appetizers with drinks and start the fire. Would you like some music? I like soft blues. It's great background for conversations. And tell me if there's something you'd prefer to eat. I've got lots of choices to select from."

Sam was giggling like a schoolgirl and shaking her head. "Slow down, cowboy. It's just us, and there's no need to be nervous with me. Take some deep breaths and give me fifteen minutes to shower and change. I can unpack tomorrow." Giving him a wink, she turned and went up the stairs, humming to herself.

Jack was enjoying watching her walk away. *Yeah, she's a keeper. Listen to the lady, Jack. Slow down and pull your shit together. You're acting like a teenager on a first date.* Looking down, he saw Thomas sitting, staring up, and purring.

His phone buzzed, rattling itself on the kitchen island. "Roy, thanks for getting back to me. I need to update you. Sam encountered some rude visitors at her house. No harm to her, but they ruffled her nerves. It sounds like the same crew Ethan ran into at his place. I've got her here with me for as long as she wants."

Roy was processing the situation. "Mansa has his crew watching your house, so the two of you will be safe. I'll come by tomorrow or Monday morning to make assessments. You should start thinking about having his team handling security for the others. If they feel uncomfortable about security, we don't tell them it's being done. Mansa and his men are trained to do their work without detection. And I might have an option for us to consider with Cynthia Jaymes. I need to sort it out before running it past you and Sam."

"Hey, appreciate the security. Go ahead and have Mansa cover the rest of the team. Monday works for assessments. It'll give Sam time to collect herself and be ready to reevaluate plans. Things are happening fast, and I see the pace picking up." Jack closed the conversation, deciding not to tell Sam about Roy's call. *She needs to have some time away from the stress. We can come up with some Sunday distractions to help her forget about the current situation.*

Sam walked into the kitchen to find Jack assembling more food than a party of eight could consume. "I know it looks like a lot, but we'll have leftovers." Looking up from his culinary creation, he gave a quiet wolf whistle at seeing Sam in her emerald-green silky sweater falling over black leggings. "Wow, you're the best-looking houseguest ever."

She admired the twinkle in his eyes and spark in his personality. *He seems happy to have us here. He's a different Jack from the one I interviewed. I like both versions, but this one is becoming my favorite.*

"Drinks are on the sofa table, and Thomas is resting on his bed. Get comfortable, and I'll be right there. Which room did you choose?"

"For now, the one with the larger bathroom and shower."

He set the tray on the sofa table, giving her a wink and nod of approval. "Ya know, bean, a fine young thing like you stayin' in a fella's home alone could be dangerous for ya."

Sam burst into laughter. "Well, fella, I remember reading bout ya havin' an appetite for new and dangerous adventures. As for this fine young thing, she appreciates the hospitality."

She had Jack laughing. "I don't think my ancestors would appreciate our attempted dialect, but I like how you think, and we're off to a good start, Sam." Jack sat next to her as they raised their glasses in a mutual toast.

Sam raised her chin, closing her eyes as she spoke. "Can we agree to leave business aside for the next day or so? I need to let my emotions settle. Right now, I'm enjoying feeling comfortable and safe with just you. I need to savor the moment."

"Agreed. We can put the project aside, but I want you to feel free to talk about things if there's a need. As for getting to know each other better, tell me what you'd like to know about Jack Gallagher."

"Tell me about your family. What do you like and dislike? I'm ready to learn what makes Jack unique."

Jack set his glass down, leaning forward to prop his arms on his thighs. "Wow. That could go on for a while."

Sam reached to massage the back of his neck, saying, "Okay, start with your mother and father. I shared my research information about them but would like to hear your perspective."

"Okay. As you know, we were a working-class Irish American family trying to claw our way through life right here in Hell's Kitchen. It's why I live here now, back to my roots. It was a miserable collection of run-down tenements and ethnic gangs back then. My old man, Aidan, was on a quest to achieve his American dream by being the toughest of the tough in the Kitchen. His way was mano a mano brutality. For him, there were only two choices in life. Be the first one to strike a blow or have your ass kicked for hesitating or asking questions. He saw using your head and being smart as weaknesses."

"He doesn't sound like who you are."

"Not now, but back then, I was just like him. Not someone you would like to know."

"What's a favorite memory about your mother?"

"My mum was on the opposite side of the coin. Full of faith, optimism, and never-ending attempts to pull me away from the old man's influence. An example of her optimism has to do with lost pennies. She loved finding them on the sidewalk or street, saying they were a blessing from above if she found them heads up. To this day, I feel she continues to talk to me whenever I find one. Heads up means she's still up there trying to help me make good decisions. She loved me despite my faults, and I never fully understood it until she was gone. She liked Chandler because he did a lot to get me turned around. It breaks my heart that she never got to see me become a better man." Jack slid back onto the couch with a sigh. Sam noticed a glistening in his eyes as he watched the fire in silence.

"I wish I could have met her."

"I wish she could have known you. She would have liked Samantha Mieras." Sighing, he said, "Okay, it's your turn to tell me things I don't but should know about you."

"Hmm. You've heard the sad part of my life and did some pretty thorough research on me." Sam adjusted her body into a crossed-legged lotus position, facing Jack as she began. "I'll start with things your research didn't reveal. Being a Scorpio, I tend to be suspicious, paranoid, jealous, and possessive. There's nothing dangerous in those characteristics, but it explains some of why I've never been in a long-term relationship. A relentless work ethic became my trusted companion because I couldn't find a man worth trusting for more than a few dates. Jack Gallagher seems to be a surprising exception, but don't let it go to your head. We haven't had an official date yet. What about you and the women in your life?"

"Are you being suspicious or possessive?"

"Neither. I'm being curious."

"Okay, like you, no extended relationships, but I've always wanted one. What I do for a living is the problem. My work takes me away. Away a lot. And I can't answer questions someone might ask about my work. You know, like 'Where are you going? Where have you been? Tell me about your clients and your associates.' Building a trusting relationship is tough when there are so many secrets I have to protect. So years ago, I resigned myself to never being able to have a serious relationship. Besides, the women I attract are more interested in a quick romp in the hay than anything long-term, and there have been plenty of those."

Sam was about to comment as Jack raised his hand to stop her. "Let me finish. So I felt it could never happen until I met this woman, Samantha Mieras. You're different. You know what I do. You know more about me than I do. So I have nothing left to hide. You know it all, Sam, and we're here having a personal conversation, not a business discussion. To top it all off, you're hot as hell, and I've wanted to cancel our agreement so I could be with you instead of working for you."

She giggled. "Are you blushing?"

"No, I think it's the fireplace being too warm, making it seem that way. I...aww, hell. C'mon, Sam—jump in and save me before I make a complete fool of myself."

Sam reached out to stroke his cheek with a shine in her eyes. "Don't be embarrassed. You're telling me what I was hoping to hear, Jack. This might sound like a fast opinion, but I think you're the guy I've been trying to find for the past twenty years." She leaned forward, holding his head and kissing his cheek. "Thank you for coming into my life and taking care of me. Especially tonight. It's been a long time since I felt so vulnerable and violated. Then you came running up the stairs with Thomas in your arms and stepped in to take charge as I felt my world crumbling around me."

"You make me sound like the guy in shining armor."

He watched as Sam stood and moved around to sit straddling his lap, wrapping her arms around his neck to pull him in for a long series of soft kisses. The firelight flickered as they continued the embrace and course of erotic exchanges.

Sam placed her hands on his shoulders to lean back. "Can I make a request, Mr. Gallagher?"

He flashed his smile, answering, "Yeah, and right now, I'll grant any request you make."

"I don't want to be alone tonight. I want to be held and told everything will be all right. Would you mind if I slept in your room with you to cuddle? I'm not a first-date easy kind of girl. I just need to not be alone after all that's happened."

"M'lady, your wish will be granted. Tomorrow is Sunday. We can sleep in, I'll fix breakfast, and we can plan the day."

"Let's start with you cuddling me for the night. We can plan tomorrow tomorrow."

Thomas raised his head from the comfy cat bed to see them walking up the stairs arm in arm. He tucked his head back in, feeling safe for the night.

CHAPTER 48

Sunday Respite

Early the next morning, a wafting, savory aroma of fresh-brewed coffee stirred Sam from a blissful sleep. Her eyes blinked as she realized she was in Jack's bed but he wasn't there with her. She sat up, finding a note on the nightstand. *I laid out one of my flannel shirts for you to wear with your leggings this morning. The weather outside is chilly, and the shirt will help keep you warm. Thomas and I are in the kitchen having a morning discussion. Come down and join us.*

She stopped on the second floor to brush her hair and see how his shirt looked on her. *Not a bad look, Sam. How about surprising him without the leggings?* Walking downstairs, she called out, "Jack, where are you?"

His voice responded, "In the kitchen. I heard you coming and started toasting bagels to go with fresh fruit and coffee for a fireside breakfast." Dancing her way into the kitchen, she turned a few pirouettes for added effect. "How does this look? I like the shirt, and you might never get it back."

"Pardon my language, but that shirt has never looked so damned good." He looked down at Thomas to ask, "What do you think, Thomas?" Sam walked over to Jack, squeezing him from behind as he tried to assemble a tray filled with their morning meal. "I like your greeting methods. Did you sleep well?"

"Like a baby. I loved talking and snuggling with you. The last thing I remember is you telling me I needed to close my eyes and stop talking so we could rest. After that, it was lights out. How about you?"

"Like a rock. Hey, I love what you're doing, but you need to turn me loose so we can move over to the fireplace. Grab the drinks and follow me, m'lady."

Thomas jumped up to the back of the sofa, trying to catch Sam's attention. "Oh, baby, I forgot about you. Are you looking for breakfast?"

"You don't need to worry about him. He found his way up to the bedroom, woke me up, and demanded breakfast before letting me start coffee. I think he likes his new digs."

She gave a giggle of delight, sitting down with Jack. "So what are we doing today? I need to shower and know our plans so I can dress appropriately."

Jack was multitasking, buttering bagels and answering Sam. "I thought we'd catch a cab and wander through the small boutiques along Madison Avenue on the Upper East Side. We could grab a late lunch, come back to relax, and cook together. I'm assuming you'd be interested in creating something together?"

Sam tilted her head. "I love cooking, and shopping at the boutiques is a favorite activity. Especially this time of year with all the Christmas trims. It's so festive. We can browse through a couple of gourmet markets to create a meal. I'm normally alone wandering through the area. Being with you will make it special."

They laughed and shared stories about living in New York as they ate breakfast. Jack glanced at the wall clock. "It's almost noon. I guess we should get ready to shop and explore. Why don't you head upstairs while I handle kitchen cleanup? It won't take me long to shower and be ready to go."

Sam shook her head. "No, no. Kitchen duty is a two-person event. I helped eat, so I get to help with dishes." She loaded the tray and headed for the kitchen as Jack followed without comment. "Are you staring at my ass? I can feel your eyes back there, Jack."

Setting the tray on the counter, she spun around to face him. "I'm not complaining. In fact, I hope you were looking." She reached up, wrapping her arms around his neck and whispering, "I said I wasn't an easy first-date girl, but this is our second-day date together." Rubbing noses with him, she continued, "So, Mr. Gallagher, how about a shower together and a morning romp in the hay with a fine young thing before going shopping?"

A smile spread across Jack's face while he held her waist. "Mr. Gallagher would love to grant your second request, m'lady." They locked into another long kissing embrace before finishing setting things into the sink.

Thomas sat licking his paws, watching them laugh and jostle each other as they playfully danced around the kitchen before disappearing up to the third floor.

CHAPTER 49

Regrouping

Standing on Jack's doorstep, Roy anxiously waited for a response after repeatedly ringing the doorbell on a snowy Monday morning. *Jack is always quick to answer his doorbell. I'll text him to see what gives.* Roy was typing his message as Jack swung the door open.

"Hey, man. Get in from the cold. I was in the kitchen and didn't mean to leave you standing out in the cold. How about some coffee and breakfast? I've got hash browns and bacon and was about to scramble eggs. Sam will be down in a few minutes to join us."

Stomping the snow from his shoes, Roy hung his hat and coat in the closet as Jack hurried back to the kitchen. "You're in a bright mood for a blustery morning." Jack was whistling and lost in his work. Roy walked into the kitchen to pour himself a coffee, looking around to ensure Sam was still upstairs. Taking a seat on one of the island's barstools, he asked, "If I didn't know better, I'd say Jack got laid this weekend. Right or wrong, bud?"

He didn't see or hear Sam walking in behind him. "Good guess, and almost accurate. Except he got laid several times." She was laughing and hugging Roy. "Good to see you, and glad you're joining us for breakfast. Hope my commentary wasn't too frisky, but I know I don't have to be shy around you."

"Damn, sorry about my question, Sam. I didn't mean it as an accusation or insult. What the two of you do is your business. I…"

Sam broke in before he could stumble through the rest of an apology. "You were just being the ever-observant investigative sleuth, making an assessment."

Jack clinked his metal spatula on the side of the fry pan. "I have food ready to serve if you two can stop bantering and trying to expose my private life."

Roy got to his feet, heading for the Keurig. "Have a seat, Sam. I'll get your coffee while lover boy serves the food. I see he's added your half-caff preference to his selections."

"Nice to see my wingman throwing me under the bus. I thought you were supposed to watch out for my backside. You know, stand up for me, not throw darts."

"A wingman can't do much when you charge ahead without consultation. From the look on your face, my report to the flight commander would read something like 'He went down in flames with a smile.'" Roy burst out laughing and clapped his hands.

Sam was blushing. "Oh my, it's spiraling out of control. Can the two of you stop long enough to eat? A prim and proper lady shouldn't have to put up with suggestive innuendos."

Roy set Sam's coffee down, giving her a side shoulder hug. "Bravo to the two of you for putting a bright note into the day. You're going to be a great couple. As Sam suggested, let's sample the good chef's work." They chatted about their weekends before Sam surfaced the need to return to business.

They refocused as Jack cleared the counter while Sam and Roy gathered file folders and notepads. "I'll start by bringing Roy up to speed on my encounter with Charles."

Sam provided Roy with a recap of her finding her home in shambles and the face-to-face confrontation with Charles. "The guy was disturbing in the way he talked and acted. He took pleasure in what he was doing, with a sadistic tone in his voice. He was like a..."

Roy took over the conversation, adding, "Like a psychopath."

"Yes, and he disabled my ability to maintain composure and control. I'm great at handling unexpected confrontations in business, but he froze me like a deer caught in headlights." Sam was closing her eyes and shuddering.

Roy handed a folder to Jack. "This is a complete background investigation for you and Sam to read and understand who Charles Abbott is and where he came from."

Jack was fanning the volume of pages. "How did you have time for an extensive dig on this guy? It's only been a few days since Ethan made us aware of him."

"What you have is three months of workup on him. Cynthia Jaymes had me do the work about two years ago when she was looking for a security director for Aegis. 'Security director' is just a cover title for a bruiser without a moral compass or conscience, and he more than fits the billing. She wanted to make sure he was capable of ruthless actions and following orders without question."

Sam was listening, propping her chin with one hand. "You make him sound like a mercenary."

"Oh, he's worse than you think. I advised against hiring him because I felt there was a significant risk he would act independently or go rogue and become more of a liability than a benefit. You nailed it when you called him a mercenary. You'll discover he developed his skills by serving three years in a private Russian military organization. The Wagner Group."

Jack looked up from reading. "Wait a minute—you gathered all this working for Cynthia? You never mentioned it to me."

"Well, you didn't ask, and it was two years ago. Back then, Cynthia was just another fee-paying client. Freelance special projects don't require sorting wheat from chaff. I didn't think her being a past client would present a problem. It was a one-time assignment and I had the contacts to get it done."

Sam looked at Jack, scrunching her face and shrugging her shoulders. Jack answered, "Okay, no problem for us."

"Thanks. I needed clarity before I tell you about a call I had from her."

Sam raised her posture. "Why would Cynthia be calling you?"

"She called me because of the work I did with Charles and wanted background investigations on you, Ryleigh, and Chandler, with options to include anyone else involved in creating trouble with David's nomination. She was clueless about my allegiance to you."

Jack tapped his pen on the island's granite surface. "I need to confirm which side you're playing for. So your answer to her?"

"C'mon, Jack. It was a flat-out no! I tried to get her to tell me what they planned to do. However, she became suspicious when I asked too many questions. Cynthia functions with a strong sense of suspicion and paranoia and didn't like my probing. When she asked if I was working with the competition, I said yes and expected the phone call to end."

Sam set her pen aside, locking in on Roy's eyes. "Well, what happened?"

"It was like she jumped out of the phone trying to grab me so I wouldn't hang up. It was a radical shift from the composed, calculating Cynthia I'd encountered before. She was panicking and started throwing out the idea of me being an intermediary, and I let her run with it."

Sam was focusing on Roy's facial expressions. "Intermediary? What the hell is she trying to do, Roy?"

"She said she wants to keep things from escalating and keep people from getting seriously hurt. As much as Charles rattled you, Ethan's article seems to have caused a significant ripple in their pool of confidence. Cynthia wants a pause. A temporary truce."

Jack reached out, tapping Sam's arm, sensing she was about to explode. He asked Roy, "What're her requirements for a pause, which I assume would also apply to them?"

"She wants assurances there will be no further articles. We let the process go forward on David's nomination, and we agree to a face-to-face meeting to negotiate a complete truce."

Sam was out of her seat, pacing. "Bullshit. No negotiating. Nope, nada."

"I'm simply carrying a message, Sam, and I agree with you."

Jack interjected, "Ethan's article accomplished what we wanted it to. It caught them off guard, and the next one will continue to pressure them into mistakes we can capitalize on."

Sam paused her pacing. "I knew she would try something, and I appreciate you making us aware. Another question, Roy. Why do I feel you have more to tell us?"

"There is more. I wasn't the only one getting a call from Cynthia. Chandler told me she called him and Ryleigh to try coaxing them into working with her."

"Jesus, she sure made the rounds."

"Sam, she was coming unhinged and willing to try to chase every chance she could."

"What were her offers to Rye and Chan?"

Roy explained the terms Cynthia had proposed and added that she had given them the same deadline she'd offered to him. "She's desperate to keep the nomination on course. My fear for our team is her turning Charles loose. We've experienced only a mild version of his capabilities. I've been going through contingencies with Mansa." Roy looked at Jack. "We may have to gather everyone here and operate with your place as a command center."

"Whatever you and Mansa feel is best."

Sam was scrolling through the calendar on her phone. "Adira and Lydia should have new information today. They'll turn it over to you for review and then on to Ethan. I have Wednesday as the due date for the next article. Am I right, Jack?"

"I changed the method of getting new discoveries from Lydia and Adira to Ethan. In the interest of expediency, they will go directly to Ethan and give him their views on what to use in the next article, since they have firsthand knowledge about things we might overlook, and time is short."

Sam listened and nodded in agreement. "Okay, call Ethan and tell him to run with the article. We don't need to approve this one. My gut tells me we have to go fast. Do you or Roy have any objection?"

Jack sat silent as Roy scrolled through his calendar. "None from me. The three of us need to be ready and available for whatever comes next. What do you think, Jack?"

"I think we should have pulled the girls from today's assignment."

CHAPTER 50

Gathering Intelligence

Adira arrived for work at David and Cynthia's Scarsdale home, the same as any other day. She found David talking with a stranger in the driveway as she approached the house. "Good morning, Adira. Let me introduce Charles Abbott. As the head of security for Aegis, he'll be improving safeguards for our computer system and physical safety because of threats over my pending nomination."

Charles extended a hand while making a slow visual assessment of Adira. "Always a pleasure to meet a beautiful woman. I've heard great things about you from David and Cynthia. Perhaps we can chat sometime and get to know each other better."

"Thank you, Charles. My schedule is busy. We'll see." Adira shook hands and walked through the office entrance without another word, thinking, *What's with the wimpy-ass handshake and leering looks? No way in hell you'll get to know me better.*

Cynthia greeted Adira, handing her a list of calls and tasks for the day. "I'm also expecting three important calls; you'll find those listed in the itinerary. Outside those, send all other callers to my voicemail."

Adira reviewed Cynthia's schedule, surprised by the names listed as important calls. *What the hell—Roy, Ryleigh, and Chandler?*

Cynthia began tapping her foot, annoyed with Adira's distraction over the call list. "Hello? Adira?"

"Oh, sorry, Cynthia. I was trying to prioritize. I'll handle calls accordingly and have one addition to the day. Lydia will stop by for reports on Society and possible new targets. She also wants time to chat and catch up with you."

"Let me know when she arrives. I need to tell her we're putting a hold on Society's activities. At least until David is confirmed as the new chief justice."

Adira raised her eyes with a questioning look. "What about pending financial commitments and communication with clients we've caught recently?"

"Keep payments coming from existing clients but put a hold on money demands from any new ones. I'll explain the situation to Lydia once she's here."

Adira made sure Cynthia had closed her office door before she started to copy Society's database of client information with names, payments, dates, and locations of encounters. Ethan had told her that the collection would validate what he would write in upcoming articles. Logging into her workstation, she found her access to the database had changed to a read-only authorization. Using her phone, she sent a text to Lydia. *We have a problem.*

Adira decided to ask Cynthia about the change to data access and knocked on her door. "Sorry to bother you, Cynthia, but I'm trying to download client information for Lydia, and it's become a read-only file."

Cynthia shot her a hard look. "Why does Lydia need client information from the database? She has her own access. Charles made the changes to make our files more secure. His number is in the system. Give him a call to have him help you with it."

"Good idea—I'll call him." Adira closed the door, thinking, *That was a bust. No way am I calling Charles.*

Adira was finishing some filing as Lydia walked into her office area. "Hi, sorry I wasn't here sooner. My Uber driver had trouble with his GPS navigation."

Adira glanced down the hall to be sure Cynthia's door was still closed. "Oh God, I'm glad you're here. You can knock on Cynthia's door. She's expecting you. They've changed my access to the database. I can't download what we want. And the guy who manhandled Ethan was here with David when I arrived this morning. What a douchebag."

"Why was he here?"

"Are you ready for this? He's the head of security for Aegis. He's the one who changed my access rights."

"Should you ask Cynthia about the change?"

"I tried already, but she got pissy, asking why I needed to copy information. I tried a quick excuse of doing research for you, but she wasn't buying it."

"Okay, let me try calming her down. Is there any other information you can gather for Ethan?"

"I have some private files on my computer and will get them downloaded while you're with her."

"I can keep her talking for as long as you need."

"Be careful. She's being super paranoid today. Just so you're prepared, she'll tell you to put new activities for Society on hold. You can use lunch with me and another friend as an excuse to get us out of here. It'll keep her from trying to tag along." Lydia nodded and walked down the short hall to Cynthia's office.

Adira finished a few tasks for Cynthia before connecting a flash drive to download files. An alert popped up on the screen, requiring administrative rights to perform the transfer. She wasn't sure what to do next, and then her workstation locked up and the screen went black. "Oh shit, this is not good."

She was taking deep breaths as the phone started ringing. "Good morning, this is Adira. How may I help you?"

"Adira, this is Charles Abbott. I must talk with Cynthia. I will hold if she's on another call. Tell her it is an urgent matter."

"Charles, Cynthia left strict instructions to send all callers to her voicemail. She…"

"Do not block my call. Why have you attached a foreign drive to the system?"

"Foreign drive? What are you talking about, Charles?"

"I'm monitoring the system and know what you're trying to do. Forget transferring my call. I'll be there in a few minutes."

"Wait a minute—I'm simply doing what Cynthia wants. I'll put you on hold and ask her to take your call." Adira disconnected the call and ran for Cynthia's office, biting her lower lip as she knocked on the door.

Leaning into the doorway, she motioned for Lydia to follow her. "Sorry to interrupt, but Lydia and I need to head for lunch. Our friend just called and had to change lunch plans. She wants to meet earlier if it's okay with you, Cynthia."

Without looking up from her reports, Cynthia waved her hand, dismissing them. "Whatever, go have lunch. Lydia and I can finish updating later. Any messages, Adira?"

"No messages other than what's in your voicemail."

Lydia looked at Adira as they hurried down the hall. "What the hell, Adira?"

"No time to talk or explain. We need to get out of here as fast as possible and head for your townhouse. I'll explain while I drive."

Adira accelerated her BMW through the property's gate, almost sideswiping Charles, who was flashing his lights as she skidded past him.

CHAPTER 51

Storm's Edge

"Adira, you're driving like a madwoman. What's going on?" Adira explained the problem with her computer and the call from Charles. "I swear, Lydia. They know what we're trying to do."

Lydia braced her right arm against the window as Adira weaved through traffic. "I'm afraid you're right. Cynthia asked about Lucas and his intentions for David's nomination. Then, she launched into nonstop questions about us and where our loyalties were. Thank God you barged in. I was on the edge of losing it with her."

They were trying to strategize as Adira's phone began ringing. The caller ID showed it was Cynthia. Adira handed her phone to Lydia, telling her not to answer until they got to her house and talked with Roy or Jack.

Adira parked her car near Lydia's townhouse, and they sat listening to screaming voicemails demanding they return to the office. Cynthia made an offer in the last one. "This is your last chance to return and avoid problems. The people you're involved with are lying to you about us. I can keep you from being harmed. Do not refuse my offer." Lydia and Adira were looking at each other, questioning Cynthia's message.

Adira sighed a slow exhale. "We need to get inside and call the boys. Are you sure no one followed us here?"

"As sure as I can be after bouncing around in the car. Besides, no one has pulled up near us."

They quickly scanned the area, feeling it was safe to go inside. Crossing the street, they were unaware of the occupants of a van parked near the house. Lydia had unlocked the door and keyed in her code to turn off the alarm system when someone shoved Adira from behind, knocking both of them to the floor.

A quartet of hooded men charged in, closing the door behind them. Adira turned toward the assailants, screaming, "What the hell, assholes?" Lydia was back up on her feet, trying to reach the panic button on the alarm panel, when one intruder grabbed her arm, bending it behind her back and slamming her against the wall. The struggle was over in less than a few heartbeats; Lydia and Adira were zip-tied to chairs, with hoods over their heads.

An ominous, low voice spoke with a heavy foreign accent. "Do not speak or make resistance, and no harm will be done."

Lydia couldn't contain her anger. "What the fuck do you want?"

"Do not speak. We wait."

Lydia and Adira sat in silence. They heard the door open and footsteps approach as their hoods were pulled off.

"Well, well. What do we have here? You may be a good hooker, but you are a terrible driver, Adira."

She was thrashing in her chair, trying to break free. "Fuck you, Charles. Turn us loose. Cynthia will have your head for this shit."

Charles swung the full strength of a backhand into Adira's face, knocking her over, along with the chair. One of the men lifted her back up. "Do you think Cynthia will save you? Who do you think sent me here?"

A wound on Adira's cheek was oozing blood down her neck as Lydia spoke. "Leave her alone. Deliver Cynthia's message and leave my house. Tell Cynthia 'Mission accomplished.'" She was trying to distract Charles and negotiate.

He turned toward Lydia. "Now, this one seems to understand what's happening." In unison, the four men laughed.

"So, Lydia. Let's make sure you understand the message and what must be done. You're going to convince newsboy he must stop being a nosy little prick. He will stop writing bad things about my associates and Aegis. If not, Adira will pay the price for his failure to comply with my directions." Lydia was quiet, not responding as her eyes darted between Adira and Charles.

He walked over to her, placing his face inches from hers. "No response? I know you heard me, and to ensure you share my message with all your friends, we will take Adira with us."

He walked over to Adira, lifting her chin to look at the wound. "As I said this morning, sweetie, I want time to get to know each other better." Adira spat in his face as he leaned in, trying to kiss her. "Oh yes, this one's feisty." He grabbed her blouse, tearing it to wipe his face, and barked commands. Motioning toward Lydia, he continued, "I'll cut that one loose. Gag and hood the other bitch and throw her into the back of the van. Leave the package in the other room but out of sight."

Lydia glared at Charles. "Don't take her. We'll do as you asked. Just leave her here with me. Tell Cynthia we'll cooperate."

"So sorry, Lydia. It's too late. Taking Adira is our leverage. Besides, I'm looking forward to finding out what she can tell us about your little group. She'll be returned once we've grown tired of her." He yelled for his men to hurry with Adira, who was kicking to resist being taken. "One more thing, Lydia. Tell Roy to take care of the bodyguards in the alley. They were so easy to locate and neutralize." He pulled a knife and cut the zip ties, leaving Lydia stunned as he and his men left, with Adira making muffled cries.

Lydia found her phone and dialed Roy's number. "Roy, this is Lydia. Charles has Adira." Her voice trembled as she closed her eyes, and tears began flowing.

"Where are you?"

"My townhouse. Oh God, they beat her. I'm so afraid for her."

"Listen to me. Lock the door and stay out of sight. We'll be there in a few minutes."

"Please hurry."

Roy turned to Sam and Jack. "The bastards went after the girls and took Adira. Grab your coats. We need to rescue Lydia before something else happens to her."

Sitting at his computer, Ethan was sifting through Lydia's files as his phone buzzed. The display showed an unknown caller, so he let it go to voicemail, thinking, *No time to deal with distractions. I've got to finish and get this to Jack for approval before tomorrow morning's deadline.* His attention to writing distracted him from seeing the mailroom clerk set a package on the floor next to his desk as his phone went off again. This call coming in was from Roy.

"Roy, what can I do for you?"

"Sam's been trying to reach you. I called, knowing you've got me in your contact listing and would answer." Roy gave him a quick rundown of what was happening and told him to proceed with the article without forwarding it to Jack for approval. "We'll be back in touch with you as soon as we have Lydia."

"Okay, is there anything I can do to help?"

"Just keep your nose to the grindstone, son. We need you to stay on schedule."

"Got it."

Jack eased into a parking space near Lydia's house. "It's useless to try finding something closer. We can hustle the rest of the way. Her house is just a couple of houses up."

Roy dialed Lydia's number as they ran to her house. When she opened the door, she sobbed as Sam wrapped her arms around her. Sam said, "You're safe now, and we'll find Adira."

"I called Lucas, and he wants me to check into a hotel or maybe come back to DC, but I want to stay here and help find Adira."

Jack began a visual search for clues. "A hotel is a good idea. Roy can keep watch over you and call the senator to let him know what we're doing." He was in the dining room, continuing his visual scan, but missed the cardboard box hidden behind the drapery.

"Charles said something about bodyguards in the back alley. I don't know what he meant. I don't have bodyguards."

Roy spun around. "How do I get to the alley?"

"Through the kitchen."

"Stay here with the girls, Jack. I'll check the alley and call Mansa."

Sam and Lydia went upstairs to pack. "You'll be away for more than an overnight, but we can come back for more things."

Heading for the back door to check on Roy, Jack found him coming back, shaking his head as he talked on the phone. "Damn it—I don't know what went wrong, Mansa. Someone hit Jimmy and Daniel with kill shots in the alley. They never knew what hit them. I don't know the answer. You need to get over here with a team to clean things up before NYPD finds out and sticks their nose into our business." He ended the call and looked at Jack standing in the kitchen.

"Who the hell are Jimmy and Daniel, Roy?"

"They're part of Mansa's security squad. He'll take care of them. We need to get the girls out of here."

Jack grabbed Roy's arm. "Is there more you need to tell me about you and Mansa?"

"Yeah, but we'll talk later."

Sam walked into the kitchen and overheard their conversation. "What's going on in the alley? It sounds like something I need to know. Can you explain, Jack?"

"Mansa sent two men to secure Lydia's house. I think Charles and his men discovered them, and it didn't go well for our side."

Turning to Roy, Sam asked, "Is Jack trying to tell me bad news?"

"Yes. I can explain in the car." They gathered Lydia and headed for Jack's place.

Roy explained that he'd had Mansa send two men to check out Lydia's townhouse, and they must have walked into an ambush. "I think Charles had men doing surveillance long before Jimmy and Daniel arrived. Charles probably radioed ahead to warn them when the girls were on their way here. His men reacted faster than our guys. I hate it when this shit happens."

With a firm grip on Sam's hand, Lydia listened to Roy's matter-of-fact description of the killings. "What are we going to do? Adira is gone. You lost two men, and you're talking about it like it's...like it's nothing."

"No, Lydia, I take losing men personally. It pisses me off, but we can't let emotions overwhelm reason. My men will have died needlessly if we let that happen. Charles wants us to panic and lose the will to fight them."

Jack pulled the car into his parking garage and turned in his seat. "Roy's right. We need to keep level heads and get back to thinking about rescuing Adira and handling attacks. Trust me, Charles is not done."

Sam put her hands on Lydia's shoulders, looking her in the eye. "Adira needs us to focus. I know you've got moxie; this is the time to pull yourself together for her."

"Yeah, I get it. I'm with you guys. Give me a few minutes. I'll be fine once we're inside. I've never had anything like this crack my outer shell."

Jack and Roy spent the afternoon making calls to see what they could learn about where Charles might be holding Adira. Sam contacted Ethan to make sure he was safe. Lydia called Lucas, assuring him she was safe and needed to remain in New York.

The evening's shadows were growing across the outdoor patio. Roy looked around at the beleaguered group and told everyone it was time to order takeout. "Troops don't function well on empty stomachs. Does anyone have a better suggestion than pizza?" Receiving no replies, he asked, "Any preferences for toppings? You have one minute before I order anchovies and limburger cheese." His announcement broke the solemn mood, resulting in a unanimous disgust for his choices, followed by a variety of more appealing suggestions. "I knew food would bring this group back to life."

Jack and Roy sat at the island finishing the last of the two large pizzas, Greek salad, and beers. Jack was asking questions about Mansa, with Roy talking quietly to fill in as much as possible for him. "There will be a time when I can explain a lot to you, Jack. Mansa and I go back to our combat days in Vietnam."

Jack motioned for Roy to stop, asking, "Wait a minute. You were a photojournalist, not a combat soldier. Right?"

Roy looked back at the group to make sure no one was paying attention. "All I can tell you right now is that being a photojournalist and being a background investigator today have served the same purpose. Those covers enable me to do what I'm good at—special projects. We're on the same side here. You just have to trust that I know what I'm doing."

Jack shook his head and said, "Okay for now. Down the road we need a long talk."

Sam was on the couch in front of the fireplace with Lydia. "Staying at a hotel alone doesn't sound good to me, Sam. I want to be with you and the guys. I need to be helping, not hiding."

Jack overheard Lydia's comment. "I agree with Lydia. My place is officially our headquarters. Roy and Lydia can stay here with us. I've got plenty of room, and we need to stick together to see if we get leads on Adira and find out what happens after Ethan's article hits. After that, we'll see if he needs to join us here."

Seeing Sam raise her eyebrows, Roy jumped into the conversation. "Hey, Lydia can stay with me instead of at a hotel. It might be more comfortable than all of us crashing in on you and Sam."

Lydia flashed a smile at Sam and poked her shoulder. "What? You and Jack? Hey, I'm not surprised." She gave a wink to Jack. "Sorry, big guy, but my previous offers are off the table now that I know Sam has first rights."

Sam smiled. "Thanks, Lydia. I'll let you know if I throw him back into the pool."

Jack's face was turning red. "Hey, hey. We need to have some sensitivity for the guy caught in the middle."

Lydia was enjoying a moment of relief from the day's stress and relished making Jack feel uncomfortable. "You're so not in the middle, Jack. You're Sam's claim for now. Treat her well, or she'll be kicking you to the curb." The teasing eased the tension of the day, letting them enjoy a laugh at Jack's expense.

Lydia stood up to reach for her phone on the fireplace mantle. "I'm feeling my moxie coming back and think it's time for me to make a call." They all looked at her in silence as she continued, "I can call Cynthia and try to reason with her. If nothing else, she might accidentally help us locate Adira."

Roy folded his arms, leaning back. "It's worth a try. I doubt you'll get anywhere, but what the hell?"

Without hesitating, Lydia dialed, getting an immediate answer. "It's about time you called, Lydia. Did you get my message?"

"Where's Adira? We want her returned unharmed as soon as possible."

"You're in no position to make demands of me. I thought she was with you. Sounds like I'm on speakerphone, but no problem. It'll save you from having to repeat our conversation."

Lydia was gritting her teeth. "You know damn well Charles has her."

"Hmm, if so, maybe you should call him. I can give you his number."

"Cut the crap, Cyn. There's no reason to harm her or keep her as a hostage."

"You still haven't answered my question."

"Yes, we got your message."

"And are you willing to stop creating problems for David?" Lydia paused, surveying the room. "All I hear is silence, Lydia. Well, I'll see what I can do to return Adira to you. It would be easier if we had an agreement to end the attacks." Cynthia disconnected the call.

Shortly after Cynthia closed their call, Lydia's phone rang, showing an unknown caller. "Hello."

"Good evening, Lydia. I believe you want to talk with me about Adira, or perhaps you'd like to speak with her? Oh, I'm sorry—she's tied up at the moment and can't talk."

"Charles, let's negotiate. What will get you to release her?"

"I thought you were an intelligent woman, but you can't even remember simple instructions. So one more time: the request was to stop creating obstacles. Adira sends her love and would appreciate your cooperation." He ended the call without letting Lydia respond.

CHAPTER 52
Second Strike

Ethan's article hit the internet with damning accusations.

COERCION TURNS TO ABDUCTION?

By Ethan Brode, reporting for the *Insider*

Previous allegations of coercion, blackmail, and illicit encounters have embroiled President Lawrence's pending nomination to fill Chief Justice Wheeler's position. Additionally, a woman has come forward with new allegations of statutory rape, impregnation, and a demanded abortion by Chief Judge David Jaymes in 1992.

The *Insider* has obtained documentation and testimony implicating Jaymes, chief judge on the New York Second Court of Appeals, in a conspiracy to silence critics of his nomination as chief justice of the Supreme Court. Senator Lucas Mathers has raised concerns regarding the allegations with the Senate Judiciary Committee. "As vice-chair of the Senate Judiciary Committee, I am calling for an investigation into allegations regarding Judge Jaymes. I am also calling on President Lawrence to remove Judge Jaymes from consideration as a nominee for the Supreme Court. As a member of the Judiciary Committee, I want to remind other members of our duty to protect the integrity of the Federal Judiciary Act."

Implementing a clandestine operation run by an organization known as Aegis, Jaymes and his coconspirators leveraged influence over political figures, using videotapes of sexual encounters and the threat of public disclosure for political favors. The *Insider* has obtained the names of the involved individuals, along with videos.

Recent coercive actions have included threats against Senator Mathers, who is willing to testify and verify such actions against him.

The *Insider* has learned of threats made against Judge Jaymes's executive assistant, Adira Tomasz, in an effort to silence allegations when the judge learned of her attempts to alert the public to his nefarious actions. Attempts to follow up with her have gone unanswered. Friends of Ms. Tomasz fear she may have been abducted and may be being held hostage to prevent further disclosures.

The *Insider* has reached out to representatives from Aegis and Justice Jaymes, but they have declined to comment.

We will update this story as additional information becomes available.

CHAPTER 53

Return Volley

Jonathan Jaymes walked onto the veranda outside his study; leaning on the railing, he squinted into the dim pre-dawn light. *This is a fine mess. I need to reset priorities and right the ship before we all go down.* Jackson, his trusted attendant, walked up behind him, placing a quiet hand on his shoulder. "Is there anything I can do for you, sir?"

Jonathan turned to say, "Jackson, I've been through so much, and you've witnessed my trials and tribulations. Current circumstances have strained my tolerance. I am at a crossroads, debating which direction to take. You've become a trusted friend despite my failures with our families. What would you do?"

Jackson paused. "The decisions we make in life produce the results we receive, which may not be what we desire. A man knows what needs to be done to achieve his desires and is the only one who can influence the results."

"Thank you, Jackson. I think it's time to have breakfast, and I extend a request for you to join me."

"Sir, you've never offered me such an invitation. You are the master of this domain and my steadfast benefactor. I will honor your request."

"Take your time, Jackson. I have a brief call to make and look forward to your company."

Jonathan returned to his desk, dialing Charles Abbott to leave a voicemail message. "Charles, Jonathan Jaymes. I'm calling about a matter of great importance and secrecy. I will be available and expecting your return call this morning at eight. Do not discuss this conversation with Cynthia or David."

He sat back in his chair, holding his hands to his lips and arching his head back. *A father's dreams for his son rest in the balance.*

Jackson and Jonathan shared a sumptuous breakfast of fluffy scrambled eggs, salty ham with coffee-infused red-eye gravy, cheesy grits, and flaky buttermilk biscuits washed down with freshly squeezed orange juice and savory coffee. They talked about their history together, remembrances of joy and pain, thoughts of family, and choices gone wrong. "I can never shed the guilt and shame of what occurred with your sister. You have been beyond generous in your forgiveness and loyalty. Your safety here is secure for as long as I live and beyond."

Jack was functioning in his familiar role of breakfast chef when Sam's phone sounded an alert from her alarm service warning of a break-in at her home. In less than a minute, Lydia was receiving a similar message. They looked at each other, wondering what was happening. Both tried to contact their alarm services as the morning television news program interrupted its broadcast with reports of multiple explosions in the city.

The commentator began a report. "This is just coming in from multiple sources. There appear to have been explosions at residences near Central Park. One was on the Upper East

Side, next to the park, and a second was on the Upper West Side. There are no immediate reports of injuries. Firefighting crews are responding to the scenes.

"We're also receiving reports of an explosion at the offices of the *Insider*, a political news service in the Garment District. Again, there are no reports of injuries, and firefighters are also responding to that alarm.

"We do not know if the incidents are related or what might be the cause. We will keep you informed as details become available."

Checking his sources with the police and fire departments, Roy said, "I'm afraid the two residences are probably Sam's and Lydia's. I'll call Ethan to make sure he's all right and see what he knows about the one at his office."

Jonathan's phone rang while Jackson was clearing the last of their meal from the conference table. He ambled to his desk before answering the call.

"Charles. Thank you for being punctual."

"I would have called sooner but waited until your requested time. How can I be of service, Mr. Jaymes?"

"To start, you can call me Jonathan and then give me your word that this conversation remains between us."

"As you wish, Jonathan."

"Good. As of this morning, I am returning to the position of CEO for Aegis. I will inform the board of my actions. From this time forward, you work for me. Any orders from Cynthia or David will require my approval. Is that clear?"

"Loud and clear, Jonathan."

"Have you read this morning's accusations by the *Insider*?"

"Yes, sir, I saw it earlier."

Jonathan was making notes before continuing. "Am I correct in assuming you have David and Cynthia's assistant, Adira Tomasz, in your custody?"

"Yes, sir, I have her detained. She's exhausted from a night of interrogation, and she's resting."

"Was her abduction ordered by David or Cynthia?"

"Yes, ordered by both of them, sir. We discovered Adira was the probable source of information for the news service publishing the original article. Cynthia and David wanted to capture her and find out what she could tell us about future obstructive actions. They also directed me to take defensive actions with the individuals assisting her."

"Did she provide anything of value?"

"Despite her tenacious efforts to withhold information, we confirmed our existing suspicions."

"Continuing to hold her captive won't serve any further purpose. I think you can release her."

"Sir, I should make you aware her current physical appearance is unpleasant, and she is not conscious."

"Damn it, Charles. Is she still alive?"

"Yes, she is alive and breathing. We're done with her and can return her, if you wish."

"Can you contact the people she's working with?"

"Yes, sir. Cynthia provided a number we can call."

"Good. Clean her up and tell them where to find her. Call me for further instructions once you're done. Just make sure she's alive when they recover her."

"Will do, sir. I'll call later this morning for further orders."

"Wait. I will call you once I decide what is in the best interest of Aegis. Until then, keep talking with Cynthia. I want her to feel she is still running things."

"I understand, sir, and will await your call."

Jonathan was dialing Cynthia's number as soon as Charles clicked off. Skipping pleasantries, he addressed her in a brusque tone. "Cynthia, I'm sure you and David are aware of the new allegations published this morning?"

"Yes, we discussed them during breakfast."

"I have grave concerns and questions about the content."

"David and I share your concerns. However, we've discovered two of the reporter's sources and have taken appropriate steps to stop them."

"You call kidnapping an appropriate action? What in the hell were you and David thinking when you ordered that girl to be taken hostage? We work from the shadows, avoiding the specter of public awareness. Your decisions have rendered the opposite effect."

"It wasn't us. It was Charles. He said we needed to make an example of her to dissuade her accomplices. David and I told him we disagreed. Charles disregarded our concerns and took her hostage."

"Balderdash, or as you prefer to say, bullshit. I know he acted at your direction, which crossed an unacceptable line. I do not want any further aggressive steps. We need defensive maneuvers. Get David and put me on speakerphone."

"He's in the shower, and..."

"Well, get his ass out of the shower and call me back."

Jonathan closed the call as Jackson walked in, telling him to turn on his television to hear about multiple explosions in New York City. "I thought this reporting might affect your decisions, sir." Jonathan watched in disbelief, knowing Cynthia and David had stretched his level of tolerance beyond acceptable bounds. *Two of our best assets have become intolerable liabilities.*

Cynthia and David were comparing thoughts and strategies before returning Jonathan's call. David was pacing the floor as Cynthia spoke. "Let's make the call, listen to what he has to say, and shore up support for your nomination. I know I have his confidence from the last board meeting and can reason with him."

Knowing his father's behaviors, David shook his head. "I'm sure he's heard about the explosions and is fuming. I don't know if we can quell his anger. Call him and let him spout his demands. We can decide what's best after finishing the call."

Cynthia dialed Jonathan's number, placing the call on speaker as she closed her eyes and took a deep breath. "Jonathan, I have David with me."

David started with a soft greeting. "Good morning, Father."

"Oh shit, David, you can cut trying to be respectful or pleasant. You've created a shit show up there, and it requires immediate damage control."

"We can manage the fallout and have supporters ready to help defend us from these false allegations."

"Good God, you are so out of touch with reality. Your defenders may have been willing to help yesterday, but today's charges and destructive attacks will send them running to save their asses, not yours. You're the one who must step up and defend your nomination. You must convince everyone the charges are false. It's time to try turning the tables, David."

CHAPTER 54

Turning Tables

David squinted, contorting his expression as Jonathan started crafting ideas for limiting damage to the nomination. After a few minutes, David's face regained its normal shape, breaking into a wicked smirk as he listened to Jonathan's agenda.

"You need to schedule a press conference for tomorrow, where you will read a prepared statement. Cynthia can create the statement while you spend the day calling the president, congressional leaders, and political allies to shore up support. Your messaging between the statement and phone conversations must be consistent. It should convey a feeling of surprise, disgust, and amazement at the brazen attack on your character. The content needs to create a vivid picture of you as the wounded victim, turning the tables on their narrative. You must make Samantha and her associates the villains. Tell people your life is being threatened because of these falsehoods. Become the victim, David. I know your flair for the dramatic, and this is not the time for it."

Cynthia, relishing Jonathan's direction, asked, "How can we get David ready to manage an onslaught of questions from the press? I know reading a statement will leave them shouting questions and clamoring for answers."

"He must tell them he will not answer questions because of investigations into the source of the attacks. Use the line of 'ongoing investigations'; this will allow him to avoid making further statements and exit the stage while they shout."

"How should he explain Adira's kidnapping?"

"I will talk with Charles about cleaning up your boondoggled mess. Again, David should not answer questions about her, the kidnapping, the accusations of an abortion, or the recent bombings. Read a written statement and tell them you have no further comment."

David was shaking his head. "I'm a skilled jurist with years of handling demands from lawyers while sitting on the bench. I think I can manage a gaggle of feebleminded reporters. Refusing to answer questions makes it look like I have something to hide."

There was a long pause in their conversation. "You may be a judge, but you are not a renowned legal scholar or skilled performer. I know your style, David. You love the spotlight and can't resist embellishing information by ad-libbing. Going off script will be a disaster. They will eat you alive and create further doubt and suspicion. Stick to a scripted statement and be done with it."

"I disagree with your assessment of my capabilities. I can manage the situation by starting with a statement and then answering their inquiries."

"David, listen to me. What I'm about to say is not advice from a father, but sage wisdom from someone who's witnessed disastrous encounters with the press. The expression 'A man who represents himself has a fool for a client' will have significant application if you attempt to answer questions. I am telling you not to take questions. It is not in your best interest, nor is it in the best interest of Aegis."

"Well, Father, we will have to agree to disagree. Cynthia will handle crafting my opening statement, and I will handle the press." David reached across the desk, closing the call.

Cynthia was wide-eyed, holding her palms up and tilting her head as David railed. "What a pompous old bastard. We'll do this my way and show him and his almighty board what I can accomplish."

"So you're going to disregard his advice?"

"Damn right I am. You will work on the content of the message. I will begin calling the president and congressional leaders. They'll have questions, and those will prepare me for facing reporters. This is my moment, and I will not hide."

Jonathan was shaking his head at David's reaction and the abrupt end to their call. He walked to the liquor cabinet to pour one of his prize bourbons, thinking, *I knew he would reject my suggestions. He will go down, as did our valiant rebel patriots at Gettysburg. I must assemble the board to explain it is time to cut our losses.*

CHAPTER 55

Imagine

Charles stood over Adira's battered and bruised body, which was crumpled on the floor like a pile of soiled linens. He thought, *It would have been much easier if you'd cooperated. I was willing to return you unharmed, but you were determined to resist. Your attitude did not serve you well, my dear.*

He turned to the man guarding her. "Get some help and clean her up. We'll be making a return as soon as I contact her friends. I have the perfect location to leave her in."

Roy returned to Jack's house after spending the day pursuing leads, trying to discover where Charles might have taken Adira. Lydia unlocked the door. "I hope you had better luck than we did making phone calls and getting nowhere."

"I don't think so. It seems like they've vanished into thin air. I've got numerous contacts scouring the city for leads. Something will turn up."

They joined Jack and Sam at the kitchen island, which had become a gloomy command post. "Since I don't have any answers, have you heard any information on the bombings?"

Jack answered for Sam and Lydia. "According to preliminary reports, the same person or people assembled all three devices, and we know the short list of suspects. Do you agree this is Charles and his men?"

"Without a doubt. Mansa has been working up information on his crew. It looks like he recruited individuals from his days with the Wagner Group. These are not common street thugs. They're ruthless, trained killers."

Sam folded her arms. "Dealing with trained killers wasn't what we expected with our project, but it's a dilemma we have to contend with if we're going to rescue Adira and stop David's nomination. I hope we can find her soon."

Lydia was nodding in agreement. "She's smart and resilient. I know she'll survive this ordeal and be back with us soon. Lucas is also trying to get help. He reached out to high-ranking FBI officials and some other agencies, telling them the abduction was a ploy to pressure him into endorsing David's appointment."

Roy looked at Lydia. "Who did he contact, and did they express a willingness to help?"

"I don't know exactly who he talked with, but they told him it's too much of a political issue for them to get involved with."

"Yeah, I got hit with sidestepping excuses with some of my requests."

They were sitting in shared silence, seeming to have exhausted all their options, when Lydia's phone started ringing. She hesitated to answer, seeing the caller ID was unknown.

Sam looked at her with raised eyebrows, saying, "Lydia, you need to answer your phone. It could be Charles or whoever has Adira."

Lydia sighed, rolling her eyes as she answered using the speaker option. "This is Lydia. Who's calling?"

"You sound distressed, love. It's Charles calling to chat."

"Where is she, Charles?"

"My, my. You always seem to be so impatient and using such a nasty tone."

"Cut the cute crap, Charles, and tell us where she is so we can get her back."

He was laughing as Lydia grew more indignant. "All in due time, dear. It sounds like you have me on speakerphone. I hope Samantha is listening. I'm so looking forward to meeting you again, Sam."

Roy motioned for Lydia to keep Charles talking as he began recording the conversation.

"Aha. A lengthy pause tells me you're trying to record or trace our chitchat. I can wait if you need extra time to run a trace. Of course, it will not work."

"You're such an ass, Charles. Tell us where we can find Adira."

"First things first, my dear. Are you willing to accommodate my requests?"

Jack signaled for everyone to remain quiet, leaving Charles to continue rambling.

"Mmm. Another moment of silence tells me we may be at a stalemate. I would guess everyone is anxious to learn where your lovely friend is. I can tell you she's resting right now. However, I will disclose her location in a moment. Excuse me one moment."

Charles's voice became muffled as he seemed to be giving instructions. "Sorry for the interruption. Where were we? Ah, yes. How do you find your sweet Adira? I hope you're a John Lennon fan. I enjoy his music, especially when he twists his lyrics into riddles. Are you aware that he was a fan of using riddles in his music?"

Lydia couldn't contain herself and began screaming at the phone. "What the fuck does his music have to do with finding Adira?"

"Oh, Lydia. Using such foul language degrades the high-class image you try to present. It reveals what a street slut you really are." He paused, waiting for a rebuttal before laughing. "I thought calling you a street slut would provoke your temper further, but alas, no. So back to my musical mystery. Using a riddle makes finding Adira a fun adventure. Like a scavenger hunt, with her being the prize if you solve the riddle. Wait a minute. I seem to have incompetent help preparing Adira for travel." This time, he muted the call.

The three-minute interruption ended with Charles's return. "Well, Adira is on her way to meet you, but where will that be? Seeing the weather is so chilly, I hope you'll solve my riddle before she gets too cold."

This time, it was Sam yelling at the phone. "Get on with the riddle so we can find her."

They could almost hear a teasing smile from Charles as he responded to the fresh voice. "That must be Sam. She sounds as feisty as Adira. Like two peas in a pod. This is such fun for me. Are you ready? You need to pay close attention to the words before I hang up."

He cleared his throat. "Imagine a field of strawberries. It's where you'll find her resting peacefully with eyes closed, where nothing seems real. Just strawberry fields forever. Imagine—it's easy if you try." The connection ended in the middle of a self-satisfied cackle.

The four of them looked at one another, trying to solve the puzzling riddle. Roy broke the trance, slapping the island countertop. "Central Park. The Lennon memorial. It has to be where he's taken her."

Sam asked, "But where? The memorial covers acres."

Roy headed for the door. "Once we're there, we can spread out and search for her."

Jack was shaking his head. "No need to search. There's a sidewalk mosaic called Imagine in honor of Lennon's song. I'm sure that will be the location. We're less than ten minutes from the Seventy-Second Street entrance to the park and memorial. Grab coats and hats. Roy, you drive."

Everyone was scrambling for the door as Sam raced up to the bedrooms. "I'm getting blankets in case we need them."

After piling into Roy's car, they raced to the park's entrance. He pulled to the curb as Jack and the girls tumbled out, and they ran into the area. Jack had guessed correctly. They found Adira curled up in the fetal position, partially covered by a black plastic trash bag on top of the mosaic.

Sam pulled the bag off and wrapped Adira in blankets as Jack lifted her off the pavement. Lydia brushed away Adira's golden locks from her face, revealing swollen eyes and her hair matted with blood. "Oh my god. Her face is still oozing blood." She looked at Jack and Sam. "Those bastards!"

Adira was motionless as Jack laid her across Sam's and Lydia's laps in the car's back seat. "Head for Presbyterian Hospital on Sixty-Eighth, Roy. It's a Level 1 trauma center. They'll be able to handle her condition."

After Adira had spent unending hours in the emergency room with a critical-care team attending to her injuries, the hospital finally admitted her. Roy provided police officers with details and played the recorded conversation with Charles.

The lead trauma physician updated the group on Adira's condition. "Your friend is in critical condition. She's fortunate to have survived, having suffered a traumatic brain injury. At this time, she is in a coma. We're moving her to the ICU, where we can treat the injuries and monitor her recovery."

Lydia began firing a series of questions. "When will she be conscious? Will she be able to tell us what happened? Can I stay with her until she wakes up?"

Sam put her arm around Lydia. "I know how close you and Adira are to each other. It may be best to leave her with the professionals, and we'll wait for their call."

The doctor continued. "We'll monitor her and hope she comes out of the coma soon. It could be within a day or two, but she may not remember what happened. Amnesia is a common outcome with someone in her condition. She's young and could have a faster-than-average recovery. You can stay near her if it will be of comfort to you, but she won't be able to respond to you. However, the brain may pick up on sounds from loved ones. Some studies suggest talking to and touching someone in a coma may help the person recover. I can arrange for one of you to be in the ICU waiting room and visit with her if you like."

Lydia's eyes were tearing up as she looked at Sam. "I need to be here with her. The three of you go back and figure out how to get him. I'll call if I need help or if there's any change in her condition. Trust me, Sam—this is the best place for me and Adira." Sam conceded to Lydia's request, and they exchanged embraces.

Jack delayed their departure, saying, "We need to set up security here."

Roy spoke out, mentioning that he had finished speaking with Mansa. "He's sending two men to be here with Lydia and Adira."

"Okay, thanks."

Roy turned to Lydia. "Mansa's men will tell you he sent them, and then they will become invisible. I know you don't like someone watching you, but circumstances have changed."

She looked at Roy, questioning. "What about the rest of you needing security?"

"We have men in place watching Jack's house. Mansa also has a team watching Ethan's editor's house."

Lydia nodded, her eyes moving to look at her partners. "I appreciate everything you're doing. Stay safe and find that son of a bitch."

Once they left, Lydia headed for the ICU, dialing Ryleigh to catch her up on developments and Adira's condition.

CHAPTER 56

Cutting Ties

The morning broadcast flashed a breaking-news alert announcing a press conference at ten by the front-running possible Supreme Court chief justice nominee, David Jaymes. "Sources indicate Chief Judge David Jaymes will address recent accusations surrounding his possible nomination for chief justice of the Supreme Court. He will read a brief statement and answer questions from the press. We will carry the event live."

Jonathan closed his eyes, shaking his head in dismay while finishing an email to his board, calling for an emergency phone conference at noon. His exception to the invitation was Cynthia Jaymes.

His relationship with Ryleigh had ended in what he thought to be irreconcilable differences. Over the past month, Jackson had encouraged him to mend fences with her. Fearing failure, he dreaded calling her, knowing that doing so could destroy the last remnants of hope for reconciliation. After hearing Cynthia's plea to corroborate her offer to Ryleigh, he reluctantly dialed.

Ryleigh answered the call on the first ring. "Jonathan, I'm surprised to hear from you and almost declined to answer. Are you calling to confirm Cynthia's offer where you grant me firstborn rights or to recommend watching David make an ass out of himself on national television?"

"Cynthia just called me to explain what she'd presented to you. She did so without my approval, but I called to hear your reply for myself."

Ryleigh rolled her eyes at Jonathan's question. "She said you would restore our relationship and grant me priority rights to your estate when you pass. The offer was contingent upon my allowing David's nomination to proceed without further interference."

"And what is your answer?"

"My answer? I can't believe you're asking after our last visit. There will be no reconciliation. It's time to stop you, David, and Aegis."

Jonathan leaned forward on his desk. "Given your final refusal to cooperate, the purpose of my call is to retract Cynthia's offer and sever all ties with you. Your conspiracy against us leaves me with no choice but to end our family relationship."

"That's so rich coming from you. I was the one who severed ties and ended our relationship. You and David deserve each other. Your bond of arrogance and entitlement is more than I ever wanted to be associated with, but scolding you further is a waste of time. So I will thank you for disowning me."

Jonathan was out of his chair, his face flushing as he walked onto the veranda. "Do you realize the power I can wield to wreak havoc against your enterprise? Of course not! However, I will take a benevolent tone in providing you with a parting holiday gift of time to prepare. Put your affairs in order, my dear. The next year will cause you extreme distress." Jonathan ended the call before Ryleigh could respond.

His cherished Glencairn glasses were getting frequent use—Jonathan poured an early-morning selection from his bourbon collection. His gait was slow as he crossed the room, thinking. *Is it worth the effort and aggravation to test*

Chandler's willpower and loyalty to his family? He dialed the number, not feeling confident Chandler would take his call.

Chandler provided a surprisingly immediate answer. "Hello?"

"Chandler, this is Jonathan Jaymes. Do you have time for a conversation?"

"Jonathan, it's been a long time since we last spoke. I'm sure this is not a cordial call, but perhaps I'm wrong. What is the purpose of your call?" Chandler's eyes were wide open as he pointed to his phone, looking at Ryleigh's astonished expression.

"This is a business call following up on an offer I believe Cynthia may have conveyed on my behalf."

"If you're calling to see what I've decided, the answer I gave her was a nonretractable no, and it has not changed."

"I'm surprised you will sacrifice family values for a losing cause."

"Times have changed, Jonathan. I discussed Cynthia's offer with my father. He and I agree: there is nothing to fear. Let me be clear by repeating that the answer remains no."

"There must be something about the environment in New York. It seems to make people unwilling to use sound reasoning when presented with opportunities. In closing, I will give you the same generous consideration as Ryleigh. I recommend you and your family put your affairs in order. Great distress will come your way in the new year." As with his call to Ryleigh, Jonathan ended without waiting for a response.

He slipped on a light jacket to go outside for a breath of fresh air, walking the long entrance road into the plantation. Two calls down, with predictable outcomes. *David's press conference will set the agenda for my call with the board. Your fate is in your hands, David.*

CHAPTER 57

Press Conference

David and Cynthia's neighborhood, driveway, and front yard were teeming with news trucks, satellite dishes, and a swarming mass of reporters. Cynthia walked back from the foyer, speaking to David as she adjusted his tie and jacket in the kitchen. "You look fine, David." She stepped back to give a final approving look. "Are you positive this is what you want to do?"

"How many times do I have to repeat my answer to you? This is my moment to rise out of the shadows of lower-court anonymity to the pinnacle of judiciary greatness. Historians will take note and write great things about me after today." He straightened his posture while shaking his shoulders.

"Do you want me out there with you? I can provide a statement of support."

"I appreciate your willingness to stand with me. Just smile, look supportive, and do not speak. I will do the talking. Sorry to be blunt, but this is one time you are mere window dressing." Cynthia stood motionless, with her mouth open, as David brushed her aside, heading for the porch with its podium and array of microphones. He turned to snap his fingers, motioning for her to follow.

Standing tall and defiant, David lifted his eyes and chin to survey the assembled crowd. He looked right and left, silently chastising the crowd for the ongoing conversation.

Like a performer, he waited for the commotion to settle into whispers. Clearing his throat, he adjusted several microphones before speaking. "I will read a statement refuting recent false accusations against me and my family. Please hold inquiries until I finish reading. Then, I will take questions."

David held his prepared statement and began reading. "I am offended, stunned, and appalled by the false attacks meant to derail my pending nomination to the highest court in the land. These accusations are nothing more than lies meant to slander my reputation. They are an attempt to prevent my nomination, the pending hearings, and the approval process by Congress. Stories of coercion, blackmail, illicit encounters, and kidnapping are the hysterical fantasies of deranged individuals." He paused, smiling as reporters started yelling questions. Shaking his head, he motioned for quiet.

"And now they make the ultimate accusation against one of the strongest pro-life proponents in the judiciary. They could not contain their lewd fantasies about my having raped a minor. They went for the jugular, propounding a hideous claim that I demanded an abortion from a woman I did not know and have never known. This woman is a false witness recruited and coached in trying to destroy my past and future professional legacies." He paused and resurveyed the crowd.

"These false allegations will be the biggest challenge I have ever faced. Once you hear all the facts, I am confident that I will prove my innocence and become the new chief justice of the highest court in the land. I can tell you I am not a villain. I am the victim facing their flailing false claims and even threats against my life." Cynthia closed her eyes, shaking her head.

David watched as reporters wrote furiously and held recording devices to capture his statement of defense. "At this time, I will answer your questions."

Back in Raleigh, Jonathan Jaymes turned away from the television to stare out the window, thinking, *And now they will have your head on a platter.*

Simultaneous shouts made it impossible to hear a single question, let alone deliver a response. David raised his arms, shouting into the microphones, "Please calm down. I will call on you one at a time."

A reporter near the front shouted without having been selected, "Is it true there are videos of sexual encounters used to blackmail politicians who might oppose your nomination?"

"I know nothing of indiscretions by politicians, and if they do exist, they have no connection to me or my work as a federal judge. Next question."

"What is your association with the organization Aegis?"

"Aegis is an independent group of citizens trying to preserve an impartial judiciary system. My family has a long history of working with this group, but it has no impact or influence on my role as a federal judge. Next question."

"Who is making threats against your life?"

"There have been a growing number of anonymous threats we will be investigating. At this time, I do not know the source of those threats." He raised his eyes to the back of the gaggle. "You in the back, waving a folder."

"If you are a true advocate of the pro-life position, why did you and your father coerce a sixteen-year-old girl to have an abortion?"

"That accusation is a total fabrication. The claim about that incident is without merit, and they are paying the woman making those statements."

"Is it true she became pregnant after you raped her at a fraternity party?"

David's face was taut, his eyes glaring at the reporter. "Again, the accusation is a lie." He tried to select another reporter, but the young man from the back continued.

"I've interviewed the victim, and she is willing to testify with supporting witnesses. What is your response?"

Shaking a pointed finger at the young man asking questions, David leaned forward into the podium. "Who are you, and how dare you make such outrageous and unfounded statements?"

The man continued as the crowd quieted to hear his questioning. "Will the charges remain unfounded if one of the corroborating witnesses is a member of your family?"

"What news organization are you with?"

"Will President Lawrence support your nomination once he learns a member of the Senate Judiciary Committee is being blackmailed into supporting your selection?"

"I will not lend credence to your ridiculous inquiries. Ladies and gentlemen, this is an example of how I am being attacked, this time by an infiltrator who is not authorized to be here. Security, get him out."

"My name is Ethan Brode. I am a registered member of the press and an investigative reporter for the *Insider*. I'm the one publishing the series of stories about you and your family's organization."

Recognizing his name from the byline in his articles, the crowd turned its attention away from David, beginning to swarm around Ethan, shouting questions about what he knew and who his sources were.

David's face flushed red as sweat beaded on his forehead. "Pay no attention to him. His statements are lies. Again, the only victim is me. Security! Remove him!"

Ethan assured his colleagues that he had valid information. "I can't divulge any sources at this time." Security fought through the mass and dragged Ethan off the property.

With Ethan gone, the crowd returned its attention to David. His hands trembled as the journalists became uncontrollable, shouting for the names of his family members, asking what fraternity he was a member of in college, who the senator was, and more, until the tsunami of questions overwhelmed him.

He turned, looking to Cynthia for help, but she shrugged her shoulders and stormed into the house. Unable to gain control, David gathered his notes and followed Cynthia, closing the door behind them.

Once inside, Cynthia turned and slapped David's face with all the force her petite stature could leverage. Her voice was shrill and chastising. "You arrogant bastard. Your father warned you about this turning into another shit show. And yes, historians have taken note and will write about you. What they write will be far from worshipping praise."

He was stammering, trying to mount a defense. "It's that reporter's fault. I was in control until he started firing accusations and questions."

"In control? Bullshit, David. He raised pointed, damaging accusations, and none of it would have happened if you had taken Jonathan's advice. You needed only to read the statement and refuse to take questions. You didn't listen to your father and had the gall to turn to me for help after ordering me to be a silent adornment. I am not your window dressing." She raised a hand to silence any response, turning to leave David bewildered and speechless.

She started for her office, shouting as she walked, "Damn it, why didn't we listen to Jonathan? No way he'll help us after this fiasco. Maybe Roy can get a meeting with the troublemakers to call a truce. I need to call Charles to see what he's done with Adira. What a fine fucking mess, David." She slammed the door, heading for her desk and phone.

The contentious two-hour call with his board exhausted Jonathan. In spite of David's embarrassing news conference, the board members opposed Jonathan's plan to have the president withdraw David's name for chief justice. They wanted to see what would happen during the upcoming Christmas recess break by Congress. Jonathan knew their direction would be a futile attempt to save the nomination, so he placed a call to Charles.

"Charles, have you returned Adira?"

"Yes, sir, we observed a group picking her up in Central Park. She went to Presbyterian Hospital for treatment and observation."

"She was alive when they found her?"

"Yes, sir."

"Good. Have you talked with Cynthia?"

"No, sir."

"Well, call and update her. You can explain that I ordered the return. I need you to keep communicating with her, but do not let her know you and I are talking. And keep me informed about what they're doing. Later…" Jonathan paused, exhaling an audible breath.

Charles interrupted the silence. "Our connection cut out as you said something about later."

"We didn't lose the connection. It was a moment of hesitation. Critical actions may be needed, but I will call once I reach a decision."

"I will be in contact, Jonathan, and alert you to questionable orders or behavior from Cynthia or David." Charles looked at his screen, which showed an incoming call from Cynthia. He ended his conversation with Jonathan before switching to her.

"Cynthia, how can I be of service?"

"I wanted to follow up with you regarding Adira. Did you get any useful information from her?"

"She didn't provide any information outside of what we already knew."

"Then let her go. Keeping her hostage serves no further purpose."

"I dropped her off to her friends yesterday after Jonathan called and told me to do so."

"What? That meddling old bastard went around me, ordering her release? You do not work for Jonathan; you work for me, and you can tell him to stop micromanaging while I'm CEO of Aegis. Am I making myself clear?"

"Your instructions are quite clear. Do you have any further assignments for me or my men?"

"Not today, but soon. Just remain available. And call me if Jonathan continues to interfere."

Cynthia ended the call with Charles. Pulling a notepad onto her desk, she began listing options to pursue. *Ryleigh and Chandler have gone quiet, meaning they'll pass on my offers. My best chance of clearing problems starts with Roy arranging a face-to-face meeting.*

Charles can terminate Samantha and anyone accompanying her to the meeting. Once she's out of the picture, he can travel to Raleigh and terminate Jonathan. It's the best way to remove obstacles and move on. The board will welcome my actions and continue with David's nomination.

With a sinister smile, she dialed Roy's number, but the call went to voicemail. "Roy, Cynthia Jaymes calling to see if you're willing to step up and be a peacemaker. We're ready to meet and negotiate a deal. I'll keep the option open until Christmas. Call me."

CHAPTER 58
Concerning Decisions

The morning light was still and dark as Sam walked into the kitchen, finding Jack with a distant look on his face. He winked, and his expression brightened into a pleasant smile as she approached him. "I was just pouring coffee for me and Roy. You look like you could use some as well."

"Thanks. Any word from Lydia on Adira's condition?"

Roy tapped his hand on the counter. "I went to the hospital around four this morning to check. Lydia said there's been no change. I tried to get her to come back here to rest, but she wasn't having it. Maybe you can talk to her about it."

"Let me get dressed so you can drive me over. I'll tell her to come back here to freshen up so I can spend time with Adira." She turned to Jack. "The safety of our team is weighing heavily on me after all the recent incidents. I feel responsible for getting all these people involved. It wasn't their fight, but they were willing to jump in for their own reasons and mine. I didn't think it would turn this violent."

She sighed, lowering her head. "Sorry if I ramble this morning, but I feel like a mother hen worrying about her brood. Sitting at the hospital will give me quiet time to process my thoughts." Raising her head, she continued, "It's my project. I need to decide what we do from here."

Jack reached out to hold her hand. "Would you like me to be there with you?"

"I would, but not yet. My life has been upside down since I heard about David's nomination. You've been the bright spot in the middle of my storm. I need to consider if my priorities should be reset. Then I'll be ready to hear what you think." She leaned forward to kiss him. "But I'd love some breakfast from my favorite private chef before going to the hospital."

She turned to Roy. "I'll be ready to go once I shower and have a quick bite to eat."

Sam walked back and forth in the hospital's hallway, having a lengthy conversation, convincing Lydia to let Roy take her back to Jack's for some rest. She checked in with the nursing station for an update on Adira after they left. "We've been telling Ms. Mathers that the patient's condition is still listed as serious, but you can visit with her."

"I know she's unconscious. Last night the doctor said she might hear my voice. I'm hoping she can, and that it might bring her comfort."

The nurse motioned for a man to come to the desk and clear Sam as an authorized visitor. "Sorry about the verification, but your security team insists no one outside our staff have access to Ms. Tomasz without their approval."

Sam looked up at the imposing figure, asking, "You must work for Mansa?" He nodded without speaking as the nurse stepped from behind the desk to lead Sam to Adira's room.

"I would recommend keeping bedside visits to only fifteen minutes at a time. You should also check with us to make sure we're not in the process of doing a treatment or evaluating her condition."

"I understand and will follow your guidelines."

Expecting to see Adira with an array of tubes and devices working to keep her alive, Sam was surprised to see her appearing to be napping. Her face remained swollen and bruised, but she seemed at peace. Sam reached out to hold and smooth her hand gently. "Oh, sweetie, what have they done to you? I did not know you would be in such harm's way."

Sam's vision blurred. "I wish I could have prevented this from happening. I wish we could have known each other sooner, under different circumstances. There will be time for us to be friends once you recover. I hope you can hear me and know how much we need you to come through this." Sam was unaware of the nurse approaching from behind until she handed Sam a tissue to dry her eyes.

As she turned to thank the nurse, her shoulders slumped, and the nurse embraced her. "I hate to interrupt, but we need you to return to the waiting area. The doctors want to make an assessment. Your friend is a fighter. She'll survive this, and you'll have opportunities to be together again."

———•———

Ryleigh and Chandler were deep in conversation about their calls from Cynthia. "I'm not willing to accept Cynthia's offer, Chandler. I don't trust her or my father, and I've traveled too far down this road to change directions. However, you face a significant risk to your family."

Chandler drummed his fingers on the table. "My father and I have had discussions over the years concerning threats to disclose that I'm biracial. Times have changed since Jonathan threatened us, and the risk is not what it was in years past. So I agree with you on refusing Cynthia's offer. My family is no longer afraid, and your father will not bully us."

Ryleigh bit her lip, pausing the discussion. "Lydia's call about Adira being kidnapped shook my foundation. I wasn't ready for it or for the bombing of homes and Ethan's office. Things have escalated out of control, and we're all in danger."

Chandler reached out to hold her hand. "You don't have to worry about Adira or Ethan. I've talked with Jack. He's enlisted the help of an old friend, who also has a connection with Roy, to protect them." Ryleigh was about to ask questions, but Chandler held up a hand to continue.

"Our friend goes by one name, Mansa. Jack and I know him from years ago when they were in Attica together. I'm not sure how he and Roy are connected, but Mansa said they work together on special projects. They've set up safe zones for all of us. Trust me—we are in excellent hands. His group is well trained and disciplined for this type of work."

Ryleigh reached for Chandler's hand. "I'm glad to know there are people trying to protect all of us. With everything happening, you and I need to talk about a long-overdue decision. We need to tell Sam the truth about the twins."

"Are you ready to go there after all these years of hiding it from her? She may not forgive us."

"Current circumstances leave us no choice, and it's a risk we must take. We should talk with Jack and Roy to tell them everything before we tell Sam."

"When would you like to meet?"

"Today, if possible. Call and see if they can meet us here, but without Sam." Chandler agreed and dialed Jack's number while Ryleigh went to the kitchen for water.

She returned as Chandler finished the call. "Yes, just you and Roy. Mansa's crew is watching your house, so Lydia will be safe while you're here. Yes, this is important. Thanks, Jack. We'll expect you at eleven."

Jack tried to anticipate the purpose of Chandler's request. "Whatever prompted him to call us seemed serious." Roy didn't offer any thought as they rang Ryleigh's doorbell.

Chandler opened the door with a solemn look on his face. "Gentlemen, thank you for being available on such short notice. If you follow me to the dining room, I'll let Ryleigh explain our situation and what must be accomplished."

Ryleigh took a seat at the end of the table, waiting for Jack and Roy to join her. "Thank you for meeting with us. Considering recent events, Chandler and I have decided we must share facts that could affect Sam's project."

Jack wrinkled his face. "Wait a minute. Shouldn't Sam be here if we need to modify the project?"

"In a perfect world, she would be here, but what you're about to learn needs consideration by the four of us about how we make Sam aware of past events. Final decisions for altering the project's course will be her decision."

Roy leaned back in his chair, shifting his focus between Ryleigh and Chandler. "Okay, there seems to be an elephant in the room, but Jack and I can't see it. Let's get it out in the open and stop using vague references."

Chandler was drumming his fingers on the table, taking the lead. "I agree, Roy. So let me reveal the elephant, and then we can provide explanations. Sam's twins are alive and well. They were not stillborn. Ryleigh and I spirited them away to protect Sam and them from Jonathan. Once he learned Ryleigh was hiding Sam and helping her avoid an abortion, he was adamant about taking the twins. He demanded custody, leaving Sam with no rights or ability to interact with them. Sam was aware of Jonathan making life difficult for her, Ryleigh, and me."

Jack leaned forward, glaring. "What the hell, Chandler? The two of you kept this from Sam for all these years? Did it ever occur to you to tell her the truth? Did you..."

Roy placed a hand on Jack's arm to restrain him from striking out at Chandler. "Hang on, Jack. Let them provide more background. Ryleigh, can you add to Chandler's explanation and try to answer Jack's question?"

She sat stoically with her hands folded as Jack eased back. "Jonathan was furious when he learned there would be no abortion. Sam and I spent months on the run, trying to stay hidden from his henchmen. I negotiated a final deal with my father after the twins were born."

"What was the damn deal?" Jack struggled to contain his growing anger.

Ryleigh gathered her thoughts before continuing. "Chandler and I had planned for them to be raised by foster families who were willing to do so without proper documentation. At first, Jonathan demanded control, but I talked him out of it. Ultimately, he allowed us to make decisions without divulging further information. However, he continued his efforts to find them. His investigators got certificates of live birth and statements from the clinical staff. We never revealed their names, location, or any information that could lead to their discovery."

Jack was shaking his head, raising the tenor of his voice. "Where were they sent? Did you and Chandler somehow raise them? How can you call yourself a friend after doing this to Sam?"

"Look, Jack, we were in a difficult and fragile situation. Chandler and I were trying to protect…"

Chandler patted Ryleigh's hand to calm her rising tension. "Let me answer Jack's questions, Ryleigh. We were scrambling to keep the twins out of Jonathan's reach. The decision to separate them made it more difficult for Jonathan's men to find them. We knew Jonathan would continue trying, no matter what we agreed upon. He never slowed the efforts to find them for over fifteen years. Ryleigh and I provided the families with funds to raise each child. The families required contractual assurances they could raise the children without fear of losing them. If Sam had known, she would have wanted them back. Everything was at risk because there were no legal adoption records. If Jonathan found them, we knew he would swoop in and take them away. It all developed rapidly, and again, we tried to do what we thought best."

Jack looked at Roy with quizzical silence, letting Roy say, "Okay, we've got the picture." Roy turned his attention to Ryleigh. "Two questions. Why wasn't Sam told about all this once they became adults, and where are they now?"

Ryleigh drew a long breath as her eyes began tearing up. She shared her secret past about Jonathan raping his wife's maid, getting her pregnant, and demanding to have Ryleigh aborted. "My mother died during childbirth; my stepmother, Elizabeth Jaymes, would not allow an abortion. She saved my life and raised me as her own. Finding out Sam was pregnant and hearing my father demand an abortion brought me full circle. I knew I had to step up and save Sam's twins."

Chandler listened in amazement, along with Jack and Roy. "Ryleigh, does that mean you're biracial, the same as me?"

"Yes."

"But you never told me."

"I never told you because of the shame I felt at Jonathan's actions and because of the promise of sworn silence Elizabeth requested on her deathbed. I didn't even tell Jonathan what I knew until last month, when I visited him for the last time. It's a secret that's clouded my judgment for years."

Turning to Jack and Roy, she said, "I could give you a long list of reasons for not telling Sam about her twins, but none would sound acceptable to you. I thought there would be a time when we could broach the subject with her and clear the air. You need to know that Chandler and I are the only family Sam has had over the years, and we simply feared that disclosing what had happened would destroy our relationship. All we can do is ask forgiveness and your help in explaining things to her."

Jack folded his hands in front of his face. "Okay, now we know the truth and motives. That leaves us with having to ask—who and where are the twins?"

Ryleigh broke into tears, raising her hand to stop Jack as she left the room. Roy looked at Chandler, who was shaking his head, waiting on Ryleigh. "I'm sorry, but this is the most difficult part of why we needed to talk with the two of you before telling Sam."

Returning with a box of tissue, Ryleigh looked at Jack and Roy as they waited. With a heavy sigh, straightening her shoulders forward, she announced, "Adira and Ethan are the twins. They are as much in the dark about their connection as Sam."

Jack shifted forward in his chair, wide-eyed, as Roy responded, "Ethan and Adira?"

Ryleigh regained her composure as the disclosure settled over the four of them. "Yes, and Adira's hospitalization was the final straw, telling us it was time to reveal the truth. We have two ways to tell Sam. Chandler and I can meet with her and tell her what we've told you. Another option would be for you to tell her and then call us to talk with her. Either way, she'll be furious, and we need an opportunity to explain our actions."

Roy's phone buzzed, showing Lydia as the caller. "Yes, we're finishing up. Whoa, slow down. Okay, take a deep breath, Lydia. Stay with Sam. Have her call us when things settle and she's ready to return to Jack's."

Ending the call, Roy froze for a moment, blinking his eyes as he tried to process what he had just heard. "Lydia's back at the hospital. Sam called her. Adira woke up. She's coming out of her coma."

Ryleigh kept crying into a fresh tissue. The sight of her dismay brought Jack out of his chair to place an arm around her as she leaned into him, saying, "Thank God. I've been afraid we would lose her." She sat back, placing a hand against Jack's chest and looking up at him. "I was a fool not to trust you, Jack. And I was selfish in hiding the truth from Sam. I hope you and she can find it in your hearts to forgive us. Somehow, Chandler and I will make amends."

"It's easy for me to forgive, Ryleigh. We need to explain all this to Sam. Maybe Adira's recovery will be the source of understanding and forgiveness for her."

"How do you recommend Chandler and I handle it?"

Jack seemed to search for an answer as Roy spoke. "I think Jack and I should talk with her and…"

Jack interrupted Roy's exchange. "No. There's no gentle way to expose this wound. As they say, it's like a Band-Aid, with the best method for removal being to rip it off. Come to my house, and we'll wait for Sam to return from the hospital. Let her tell us what's happening with Adira, and then you can tell her the truth. Roy and I can try to help, but it's up to Sam how she reacts."

Ryleigh agreed with Jack's assessment and plan, with one addition. "Can I call Ethan and have him there when we tell Sam? He's out on a limb, researching and writing alone. This is a good time for us to come clean with him and Sam."

Jack looked at Roy, who was shrugging his shoulders without voicing an opinion. "Well, I'll speak for Roy and me and say yes. Nothing to continue hiding from anyone."

CHAPTER 59

Coming Clean

Chandler and Ryleigh arrived at Jack's house to find Ethan opening the door for them. "Have you guys heard the news about Adira?"

Ryleigh hugged Ethan, saying, "Yes, and we're here to learn details from Sam."

They followed Ethan to the kitchen area. Ryleigh asked, "Any further updates from the hospital, Jack?"

"Yeah. Some remarkable stuff is happening, but I'll let Sam sort it out once she arrives. She gives me information in small, exuberant sound bites." He gave Ryleigh a wink and smile. "I can tell you this much: Sam is in a great place with her emotions."

Everyone was getting comfortable, talking in front of the fireplace, as Roy and Sam arrived with Lydia. Sam was bright-eyed, almost skipping in through the kitchen area. "Rye, Chan, and Ethan! Oh my God. So glad you're all here. You will not believe what's happened. I even talked Lydia into joining the party while Adira settled down for some rest."

She turned to Jack, giving him an extended hug and kiss. "Honey, break out drinks for everyone to celebrate with while I hit the little girls' room." With a twirling move, she bounded up the stairs, humming a happy melody.

Roy laughed. "She's sky high, folks. You need to let her tell the story. It will all play well for what she'll hear later."

When Sam returned, Jack and Roy were filling drink orders as they gathered around the kitchen island command center. She cozied up to Jack while everyone looked on, waiting to hear her tale. "Okay. Where do I start? Oh God. Adira is out of her coma. The doctor said she's doing much better than expected. She's still disoriented but improving with each hour."

She stopped to catch her breath. "Here's the best part of what happened. I was holding her hand, talking to her, and hoping she could hear me. Suddenly, she blinked her eyes and squeezed my hand gently."

Lydia chimed in, saying, "The way Sam squealed over the phone, I thought something bad was happening."

Sam's eyes welled up. "That's when she smiled, and I thought my heart was going to jump out of my chest. I felt excitement like...like a mother holding her newborn for the first time. The way she looked at me melted my heart. I yelled for the nurse, and it seemed like half the hospital came running down the hall. It felt like a miracle."

Roy raised his glass. "Here's to Adira and a speedy recovery."

Ethan shouted an emphatic "Yes," launching a unison cheer of "Hear, hear!"

Jack turned to Sam. "Did the doctors give you any idea when they might release her?"

"They said it could be in as little as a few days based on her initial progress. On the way over, I talked with Lydia about the two of them staying here until Adira is stronger and it's safe to be away from here. I didn't think you'd have a problem with it, Jack."

He smiled down at her. "I'm good with whatever invitations and orders you propose. Mi casa, su casa."

"Thanks, sweetie. Oh, one last note. As we were leaving, I encountered Mansa talking to one of his men. He assured me they would keep watching Adira, so we shouldn't worry about her safety."

Chandler nodded, saying, "He's a good man to have on our side."

Sam chuckled. "And he's an imposing mountain of a man with incredible manners. He kept saying 'Yes, ma'am,' while I kept trying to get him to call me Sam."

The group grew quiet with sighs of relief. Ryleigh steepled her fingers in front of her mouth, exhaling. "Sam, this is one of the happiest moments I've ever seen in your eyes. You deserve joy and relief from the stress you've endured over the past twenty-seven years."

After hesitating, she said, "I need to move us on to a different topic, but one I hope will provide an equal moment for celebration. Chandler and I had a discussion with Jack and Roy regarding matters we need to tell you about. I'm fumbling for the right words and how to explain. I, uh…"

Sam tilted her head as she looked at Ryleigh. "No need to hesitate or stumble. Just tell me. We're family, Rye."

Chandler began speaking. "Sam, do you recall the pressure from Jonathan when you were pregnant and on the run with Ryleigh?"

"Of course I do. It seemed like a never-ending stream of threats and attempts to find us. Discovering I wasn't having an abortion turned Jonathan into an enraged maniac. I've never shared with anyone how much you and Rye sacrificed to keep me out of his clutches. I'm forever grateful to you for caring for me and almost saving the twins." Sam reached for Ryleigh's hand. "I never understood why you took me under your wing and fought your father. You and Chandler are my guardian angels."

Chandler was about to respond, but Ryleigh took over. "Well, Sam, the true ending to the story has details you weren't aware of. Let me start with why I did what I did." Ryleigh recounted the secrets behind her origins: her mother being ordered to have an abortion, Elizabeth refusing to let it happen, and Ryleigh finally disowning her father.

The group sat listening without speaking a word. Sam broke the silence. "You were trying to do for me what Elizabeth did for you. You were paying it forward. I had no idea."

"Yes, but there is more to tell you."

Sam laughed softly, saying, "More? I don't know if Jack has enough Kleenex."

Ryleigh patted Sam's hand. "We may need them. So here is the true ending to the story of saving you and the twins."

Jack reached out to hold Sam's other hand as she asked, "What do you mean by 'the true ending' and 'saving the twins'?"

"I don't know how to start other than by telling you the twins survived delivery. Chandler and I sent them off into hiding, with little time to spare. Jonathan's men showed up at the birthing clinic within an hour of their birth, trying to take them."

"Wait a minute. My twins weren't stillborn, and you never told me? You lied to me?" Sam's vocal volume was rising with each word as she pulled her hand from Ryleigh's.

"Yes, we did, but we were trying to protect you and the twins. I knew Jonathan wanted to harm them, and sending them away was the only solution. We never meant to hurt you and have no excuse for keeping the truth from you for all these years. I was terrified you would disown me."

Sam pushed Jack's hand aside and began pacing behind the counter. "My children are alive, and you never told me.

Rye, I've always wanted to believe they were alive. I daydreamed about them being happy, off safe somewhere." She glared at Chandler. "And you knew everything?"

"Yes. We can only ask for your forgiveness."

Sam stopped her pacing, standing inches from Ryleigh. "I want to scream, rant, and beat the shit out of you for this, but I know what we went through from the time Jonathan ordered me to have an abortion. I remember you telling me I'd be okay because you had a plan. I know you and Chandler love me like a little sister. I'm angry, pissed beyond belief, but I know I need to forgive you. It hurts."

She backed away with her hands on her hips. "Hold on. If the twins are alive, where the hell are they? Can I contact them?"

Ryleigh turned to her right, putting an arm around Ethan, whose mouth and eyes were wide at what he was witnessing. "Sam, I'd like you to meet Ethan Brode, your son."

Ethan darted his look to Ryleigh. "Sam's my mom? My mother and father told me I was adopted, and they didn't know the identity of my birth mother. They said it was an illegal adoption with no traceable records." He was trying to talk as Sam embraced him, burying her face into his shoulder, crying. Ethan cried as he wrapped his arms tightly around her, saying, "I never thought we'd ever meet."

Everyone in the group was stifling tears as Lydia spoke up. "Wait! If Ethan is Sam's son, why am I getting the feeling I know his sister?" She looked at Chandler. "Is Adira Sam's daughter and Ethan's sister?"

Chandler nodded. "Yes, Adira is the other twin."

Ethan shook his head, trying to grasp the realization of having found his mother and a sister he hadn't known existed. He turned back to Ryleigh. "You were always around, sending money to help my parents and me. They kept referring to you as Aunt Ryleigh. And all the time, you were my aunt."

"The reference was your parents' idea. They hoped one day you'd be able to learn the truth about me. Chandler and I were always in the background with the adoptive families. We never wanted to create conflict." She turned back to Sam. "We always wanted to tell you this secret we've carried for so long. There is no excuse for hiding the truth, and I'm relieved that it is no longer a secret."

Sam sat down on a barstool, leaning her elbows on the counter. "I'm exhausted and wondering how to tell Adira. Will she be able to handle this after what she's been through?"

"I think I can help you answer your questions." Everyone watched as Lydia started talking. "Adira and I have become more than just friends. We've shared deep feelings, questions, and wishful dreams. She's often wondered if she might ever find her birth mother. I know she, like Ethan, was told about her adoption and talked about Ryleigh always being there to help her family. She's tough but has a soft side. It will be a relief and uplifting revelation for her."

She turned to Ethan with a laugh. "As for learning you're her brother? She'll love it and probably break into a hysterical laugh, thinking about how the two of you ran into each other. She said there was something familiar about you."

"Thanks for reminding me about running her over, Lydia." He looked around the room. "If it's okay with everyone, I'd like Sam and me to be the ones to tell her."

Sam was dabbing her eyes with a tissue. "I like your idea, Ethan." Looking around, she asked, "Does anyone have an objection or a better idea?" No one responded as she turned back to Ethan. "Let's see how she's doing tomorrow."

Jack tapped the side of his glass with a spatula. "I'll put some snacks together while everyone returns to earth. The house is open for mingling, crashing, and hanging out. You may not discuss or make any project decisions for the rest of the night. We'll save it for tomorrow."

Sam stood to speak. "I agree with Jack and will add two things. Thank you to Ryleigh and Chandler. Your revelation caught me off guard. Considering the circumstances, I know what you did was in the best interests of my children and me. Learning they are alive and who they are has softened my anger. You were my family back then, and we remain family today." She walked over and hugged Ryleigh and Chandler. Roy started applauding, with everyone following his lead.

Sam raised a waving hand. "And now I have this incredible extended family." She motioned to Jack. "Do your magic, Chef Jack."

CHAPTER 60

A Provocative Morning

Sam glanced at the clock with its six o'clock display as she stirred in the bed, spooning behind Jack and whispering in his ear. "Are you awake?"

"Not quite, but your cuddling is getting me there."

"I need to talk and have you hold me."

"Let me turn over, and I'll take care of your request." He wrapped her in his arms, pulling her in close. "What's troubling your mind at this early hour?"

"I'm caught up in a storm of emotions. Part of me is still angry with Rye and Chan, but I know that will subside. Part of me wants to hug my kids and get to know them better. Part of me wants to run away with you and them, to get as far away as possible from the trouble and conflicts. Then..."

They were nose to nose, his hand caressing her face. "Okay, finish your thought, and I'll try to help you work things out."

She buried her face in his chest of soft salt-and-pepper hair. "Then there's us. It's the best part of what's happened to me over the past two months, and I don't want what we've discovered to get lost in the madness. Being here with you is more than I thought I'd ever have with a man. So I'm not letting you get away, Jack Gallagher."

"Same for me, Sam. I never thought I would ever find a woman like you. There will be time for whatever we want once the craziness is done, and we won't let it distract us from being together." He kissed her and slid his hand down over her firm butt, giving it a squeeze.

"I like what you're doing, but it's not going to happen this morning. We have a house full of guests, and I might get noisy."

"No guests left in the house. Chandler and Ryleigh left after you fell asleep on the couch. Ethan caught a ride with Roy and Lydia before I carried you up the stairs."

Sam pushed against his chest, looking surprised. "Wait. Roy and Lydia? Her house is in shambles. Was he dropping her at a hotel?"

Jack was grinning like a Cheshire cat, revealing a secret. "Nope. She was spending time talking with him in front of the fireplace. I think they were trying to give us some privacy. They offered to take Ethan to Ed's place, and then they'd be off to Roy's."

"So we're alone?"

"Well, you, me, and Thomas, but he's sleeping downstairs."

Now, it was Sam flashing a mischievous look as she reached under the sheets. "Think you could be up for a morning romp?"

He brought his hand around to cup her breasts, feeling their nipples firming as she kicked the blankets away. "They're hungry for your kisses and attention, Mr. Gallagher." It became an exotic dance of passion as they coursed over the king-size stage in a private performance of erotic skills and dexterity.

Sam was catching her breath, sitting on top of Jack. She smoothed his chest as beads of sweat glistened on their bodies. Leaning down, she locked eyes with him. "We should think about showering and cooking breakfast. I don't know about you, but I've worked up an appetite."

"Yeah, I don't want this to end, but we'll probably have guests returning soon."

"They're coming back? When?"

"I told Roy we'd have breakfast around nine."

She glanced at the clock on the nightstand. "Well, it's eight o'clock, sweetheart. We better get into high gear to look like innocent, respectable hosts when they arrive." Jack burst into laughter as Sam bounded out of bed, heading for the bathroom. He swung his feet onto the floor thinking, *You're a lucky man, Jack.*

CHAPTER 61

Resolution

Thomas was finishing his breakfast, watching them coordinate culinary activities while accompanied by soft, bluesy guitar music in the background. Jack poured orange juice, remarking, "I like the way we cook together. It's like rehearsed dance moves to avoid crashing into each other. I'll call it kitchen dancing."

She crossed behind him, patting his ass. "Call it what you like. I love being in the kitchen with you. In fact, I love just being with you."

They were so engrossed in their kitchen dance that they didn't hear Roy and Lydia walk into the kitchen until they applauded and Lydia said, "Bravo! No mystery to what you two did this morning."

Jack's face flushed as Sam beamed. "Nothing more than a choreographed performance during morning meal prep."

Lydia was quick to respond. "Leave it to Sam to be a girl who kisses and doesn't tell all."

With his trusty spatula in hand, Jack said, "I don't know what you two are chattering about, but I'm looking forward to eating. Nothing fancy this morning, just scrambled eggs and toast. I'd offer a better variety, but my pantry needs replenishing. Pour yourselves some OJ or coffee and help Sam set the island while I finish scrambling."

The four talked with a lighthearted banter, maneuvering around looming uncertainties.

Lydia explained they had stopped at the hospital. "Adira's looking and doing even better today. She must get her grit and fight from you, Sam. Looks like they're going to release her tomorrow. I called Ethan. He's still planning on the two of you picking her up but not telling her anything until she's here with all of us. I told him I'd leave the details for you and him to work out."

Sam put an elbow on the counter, propping up her chin with one hand. "I know she'll be happy once she's back here with everyone. I'm nervous, excited, and not sure how I'll tell her she's Ethan's sister and my daughter. Until then, I'd like to hear opinions on my original objective, stopping David, and any thoughts on continuing or changing the project."

Lydia spoke first. "My vote goes to finding Charles and his band of outlaws. They can't get away with what they've done to Adira, Ethan, and our homes. He's an arrogant, sadistic son of a bitch. For what it's worth, I'm a skilled marksman and could put a few well-placed rounds into him. As for stopping David and Jonathan. I'm still on board, especially after hearing Ryleigh's story."

Knowing Jack's front door security code, Ethan walked unnoticed into the conversation. "I'll second Lydia's motions. Not sure if I have a voice in your decision-making, but I'm for taking them all down."

Sam jumped up from her seat to hug him. "Of course you have a voice in what we decide. We're all in this together."

Jack was watching Sam beam with pride as she embraced Ethan. "Pour yourself some coffee or juice and pull up a seat. I'll throw my thoughts into the ring and give Roy the final opinion." He walked around behind Sam, placing his hands on her shoulders.

"When I first interviewed with Sam, she was all about burning David and the whole damn clown circus to the ground. She was out for vengeance with no holds barred. After this week, I think she has a fresh feeling about physical harm and violence. I know I do. I agree David, Cynthia, and Aegis cannot continue with this nomination. Are we the ones to bring their progress to a halt? Yes, and as Ryleigh put it, each of us has reasons to stop them. It's become more than Sam's fight—it's a collective fight."

He looked around the island. "Just tick down the list. Ryleigh survived her father's efforts to have her aborted. Sam was raped as a minor and ordered to have an abortion. Ryleigh, Sam, and Chandler scurried, hiding to protect her unborn children. Then, there were the threats against Ethan and Lydia. Ethan being mugged. Adira being beaten within an inch of her life. Senator Mathers being coerced to allow David's nomination to succeed. And something you've not heard yet: direct threats against Ryleigh and Chandler. My vote is the same as Lydia's and Ethan's."

They all looked at Roy, who was patting his hands together and turning to Sam. "I have nothing new to add other than that we should make a run at hitting our objectives without further violence. It's back to you, Sam."

"Hearing your solidarity tells me we keep going but also try negotiating. I'm determined to see it through to the end." Pursing her lips, she paused. "Roy, Cynthia asked if you'd be a peacemaker. Have you heard any more from her?"

"She left a voicemail the day we recovered Adira. She wants to schedule a meeting to negotiate a deal. I don't know what she means by a deal, but she said the offer was open until Christmas, which is closing in on us."

Sam looked at Jack, who nodded and motioned for her to continue talking. "This wasn't my original intent, but I have to be open to change. What's the acceptable outcome of meeting with them?"

Roy grabbed pen and paper, saying, "Give me a list of options. Then we can see what's reasonable or unreasonable." Lydia insisted Cynthia turn Charles over to them to face prosecution. Ethan wanted assurances about ending further violence. Sam was unwavering in her demand for David to withdraw from consideration for the nomination.

Jack commented that Cynthia would look for concessions before granting their requests. "One-sided negotiations are unrealistic. What are we willing to give them in return? I think we'd have to stop further articles on Aegis and David. It's what they see as our form of violence against them. Turning Charles over to us may be beyond their control. He operates as a rogue individual." He looked at Sam, asking, "Would you be willing to let David's name go forward? After the firestorm Ethan started, there's a strong possibility the president might back away from him or the Senate committee will nix it."

Sam sat in contemplation as Lydia added, "Lucas told me David's name will never get past the Judiciary Committee. He said Aegis has created more than enough enemies to defeat a David Jaymes nomination."

Roy looked up from writing as the suggestions ended. "I don't know how they will respond to the demands. Jack makes good points to consider. Sam?"

She placed her hands on the counter, closing her eyes. "I hear all of you. My heart and head are wrestling with twenty-seven years of conflict. So here's my perspective. It's a three-point plan. They turn Charles over, both sides stop the violence, and David withdraws his name. I'm willing to give ground and risk letting them continue with his nomination. Lydia's sharing what Lucas said and the concerns Ethan's articles have raised tell me they'll fail to get David through the process. To me, it's a low-risk concession. If they refuse to or can't deliver Charles, we have the right to pursue him." She opened her eyes, looking for Roy's reaction. "You're the negotiator, Roy. Am I giving you room to work?"

"Yeah, I think your demands and concessions are a reasonable balance that still achieves your original aim of stopping David. The upside is an end to the escalating violence."

Sam reached out to place a hand on his shoulder. "Okay, we'll see what happens with calling Cynthia. Just to be clear—you can give ground, but not beyond what I said."

Ethan asked, "What happens if they refuse your terms?"

Sam smiled. "I hope it doesn't go there. If it does, we go nuclear. You do a press conference with Lucas followed by a series of articles exposing them and whatever other cockroaches there are. So keep digging and writing. We need to be prepared for the worst while hoping for the best."

"Got it."

She turned to Roy. "I'll talk with Rye and Chandler to bring them up to speed. I want this over with by Christmas. Let's schedule the meeting for Christmas Eve. It could give us another reason to celebrate the holiday."

Jack broke into the conversation, asking, "Since our goals are set, can everyone be here tomorrow when Adira returns from the hospital?"

Sam added, "I'm sure Ethan and I will have to wait for the doctors to complete their paperwork and final evaluations. Noon would probably be a reasonable arrival time for us. We'll let Jack know if it's sooner, but hospitals don't move fast."

Jack looked at Roy. "You can coordinate getting everyone here. I'll plan a grocery run while Sam and Ethan are at the hospital. Thomas can guard the fortress while I'm out."

Ethan and Sam were ready to head for the hospital bright and early while Jack was finishing his shopping list. "Anything either of you'd like to add before you leave?"

Sam looked at Ethan as he shook his head. "I don't think so. We'll call once we're on our way back with Adira." She gave Jack a quick kiss and turned to leave with Ethan.

Jack finished kitchen cleanup before leaving for the store. He walked down the outside steps as two men stepped out of a car to confront him. Jack watched them approach, asking, "Can I help you?"

Without a word, one of them shoved Jack while the other took a swing. Jack dodged to the right, lost his balance, and fell to the ground. Looking up from the sidewalk, he yelled, "Hey, what the hell do you want?"

Looking around, the assailants saw three men running toward them, and they turned to sprint away. Two of the rescuers chased in pursuit while the third man helped Jack to his feet. "Are you okay, Mr. Gallagher? My name's George. We're the security team for the house."

"Yeah. I'm fine, George. Thanks for being here and watching out for me. Your buddies may need your help if they catch those two. Go ahead and help them. I think I'm safe now."

With a quick nod, George was on his way to help his partners.

CHAPTER 62

Reunion

Getting Adira released from the hospital took the entire morning. She was full of questions, trying to understand what had happened. "The last thing I remember is Lydia unlocking the door and being pushed from behind. From there, my memory goes blank." Ethan provided a synopsis of the attack without going into the gruesome details.

"C'mon, Ethan. I know you're trying to be gentle, but at least tell me who was responsible for my beating."

He was hesitant, and Sam answered. "Do you recall meeting one of Cynthia's associates named Charles?"

"That creepy bastard did this to me?"

"Yes, and we're working to hold him accountable."

"Oh, hell! Just put me in a room with that prick. A swift kick in the nuts would be a good start. From there, I can use my martial arts training and beat him to a pulp."

Ethan looked at her with surprise. "Martial arts?"

"Damn right. I'm a second-degree black belt in Tae Kwon Do. Three years of training and ready to kick his ass."

Sam smiled. "I'm sure you'd bust his balls, but we're going with less aggressive methods like arrest, prosecution, and incarceration."

As they waited, Adira kept peppering them with questions about the project, what was happening with David and Cynthia, and what everyone on the team had been doing.

Sam and Ethan did their best to answer cautiously, trying to keep her from becoming too agitated.

"Where are we going after leaving here? I'd like to see Lydia. You can drop me at her house." They explained about the bombings and the need to use Jack's house as an operations center and crash pad. "Man, you've had a lot of shit to deal with while I was out of it."

Sam called Jack from the limo she'd ordered to drive them to his house. "Is everyone there? Good. We should be there in a few minutes." She ended the call, explaining to Adira, "Everyone wanted to see you, so Jack has the whole group at the house."

"Wow, I feel like a celebrity with a private car and fans waiting to greet me." She laughed at Ethan and Sam. "Hey, guys, I was being sarcastic. However, I do feel special."

Ethan put his arm around her for a hug. "You are special in more ways than you can imagine."

"Hey, don't get amorous. You're cute, just not my boyfriend type. We're more in the brother-sister category of friendships."

"I, ah…"

Sam jumped in to rescue Ethan. "Ethan is just expressing how all of us feel about you." The car pulled up in front of Jack's. "And here we are."

Lydia was waiting with the door open and ran down the front steps to greet Adira. "Damn, you look good for what you've been through, honey. Let's get you inside."

Adira walked into a party atmosphere of balloons, streamers, cheers, and an overwhelming surge of hugs. "Oh my God. This is beyond a great homecoming." She worked her way to the kitchen, finding Jack the last in the receiving line, waiting with open arms.

"Let me get you comfortable in front of the fireplace."

"No way. I want to sit at the infamous kitchen island command center to hear updates and how we're going to bust Charles's chops." They broke into a mixture of cheers and laughter at Adira's desires.

The group took turns explaining events and voicing opinions. Eventually, the excitement settled, leaving Sam to take center stage. "I want to share some revelations that came to light while you were in the hospital. Lydia said you wanted to find your birth mother and learn more about your ancestry. Am I right?"

"Yes, and yes! Not sure where you're going, but I'm feeling tingly. I know you couldn't have found my birth mother in the few days I was gone. But go ahead with whatever it is. I love surprises."

Sam looked around the kitchen, getting affirmative nods to continue. "It took only a day, but we found your mother and discovered you also have a twin brother."

"Holy shit!" She blushed and apologized for the verbal exuberance. "Okay, okay. So who is she, where is she, and a brother on top of it all?"

Lydia couldn't contain herself. "They're here and waiting to meet you."

Adira jumped up from her seat, scanning the room and front door. "Where?"

She was standing next to Ethan, who was beaming with pride. He tapped her shoulder to get her to face him as his eyes glistened. "Hi, sis."

Adira reached out to place a hand on Ethan's chest. "Really? You're not screwing with me?"

"Nope. And to top it off, you're my baby sister since I was born first."

She wrapped her arms around his neck, pulling him close. "I knew we had a connection from the day you dumped my ass on the sidewalk." Again, the group was laughing and celebrating, the joy filling the house.

Suddenly, Adira straightened, locking eyes with Ethan. "Okay, big brother, where are you hiding Mom?"

"I'm standing right behind you." Adira spun around, finding Sam with outstretched arms. They locked into an embrace before either of them could speak.

"Oh my God. Ever since I discovered I was adopted, I've wanted to find you. This is the greatest party ever. And the surprises are beyond my wildest imagination." She put an arm around Sam's shoulders and then Ethan's. "Lydia, get a picture of me with my family as the three of us stand here blubbering. I want to capture this moment forever!"

Chatter and happiness filled the next hour. Ryleigh and Chandler sat with Adira, Ethan, and Sam, reviewing histories and apologies.

Adira sat quietly for a moment, looking at Ethan. "Holy shit! What the hell do we call David? After hearing everything he and Jonathan did to Ryleigh and Sam, trying to have us aborted, there is no way I will ever acknowledge them as my father and grandfather. They're fucking bastards, just like Charles." She looked at Sam. "You're my mother, and I'm so excited to be here with you. I have no father worth acknowledging. We're shutting his fucking nomination down. Are you with me, Ethan?"

"Damn straight, sis."

CHAPTER 63
Disturbance

Lydia was listening to Adira's rant over David as her phone signaled an incoming call. Roy caught the distressed look on her face and followed her as she left the room to answer. She put the phone on speaker mode once they were away from the group.

"Lydia, darling. I see Adira and her bodyguards have left the hospital. I'm sure there's a festive gathering at Jack's, welcoming her back."

"What the fuck do you want, Charles?"

"What do I want? I want to hear you've come to your senses and decided to stop attacking my friend David. After all, I returned Adira alive, which I thought was a generous gesture."

"Adira was alive, but barely. As for the attacks on David, no way in hell we'll stop." Lydia looked at Roy as he motioned for her to calm down.

Charles rolled his eyes at Lydia's response. "Well, I recommend you talk it over with your friends. Think of my returning Adira as a holiday peace offering that deserves a reciprocating gift. However, things will return to being very dangerous if you choose not to respond appropriately. Let me be clear. None of you will be safe. I'd love to keep talking with you, but I have another call to make."

Lydia and Roy were returning to the kitchen when Sam's phone buzzed. She answered the call. "Hello?"

Charles was cackling into his phone. "Well, hello, Samantha. It's Charles Abbott. I've looked forward to talking with you again. Our first meeting was a bit awkward."

"Why are you calling, Charles?" Everyone looked up at the mention of his name.

"Put me on speakerphone. I'm sure everyone will be interested in what I say."

Sam switched modes on her phone, asking again, "Why the call, Charles?"

"I was just talking with Lydia about ending your nasty attempts to prevent David's nomination, but she was rude and uncooperative. Then, I realized you're the decision-maker and I was wasting my time talking with her." He paused before continuing. "Am I correct in believing you make the final decisions for your group?" Jack motioned for Sam to remain quiet.

"Oh dear, I always seem to get an awkward silence when talking with your friends, and now the same from you. I felt confident you were the one capable of deciding what the group does. I would call Jack or Roy, but I have phone numbers only for you and Lydia."

Sam couldn't contain her growing exasperation. "How did you get my number?"

"How? It's the number printed right here on the tag attached to Thomas's collar. It tells me who to call so I can return Thomas to his owner."

"What? When did you get the information from his tag?"

"Oh my. It appears you're not aware he's missing."

Sam jumped from her seat as she and Jack frantically searched the kitchen and laundry room for Thomas. Her nostrils flared as she clenched her teeth, glaring at her phone.

"Goddamn it, Charles. I will hunt you down and kill you with my bare hands if any harm comes to him."

"Oh my goodness, Sam. Calm yourself. You may think I'm cruel, but I wouldn't harm an innocent pet. Actually, I've grown quite fond of Thomas and may decide to keep him. So be nice to me, or you may never see him again."

She pounded a fist onto the counter. "You son of a bitch!"

"Now, now. No need for tantrums. And don't worry about his diet. We gathered all his food before leaving with him."

"What? When were you here?"

"We created a convenient distraction when Jack left the house, and your bodyguards rushed out to rescue him."

"I want him back, unharmed, now!"

"Let me see what Thomas thinks I should do. Hmm, he seems so content and happy being with me."

"Damn it, Charles. Return Thomas to me."

"No can do, Sam. Losing Thomas will be the least of your worries if your attacks continue. I recommend doing all you can to avoid causing me to intensify actions."

Sam drew a sharp breath, closing her eyes. "Okay, how do I get him back?"

"I can't believe you've forgotten my request so quickly. Lydia can help you remember. Talk it over with everyone, and have Roy call Cynthia to arrange a truce. The deadline is Christmas. He has her number. Say goodbye to Mommy, Thomas." The call ended with Sam gritting her teeth and cursing into the phone.

CHAPTER 64

Taking Charge

The kitchen was ominously still as Sam straightened her posture and addressed her team. "We've allowed them to keep us reacting to what they do. Well, they made the wrong move taking Thomas. We're getting him back and flipping the tables on them."

She looked at Roy and Jack. "We'll learn from the lapse in our focus and adapt. Here's what we need to do."

They all leaned in for assignments from Sam. "Chandler and Ryleigh, work with Mansa to see if we can pinpoint a location for Charles and how many goons work for him. We need to know what we're up against in order to be ahead of them. Also, ensure that he properly secures the house this time."

Roy said, "I know Mansa has resources working to discover a location for Charles. Let me coordinate with him, and I'll get back to you as soon as we have information."

Sam pointed a finger at Roy. "I need you to follow up with Cynthia. Chandler and Mansa have a good relationship. He and Ryleigh can handle working with him. Jack can work with you on a meeting with Cynthia. Tell her whatever you feel will get us face to face with her. Phone conferences are unacceptable, and David has to be there too. You and Jack pick a day and location so we're in control. The sooner, the better." She looked at Jack. "One more thing—tell that bitch they return Thomas unharmed, or there's no truce, and we go with the nuclear option, and you can explain what that means."

She shifted her attention to Ethan. "Keep working on the next two articles. I want to be ready to fire shots if we have to go nuclear. Contact Senator Mathers to see if he will hold a press conference with you. Lydia, you can help Ethan with the content for his stories and coordinate with Lucas."

Lydia patted Ethan's shoulder. "We can work from your office. I'll contact Lucas to link the two of you for a press conference." She walked over to hug Adira. "You stay with Sam. She'll keep you safe and can use your support running the command center."

Sam's rapid-fire delegation had mesmerized Adira as she watched. "I want to help. What can I do, Sam?"

Sam reached out to grasp her hand. "You have the toughest job, sweetie—keeping me focused and thinking strategically. You'll be our central coordinator to keep me in the loop with everyone's progress. This is where we take charge and put Cynthia and Charles on their heels."

She looked around as Jack and Roy were nodding in agreement. "Hey, you two! Get going while Adira and I plan options to deal with the unexpected. You can work here or from Roy's place."

Roy pushed his seat back from the counter. "Looks like our commander needs us on the move."

Jack gave Sam a quick kiss. "Good to see you being large and in charge. Call when you need us back here."

Adira was shouting as the boys headed out the door, "I'll keep everyone up to date on developments."

Sam retrieved her briefcase from the living room and handed Adira a notepad and pen. "Are you ready for this? I know you've been through a lot, and I don't want to stress you."

"I can rest on the couch in front of the fire if I get tired. Right now, I'm pumped."

Sam gave her a hug, saying, "I love knowing you're mine and promise we will stop his fucking nomination."

Adira was making notes, watching Sam place her laptop on the counter. "You're amazing, Sam. The way you flipped a switch to go into action mode energized me."

Sam handed her phone to Adira. "Addressing conflict and problem-solving are what I do best. You and I are going to be a great central command team. Send messages to have everyone back here around eight with updates." She started compiling a list of contingency plans to ensure they would stay two steps ahead of Cynthia and Charles.

The route to Roy's place required a detour through Harlem, with Jack navigating. Roy drove into an abandoned construction site, asking, "This is where you want to have a negotiation meeting?"

"Yeah. Over at the far end of the site, there's an abandoned parking structure they were going to demolish but didn't. The entire project shut down before they could demo it. I've used it several times when I needed an upper hand. It makes people uncomfortable, but it's my kind of environment."

"Okay, but Cynthia and Sam might not see it your way."

"I can handle Sam. As for Cynthia, I don't give a damn what she thinks. This is where we meet. The place has great hiding spots, allowing you and Mansa to stay well concealed but within reach to cover us if needed. Think you can handle it?"

Roy turned in his seat to face Jack. "I'll cover your ass, but Mansa needs to buy into the location, or we find a second choice. He's the one I lean on for tactical maneuvers."

"No problem. I'll explain it to Mansa while you get Cynthia on board to negotiate with us. We'll wait to give them the location until the day before the meeting to keep them off balance."

They went through Sam's options one more time before calling Cynthia. "Cynthia, it's Roy. I'm calling to accept your offer to act as negotiator."

"Roy, I had a feeling you'd be calling. What do you have in mind?"

"We want a face-to-face meeting as soon as possible. Will the twenty-fourth work?"

"Christmas Eve? Are you serious?"

"Yes."

"Let me check." Cynthia placed the call on hold to talk with David and Charles before returning to Roy. "The twenty-fourth will work. Who will be there? What are we trying to accomplish, and where?"

"Four participants. You, David, Samantha, and Jack Gallagher. He's her operations man."

"Hang on." Cynthia's voice became muffled as Roy waited.

"Cynthia, just put the phone on speaker, and I'll do the same, so we don't have to explain to others."

"Who's there with you?"

"It's just Jack and me from our side. I'll assume you have David and, perhaps, Charles with you?"

"So what are you expecting to accomplish?"

"You wanted us to pause with news articles, leaving David's nomination to go through congressional hearings. We want Charles to stop the violence and have Jonathan refrain from his threatened actions against Ryleigh and Chandler."

The discussion paused before Cynthia responded. "We agree with having all parties stop hostile activities, and the nomination process continues. I do not have any influence over whatever Jonathan may have threatened. You need to take those issues up with him. If we're agreeing on a basic cease-fire, there's no need to meet."

"Wrong answer, Cynthia. We need an in-person meeting to discuss additional points."

"What additional points?"

"You'll hear them once the four of you are together. And one last requirement from our side before we agree to a meeting. Return Thomas, or everything is off."

"Roy, this is Charles. Tell Sam her precious feline will be at the meeting for her to see him."

Jack shook his head, saying, "That's a no-go, Charles. Thomas has to be at my house before the twenty-fourth. I think you should encourage the return, Cynthia. If not, there will be a national press conference on Christmas Day, a series of nonstop articles, and the release of some pretty embarrassing video clips."

Charles was yelling. "Don't do it, Cynthia—they're bluffing."

She cleared her throat. "We will return the cat unharmed. What's the time and location for the four of us to talk?"

Jack answered, saying, "Two in the afternoon. We'll contact you tomorrow with the location."

Cynthia responded, "We can meet at our home. It's secure."

Roy took the lead. "We'll select a place and get you the information tomorrow. There's no room for negotiating the location." He hesitated and asked, "Do you want to save David's nomination or not? If not, we can call everything off and schedule the first of many press conferences."

Charles was still objecting when Cynthia raised her voice to stop him. "Fine, Roy. Call me tomorrow, and we will be there the next day." As she ended the call, Charles could be heard arguing to keep Thomas hostage.

Jack and Roy high-fived, feeling they had maintained control and gotten what Sam wanted. They contacted Mansa, asking him to come to Roy's apartment to discuss the location and steps to keep Sam and Jack safe.

Ryleigh and Chandler were the first ones back, followed by Ethan and Lydia. Sam was getting everyone settled. "I'm not sure where the boys are, but they should be here soon." She was finishing her statement as Roy and Jack walked through the patio doors into the kitchen.

"Nice of you to ask, Sam. I'm not sure where the boys are, but the men thought picking up an assortment of pizzas was worth being a few minutes late." They all laughed at Jack's sarcasm about being called "the boys."

Dishes were being passed around when the doorbell rang. Chandler went to answer, opening the door to find a box on the porch. He carried it into the house, opened the loosely folded top, and announced, "Oh my God! It's Thomas!"

Sam rushed over as Chandler handed Thomas to her. His purring was loud enough for the entire group to hear. Sam lifted him above her head. "You are a sight for worried eyes. Look, everyone. He's smiling, happy to be away from Charles the Grinch."

They began passing Thomas around, giving him affectionate cuddles and morsels of pizza as Sam caught everyone's attention. "We can keep welcoming Thomas back. While that continues, Adira and I are eager to hear progress reports."

CHAPTER 65

Reports

Ryleigh offered for her and Chandler to start. "We met with Mansa to find out what happened with Thomas being taken. As Jack has shared, Charles had his men attack Jack out front to draw the security team away, which left the house unguarded. He apologized for the lapse and said it won't happen again. I'll let Chandler cover what we learned from Mansa about how Charles operates."

Chandler said, "Charles has a core group of five men he recruited through his contacts within the Wagner organization. They scour New York bars and hangouts known to be frequented by individuals offering criminal services for hire. So his team is a collection of trusted associates and a rotating group of freelancers.

"Names of potential recruits go to Charles, who does one-on-one interviews. He prefers hiring foreign nationals, many of whom are here illegally. There's no structure or hierarchy beyond the core group. Charles calls all the shots and micromanages. Once an assignment is complete, payments are made in cash. So far, there are no repeat hires from the freelance group."

Sam let Adira finish taking notes while she pondered a question. "Any idea of where he's operating from?"

Chandler shook his head. "The short answer is no. He moves to a new hotel or other location daily. Mansa said

Charles is someone skilled in black-ops methods, which Roy's background files confirm."

Roy chimed in, agreeing with Chandler's assessment. "I've talked at length with Mansa, and he characterizes Charles as elusive, ruthless, and without moral conscience."

Sam looked around, asking if Ethan and Lydia had been successful in their assignment. Ethan passed out draft copies of three articles to use before and after a press conference with Lucas. "I welcome suggestions on the articles once you have time to review them. I'll let Lydia give an overview of her conversation with Lucas."

Lydia turned pages in her notepad before starting. "Lucas is ready to help in any way we feel is necessary. He's been in discussions with colleagues snared and coerced by Cynthia and Society. Several are willing to participate in a press conference and, in Lucas's terms, blow the lid off to expose Aegis for its high-handed political meddling with the court system. Lucas feels a press conference will be an excellent follow-up to one or two of Ethan's articles. Just give him a heads-up three to four days in advance. His office will make the announcement and conduct the conference. Lucas feels the lull in political news over the holidays will give the press a hot topic to run with."

Adira paused her writing to ask, "What if David is nominated, and we let it go before the Judiciary Committee?"

"We discussed the possibility of letting the nomination proceed. Two senators, besides Lucas, who are willing to take part in a press conference also hold seats on the Judiciary Committee. Ethan's first two articles have raised concerns with other committee members. Lucas feels they can defeat David without further objections if we let the process happen."

Sam gave a thumbs-up to Lydia and Ethan. "Nice work. Looks like we have torpedoes loaded and ready to catch Aegis by surprise. You and Roy are up next, Jack."

Jack extended his hand to Roy. "I'll let you cover the call with Cynthia."

Roy recounted the conversation and apparent agreement for a meeting. "I would say the return of Thomas shows we've gained the advantage. Cynthia will do whatever it takes to keep David's name as the front-runner for the nomination and avoid further interference from us. I can tell you that Charles was not in favor of returning Thomas. His return was a decision driven by Cynthia. As much as Sam has taken charge here, Cynthia seems to call the shots for their side."

Sam asked, "What about turning Charles over to us?"

"Getting them to turn Charles over for prosecution is up in the air because we didn't discuss it. I felt it would have halted everything and left it as a demand for you and Jack to handle. Our moves have them reacting to what we do, just as you wanted. Pushing for Charles's arrest is worth trying, but we might have to chase him down on our own. Mansa and his team can handle that if needed. The bottom line is they're willing to talk. The only item left to clarify is the location, which I'll let Jack explain."

He nodded to Jack as he placed his folded hands on the counter. "Sam and I will meet with Cynthia and David. We talked with Mansa after he left Chandler's place to review the location and security. Mansa and Roy will provide cover for Sam and me in case things go astray."

Sam spoke up before Jack could continue. "Wait a minute. You're leaving out some important details. Where are we meeting, and how are Roy and Mansa covering us?"

Jack rubbed the side of his face. "The location is an abandoned construction site in Harlem."

Sam's eyes looked sideways at Jack as she tilted her head. "An abandoned construction site? I can't believe Cynthia agreed to it."

"We didn't tell her the location. I said we'd let her know tomorrow."

Adira asked, "Why did you pick this location?"

"I've used it before to give myself an advantage because people didn't want to be there for long. Taking Cynthia and David outside their comfort zone continues to play to our advantage."

Sam placed her elbows on the counter and rested her forehead on her hands. "Okay, okay. I'm trying to get comfortable with your choice. How are Roy and Mansa going to cover us?"

"We worked it out for them to arrive well before the scheduled time. The structure is a maze of pillars and growing shadows in the fading afternoon light. It will help conceal their location while giving them a clear view of us."

Sam looked at Roy. "Is all this good with you and Mansa?"

"I had reservations, but Jack and Mansa worked things out to help me feel more comfortable. My initial concern was the location. After Mansa did a recon of the site, he felt Jack's choice was good and convinced me it gives us an advantage in providing cover for you and Jack."

"I have to go with the experts but feel like bait luring in the sharks. Maybe I'll gain confidence after a good night's rest."

Sam pointed and asked Adira to address their discussions while everyone was out working. Adira said, "Sam and I see this unfolding in two ways. Of course, we expected them to agree to meet, and Lydia's report on Lucas puts us in an excellent position whether they accept our terms or refuse."

She read her notes before continuing. "Our soft approach will have Sam offering to pause news articles and other actions provided they stop the violence from their side. The offer also requires Charles to face prosecution for the bombings and attacks on me and Ethan. So the first option is to offer to hold off on our work and get them to hand over Charles. Sam and I agree that the requirement to turn him over may not be something they can deliver on. As Roy explained, we would then go after Charles without their cooperation."

Adira looked up for comments. "Okay, next is the strong-armed or, as Sam calls it, nuclear approach. Sam tells Cynthia that, without a truce, we go hard. Now, thanks to Lydia's coordination with Lucas, we can add the press conference. It would include several members of Congress standing with him and making similar accusations. We feel this threat will put a fire under Cynthia to strike a bargain. Sam and Jack would wait for reactions from David or Cynthia. We expect this approach might create a caustic response."

Roy's eyes squinted as he asked, "What if Cynthia agrees to everything else but refuses to hand over Charles?"

"That's when Sam could talk directly to David, telling him the truth about me and Ethan. I doubt he'll care. The one thing I learned while working for them is that he has no concern or compassion for anyone else, but it's worth trying to pull emotional strings to see if he responds."

Sam thanked Adira for her explanations. "Obviously, the strong approach means we leave the meeting without resolution. It includes turning Mansa loose to hunt down Charles and possibly eliminate him. It's a last resort, but it will end the nomination and remove the threat of physical violence against us."

Adira turned her notepad to a blank page. "I'm ready for comments and suggestions."

Ryleigh started talking first. "Roy will have to give Cynthia a good reason to go to Harlem. I think sparking her curiosity will help. Tell her you will provide them with the twins' identities and locations and how their existence may affect David's appointment. It's like writing a novel. Give the reader a reason to turn the page and see what happens next."

Roy was smiling and writing a note. "I like the idea and the analogy. It might get her past any objections to the location."

Ryleigh was nodding. "Yes. Manipulate her into doing what we want. Trust me, it will work. I'm a master manipulator and know how to pull people's strings."

Chandler raised a hand to speak. "I'd like to see something added to prevent Jonathan from acting on his threats against me and Ryleigh."

Ryleigh interrupted Chandler's comment, saying, "What Chandler means is that we'd like to have Cynthia stop Jonathan. However, we have an alternative method of stopping him without complicating what's planned for Harlem."

Agreeing they had accomplished their refocusing of the project, the team transitioned into casual conversations. Chandler and Ryleigh excused themselves, saying they needed to finish plans to confront Jonathan and convince him to reconsider his threatened actions against them.

CHAPTER 66

Scheduling

Roy was with Jack, Sam, and Adira the next morning as he reviewed thoughts about scheduling the Harlem location with Cynthia. "This is going to be a group call. I plan to let Cynthia know who's with me. I'll tell her we're not negotiating on the phone. The purpose of this call is to confirm the location, time, and participants. We keep this as short and nonconfrontational as possible."

Adira was making notes and spoke. "Knowing Cynthia, she's going to push for more information. She gets freaky when she's not the one controlling situations."

"It might be what she wants, but I'll keep asking if she wants to pause the conflicts or risk losing the nomination. I think she'll back down from demanding control." He looked around before gesturing to Sam for her thoughts.

Sam tapped her pen. "Let's keep the pressure on her. Her primary focus as CEO of Aegis is to ensure David's success. I'm convinced we have good options to prevent it from happening. Any other ideas before we make the call?" Exchanging looks, the group remained quiet.

Roy dialed Cynthia's number and waited while the phone rang numerous times before she answered. "Good afternoon, Roy. I was beginning to think you might have changed your mind about getting together."

"No change of heart here, Cynthia. As Jack and I said on the previous call, we're just confirming arrangements. I have Samantha and Jack with me, listening."

"No problem. I have David with me for the same purpose."

"Okay, the time remains the same, two o'clock on the twenty-fourth. I trust you received my email with the location and map of the site?"

"I have it in hand. It raises questions and problems. We would prefer to use our home or a neutral location. I don't know why this is the choice and disagree with using it."

"While I understand your hesitancy, the location is non-negotiable." Then Roy sat silent.

"Let me put you on hold." Cynthia returned and said, "Your choice is unacceptable. I gave you the option of using our home and would be open to other selections from you."

"No negotiating on this, Cynthia. We have a meeting and a break in violence. If not, our team will move forward with more articles and press conferences. Let me remind you our offer allows David's nomination to proceed. We're willing to roll the dice and see what happens. It's your call. Meet in Harlem or watch his chances for chief justice crash."

"You're guaranteeing no more scandalous articles if we meet?"

"No more attacks if we talk face to face and reach an agreement."

"You mentioned additional terms. What are they? I want to know so we have time to consider counteroffers in the spirit of a true negotiation."

"The basic terms are the same as those we offered yesterday. Yes, there is an additional item due to our having discovered the identity of Sam and David's twins."

"What the hell are you talking about?"

"Look, I'm not revealing anything more on this call. The additional terms involve Sam and David's children."

Cynthia looked at David with raised eyebrows, but he listened without speaking after hearing the news about the discovery of the twins' identities. "David and I are not pleased with going to Harlem, but we'll be there."

"Jack and Sam will be there, waiting for your arrival. They will be on the second level of a parking structure at the far end of the site. He will signal for you to drive up."

Roy ended the call, setting his phone down. "Okay, team, we're at the cliff's edge. I want to fine-tune our plan for Harlem. Let's get Mansa here to clarify how he and I will cover the two of you. We also need to think through contingencies. There's a good chance Charles will be with them. He's the wild card."

Jack suggested calling Ryleigh to let her and Chandler know where things stood. Sam gave a nod, saying, "I'll make the call."

Ryleigh answered Sam's call and thanked her for the update. She turned to Chandler after ending the brief conversation. "Are we still heading for Raleigh on Christmas Eve to make a last attempt at bargaining with Jonathan?"

Chandler drummed his fingers on the table. "Yes. I've chartered the flight. First, call him to see if he will meet with us. I'll call Mansa to confirm he has two men to accompany us."

Ryleigh hit Jonathan's number in her contacts. "Jonathan, I wasn't sure you'd accept my call after our last conversation."

"I hesitated to answer, but curiosity got the best of me. What is the purpose of your call?"

"I'll be brief and direct. Chandler and I are reconsidering your offers and would like to see you on Christmas Eve to try reaching an amicable agreement."

"At this point, I'm not sure such an agreement is possible. What do you have in mind?"

"We'd prefer to talk in person."

"On Christmas Eve? What time?"

"At 2:00 p.m. – would it be a problem for you?"

"Not for me, but all my staff, except for Jackson, will have the day off for their family celebrations. So I cannot provide lunch or overnight accommodations. What time should I expect you?"

"I'm well aware of your holiday routines. Our goal is to negotiate, not to be entertained or waited upon. We will be there around two."

"Fine. I will be waiting."

Jonathan rocked back and forth in his chair before trying to reach Charles.

CHAPTER 67

Conflicted

Having closed the call with Roy, Cynthia moved forward in her chair, looking at David and Charles. "You were correct, Charles. They were adamant about using the crumbling parking structure. What are your thoughts after visiting the site?"

"I see it as an intimidation factor. They want you to feel pressured, uncomfortable, and willing to agree to whatever they want so you can leave. They have more requirements before a truce can be reached, but you won't know what they are until you're face to face. I'm surprised they've not asked for my head yet, and that may be their position in allowing David's nomination. In my opinion, they have the advantage, but it's nothing I can't overcome."

"Will you be able to avoid detection until we're ready for you?"

"Concealment is no problem. I also expect them to have security there to protect them, but I can shield myself from attack. Their security people will probably go through the area well ahead of the meeting, looking for me. I have a route that will let me slip in shortly before you arrive so they will not know of my presence or location."

David leaned forward. "The light will fade at that hour. Are you confident you can target them well?"

"I have a laser sight that enables me to shoot without raising the gun to eye level. Accuracy is not a problem unless the target is moving too quickly. Then it may require multiple shots, but I can eliminate them."

Leaning back to look at Cynthia, David pointed out that killing them might be a PR risk. "Are you sure about being this aggressive?"

"This is not the time to get cold feet, David. We debated and finally decided to have Charles kill Samantha and Jack, or whoever shows up with her, if her demands were excessive. We have reason to believe they will be excessive since they're unwilling to disclose their additional terms. Once we're done in Harlem, Charles can take care of Jonathan. As you said, he's become a pain in the ass and an obstacle to having full control of Aegis. So in answer to your question, I'm sure."

Cynthia looked from David to Charles. "My only concern is whether payment of $50,000 seals the contract for Jonathan's elimination."

"Yes, and I appreciate the generous compensation. It's what ensures allegiance from a mercenary like me. Just make the wire transfer prior to the event. Not that I don't trust you; it's just the way I do contract killings."

"Good! David and I will meet with Samantha and Jack. We'll listen to their proposal and demands. If the terms are acceptable, you can remain hidden, without killing them, and travel down to North Carolina to take care of Jonathan. If we can't reach an agreement with them, you have a green light for terminations."

"I understand."

Charles looked at his watch, waiting to see if Cynthia or David had further instructions. "It appears we've completed our arrangement. I will be in place at the parking structure before your arrival tomorrow. Text me if there's a last-minute change."

Having repacked his duffel bag for another daily move, Charles sat in his room, thinking. *Will Jonathan be willing to make a better offer? Working for him could be more lucrative. Perhaps there's an opportunity to collect from both parties.*

He jotted a few notes, knowing an offer from Jonathan would probably exceed what Cynthia had provided. *Money will determine the winner of my services. Who will be my prey to hunt and kill?*

He dialed Jonathan's number. "Jonathan, Charles here. Is this a convenient time to chat?"

"Yes, tell me what David and Cynthia are up to."

"Well, I just left them, and they have agreed to negotiate a cease-fire allowing David's nomination to proceed without further interference."

"Sounds like a snowball's chance in hell for success. Do you think it will happen?"

"Perhaps, but we won't know until they meet. Cynthia has engaged me to be at the meeting. They have paid me to kill Samantha and her accomplice if their demands exceed more than the initial offering of a cease-fire."

"Hmm. This is an interesting development."

"Have you reached a decision on David and Cynthia?"

"I have a reluctant consensus from the board to end the ongoing embarrassment. Originally, they wanted to wait and see what happened until after the holidays. I finally convinced them that we could not wait. They've allowed me to provide you with a payment of $150,000 to kill David and Cynthia, along with Samantha and anyone with her."

"Just to be clear—all parties are to be terminated?"

"I didn't think using the term *kill* required clarification. No witnesses or survivors."

"What if they negotiate a truce and allow the nomination?"

Jonathan stifled a laugh. "A truce will not happen. It doesn't matter. I want an end to all the disruption so we can regroup around another candidate. Can you accomplish the task?"

"Yes, and I appreciate the guaranteed payment. It will keep me from having to make difficult decisions."

"When is the meeting?"

"Christmas Eve, which seems ironic given that it's a time of peace, even when countries are at war."

"Sometimes war preempts traditions, Charles."

"I will contact you once my work is complete."

"I will wait for your call." Jonathan rose from his chair, heading for another contemplative walk down his drive. The azure sky and sunshine provided warmth as he thought of the coming days. *Ryleigh will be here while her friends are meeting with David and Cynthia. Is it a coincidence or a plot?*

CHAPTER 68

Eleventh-Hour Distraction

Sam's petite frame bolted upright after a fitful night's sleep. The bedside clock flashed six as Jack snored softly. She threw the covers back, feeling that whatever thoughts raced through her mind wouldn't let her sleep any longer. She gathered her robe and slipped quietly down the stairs, finding Thomas looking to be fed.

"Did something disturb your sleep too? Let me start some coffee, and then I'll fix your breakfast, but we need to be quiet so we don't disturb Jack."

Tiptoeing behind, Jack wrapped his arms around her. "What's this about not disturbing me? I felt you get up, hoping you'd return, but it didn't happen."

Sam twisted around, still in his grasp. "You shouldn't sneak up on me like that. I love the hugs, but not being startled out of my wits." She looked up, giving him a kiss and a quick jab to the ribs.

"Ouch. Your nails are almost a pointed weapon." Jack stepped back, feigning injury while laughing. "How about breakfast down the street at Westway Diner? They open at seven and have a great pancake breakfast. They also have lighter fare if you prefer."

"I might surprise you and order the same as you. But I mentioned breakfast to Thomas. Let me take care of him.

Then I can clean up, change, and be ready to take a cold walk to Westway with you."

"I'll call Roy from the diner to find out when he'll be stopping by with Mansa. They wanted to finalize plans before they head over to Harlem."

Sam was thinking about Jack as she watched Thomas devour his morning meal. *I love Jack being relaxed and spontaneous. How did I get so lucky to find him?*

The diner was bustling with an early-morning crowd as the hostess seated them in a booth. The smell of bacon and freshly baked cinnamon rolls stirred their appetites. "What can I get for the two of you?"

Sam answered, "Two coffees with waters, eggs over easy, buttermilk pancakes, bacon, and hash browns instead of toast." She looked over to see Jack laughing and closing his menu.

"You were serious about what you planned to order. I hope we don't have to wait too long."

"I don't mind waiting. Your company is more enjoyable than food." Sam reached across the table to hold hands. They spent the time chatting about the coming holidays and making plans for being together.

They were finishing when Jack's phone rang. "Roy, I was going to call and see when you'll be over. Sam and I are at breakfast and should be back in about fifteen. Nope, we haven't been paying attention. Are you sure? Damn it. Yeah, see you shortly." Jack set his phone on the table, looking at it curiously.

"Is something wrong, Jack?"

He pulled money from his wallet, saying, "Nothing we need to be concerned about right now. It was Roy saying he'll be at my place soon."

They were opening Jack's door as Roy and Mansa walked down the sidewalk. Sam waited on the porch while Jack went into the house. She hugged Roy and shook Mansa's hand, saying, "Good to see you again. Our brief encounter in the hospital didn't leave time for me to thank you for all you've been doing."

Mansa pressed her hand between his two massive hands. "Keeping watch over Adira and the rest of your team has been my honor, ma'am."

"Mansa, my name is Sam. Remember our talk in the hospital?"

"Old habits are hard to break, but I will replace *ma'am* with *Sam* in my vocabulary." His chuckle over the unintended rhyme was louder than her laugh as they continued into the house.

The four gathered at the island as Mansa motioned toward Roy, conceding the opening of the conversation to him.

Roy asked Jack, "Have you told Sam about the breaking news?"

"Nope. I wanted to wait until we were back here and let the two of you tell her."

Sam's posture stiffened as her eyes darted between the three men. "What breaking news? What are we talking about?"

Roy shook his head, speaking slowly. "You won't like this, but Justice Wheeler passed away in the hospital around six this morning. He…"

Sam slammed a hand on the counter, interrupting Roy as she jumped from her seat and started waving her arms erratically. "Of course he died at six. Oh my God, that's what woke me out of bed. It was a premonition. How the hell?" Jack tried to hold her as she beat her arms against his chest.

He pulled her close, caressing the back of her head as she shuddered. "Why are we hitting obstacle after obstacle? Damn it—this gives them the upper hand. They don't need to negotiate a truce or make any concessions. What do we do now, Jack?"

"Calm down, Sam. We need to step back and think it through."

She turned her head, resting it against Jack as she looked at Roy. "What do you think?"

"Mansa and I talked about this before calling Jack. We feel Justice Wheeler's passing strengthens our position."

Sam sat back down, wiping her eyes. "How? Help me understand how."

"Look, they wanted a cease-fire to allow hearings on David's nomination, but they didn't know when it would happen. Before today, they could string us out, let controversies die down, and wait for Wheeler to resign or die. This jumps the timelines. A hearing could happen within the next month. Cynthia has lost the ability to string us out. She needs to end the fight and concentrate on a congressional hearing, which will be difficult or impossible if we're still attacking. What's your take, Mansa?"

"Listen to Roy, Sam. He's right. They need your cooperation because they're closer to the finish line than they were yesterday. They may even be willing to turn Charles over if they feel it gives them a chance to win. It definitely improves your chances for success."

Jack placed a hand on Sam's shoulder. "I agree with Roy and Mansa. We go ahead with the meeting and negotiate. If we let the hearing happen, Lucas will step up. He feels there are enough committee members willing to deliver the votes to defeat a nomination without more violence. In the meantime, I like Mansa's feeling that Wheeler's death might convince them to surrender Charles."

Sam took several deep breaths. "Okay, I'm listening and beginning to agree. Walk me through your plans to protect us. This kind of shit might be your comfort zone, but my stomach churns with fear when I think about it."

Roy motioned to Mansa, saying, "You've developed the plan. I think she'll feel better hearing you explain it."

Mansa talked about his reconnaissance of the site and his expectation that Charles would be there to provide cover for David and Cynthia. "Roy and I will be in place hours before the meeting to make a clean sweep of the second level. Roy feels we'll be well ahead of him if he's planning to attend the party. The structure has lots of nooks and crannies for us and him to use for concealment. Distance and visibility are a problem, which is why Roy's arming us with AR-15s and laser sights. I hope we won't need them. However, the two of you must be prepared to hit the floor if we have to defend you."

Sam asked, "Hit the floor? I think I know what you mean, but when?"

"If Charles takes aggressive action, like shooting, you must get as flat as possible as quickly as possible. Just remember to act without stopping to think. Roy and I will go after him, and we don't want you or Jack caught in the crossfire."

Sam looked between Roy and Mansa, asking, "There's more going on with the two of you than you're letting us know. Am I right?"

Roy smiled as he answered, "Like I told Jack, there is a lot more, and the time will come when Mansa and I can explain things for you. We're part of a special group, and you just need to trust us."

She reached for Jack's hand. "Are you ready for this, or should we scratch?"

"Everything will be all right, Sam. We're in expert hands with these two watching over us. Mansa's just trying to have us prepared for the worst."

Roy looked at his watch and at Mansa. "I think we've covered our responsibilities and contingencies. We need to head for my place to change into warm gear and pick up our tools." He shook Jack's hand and gave Sam a quick hug. "Stay close to Jack. He'll help you to be ready. Like he said, everything will be all right." He gave her a wink and a nod.

Sam's eyes blinked as she nodded back. "I'll pull it together and be ready."

CHAPTER 69

En Route

Sam and Jack were heading for Harlem as she stretched her head back against the passenger headrest. "Thanks for driving, Jack. I couldn't handle the traffic on top of my nerves about seeing David and trying to handle Cynthia."

Jack tried to ease his tense grip on the Audi's steering wheel. "I understand where you're at, Sam. As Adira suggested, you need to focus and handle it like a high-stakes investment meeting. You've done it many times and are a wizard at getting positive results. Remember, I'll be there with you, along with Roy and Mansa, ready to protect us."

She reached into the center console, retrieving her Glock 43. Jack watched her out of the corner of his eye. "Whoa! Where did you get that?"

Sam smiled at Jack's surprise. "She's always with me. Mostly in my briefcase or purse." She slid the gun into her coat pocket, asking, "Does it make you feel uncomfortable?"

"Not really. It's a good pairing for mine. I was caught off guard because I've never seen you with it. I mean, most women don't carry."

"Oh, Jack. You need to update those old-school notions. I've carried for several years. It was Ryleigh's suggestion. She loves to say it's the best companion a woman can have in a tough situation. Our shooting range work has turned me into a pretty damn good shot."

"Good information for me to know. I'll try to behave better so you never point it in my direction." He started slowing the car as they approached the site.

"Jesus, Jack. It looks like a battleground. Cynthia's going to have a cow when they pull up here."

Jack was smiling as they drove through the growing afternoon shadows. "We're headed for the second level in the parking structure down there. Our boys have been in place since they left us this morning."

"Why the second level and not the first?"

"It's a psychological thing, being able to see people before they see me. Looking down at them while they have to look up is a power play. It damn sure gives us the upper hand. We'll park in a front center spot. Mansa said it will give them clear sight lines to see the four of us as we meet."

Sam was looking around. "Jesus, this place gives me the creeps. We should have brought some bourbon to calm our nerves. Maybe you don't need a boost in courage, but I sure as hell do."

Jack laughed, retrieving a flask from the breast pocket of his jacket. "Well, you're in luck. This is Jameson, not bourbon, but it should work just as well." Taking a drink, he handed it to Sam. "Feel free to imbibe. It'll calm your nerves and warm you at the same time."

She took a hesitant sip to appraise the taste. "Not bad, Jack. Thanks for bringing the courage in a flask."

He crept the car up the parking ramp and swung around to face out onto the yard below. "Well, bean. 'Tis time we stepped from arr fine carriage ta be ready fer greetin' our guests."

Jack's attempted Irish accent made Sam smile and shake her head. "You just couldn't resist trying to make me laugh. Thank you. I love it."

Cynthia sat in her expansive dressing area, preening, as David walked in. The idea of challenging her decision was fraught with danger. He felt her conceding the choice of location for the meeting with Samantha was a bad snap decision she had made after being outmaneuvered by Roy.

David Jaymes despised snap or breakneck decisions. His preference during the early years of practicing corporate law had been to function in the comfortable domain of cautious deliberation. That preference had continued into his role as chief judge for the US Court of Appeals for the Second Circuit. He knew this meeting veered outside his established boundaries. An empty feeling in the pit of his stomach had him on edge and willing to challenge Cynthia's decision.

"We should cancel. Wheeler's death puts us in a position to push my nomination through without their cooperation. Besides, meeting in Harlem at an abandoned construction site presents a significant personal risk, given the lack of security. I can't believe you, of all people, agreed to it."

Without changing her focus from the makeup mirror, Cynthia lifted an eyelid to finish applying mascara. She spoke in a quiet, measured tone. "It doesn't matter what you believe, think, or feel, David. Until your appointment is approved, our priority is to stop the attacks. Once you're confirmed, whatever they decide to do can be dismissed as coming from disgruntled political hacks. So go warm the car while I finish."

"Not doing it, Cyn." David raised his phone, starting to search his contacts file. "I'm calling Charles to tell him we're canceling. He can get out of there, and we'll change our plans with him."

Cynthia whirled, snatching the phone from his hand and throwing it to the floor. She glared at him, pointing her mascara brush like a knife. "You are not calling anyone. You are not canceling anything. They will destroy you and your nomination in less than a heartbeat if we don't meet and negotiate a truce. You fucked up the press conference and put us in a difficult position. I will not let you create more problems. Now, go warm the damn car and be ready to leave."

"You're not thinking this through, Cyn. If Charles kills them, we lose because the rest of their group will still work against us, and we'll have to handle questions regarding their deaths."

She turned her attention back to preening. "Listen, if Charles takes them out, we can say he defended us as part of our private security team after trying to reach a peaceful resolution to stop their false accusations. I also believe the rest of Samantha's group will abandon their efforts without someone leading the way. I wish you'd learn to trust what I do—like thinking things through and planning. Now, get your ass out of my dressing room and warm the car. We need to be there soon."

David drove to Harlem with Cynthia sitting in frosty silence. He knew another confrontation would risk reigniting her rage. He considered confrontations with her similar to facing a wounded wolverine. Cynthia's public image as a petite and delightful woman masked her vicious capabilities. David often warned associates, telling them that 'Never judge a book by its cover' should be a must-read warning label when they were dealing with Cynthia.

Mustering the courage, he thought, *A head-on attack may work as a foil to her sting. Be a man, David. Step up and fight fire with fire.* He pulled the car to the curb, stopping a half block from the site's entrance. "This is bullshit, Cynthia. We cancel and negotiate over the phone. Meeting them here was an ill-advised decision."

She raised her chin, staring out the window at the road ahead. "I will tell you one last time, David. We're doing the meeting and saving your nomination." She spun in the seat, facing David with a scowl known to make men cower in fear for their lives. "Don't make me walk the rest of the way without you."

David eased the car forward, entering the construction site.

Ryleigh and Chandler were pulling up to Jonathan's home. As always, Jackson was there to greet her. "Your father said you'd be here, and I was surprised to learn of it. I was told not to provide anything because he feels it will be a brief visit. He is in a vile mood, Ryleigh." He shook Chandler's hand and watched as two men exited the back seat of the rental car.

Ryleigh put her arm around Jackson, walking him away from the car as she talked. "This is not a social visit, Jackson. Chandler and I have unfinished business with Jonathan."

She explained the threats hanging over her and Chandler and Jonathan's unyielding position. "What I am about to tell you is the only way left to have justice for my mother, your sister. For Samantha, and to prevent him from destroying more lives. I wish it could be another way. You may want to leave and not be here until later. I do not want any implication of your participation."

Jackson stopped. "I believe you are trying to tell me you're here to take his life. Am I correct?"

"Yes, the men with us are here for that purpose." Jackson lowered his head as she continued. "I know there is a trust fund in your name, so you will be able to retire comfortably. Chandler and I will also help with anything you need."

"What if I oppose what you want to do?"

Ryleigh looked around, seeing Chandler and their companions waiting beside the car. "We will leave if you wish."

"I have wished for the strength to end his life for years. What he did to my little sister and tried to do to you is beyond my ability to forgive. I will take my car and leave. No one will know you were here. It will be unfortunate if, upon my return, I discover that vandals have been here and taken his life." He hugged Ryleigh. "I should ask you to leave, but my past pain desires a final justice for Tilly. Did you know that was Mother's name?"

"Yes, and I've always cherished knowing it."

"I will take my leave and hope to see you again, soon and under better circumstances."

Ryleigh talked with Chandler as Jackson drove away, explaining they would try talking with Jonathan one last time. "I owe it to Jackson and my mother to try, one last time, for a peaceful resolution." She turned to Mansa's men, telling them to wait until she and Chandler returned. Walking up the stairs, she said, "We will know what to do shortly."

Chandler knocked on the door to the study and heard Jonathan's voice booming, "Open the damn door and tell me why you're here. Be quick about it."

Ryleigh entered ahead of Chandler. "You sound impatient."

"I don't care to listen to whatever you want to say."

"All right, I can make this direct and brief. We want you to assure the threatened actions against us will not be taken. We are not here to bargain. It is a demand."

"I do not think you are in any position to make demands of me. My patience with you, Chandler, and David is exhausted."

"Chandler and I do not care about David. He is about to become what you have envisioned for years, and I cannot stop it from happening. I want your threats removed!"

Jonathan gave a boisterous laugh. "Again, you cannot demand anything of me. There is nothing you can do if I refuse."

"I can't believe you are callous enough to destroy the life of your only daughter."

"I have no daughter. She disowned me. If I can order the killing of your brother, I can damn well destroy your life. You should never have been born."

"You've done what?"

Jonathan continued laughing at her. "At this moment, David and Cynthia, along with Samantha, are about to breathe their last breaths. I am done with all of you." He started shaking a finger at Chandler. "You and she are two worthless half breeds. It disgusts me to have you in my presence. Get out of my home."

Ryleigh stood speechless as Chandler grabbed her arm. "We are leaving." He scowled at Jonathan. "As you have ordered, so will we."

They walked out of the study, Jonathan yelling obscenities after them. Chandler waved the two men to enter as he and Ryleigh exited the house. He turned her to face him, saying, "We knew this would be the likely outcome. There was no other choice to end his reign of tyranny." Ryleigh cried, shuddering, as lethal gunshots rang out from the house.

CHAPTER 70

Waiting

Jack and Sam stood behind the retaining wall's crumbing remains, looking out across the bleak landscape. "This is why I picked the second level. From here, we can see them before they see us. It puts us in a dominant position." They were unaware of the lurking figure behind them drawing practice beads, creating red flashes of laser light on their backs.

Mansa nudged Roy, pointing at the flickering dots. "Did you see it? It's coming from the other side. I told you I heard scuffling over there about an hour ago."

Roy stretched forward, trying to locate the source without disclosing their position. "Okay. It has to be Charles. One of us needs to try getting behind him. I've got a bad feeling about this." Mansa held a finger to his lips and pointed to his chest before slipping back and disappearing in the cavernous shadows.

Jack continued gazing at the construction yard with its collection of derelict equipment and towering weeds. Drawing his flask, he raised it in a toast. "Here's to you, Aidan Gallagher." He handed it to Sam, explaining, "My old man loved this kind of shit. Being here takes me back to the day I lost him and my brother when we made a play for another gang's territory. It didn't end the way he planned." He lowered his head, spreading his hands as he pressed back from the wall.

Sam watched as he seemed to fight the recollection. "You've not shared much about them. Someday, I'd like us to sit and talk about our families. There's so much I want to know about Jack Gallagher beyond the background reports. And you deserve to know more about me."

Jack turned to face Sam, pulling her in and resting his chin on her head as he spoke gently. "We will have time for many discussions once this is over. I plan on us being together for a long, long time, Sam."

The running lights on David's car caught Jack's attention as the car crept through the desolate yard toward the decaying parking structure. He raised an arm, waving for David and Cynthia to proceed.

He took a half step back, placing a hand on each of Sam's shoulders as he looked at her somberly. "My head is telling me everything will be all right. But before anything happens, my heart has to tell you...I love you, Samantha Mieras." He kissed her forehead and turned, holding her hand to wait.

Sam was speechless, turning with him as tears trickled down her cheeks. She shook her head, brushing them aside, thinking, *Pull it together, Sam. Everything will be all right.*

CHAPTER 71

Waylaid

David slowed his Mercedes to a stop next to Sam's Audi. Stepping out, he nodded to Jack as Cynthia walked around, joining him on the driver's side. He turned toward Sam with a quizzical look, knowing who she was and trying to recall images from twenty-seven years ago. The scene moved slowly, everyone going through awkward, silent visual assessments.

David finally broke the tension. "We're here as you requested. This is a good time to disclose your requirements beyond agreeing to a truce."

Stepping ahead of David, Cynthia glared, asserting a position of dominance. "Let me clarify David's request. You told us this meeting would stop your outrageous attacks. You said we would negotiate..." She paused, turning toward Sam. Her eyes tightened as her lips pursed. She pointed an accusing finger at Sam, saying, "So this is the bitch behind all our problems? I know you want more than the simple terms we discussed on the phone. It's your chance to speak up, hon, or will you be hiding behind your man?"

Jack's eyes blinked shut. *You didn't need to go there, Cynthia.* He knew her snide challenge would trigger the worst of Sam's instincts.

He was about to speak when Sam placed her arm across his chest, widening her stance. Placing her hands on her hips, she took a step forward, assuming the personality of a drill sergeant about to address a class of raw recruits. Jack remained silent, knowing Sam had shifted into battle mode.

"Thanks for the opportunity to speak, and never make the mistake of calling me a bitch or *hon* again. I'll fill in the blanks for you. Yes, I'm the reason you're here—because David raped me and, with his father, demanded that I have an abortion. As for Jack, he's my associate, working under my direction. However, I'll speak for myself."

Sam jabbed the air with her finger, exchanging fierce eye contact with Cynthia. "And as for you and your arrogant attitude, put a cork in it, bitch."

While Cynthia and Sam were raging, Mansa scrambled back to Roy, whispering, "There's no way to get behind him. He's taken a position just past where we saw the structure's decking had collapsed."

"I'm not surprised."

Mansa was rubbing his face, trying to generate an alternative solution. "If their negotiations work, we may have nothing to worry about. We listen, stay put, and wait for everyone to leave."

Roy looked at him with raised eyebrows. "I don't think that's going to happen. From the sounds of the initial greetings, this is not going according to plan. We sit tight. If our intruder starts something, we counterattack to take him out. I'm not sure we can avoid casualties. Are you up for fire and movement?"

"Yes, sir. You make the call."

Cynthia looked at Sam. "Jack and Roy said we would be agreeing to call a truce and allow David's nomination to run its course."

Sam nodded. "We also told you there was an additional requirement."

"Yes, but you never said what it was. Tell us what you're adding." Cynthia placed her hands on her hips, mirroring Sam.

Sam looked at Jack, letting him explain. "We call a truce on both sides. The nomination proceeds, and you turn in Charles to be arrested for the bombings and for taking Adira hostage."

Hearing Jack's demand, Charles squinted with a scowl, leaning forward to listen for a response as David began laughing.

"Your demand is ludicrous. You have no proof of his involvement in any of those incidents."

Jack began raising his volume. "Proof? Here's proof for you, David. Eyewitness accounts from Ethan and Adira about the threats and beatings Charles conducted. Not by his henchmen, but by him."

"Eyewitness accounts from people I have no connection with and, quite frankly, don't care about. They're your operatives, willing to spew whatever lies you create for them. The demand is unacceptable."

Sam interjected, "There's more behind the requirement."

Cynthia shrugged her shoulders. "What? More false information and accusations? David's right. Acceding to the demand is out of the question."

Sam took a breath as she shifted her focus from Cynthia to David. "Ethan and Adira are our twins. I learned about it from Ryleigh and Chandler. You can ask Cynthia if it's true. She has documentation of the live births that Jonathan gave her. Our children are more important to me than our differences and should be to you as well. Think about it, David. Charles must be held accountable for what he's done to them."

Cynthia looked at David, shaking her head. "Don't listen to her, David. It's a desperate attempt to sway you with lies. We are not caving to their demand."

David's eyes moved between Jack and Sam, trying to sense the validity of Sam's revelation. "You and my sister have spent years lying and conniving to destroy me. I do not believe your claim."

"How about hearing details from Ryleigh and your father? We can pause further actions so you can talk with him for verification. Once you're satisfied we're telling the truth, you can turn Charles in for prosecution."

"Okay, I'm willing to hold until I talk with my father. If what you're saying is true, I will consider surrendering Charles."

Roy looked at Mansa. "Lock and load. David's statement won't sit well with our uninvited guest."

Charles's nostrils flared as he fired a shot, shattering David's head, sending his limp body back against the car. Cynthia turned to reach for him as a second shot struck her back. Jack pulled his gun while pushing Sam to the pavement, diving on top of her as a third shot caught his left shoulder, exploding tissue and bone as it exited his back.

Roy and Mansa were on their feet, charging to reach Sam and Jack while firing repelling shots toward Charles's location. Charles stepped forward to engage as bullets ricocheted around him. One round struck his arm. He dropped his weapon and turned to escape out the back of the structure while his attackers diverted to help Jack and Sam.

Roy pulled Jack's body off Sam. She started screaming at the sight of his shoulder spurting blood from its wound. Mansa was phoning 911, calling for medical aid and police assistance. He gave their location, saying, "We have multiple people with gunshot injuries. One of them is a Supreme Court nominee."

Roy tore off his jacket, using it to improvise wound management for Jack until help could arrive. Sam cradled Jack against her, trying to use her body to hold the makeshift dressing in place across his back. "Hold him tight against you to keep compressing the wound. He's tough. He'll make it, Sam."

Jack's eyes fluttered as he began losing consciousness, and the sound of their voices started fading. Sam was squeezing him as tight as she could, rocking back and forth, pleading, "Jack! Goddamn it, listen to me. Stay with me, Jack." She was sobbing uncontrollably, looking at Roy.

Mansa began checking for pulses on David and Cynthia. "David's gone. Cynthia is still alive and needs medical attention. I'm contacting our squad and going after Charles. You need me out of here before you have to explain why a felon with a weapon is working with you. We don't need unintended exposure."

Roy waved at Mansa. "Get going. You were never here."

"Yes, sir." Mansa was back on his feet, following a trail of blood to a back stairway with no sign of Charles. He continued pursuit to the sound of wailing sirens and flashing lights arriving behind him.

Police cruisers and first responders swarmed the site as Roy frantically waved them to the second level. Sam was smoothing Jack's hair with one hand, whispering to him, "Jack, you can't leave me. I love you. Do you hear me? You can't leave. Not now, never."

EMTs were assessing Cynthia's injuries. "I've got a pulse on this one. Get the wound dressed so we can transport her." Another team pulled Jack off Sam's lap as they tore into packages of dressings. "We've got him, miss. Do you have any injuries?" She shook her head as an officer helped her stand. He walked her to the back of the EMTs' vehicle for evaluation, telling her to allow the team to do its work.

She was twisting around, looking back at Jack. "I'm fine. I need to stay with him."

"You need to come with me while they try to save your friend. We'll have you back with him once he's stabilized and ready for transport."

Sam sat on the edge of the rig's doorway, watching Roy talking to officers as they patted him down. He raised his hands, and Sam could hear him talking. "Reach in my back pocket and check the ID. I can give you an emergency number to call for verification."

One officer retrieved a leather wallet, revealing a shining metal object as he opened it. Sam squinted in the dim light, noticing a significant change in attitude once the officers passed the wallet around for inspection. She tried to get Roy's attention, but he waved her off, continuing to talk and gesture with several new individuals gathering around him.

Sam observed Cynthia being placed onto a stretcher as David's lifeless body was covered with a sheet.

While Jack was being loaded onto a stretcher, one of the EMTs approached Sam to check on her. She told the technician she was unharmed. "Okay, miss. I need to make a quick assessment. Sometimes people are in shock and don't realize they're injured."

"You don't have to call me *miss*. My name is Sam. Is he going to be okay?" The technician handed her a box of tissues, and she began crying again.

"We have him stabilized, but he's suffered a serious wound and lost a lot of blood. We're taking him to Presbyterian Hospital. Are you his spouse or next of kin?"

"No, but yes. I'm all he has for family. We…"

"Good enough for me, Sam. Once they get him in place, you can ride along as we move him to the hospital for trauma care."

Roy walked over to check on Jack, following the stretcher to the rig. He put an arm around Sam. "You go with Jack. I'll take care of things here."

She looked up at Roy as tears clouded her vision. "What were you telling the police?"

"I was telling them what happened and identifying everyone for them. Standard protocol, Sam."

"I thought I saw a badge, and it seemed to calm the police down when they searched you."

"It was special identification, and they needed to check it out."

Sam's eyes blinked as she tried to see a clear image of his face. "You're more than a guy who checks backgrounds on people. Who are you, Roy?" He ignored her question as one of the technicians extended a hand to help her into the rig.

"They're ready for you to join them, Sam. Go with Jack and make sure they take good care of him. We've called ahead to tell them you're his next of kin, so you won't have any problems being with him. I'll call Lydia and tell her to meet you there with Ethan and Adira." He patted her hand, saying, "We'll talk about who I am later. Everything's going to be all right."

CHAPTER 72

Reassignments

It was later in the evening when Mansa called Roy to tell him Charles's trail had gone cold outside the construction site. "He must have had a car waiting. The trail of blood stopped in the middle of the street, where they must have picked him up. How's Jack doing?"

"I believe he's still in surgery. Sam's there with Lydia and the twins. He should be okay once they do all the repairs."

"Does Sam know who we are?"

"No."

"Are we going to tell Jack and Sam the full story behind us and Chandler?"

"Mansa, when I recruited you for the task force, I told you people would ask those questions whenever we worked together. Who we are and what we do is not subject to disclosure."

"Yeah, I know and don't have a problem with it. It's just, you know, they're more than ordinary people."

"Okay, back to business. Tell Curtis and Matt to pick up with finding Charles and his crew. Those two are the best bloodhounds you have in the squad. Tell them to keep a low profile. I don't care how long it takes. They'll report directly to you, and you can keep me updated. The rest of our squad needs to maintain security for Sam and her group. I can get more men if we need them. Priority one is finding Charles before he pops up and starts causing trouble again."

"Got it. Before I go, I have one last question. We talked about recruiting Jack when this assignment was over. He'd be a great asset for us to have on board. You said maybe. Is it still up for consideration?"

"I'm kicking it around, but you'll be the first to know if I decide to consider having him join us."

CHAPTER 73

Recovering

Two days after Harlem, Sam was returning from a long breakfast discussion with Roy in the hospital cafeteria as a nurse left Jack's room. "Mr. Gallagher is looking for you. He buzzed the nursing station about an hour ago, demanding we clean him up, insisting he needed to look presentable before you came back. I put his bed up and told him only for a little while. He kept asking where you were and what day it was. Safe to say he's feeling better."

Jack tried to interrupt their conversation with a raspy voice from inside the room. "Hey. Quit delaying my girl. I need to talk with her, and I could use some real food for breakfast when you get a chance."

The nurse turned to Jack. "Liquids for now, Mr. Gallagher. You'll get something solid if you behave and rest. Don't be one of those cantankerous patients."

Sam looked at the nurse and laughed. "Yes, he can be cantankerous. Hearing him asking for real food tells me he's on the road to recovery."

Jack was reaching for Sam, motioning her to come closer. "Hey, bean, come over here, and let's be gettin' on with the details of what happened."

Sam was shaking her head and laughing. She walked up beside Jack's bed and kissed him on the forehead. "You better be nice to the staff. They put in a lot of work to save you for me." She knew the bluster was Jack Gallagher's way of letting them know he would make it.

"Yeah, you're right." He looked at her sheepishly, telling her, "I'm sorry, but being stranded here got the best of me." He looked past Sam to remind the nurse, "A piece of toast with some jelly would help my disposition."

The nurse placed Jack's chart into the door pocket. "No toast until later." She told Sam, "Maybe twenty or thirty minutes, and then we need him resting. I'll have the doctor order something to help him sleep."

Jack reached for Sam's hand. "I could hardly wait to see you. I have so many questions. My shoulder feels like a bear tried to tear it off. The last thing I remember is seeing David and Cynthia go down. Where are Roy and Mansa?"

"We'll have time for details once we get you back home."

"Tell me Roy and Mansa are okay. No need for a play-by-play commentary, but a short recap would be good."

"They're fine. Two of Mansa's men are looking for Charles, who killed David and wounded Cynthia before taking out most of your shoulder. Roy's been amazing, coordinating with the police, working with Ethan, and quieting rumors about us being responsible for the shootings. Somehow, he's able to pull the right strings to make things happen. I just finished having breakfast with him and learned a lot. He and you will talk, but enough with the updates. I want to talk about us."

"Well, so do I, but I'll let you start."

Sam reached out to smooth his hair, letting her hand rest against the side of his face. "I was so afraid of losing you. Over and over, I kept hearing your voice telling me everything would be all right and your heart telling me you love me. We didn't get the chance for me to say I love you. So you're hearing it now."

"Okay, my turn?"

"Not quite. Thomas and I have been talking. He loves living at your place and doesn't want to leave. I told him I was feeling the same way. So, Jack Gallagher, do you think you're willing to let us move in for good? I don't mean to stress you, but I'd love to have us under one roof."

Jack's eyes widened as a teasing look filled his face. "Are you proposing to me, Ms. Mieras? Living together would require me, as it's said, to make an honest woman out of you."

Sam wanted to hug him, but tubes and monitors were in the way, so she squeezed his hand as hard as she could. "Let me clarify my intentions for your foggy brain to comprehend. Will you marry me, Jack Gallagher?"

"It would make me the happiest man alive if you're willing to put up with a cantankerous man. So the answer is yes. I want to make it happen as soon as I can get out of here and have the strength to stand and say 'I do.'"

The nurse walked into the room as Jack pulled Sam in for a kiss. "Looks like you've found an appropriate use for your good arm, Mr. Gallagher. I hate to interrupt, but I need to deliver a medication the doctor ordered to help you rest."

Sam turned, beaming, to look at the nurse. "We're getting married!"

CHAPTER 74

A Toast

Three Months Later—Jack and Sam's Home

The wedding celebration was in full swing, with guests congratulating Sam and Jack. The weather was warmer than expected for an early New York spring day as the party spilled out of the house and onto the patio.

Sam was radiant, dressed in a cream-colored satin dress, while Jack sported a formal-looking navy-blue sling to support his shoulder. Even Thomas got into the formal attire with a black bow tie collar.

Roy was in the kitchen, talking with the caterer about making a best man's toast and having the bride and groom cut the three-tiered wedding cake. An incoming call interrupted their conversation.

Roy looked at the screen, which showed a call from Curtis. He excused himself and walked into the laundry room for privacy.

"Curtis, you should be calling Mansa. I'm in the middle of an important event. What do you need?"

The cackling voice on the other end of the call sent a shiver of fear and anger through Roy's body. "Roy, it's Charles, not Curtis. I knew you'd answer if I used his phone to call you. However, he's tied up and unable to talk with you at the moment."

Roy's hands shook as he tried to maintain a level of composure, holding the phone to his ear. "What are you doing with his phone?"

"Well, Curtis didn't seem to mind me using his phone. We discovered he's been trying to locate me ever since our incident in Harlem. However, he and his partner became careless and let us capture them. Oh, before I forget, his partner is deceased. I believe his name was Matthew."

"What do you want, Charles?"

"Oh dear, what do I want? Well, several things. First, I wanted to apologize for not making the wedding reception. I suspect my invitation got lost in the mail. Tell the newlyweds I wish them all the best. I want them to be happy. At least for today."

"What else, Charles?"

"Hmm. You can tell them. No, you need to tell all your little terrorist friends: I have grievances to settle with all of you."

"Where is Curtis?"

"I'll answer your question in a moment. Before doing that, I have a curious question for you. Have you told your friends who you really are? It took some work before Curtis told us about you. I did not know you held such a powerful position. I feel honored to finally be up against a worthy adversary."

"Cut the chatter, Charles. Where is Curtis?"

"Oh yes, back to answering your question. Personally, I don't like it when one of my men talks and reveals secrets, and I'm sure you feel the same way. So as a favor, I will take care of disciplining Curtis for you."

Roy's face bunched into a painful grimace as he heard a sudden burst of commotion before hearing Mansa's voice shouting commands. "Drop the phone, Charles. Turn around and spread-eagle with your hands against the wall. Li'l

John, cut Curtis loose and evacuate him." There was a break in commands as Roy strained to hear what was happening after the phone tumbled to the ground.

He heard another familiar voice shouting, "Mansa, he's got a gun."

There was a rapid two-shot burst before Roy could hear Mansa shouting again. "Target's down." Another series of shots and commotion followed his commands: "Watch out, Li'l John—they're coming to recover him. Get Curtis and withdraw. Repeat, clear, and withdraw."

Roy clicked off the call as Jack leaned in through the doorway. "Hey, bud, we're waiting for your best man's toast. Are you okay?"

Roy looked up, nodding with a glazed look in his eyes. "Yeah, I'm fine. Everything's all right. Let's make that toast to you and your gorgeous bride."

COUNTER VENGEANCE

A past adversary challenges a reunited team trying to defend themselves from escalating threats, intimidations, and killings.

Samantha Mieras and her team regroup in the aftermath of Jack Gallagher being shot by an assassin. Their opponents from the privilege-minded organization Aegis are seeking retribution for the shooting of their Supreme Court nominee David Jaymes and his wife, Cynthia.

Opposing desires for vengeance create a crossfire of dangers. The original master manipulator in Collective Vengeance is no longer hiding. He is the assassin on a vengeful rampage to appease his injuries. Samantha and her team are frantic to find him before he strikes again.

Can Aegis and Samantha's team form an alliance to thwart the would-be assassin? Who will be the peacemaker attempting a truce? Can common ground be found to stop the rampage?

Follow Samantha and her team as the navigate unchartered waters seeking an accord with their political archenemy?

Counter Vengeance

The second novel in
The Vengeance Series

by
Joseph Stanley

Available in 2025

SERIAL VENGEANCE

A reporter's investigation and a killer's psychotic pleasure are drawn into a strategic game to prevent the next kill.

Miriam Wilson is a serial killer driven by distorted passionate beliefs in pursuit of personal justice for childhood abuse. She lures an investigative reporter, Bree Walsh, into a series of strategic chess-like games to try and save the next victim.

Miriam taunts with arrogant contempt as Bree battles to win. Each new game's objective is to avert another kill before it can pleasure the sociopathic personality of the killer.

Bree joins forces with Detective Chief Inspector Patrick Hanks as they're drawn into the killer's web of deceit. They enlist help from Larry Monroe, the coroner, Robert Myers, a criminal psychologist, and Bree's editor, Angie Landings, to form an elite team attempting to defeat Miriam at her own game.

Can Bree and her team make the right moves to discover the intended victims and stop another killing? What drives Miriam's insatiable hunger for vengeance? Is she acting alone? Where and when do the games end?

Serial Vengeance

The third novel in
The Vengeance Series

by
Joseph Stanley

Available in 2026

About Joseph Stanley

In the interest of full disclosure, I will explain my pen name, **Joseph Stanley**. My birth name is Joseph Stanley Suchocki. My father's name, Stanley, is the origin of my middle name. So in a respectful nod to my father, I am using Joseph Stanley as my pen name. I know he would have enjoyed our names being together in my literary endeavors.

My personality and writing characteristics are based on a variety of experiences. Being a baby boomer and Capricorn started the ball rolling in January 1946. High school and two years of college were highlighted by my playing in a true-to-form sixties garage band of western Michigan fame.

The next major influence was five years (1966–1971) of service in the army; I spent two years in Vietnam and reached the rank of captain. My claim to fame in service was coming home in one piece and of sound mind. While I appreciate and understand people thanking me for my service, I simply saw it as an expected duty to be fulfilled.

After military service, I started working in medical sales and sales management, eventually becoming an independent entrepreneur. That chapter started with my founding a national consulting company, where I spent thirty-five years conducting hundreds of seminars throughout the country and writing policy manuals, newsletters, training programs, and more.

Heading into retirement, I battled depression (see the preface), which launched my journey into being a fiction writer. I began studying the art of writing, with a goal of creating and publishing stories in various formats. And as you read this, my journey as an author continues to be a work in progress.

I invite you to check out my author's website (www.stanleywrites.com) and follow me on Facebook (JosephStanleyWrites). I hope you've enjoyed or will enjoy *Collective Vengeance*, and look for the sequels, *Counter Vengeance* in 2025 and *Serial Vengeance* in 2026.

JOSEPH STANLEY